The Rat Catcher

a novel by

Andrew Laszlo

To Howard:
My good friend and buddy.
I hope you'd enjoy The
Rat Catcher.
With kindest regards,

Andy

The Rat Catcher is a work of fiction. All incidents, events, and persons in the story are fictitious, even in those instances when the events depicted are based on known historical incidents, and the names of the players in the story are similar, or identical, to those who actually played a part in those historical events.

Dan River Press
PO Box 298
Thomaston, Maine 04861

CONTENTS

"... the Angel heard the cries and witnesseth the horrors, and the anguish of the tormented, and the death that befell on them. And the Angel took up the shield and sword, and anointed the palms of her hands with the milk of ewes, and drank the nectars of the orchard. And she looked upon the blood of wolves on her shield, and dipped her sword in the serpent's venom. And she raised her arms to the Almighty in Heaven, and said the prayer for the dead. She cleansed her feet and soaked the straps of her sandals in the pure water of the mountain spring, and set out on the journey to seek the path of the righteous, so the sins of the tormentors of the meek shall not go un-avenged ..."

... from the writings in the "Book of Sorrows" ...

Book One

§

Prologue

Violetta Kuhle was a happy woman for the first time in many years. She spent the better part of the day cooking up her favorites; steamed dumplings, breaded schnitzels, white wurst, loaves of dark bauern bread, and a huge pot of sauerbraten from a slab of fresh meat Ferdie had brought in just the day before. She cured the meat in her favorite marinade, with beer, vinegar, seedless raisins, onions, and plenty of black pepper to give the meat a tinge of authority. She was pleased that her hoard of spices and marinades, though she seldom got to use them these days, was still there in the sealed porcelain jars, ready to be used for an occasion like the return of the film crew. She was looking forward to the feast this evening. Although she would have liked to use real beef, the plane was not due till the morning, and the beef could only have come in on the next plane two weeks later. She had gotten used to this kind of life—an "existence" she called it in quiet resignation—deep in the jungle, far from any civilization and the pleasures of life that she loved in the good old days.

This was their fourth year living in this remote spot. As beautiful as Kaneima was, and as much as she liked it the first couple of weeks, the endless days without anything to do but try to escape the heat and humidity, made her life monotonous, her days endless, and made the weeks, months and the years weigh on her like a life sentence in paradise.

At first, she tried to tell herself that their stay in Kaneima was temporary and for a short time only, but now, four years later, she knew it was not so. When they left Germany just weeks after the war was over, she knew they were going into exile under assumed names and identities, but there was no other choice. They couldn't have stayed in Germany. If they had, they would have been hunted down like animals, thrown in jail, tried and sentenced to possibly long prison terms, or even worse, taken to Russia to a gulag, or wind up on the gallows. Most of their close friends were already arrested, and it was only a matter of time before they would have been also. She never understood what was so bad about her husband's work. He was a scientist, a doctor in the service of the Fatherland, doing work that was to benefit all mankind forever. She was sad to leave the old country, her parents, childhood friends, and all who became good friends during the long years of the war. But her fears of living in a strange, far-away part of the world evaporated quickly. Caracas was a beautiful city, with wonderful climate, beautiful beaches nearby, and all the comforts her husband's new job, managing one of Latin America's newest and most beautiful hotels, The Humboldt, on top of Mount Avila, afforded them. It was the good life. She found learning Spanish difficult, but with all the German people around them, most of whom were also recent arrivals from the old country, there was no shortage of opportunities for a full and pleasant social life.

But then her world crumbled. She could only suspect the reasons, when one day, they were told to pack quickly, and only the most essential necessities, and they were taken deep into the jungle in a small plane. The place was beautiful at first. Three huge waterfalls in the distance on the far side of the lagoon, a beautiful, pristine crescent beach at the waters edge, and some small, thatch-roofed huts that were to be their home from then on. Most of their personal belongings came after them, shipped by whoever arranged their departure from Caracas, but her beautiful furniture, made from aromatic tropical hardwoods, never arrived. But even if it had, she wouldn't have had the place for it in the small hut a ways up from the lagoon, amongst the huge trees of the jungle.

There was a village nearby with primitive natives, hunters who lived a simple, happy, stone-age life. But Violetta wasn't happy. As the days went by, without her friends and the commotion of a big city around her, she became bored, unhappy, and desperate with her situation. Though she tried deceiving herself that it was temporary, inwardly she knew that the rest of her life might be spent by the lagoon, surrounded by half naked native Indians, flies, spiders, lizards, snakes, wild animals, and the dense jungle all around her. There were a few others she could socialize with. Ferdie Witt was an old friend, though in the good old days during the war, Ferdie was only a noncommissioned officer, and they seldom interacted socially. Ferdie worked with her husband, Dr. Anatole Hubert, now going by the name, Senor Alfred Kuhle. There was one other couple who lived in the area, but they seldom got to see each other. Violetta suspected they were also Germans, though the man insisted on being Latvian, who spoke German and a little Spanish, but his wife, a ravishingly beautiful young woman claimed to be an Austrian countess. The Latvian man was thought to be a diamond prospector, who, as the rumors had it, discovered diamonds under the waterfalls of the lagoon. He lived a solitary, secretive life, and seldom came around.

To Violetta, life at Kaneima quickly became dreadful. Endless hot and humid days of lying in the hammock, chasing gnats and mosquitoes, waiting for night to fall, and hoping for the air to cool a bit, but it seldom did. Day followed day, and night came without relief, as the cycles repeated without letup in endless monotony, except during the monsoon rains that made the air heavy and covered everything with mildew. Only the early mornings were bearable. Just after the first light of the day brightened the sky, but before the sun broke over the horizon and steam rose from the ground, was the best part of her existence, and the best time to make love with her husband. She tried to seduce Ferdie once, a couple of years ago when her husband went hunting with some of the natives, but Ferdie was shy and wouldn't cooperate. She figured he was still conscious of the separation between officers and non commissioned personnel, or perhaps, he just liked younger women, like the Indian girls who lived with him. But when the plane came in every second Tuesday, bringing their bi-monthly supplies, it was fun to go swimming in the lagoon with some of the handsome pilots, and occasionally sneak off into the jungle and make love to them. She suspected her husband knew about it, but said nothing, because he probably understood her unhappiness, and because he also chased every skirt that occasionally came by, even if it was only a young Indian girl from the native village.

But everything had changed about three weeks ago, when the movie company arrived. Almost six months before a man had come on the Tuesday morning plane, and explained that he represented a motion picture company that wanted to come to Kaneima, use it as a base camp, and go on trips from here to photograph Angel's Falls, a little known natural wonder though it was believed to be the highest waterfall in the world. When the company arrived, life at Kaneima changed dramatically for Violetta. Most of the people in the film crew were young American men and women, had crates and crates of interesting equipment, delicacies like rich chocolate bars that didn't melt in the heat, and canned delicacies like Portuguese sardines she loved all her life, but couldn't get in Kaneima. They also had crates of the most fragrant, newest kinds of American cigarettes that tasted mellow and smelled great; pleasures of life she had given up long ago. There was a naturalist and famous explorer amongst all the other interesting people who was the leader of the expedition, and the figurehead of the movie that was to be photographed in part at Kaneima. In anticipation, Violetta had her house cleaned spotlessly by her native maids, and she unpacked some of her favorite clothes she had not worn for years.

The movie people were fun, uninhibited and carefree; enjoyable and entertaining to be around whether they were working or not. When she got to know some of them well, a makeup artist showed her the latest in cosmetics, and a hairdresser styled her hair in the current fashion of Hollywood. The evenings, when the crew converged on the veranda of the Kuhle house after work, were filled with music, drinking and laughter. Relationships developed. It would have been impossible not to notice the play Alfred made for the good looking, young script supervisor, and Violetta couldn't have cared less if anyone noticed her interest in the director of the movie.

She was humming an old German tune as she was cooking up a storm, thinking of the crew's return, and looking forward to the fun until the crew left the following morning. Alfred, who guided the movie people, sent one of the Indians back to Kaneima to let her know that they were on their way, and would be back at Kaneima by mid day. The crew had been gone for ten days, filming Angel Falls, the last of their objectives around Kaneima. They were to leave the following morning and Violetta was not going to waste any of the time that remained to her.

*   *   *

Full daylight was descending over Kaneima, as the first golden rays of the sun were beginning to kiss the top branches of the tall hardwood trees, and the thunder of the waterfalls, tamed by the distance, drifted in over the lagoon. Violetta was pleasantly exhausted. She was half asleep in one of the big, comfortable wicker chairs, her eyelids heavy from the nonstop drinking, dancing and lovemaking throughout the night. But the veranda was empty. There were no people around, and the few stray mongrel dogs that came up from the village fought for the scraps of food they could snatch from the tables. She didn't care about the mess, the dirty dishes and leftover food and drinks; the Indian girls were going to clean up in a little while, and she thought sadly that shortly the veranda would look like it always did, empty and devoid of people, and her life was going to quickly revert to the pointless, mundane and boring existence of the past four years.

The music still reverberated in her mind, American tunes played over the loudspeakers the movie company's sound engineer set up the night before, and played throughout the night. But she watched sadly this morning, as daylight was coming up, and the tired, sleep deprived and hung-over crew of the film group were taking a last swim in the cool waters of the lagoon, and quickly packing the loudspeakers in cases, ready to be put on the plane. Before the last jeep-load of people and gear left a few minutes ago to go to the airstrip, some of the men and women came over to her, shook hands and kissed her on the cheek, and thanked her for the hospitality. Within minutes, Violetta was alone once again. Most of the Americans gave her some going away presents, some nicely wrapped, some improvised, a few photographs, and all promised to write and possibly, even to come back sometime.

She vaguely recalled one person, a shadow without a face during the night, who mixed her a drink of raspberry syrup and seltzer, her favorite drink that she seldom had these days. It was always a special treat when her mother mixed some raspberry syrup with cold seltzer water for her on hot summer days, as she grew up in Germany. It was her favorite. She couldn't recall if she was exhausted from dancing, but the drink refreshed her, and she was grateful to whomever it was that gave it to her. She spotted the small bottle of syrup on the table and reached for it. Now, as daylight was coming up, she recognized the bottle. It was the same brand her mother always looked for, Hungarian Raspberry Syrup, that was the best. She was examining the bottle, wondering who might have given it to her, and how did they know that raspberry syrup, particularly this brand, was her favorite. But she couldn't recall who gave her the little bottle any more than she could remember who she danced with, or who she slept with during the all night long party. Her head was pounding, her eyes were burning and her tongue felt swollen in her mouth that was parched by the tropical heat, and the nonstop drinking of alcohol for the past 12 hours or so. She reached for a glass near her on the table, dumped whatever it was that was still in it, and her fingers fished for ice that hadn't melted and was still floating in water next to some dead flies in the big crystal bowl in the middle of the table. She dropped whatever ice she could scoop from the bowl into the glass, poured some of the syrup and filled the glass to the rim with seltzer. The aroma of rich raspberry syrup flooded her mind with childhood memories, and she savored the rich flavor of the cold drink. It tasted so good. It was sweet and refreshing, and she drained the glass to the very last drop. She closed her eyes. She heard the DC-3's engines start up in the distance, and a few minutes later the old plane came circling over the lagoon, and flew low over the veranda with engines roaring, rattling the dirty dishes and glasses on the table. Seconds later the plane's noise died away, allowing the murmur of the waterfalls to return, and Kaneima was once again quiet, desolate and depressing. Her eyelids became heavy and her legs felt like lead, but she got up, and in her stupor she mixed another drink of syrup and seltzer. Then, with her head spinning and holding onto things, she slowly made her way to her bedroom.

Chapter 1

The Rat Catcher.

Ben "The Doorknob" Chapman swung the wheel of his La Mans into the seven story Municipal Parking structure that ran the entire block on Eighth Avenue between 53rd and 54th Street, and took up the better part of the block between Eighth Avenue and Broadway. The fellow in the car in front of him gave him the finger, as Ben tapped his horn three short blasts, and he just smiled knowing that the fellow was waiting for someone to pull out of a parking space, but probably thought that Ben was honking his horn to get him moving. But Ben was in no hurry. He was already late for his job and didn't care. He wasn't honking at the guy in the car in front of him, he was just signaling the young Salvadorian kid in the ticket booth to alert him that he was on his way. The kid smiled and waved, as he recognized Ben's car and stepped out of the booth to pick up the red plastic cone from slot number one, Ben's reserved parking place right next to the elevator and the staircase in the corner of the ground floor by the 54th Street entrance. He shook hands with Ben and hurried back into the ticket booth to let a line of cars that had built up while he was helping Ben park, out of the garage. Ben parked his car and got out and smiled at the kid, knowing, actually sensing more than knowing that the kid was probably an ex-con, juvenile delinquent at best, and very probably an illegal, one of thousands employed by the City of New York, mostly to keep them off the street and out of jail.

The stench, the unbelievably foul smell of rancid urine and defecation hit his nose, as he knew it would, and he looked down at his feet so as not to step into anything as he got out of his car. He loved the convenience of having his own, private spot waiting for him whenever he pulled into the garage, but even though he knew that the floor, even the walls were hosed down every morning, the smell was awful and he was hoping to arrange for another spot within eyesight of the ticket booth and the Salvadorian kid, who would keep the space reserved for him. This slot, number one in the garage was probably the worst. It was alongside the men's room that had been locked up long ago, and it was possible that no one knew where the key was. But now that the men's room was locked, the staircase in this corner of the garage became the favorite spot of every derelict, every bum, between 42nd Street and Columbus Circle, to relieve themselves. He smiled, as he caught himself thinking that if he had to make a report on some crime that had taken place in the garage and had to describe the condition of this corner, for reasons of political correctness he could not have referred to those who urinated and defecated in the staircase, as derelicts and bums; he would have to describe them as "homeless persons".

But fresh, cool air replaced the acrid stench of the garage as soon as he stepped out of the structure and headed west on 54th Street across Eighth Avenue. He smiled at the familiar sight of police cruisers taking up every inch of parking space, double and triple parking everywhere, and smell and all, he was grateful for the convenience of not having to deal with finding a parking place. Until just about six weeks ago he had his own reserved spot in the little courtyard right next to the precinct, but now that he was considered a 'short timer,' his space was given to the guy who was about to replace him. He had no problem with this. He knew the routine and now that he was about to retire, he no longer got urgent assignments, and the garbage cases that piled up on his desk did not call for a parking place he could pull in and out of at a moment's notice. He also smiled inwardly as he observed the activity; uniformed cops, plain clothes people coming from and going into the building, and he knew that no one would notice that he was about a half hour late again this morning. He loved this place. It had been his home for the past 12 years, and he was proud to be serving in this old building, the 54th Street Precinct, or as it was known to cops on the Force, "Midtown North." It was one of New York City's busiest and most important precincts, and although parking was difficult, most who served in Midtown North were proud to be there.

As usual, Sergeant Finnell was busy behind the large, elevated desk in between two huge columns and behind the iron railing and didn't even lift an eye, or say good morning, as he walked by. He was almost in the corridor, when Finnell called after him: "Lieutenant Doorknob." Ben stopped in his tracks. It was mostly the old timers like Sergeant Finnell, who occasionally still called him by that stupid nickname, "Doorknob," which referred to the size of his nose, and which he didn't much like but lived with since he joined the department 23 years ago. In fact, his oversized nose became somewhat of a trademark for him, and the mostly good natured talk behind his back attributed his brilliant detective work to his oversized nose, which—the talk had it—was behind his success in solving the most difficult cases. Some claimed he could smell a "rat"—police talk for a criminal—from a mile. Even he was beginning to believe it, until just nine months ago when a hop head stabbed him with an ice-pick twice in the chest and once in his side, narrowly missing his kidney. He shot and killed the perp, which is probably what saved his life, but when he was reinstated for active duty after almost four weeks in the hospital and six more weeks at home, he knew he wasn't the same cop he used to be. When a new early retirement incentive was offered, he took it.

He walked back to the desk where Finnell was shuffling papers. "What is it, Mike?" he asked the desk sergeant. "Late again!" Finnell threw him a glance. "Yeah?" Ben acknowledged Finnell's crack a bit irritated and as Sergeant Finnell, concentrating on shuffling papers, did not reply, he asked: "What about it?"

"The old man wants to see you." Finnell finally said without looking up, still shuffling the papers on his desk.

Ben turned and walked into the narrow corridor to his office and went through his morning routine of years, stopping at the coffee maker for his bagel and morning cup of black coffee, and looked at the new files and correspondence in the in-box on his desk even before taking off his coat. Aside from some junk mail and a couple of new files, nothing caught his interest and a little while later with coffee cup in hand, he knocked on the patterned glass panel of a door that said "Precinct Commander." "Inspector William H. Fredericks." Ben had seen this sign hundreds of times, but it just now occurred to him how convenient and practical the sign was. When the occupant of the office retired, or was reassigned, or left the precinct for any reason, only the name of the occupant had to be repainted.

"Come on in, Lieutenant." He heard Inspector Fredericks call out and Ben pushed the door open. "How did you know it was me?" Ben asked.

"I asked Finnell to tell you to see me, besides. . ." he smiled at Ben, "you are the only one in this den of thieves that has enough good manners to knock." Ben sat down in one of the rickety old wooden armchairs to one side of the desk, a routine he had done hundreds of times in the past. "You aren't going to chew me out for being late, are you Bill?"

Fredericks put on a mock severe expression; "How did you know that's what I called you in for?"

"Finnell already talked to me about it."

"Since when does a sergeant reprimand a superior officer in this precinct?" Fredericks asked with mock indignation.

"Well, he didn't exactly reprimand me, just reminded me."

"As a matter of fact, that's what I wanted to talk to you about Ben. I understand that you've been showing up late more and more, and I want to know why!"

But Ben didn't fall for the playacting. The two had been good friends since graduating from the Academy in 1953, when both of them were 22 years old, and served side by side almost uninterruptedly throughout these years. "Well," Ben answered, "if you really want to know why, it's because the shit that I get to work on these days could bore a three month rookie to tears, and because I clear up all the garbage paperwork by four in the afternoon, which incidentally," he smiled at the Inspector, "is, why I also go home early every day." They both laughed.

"Not a bad detail to be a short timer!" The Inspector remarked.

"You ought to try it sometime. It's boring enough to make one wish for retirement." He sipped his coffee.

"How much time do you have left?" The Inspector asked.

Ben looked at his watch. "Five weeks, three days, seven hours and eight minutes."

The Inspector laughed. "Maybe I should have asked you sooner."

"Asked me what sooner."

"Asked you to have lunch with me."

"To have lunch with you?" Ben repeated the Inspector with a skeptical expression.

Inspector Fredericks feigned surprise. "Well, yes. We haven't had lunch for some time now, and I thought that…"

Ben cut him off. "Bill! We've had lunch once or twice a month for going on eight years now. But some times when we have lunch, I find myself on some shit detail, like pulling soggy stiffs out of stolen cars from under the water by the 37th Street pier. . ."

"No, no Ben." The Inspector cut him off. "Today it's strictly social. Honest." He sounded almost convincing.

"Yeah. Right!" Ben leaned forward. "And if I believe that, the next thing you'll tell me about is the bridge you want to sell me in Brooklyn. Right?"

"No, Ben. Honest. Just a nice social lunch for two old fart New York City cops."

"This nose," Ben tapped the side of his nose, "smells a rat."

The Inspector's phone rang. He picked it up and listened. "Yes. Put him on." He scribbled on a piece of paper and handed the note to Ben. "Have to take this. It's the big C. The Greeks at noon." Ben took the note, nodded, and as the Inspector started talking, got up and walked out of the office.

*   *   *

Inspector Fredericks was already at his table by the big plate glass window looking out onto Ninth Avenue. Ben spotted him as the light changed and the traffic started, cars and trucks eight abreast, and it seemed they were all honking at him to get out of the way. I should give some of these bastards a ticket, he thought, but Bill was waiting and he was also hungry.

"Have a seat, Lieutenant." Bill said as Ben got to the table.

"You know, I thought it was strange you called me lieutenant when I came to your office this morning. Now I know you are pulling rank. Why? What gives, Inspector?" He underlined the "Inspector."

"It's just a way of speaking, Ben." He started fidgeting with the menu.

"I'd believe you if you weren't looking at that Menu. You know it by heart Bill. What's up?"

"Let's eat first." Inspector Fredericks looked a bit uncomfortable.

"You mean I might lose my appetite if we talk first?"

Fredericks waived the waiter over. "What you gonna have?" He asked Ben. "Order whatever you want. The treat is on the Department."

"In the first place, eating in this dump is no treat. Second, now that I know it's on the department, I know you want something from me. Right?"

"OK. But let's order first." He turned to the waiter. "What's the special of the day?"

The waiter looked annoyed. "The same as every day. Mussaka, Souvlavki, gyro . . ." Fredericks cut him off. "I'll have the special."

The waiter looked at him. "Which one?"

"The Souvlaki." Fredericks folded up the menu.

This was not a new experience for the waiter. He looked exasperated. He knew Fredericks was a Police Inspector and whenever he was with somebody, he went through the same, annoying routine. He wasn't going to argue. He turned to Ben. "What's yours?"

"What is the soup d'jour?" Ben asked him.

"We have some lamb stew."

"Is it fresh?" Ben asked.

"It's better the second day." The waiter answered.

"In other words," Ben said, "It's fresh. I'll have a bowl."

Now it was the waiter's turn. "You want some psomi sta karvouna with the stew?"

"What the hell is psomi . . ."Fredericks tried to repeat the waiter who shot him a dirty look.

"It's bread," the waiter said with contempt. "Toasted."

Ben turned to Fredericks. "You said I could have whatever I wanted?"

"Yeah. That's what I said. Lunch is on the Department."

Ben looked up at the waiter: "I'll have the toast."

The waiter turned on his heels and left without comment. "I don't think he likes cops." Fredericks said and they both broke up. "Yeah." Ben nodded. "I wonder why." He was a bit embarrassed by both of their behaviors, yet, at the same time he sensed that the camaraderie of the old days was still there. As a New Yorker it was almost natural to be a bit of a Smart Aleck, but it was a prerequisite for a New Yorker, who was a cop. Yet, the one-upsmanship, the sarcasm that was so much part of the job and of his life, slowed down after he lost the fight with the strung-out druggy that put him in the hospital. Somehow, being a wise guy cop just wasn't the same after that. He was slowing down and was looking forward to retirement. He knew he was going to miss the streets, an occasional wild car chase going the wrong way in a one way street, and the adrenalin pumping every time he had to reach for his gun. Just now, as he and Bill gave the waiter a hard time, he knew he was going to miss the camaraderie, the strong ties with his partner, who, he would give his life for, knowing that his partner would do the same for him. Bill Fredericks and he were partners for almost eight years after his rookie training was over, and both of them were assigned to Traffic, and later to Vice in Chinatown.

They studied for the Sergeant's test together and four years later both of them were promoted to lieutenant. That was the end of their partnership. They continued to remain friends, but Bill became a politician. He played the advancement game and the two separated as Bill was assigned to better and better political positions and eventually the two came together again as Fredericks, now an Inspector, took over Midtown North, first as an assistant Precinct Commander, then a few months later, as commander.

But Ben wasn't envious of Bill. He was a loner, and he knew that some of the other cops referred to him at times as 'Mr. Independent,' because he considered himself a street cop who preferred to work alone. Working without a partner was against departmental regulations most of the time, but working on a case with a partner who might not have been as interested in the case as he was, was always a pain. Working alone, he could follow his hunches without explaining them and didn't have to listen to someone else's theories, which most of the time didn't fit his thinking and bored him. The downside was that without a partner, without backup, he was on his own. If it weren't for the screaming, hysterical black woman, a homeless derelict bag lady who found him, he would probably have bled to death at three o'clock on a freezing November morning. But working alone had one other advantage; he didn't have to listen to his partner's wisecracks, which after a while wore thin and became annoying.

The waiter's voice brought him out of his reverie: "Who gets the stew and the toast? Ben held his hand up and nodded. "I do." "Who gets the special?" Fredericks looked at the waiter, then looked around the table with an exaggerated, mock puzzlement. "I guess I do." He said. "I don't see anybody else around . . ." The waiter slapped the plate in front of Fredericks, "Enjoy." He said in a way that could have meant "I hope you'll choke on it," and walked from their table.

Ben was dipping a piece of his toast into the stew. "You ready to talk yet, or you want to finish your special first?" The Inspector looked at the plate. "Doesn't look very special to me." Fredericks kept looking at his plate. "You make any retirement plans yet? Figure on taking some time off? What?"

Ben thought a while. He had been thinking about what he was going to do in retirement, but now that somebody asked him, he wasn't prepared to give a definite answer. "I've been in contact with a couple of friends at the City Wide Detective and Surveillance Agency, but yes, I'm definitely going to take a little time, make a few trips." Then he thought and added. "I want to see a little more of this world then Broadway, 42nd Street, and Hell's Kitchen." He dug into his stew.

"A cruise maybe? Where're you thinking of going?" Fredericks asked.

"I've been thinking about going over to Auschwitz . . ."

Frederick's look and sharp voice stopped him. "Auschwitz? Did I hear you say Auschwitz?"

"Yeah. What's wrong with that?"

"Nothing." Fredericks looked at his special. "Nothing at all." Then as they both ate their food quietly, Fredericks started talking. "What if I could arrange an all expense paid, unlimited, no questions asked, vacation for you in Auschwitz?"

Ben's fork stopped in mid air somewhere between his plate and his mouth. "Don't be a turd, Bill. My wife's entire family was murdered in Auschwitz." The smile disappeared from Fredericks' face. "Sorry about that, Ben. That was a dumb remark, but I didn't mean . . ." Ben waived him off and swallowed his mouthful of stew. "I promised Goldie before she died that I would go and put a small stone on her parents' graves." Fredericks looked puzzled. "Put up a headstone?" Ben shook his head. "No. Not a headstone. It's an old Jewish tradition to put a small stone, a pebble, a small rock on someone's grave, like a calling card," he explained, "to show that the person is not forgotten." He added. "At least that's what I think it means."

Fredericks looked at him. "I am sorry about that dumb crack. I really am." But before Ben could stop him again, he continued: "I didn't mean to be a smart ass, but there is something I need to talk to you about, that might fit in with your plans."

"Fit in with my plans of going to Auschwitz?" Ben looked puzzled.

"Yes. I think it might."

"I knew it!" Ben mopped some of the last of his stew with a piece of toast. "I knew there was more to this lunch than stew. Go ahead Bill, I am all ears!"

"Well, there is no point in talking about it, if you have your heart set on retiring." He feigned emphasis to his words.

Ben shook his head. "But you'll tell me anyhow! Right?"

"OK, Lieutenant, listen up . . ."

But Ben cut him off. "What's this Lieutenant shit about? You have been calling me Lieutenant since I walked into your office this morning."

Fredericks smiled and let it hang. "Would you like to be," he dragged out his words, "promoted to captain?"

"What?" Ben wasn't sure he heard right. "I am retiring! Remember?"

"I do, Ben. I do. But I have something to tell you. Hear me out. Please."

"OK. But hold it a second." He held up his hand stopping Bill. "I think I'm going to need something to help me through with this." He waived to the waiter. "Let me have a Metaxa."

Fredericks interrupted: "You want the seven star?"

"Or what?" Ben asked.

"Metaxa," Fredericks touted his knowledge, "goes from one star to seven stars. Seven stars is the most expensive."

"But it's on the department, right?"

"Right. I just mentioned it because it might be a matter of taste."

"OK." Ben said, "As long as it's on the department." He turned to the waiter: "I'll have the seven stars."

"We don't have seven stars," the waiter replied tersely.

"I'll have the six, five, or the four stars then," Ben nodded to the waiter.

"We don't have six, five, or four stars either."

"How 'bout three stars?" Ben asked.

"Lieutenant," the waiter said patronizingly, "if I had three stars, you would have had your four stars by now."

"I get it." Ben said. "I'll have a Metaxa. No stars, but make it a double."

"Make that two." Fredericks called after the waiter. He turned back to Ben: "Have you had any interesting cases lately?"

"Yeah. Mr. Higgins' golden retriever is intimidating Mrs. Snyder's poodle."

"Well, it's fun to be a short timer," Fredericks said and they both laughed.

Ben took a sip of his Metaxa and turned to Bill. "OK, Bill. What's this free lunch about?"

Inspector Fredericks took a bit longer than usual to get started. "Here is the deal Ben. Two days ago I got a call from the big "C", the big Cat. The Commissioner called me directly and wanted me to assign you to him to work on a high profile case." He stopped to gauge Ben's reaction. "Now, I don't know why, frankly I think it's political, but the big "C" wanted you on this case and wouldn't take no for an answer when I told him you were leaving the Department in six weeks."

"In other words," Ben butted in, "The case can wrap in six weeks?"

"From the little Commissioner Katz let on, frankly, I doubt it."

"You mean, you know it won't."

"I honestly don't know Ben, but I doubt it." He looked Ben straight in the eye and Ben knew that Bill was leveling with him. Fredericks went on, "Personally, I think this case will go on much longer than six weeks, but . . ." he added, ". . . it sounds interesting."

Ben took a sip of his Metaxa. "I'm all ears." He said with more than a little ring of sarcasm.

"According to Commissioner Katz, The Hungarian Security Agency, or whatever their name is, the Hungarian equivalent of our FBI, contacted our FBI asking for assistance. The little the big "C" told me was, that during the past ten or so years there have been a series of murders throughout Europe, and that the Hungarian Security . . ., the Hungarian FBI, believes that all of them are connected. The Hungarian Security Agency, or whatever, believes that they were all committed by one person, or organization, and that at least one of the perpetrators might be living in the United States, possibly in the New York area.

"So why not the FBI?" Ben asked.

"The FBI washed their hands," Inspector Fredericks looked at Ben, "wisely and smartly, I might add, claiming jurisdictional problems and other legal horse-crap, and suggested to the Hungarians that they contact the NYPD. The Hungarians did, their ambassador called the big Cat, and the big Cat called me. Commissioner Katz wants you on this case Ben. He even authorized this gourmet Greek lunch."

Ben pondered this a bit and ordered another double Metaxa. "Sounds like quite a case! Something I probably would've jumped on a couple of years ago, but this close to retirement," he shook his head, "I don't think so." Fredericks stayed quiet. "Why me?" Ben asked after a bit. "There are fifty-six hundred detectives on the Force in New York City, why me?" he repeated.

Fredericks took his time answering. He kept looking into his Metaxa shot glass as he spoke quietly. "I have something to tell you, Ben. I recommended you."

Ben threw the remains of his Metaxa down his throat. "Well, thanks for the gourmet lunch Bill, but no thanks for the offer. I'm retiring!"

Fredericks held up both of his hands in a calming gesture, "Ben, wait a second." He motioned to the waiter for another round of Metaxa. "There is more to this. I know you're looking forward to retirement. I know you've earned it. But there is one angle to this case that points right at you."

The new round of Metaxa was brought over by the waiter. "Yeah," Ben pointed at the shot glasses, "and that's why you're trying to get me drunk. Right, Bill?"

"Hear me out, Ben. I don't know all I should about this case, but it seems like just the kind of a case you used to love to work on, and, I might add, were so good at."

"Cut the crap, Bill!" Ben stopped him. "It won't work."

Fredericks held up his hands again. "From what I've heard, the murderer leaves a note at each scene, signed 'The Rat'." Ben looked at the Inspector with a puzzled expression. "So what?"

Fredericks smiled. "You are known as the 'Rat Catcher,' aren't you?"

Ben rolled his eyes. "For Christ's sake, Bill! Can't you do better?"

Fredericks nodded. "I think I can, Ben." He took a couple of sips of his Metaxa. "You see, I knew about your wife's family before I made that stupid wisecrack about paying for your vacation in Auschwitz. You know I didn't mean it the way it sounded, but I had a reason for saying it." He paused for a second and sensed that he connected with Ben. "I don't know too many of the details, but some of the murders took place in Auschwitz." Ben looked up, and his expression was asking for more. "All the murder victims," Bill spoke with emphasis, "were ex-Nazis, or were suspected of having been Nazis, or had something to do with the mistreatment, torture and slaughter of the Jews during the Holocaust." He stopped talking. Ben was also quiet, but it was obvious that Bill had gotten his attention and he wanted to hear more. "So far," Bill continued, 'The Rat'— that's how he signs his note at every site—has murdered 19 people, and claims that he has six more to go." Ben listened quietly. "Actually, the young fellow . . ."

"What young fellow?" Ben cut him off.

"A young captain from the Hungarian Police Bureau, or whatever," Bill explained, "claims to have a list of the next 6 targets, all of whom are Hungarian, and all of whom had something to do with the Holocaust in Hungary."

Ben cut in: "And how does that connect to me?"

"I honestly don't know, Ben. But a murder is a murder and, as the police, it is our job not to let killers go free and murder again and again."

Ben cut Fredericks off. "We pinned an awful lot of medals on our boys, including the Medal of Honor on some for killing those bastards over there."

"The war has been over for a bit, Ben. And the boys we pinned medals on were soldiers. This guy is a killer and it makes no difference who his victims may be. There are probably a hundred or more reasons why you should be the guy to handle this. Think about it and let me know. But don't wait too long. The big "C" is impatient, and you might also consider what it would mean to retire with captain's pay and benefits." He let it sink in and added: "Why don't we have lunch again tomorrow? You can let me know then."

"Is it gonna be on the Department?"

"Yes. We'll meet here at the same time. 12:30."

"No thanks. One Greek lunch without seven star Metaxa a year is enough. But the next time I'll pick the place. Maybe the Stage Deli, or Gallaghers." He thought a bit and added: "If the Hungarian police captain is around, I'd like to have a talk with him."

Fredericks nodded, waved to the waiter and smiled broadly when the waiter handed him the check. "My compliments to the chef, the special was superb." The waiter took a deep breath and looked off to the side. "Yeah. I'll tell him." They both got up, and headed out of the restaurant. As they waited for the green light on the corner of Ninth Avenue and 54th Street, Fredericks turned to Ben. "So when the big "C" calls, I can tell him you'll take the case?"

"It depends on two things: One," he patted his stomach and pantomimed gestures of throwing up, "he agrees not to buy me any more lunches at this dump, and two, what the young Hungarian "G" man has to tell me." Fredericks nodded, but Ben held up his hand stopping him. "And there is one more thing." Bill stepped back up on the curb.

"Here is the deal. The promotion to captain, and all related benefits will be effective immediately, not when I retire. I'll do this one case only before retiring, and I make and approve my own schedule. The Department will advance me an appropriate budget for this investigation. If the investigation goes longer than a year, at my discretion I'm to be released, and immediately retired with the rank and benefits of captain." He looked at Bill, but it was some time before Fredericks answered. "Wow," he said. "When did you pass the Bar exam? You sound like a shyster lawyer trying to cop a plea." He looked at Ben and added: "Can you come down a bit? If I bring this to the big Cat, we'll both get fired."

"Hey!" Ben cut him off, "I didn't ask for this! Remember? I wanted to retire and the Captaincy wasn't my idea!"

They crossed Ninth Avenue without talking, and headed East on 54th Street towards Midtown North.

Chapter 2

The Hungarian Super Sleuth.

The Stage Delicatessen was in full swing with the usual lunchtime crowd when Inspector Fredericks and Lieutenant Chapman entered and bumped their way through the multitude getting their take-out orders at the crowded sandwich counter. The tables were just about all taken even though it was still not quite noon, and true to their reputation, the waiters were getting nastier and more obnoxious as the restaurant was filling up. Fredericks led the way to one of the back rooms. "We are a bit early," he said, "Kapitan Gabriel Kerek . . ." he played the word 'Kapitan' to the hilt, ". . . won't be here for another half hour." He waved, and flashed a big smile at one of the waiters who knew him, and headed straight for a table in the back corner.

"So, how do we talk with this guy?" Ben asked. "Does he have an interpreter?"

"Doesn't need one. Speaks English, I hear, as good as you, maybe even a little better." Then added, "He doesn't curse and isn't a wise-ass."

"How do you know?" Ben asked.

"Commissioner Katz briefed me. The *Kapitan* is anxious to meet you and start working with you."

Ben cut him off: "I didn't say I would be working with him."

Fredericks held up his hands in his usual condescending manner. "OK, OK. I know, I know. I explained that to the big Cat, but he doesn't want to take no for an answer. He accepted all your conditions." He looked at Ben with a mischievous smile. "And wants to talk to you after you meet the *Kapitan*, Captain." He seemed disappointed, as he noted that his reference to the Captain went over Ben's head.

"Today, you mean?"

"Yes. He wants you downtown before four, Captain."

Ben still didn't catch the 'Captain'. . ."What's the rush?"

"I don't know, Ben. Maybe he has an early date with his girlfriend."

"What if I don't like what this Hungarian flatfoot has to say?"

"Ben . . . listen," Fredericks said condescendingly, "he wants to see you this afternoon. As far as he is concerned, you're already on the case, Captain." When Ben still didn't catch the 'Captain,' Bill threw up his hands in frustration, "I don't know Ben, I'm only the messenger here."

"Yeah. Right! I'll see what the Hungarian super sleuth has to say first."

"Do what you have to, Ben." Fredericks turned serious, "but remember one thing."

"What?"

"When the big Cat first called me and briefed me about this case, I honestly thought you'd like it. I knew you were bored with the crap, garbage cases you had to work on and I thought you'd jump on a real case again. I knew you wanted to travel, and I thought that this case would probably have some travel built in. And," he added, "I also thought that you wouldn't mind the extra money a promotion would give you for your retirement." He reached for the menu. Ben didn't know what to say.

"I think I'll have the corned beef on rye," Bill finally said, "take the leftovers home in a doggie bag and eat it for lunch for the rest of the week. "What you gonna have?" he asked. The tension was broken and Ben was grateful to Bill for letting him off so easily. "I hope you have your Mylanta with you." He smiled at Bill. "I'm going to have the pastrami on a Kaiser roll and have the leftovers for lunch tomorrow."

The sandwiches at the Stage Delicatessen on Seventh Avenue were legendary for their taste, the wonderful quality of the fresh meats, and bread hot out of the oven, but were known mostly for their enormous portions. An average sandwich was at least five times the size of a normal sandwich served in an ordinary deli, almost impossible to finish, and if one did, it was heartburn time for the rest of the afternoon. "What are you gonna drink?" Bill asked.

"I'd like to have a beer but I don't want the Hungarian super sleuth to think I'm a rummy, so I'll just have the Cream Soda. How about you?"

"I think I'll have the same," Bill said and looked up when someone stopped at their table.

It was a well dressed, attractive woman, mid to late thirties. "I am Captain Kerek." She held out a hand. Fredericks stood up to shake hands and after the surprise of seeing that Captain Kerek was a woman sank in, he pointed to Ben. "This is Lieu . . ." He corrected himself, "Captain Chapman."

"Ben threw a look at Fredericks, as it suddenly dawned on him that Fredericks had been calling him Captain. He was about to say something to Fredericks, but the woman was just standing there, looking at him, and he stood up and shook hands with her. "Chapman," he said simply.

"You are exactly on time," Fredericks stuttered and indicated a seat,". . . have a seat, *Kapitan*."

"If you wouldn't mind," the young woman said, as she seated herself, "I would prefer to be called Gabriella, actually Gabi would be best. Gabriella is my given name but all my friends call me Gabi." Fredericks and Ben sat quietly, alternately looking at each other, the menu, and the Hungarian Captain who turned out to be this good looking, young woman. She must have sensed their shock and explained further, "Gabi is spelled G-A-B-I but pronounced as Guhby." She laughed lightly, "Most Americans pronounce it Geby, so take your pick." Then she added, "I guess you are surprised that I am a woman?" Both Ben and Fredericks shook their head, but it was obvious that they were surprised. Ben already didn't like this turn of events. He had never worked with a woman. There were women in the NYPD, more and more in fact lately, but he had never worked with one, and now that he was about to retire, he didn't think this was going to be a good idea. Fredericks also didn't know what to make of the situation and was wondering why the Commissioner hadn't prepared him. Knowing Ben as well as he did, he figured the deal was off, and was already thinking about what he was going to say to the Commissioner when he went back to his office after lunch.

"We'll try Gaby," Fredericks said with a forced smile. "We were about to order Capta . . .," he caught himself again, ". . .Geby, why don't you look at the menu." This is a very special place," he swung into an explanation, "the sandwiches are wonderful."

"Yes. I've heard," Gabriella said. "I will have pastrami on rye bread, and a Budweiser." Ben and Bill looked at each other. "You shouldn't eat Pastrami without some alcohol to chase it," she explained, "Something has to break down the fat."

"You know a lot about American food?" Fredericks asked.

"Actually, pastrami is an eastern Hungarian food. The Romanians claim they invented it, but it is not true," she said with a smile. She indicated the pictures on the pages of the menu with a sweep of her hands, "Most of this stuff is Middle and Eastern European, mostly Jewish, Russian, Polish," she looked at Fredericks and Ben, "Except maybe the corned beef, which the Irish claim as their own." She laughed, as did Fredericks, but Ben just smiled. "What about the beer, the Budweiser?" Bill asked.

"Budweiser is the second best Czech beer, in Czechoslovakia. I mean in most places in America you can't get the best Czech beer, the Pilsner Urquel, and I am sorry to have to tell you that the American Budweiser is not as good as the Czech Budweiser, but it will have to do for now."

"Well, I learned a lot today," Bill remarked.

Ben was beginning to warm up a bit. All his life he lived by his own principle that if he didn't like somebody the first few minutes after he met them, the chances were he would never like them. He never made any bones about this. He lived by his instincts, and he knew that was one of the reasons he was a good cop. He could sense pretension, deception, when somebody tried to con him, but when somebody was straight forward and honest, like this young woman, at least at this point his instincts didn't set off a warning. The young woman was good looking, nicely groomed and tastefully dressed, and he realized that there was nothing about her that turned him off. He was even more convinced when he turned to the young woman: "You are a long way from home, Captain." She came directly to the point. "Gaby, or Gabriella if you'd prefer, please. I came to see you, Lieutenant Chapman."

Ben nodded. "In that case you might as well call me Ben."

"Thank you." she smiled. "I will."

"I briefed. . ." Fredericks stopped, thinking that perhaps he should use simpler language, or explain what he meant by 'briefed.' "I told Ben as much as

I could about your case. He knows as much as I do." Then he stopped for lack of anything else to say.

"Yes." She hesitated a moment. "My organization has been pursuing this case for a little over ten years now, but aside from a few hunches, we have nothing."

"Well, a few hunches are not a bad beginning," Ben nodded.

"After ten years," she looked at Ben, "it's difficult to consider it a beginning, Capt . . . " she corrected herself, "I am sorry, Ben. Besides the hunches, I'm sorry to have to admit, we are no closer to solving this case than we were over ten years ago." She looked at Ben. "That's why I am here.. . .to ask for your help."

"Why me?" Ben asked.

"Inspector Fredericks and Commissioner Katz think you are the best man to help us with this case. They said you have a perfect record."

Ben could tell the young woman wasn't buttering him up. "That's not quite true. I came off second best in one case."

"That would be when you were stabbed?" Gabriella asked earnestly.

"Right." He nodded, but he didn't want to talk about being stabbed. It was not a good memory, and unlike other cops who seemed to revel in talking about their injuries, showing their scars, gunshot wounds, he never talked about the morning when the spaced out drug addict sank an ice-pick in his chest. He changed the subject. "Your perp knocked off nineteen people, I think Bill mentioned."

"Actually," Gabriella answered with some hesitation, "Twenty." She reached into her purse and pulled out a sheet of paper. "My consulate delivered this to my hotel this morning." Both Bill and Ben perked up. "It is in Hungarian," Gabi explained, "but the murderer struck again two days ago. Our consulate in Los Angeles was contacted by the Los Angeles Police Department for information on a Hungarian alien resident of Los Angeles, who died of mysterious causes, under very unusual circumstances," she looked at both Bill and Ben "which, incidentally, has been the case with some of our other victims. The actual cause of death is unknown in this particular case. There was no indication of any physical cause, no gun shots, strangulation, poisoning; in fact the coroner's report lists the cause of death as heart failure."

Ben held up his hands and cut in. "Whoa! If the victim died of heart failure, why was he considered murdered?" Fredericks nodded in agreement.

"As in all the other cases," she continued, "the murderer left a note, taking responsibility for the person's death."

The cop in Ben was coming to the surface. "That is kind of unusual, if you ask me, for one murderer to claim nineteen," he corrected himself, "twenty victims. What makes you think it's just one perpetrator?"

"There was no doubt about that from the very beginning." Gabriella explained. "Every person murdered was identified in a note left by the murderer. The note explained who the victim was, why he was picked to die, and most importantly, every note was signed by the murderer as 'The Rat'."

"Wow." Ben sat back and the "wow," which he repeated was in reaction to the immense sandwich the waiter just brought to the table. But he was no longer hungry. He wanted to hear more, and inwardly had to admit that he was hooked.

"You tell me that no foul play, . . ." he smiled inwardly at the expression, 'foul play,' which he detested as a dumb phrase reporters and TV script writers used when they wanted to sound like the police, ". . .was suspected? That the victim was believed to have died a natural death?"

"Yes," Gabriella emphasized, "if it were not for the notes the murderer left behind, a number of the cases would have been classified as death by natural or accidental causes, and could have gone unnoticed. Of course there were the cases where there was no doubt," she looked at Ben and repeated him. "Indeed, there was 'foul play.' But even in those cases, not one single individual was killed simply by a gunshot, or stabbed, or beaten to death. Everyone killed so far died under very unusual circumstances, and no two cases were alike." Ben made a mental note to ask her later about what the unusual circumstances were. Bill noticed Ben's interest perk up, and had an almost imperceptible smile on his face, realizing that Ben was on the case. Gabriella continued, "The first victim, an ex-gendarme in the old Hungarian Gendarmerie, was found buried in human manure in an old boxcar, . . ." Ben cut in. "Wow!" He shook his head. "That's a lot to start with. Why don't we tackle this," he indicated the untouched sandwiches, "and continue talking back at my office." He turned to the Hungarian captain. "You free this afternoon?"

"Yes sir! That is what I am here for." She picked up the immense sandwich. "I should take some of this back to my hotel for dinner."

Fredericks didn't comment. They all dug into the food.

*   *   *

It was exactly 3:30 when there was a discreet knock on Ben's door and the door opened a crack. Inspector Fredericks stuck his head into the office. He looked at his wristwatch. "It's half past three, Ben," the Commissioner is expecting you before four."

Ben almost looked annoyed, like when a man is interrupted in the middle of something very important. "I can't go right now." He paused and looked at the Hungarian Captain. "We are in the middle of . . ." he didn't know what to say. He knew Bill was already convinced that he would take the job, but he never liked to be taken for granted, and he didn't want to give in that easily. "Why don't you call the big Cat, . . ." he corrected himself, ". . .the Commissioner, and tell him, I'm talking with Captain Geby, I mean Kerek." He threw an apologetic glance at Gabriella. ". . .and that I'll come to see him tomorrow." Fredericks shook his head. "The C is gonna be pis. . ." He didn't finish. "But I'll tell him."

"Would you prefer for me to call him?" Ben asked. But Bill shook his head. "No, I'll call him." He didn't wait for Ben to say thanks, or anything, just closed the door and left Ben and the Hungarian captain to themselves. He knew that Ben was on the case. He knew Ben long enough to know that even if Ben was playing hard to get, he was hooked and on the case. The chase was on, and when Ben started a chase, he wouldn't stop until the perp was in custody and the case was put to bed. He didn't think it was going to be difficult to explain to the Commissioner that Ben was in a "heavy" conversation with his Hungarian counterpart, and hearing that, he was sure the Commissioner would not mind waiting till tomorrow to talk with Ben.

*   *   *

Ben reached behind him and picked up an empty file box, the kind that usually holds dead files intended for storage. "This is my 'Barf Box'." He showed the box to Gabriella and indicated that it was empty. "B.B. I call it for short." He made like he was throwing up, sticking his tongue out, holding his stomach, and leaning over the empty file box. When he saw Gabriella's puzzled expression, he explained. "Whatever comes up, goes into this box." She listened, still looking a bit puzzled, but it was obvious that she was interested in anything Ben had to say. "When the box is full, . . ." Ben continued, ". . . or when some key item comes up, I sort through everything in the B. B. and if two pieces of the puzzle fit together, I put them on my Barf Board." He pointed to a good size bulletin board on his wall to one side of his desk. The board was almost completely empty, except for a few pieces of obviously unimportant sheets of paper, a menu from a Chinese take-out place with a large red dragon and the telephone number in green; a 'Do List' with nothing on it, and some more sheets of faded paper that should have been discarded long ago. He felt, though he was a bit embarrassed, that he had to explain why his Barf Board had nothing important on it. "I have been clearing it off, . . ." he started feebly, ". . . now that I am getting ready to retire, I am not taking any new cases." He caught himself thinking that he might have said too much.

"Inspector Fredericks mentioned, you were retiring but he had hoped you might be persuaded to help us out." Gabriella looked at Ben with anticipation.

"It's true," Ben said. "I told Bill when he first brought this to me that I would talk with you." After a moment he added, "But I didn't promise him."

She remained silent. Ben seemed to be in deep thought and the young Hungarian captain sat quietly, not wanting to disturb him. They sat in silence for a while. "Well . . ." Ben slapped his knee, sat up straight in his chair and smiled at her. "Why don't you give me a little more. How 'bout," he suggested, "you give me some detail?" She nodded her head in agreement. "Why don't we start with case number one, the first murder."

Gabriella reached into her large purse and pulled out a file folder. "Murder Number One, as it is officially called now, happened on July 4th, 1968, and it involved an ex-gendarme in the old Hungarian Gendarmerie who was found buried in human manure in an old boxcar. He was involved in the deportation of Jews from a small western Hungarian town, Pápa." She looked up at Ben, who was leaning way back in his chair, looking at the ceiling, chewing on his pencil, but his expression left no doubt, he was listening.

"It was a very unusual case." She continued. "Even before the local police found the murderer's note, it was obvious the man was murdered. The local police called it," she seemed a little uncomfortable to say it, "the shit case." There was an embarrassed smile on her face as she continued. "The corpse was found in an old boxcar that had been side railed and unused for many years, in a heap of human manure that was dried almost as hard as cement, but it apparently helped preserve the body to the point that it could be identified." She looked up at Ben who didn't comment or ask questions, but he made circles in the air with his chewed up pencil, indicating for Gabi to go on.

"But even if the body had been decomposed, his identity was fully explained by The Rat's, the murderer's note, as Köröndi Pál. According to The Rat," she turned to Ben to clear it up, "I hope you don't mind but we have been referring to the murderer for years now as The Rat." Ben nodded. "In any case," she continued, "according to The Rat, Mr. Köröndi . . ." Ben interrupted her: "Is that his last name?" "Yes." She explained, "In Hungarian the family name comes first. Köröndi is his family name, and Pál, Paul in English, is his given name." Ben seemed to be transfixed on the ceiling, and kept chewing on his pencil. "Mr. Köröndi," she went on, "was the man responsible for organizing the deportation of three thousand Jews from the town of Pápa to Auschwitz. He loved his job, and left no doubt that he was in full favor of sending the Jews to their death, even more than the Nyilasok—that's the Hungarian Nazis"—she explained. "Mr. Köröndi did everything to make the life of three thousand people miserable. When some of the lower ranking railroad people put a few buckets of water and some empty buckets for sanitation in some of the boxcars, Köröndi made them take them out of the cars and threatened to send the men to Auschwitz with the Jews." She stopped for a while and opened the file folder. She pulled out a sheet and handed it to Ben. "This is a copy of The Rat's note. I hope you don't mind, but I have taken a chance on your involvement and had translations made, with appropriate explanations." She handed Ben the two sheets of paper. "As you will see, The Rat's note points out that Mr. Köröndi was murdered on the anniversary of the Jews having been taken from Pápa, twenty-four years before the murder. The note also indicates that Mr. Köröndi was one of twenty five people amongst those who had something to do with the murder of the Jews, and who were still alive, and like Köröndi, were marked for execution."

Ben took the sheets of paper from Gabi, opened one of his desk drawers and pulled out an empty file folder. He put The Rat's note into it, and put the file folder into his Barf Box. "There seems to be a lot of good clues in there," he said to her.

"That's what we thought also," she agreed, "but one by one the clues dried up." Ben looked at her. "Dried up." Gabriella smiled. "It's a little bit of literal translation from Hungarian. The clues didn't pan out," she used American slang.

"You said the victim, Mr. Koro . . . Kormi. . ."

"Köröndi." she helped out.

"Right, Köröndi, you said was covered with human excrement, manure?"

"That's right. The forensic people thought that as the shit," she corrected herself, "the manure, dried, it helped preserve the body that they figured should have been pretty badly decomposed by the time it was found."

"That's something. I would have thought that all that shit," he emphasized the word, "shit," noting, and hoping to ease the young Hungarian captain's discomfort with using the word, "would have sped up decomposition. By the way," he turned to her, "it must take a lot of shit to cover an entire body. Where does one get all that shit?"

Gabriella smiled. "That was the first question we asked the local constable, but in Hungary it isn't really hard to get hold of human manure." Ben waited for more. "A little town like Celldömölk still has a lot of homes without indoor plumbing . . ." Ben cut in, "What does this town Sell something have to do with this case?"

"Oh, I guess, I didn't tell you. Celldömölk is a town twenty seven kilometers, less than twenty miles from Pápa. It is a much smaller town than Pápa, but its railroad station is bigger because it is a rail junction. The lines branch off at Celldömölk and some of the old railroad equipment, like old engines, locomotives and cars are kept there on old, unused sidings. Almost like a museum. The government that owns the railroad in Hungary doesn't have the money to have a proper museum, they just keep the old trains at Celldömölk."

"So what does Selldo...." He still had trouble with the name of the town, "have to do with this murder?"

"Mr. Köröndi's body was found in one of the old boxcars at Celldömölk."

"Didn't you say something about Mr. Köröndi being in that town Pápa?"

"Yes, sir, I did. But as The Rat's note explains, Mr. Köröndi was murdered in the same kind of boxcar the Jews were transported in from Pápa."

"And why the shit?" Ben asked.

"The note also explains that. By the time the Jews reached Auschwitz, most were sick, and many of them had died in the superheated boxcar. It was July. With more than a hundred people in a single car without food and water, and without any place to relieve themselves for ten days, most of the dead bodies, in fact all the people in the car were covered with shi. . ." she corrected herself, "with excrement, which is why, as The Rat's note explains, Köröndi was to die, covered with shit."

Ben was about to get sick. He turned away from her, and wiped his face with his handkerchief. "You know, my wife's entire family were murdered in Auschwitz."

Gabriella remained quiet, but her expression left no doubt how sorry she was. Ben continued: "Goldie, my wife, let her rest in peace, somehow survived, but never wanted to talk about what it was like. I picked up a little something about her experience, when she talked with friends about it now and then, but I didn't think she wanted to tell me about it, so I let it be. I didn't press her. I didn't want her to remember those things, and I guess, she didn't tell me because, maybe she didn't want me to feel bad. Besides, even now as you are giving me some of the detail, I guess she would have thought I wasn't going to believe her. How can you believe something like this?" Gabriella nodded her head in agreement. "She never talked about it," Ben said again. They sat quietly for some time. It was Ben, much to Gabi's relief, who broke the silence. "So, where does somebody get hold of enough human excrement to cover a body?" Her answer surprised him.

"Well, actually, like I said, it's not that difficult in Hungary. Celldömölk is a small town and still has lots of homes without indoor plumbing. They have outhouses built over cesspools that have to be cleaned out whenever they fill up."

"So, what do they do with all that shit?" Ben smiled, trying to make the use of the word a little easier.

"Most just gets dumped. There is a law now forbidding the use of human manure in agriculture, but some of the village people, particularly those who have no animals and no animal manure, still try to use human manure."

Ben thought all this was interesting but he wanted to get back to the case. "So, if somebody wanted, let's say I wanted, to come by enough human manure to cover a body, how would I go about it?"

"There are several ways," she started to explain. "There are people who clean cesspools as a profession, and some people clean their cesspools themselves because they can't afford the professionals. If one knew any of these people, professional or not, I don't think it would be very difficult to get hold of a load of manure."

"Would this be an expensive undertaking?" Ben wanted to know.

"I doubt it. Its getting to be more and more difficult to dispose of unprocessed human waste, and anybody who has it, I imagine would be happy to get rid of it."

"Was this followed up? I mean did anyone try to get to the buyer, or . . ." he was groping for a word, "the disposee, or the disposer, of the manure?"

"We made a small effort, but more for show than for anything else, because we knew it was going to lead nowhere." Ben's expression was asking for more. "The forensic people knew from the murderer's note that the murder took place three months before the body was found. The local constable—a little town like Celldömölk," she explained, "has no police department. They have a couple of constables who don't want excitement. Neither do the people in town. '*Ne szólj szám, nem fáj fejem.*' " Ben was puzzled. "Meaning?"

"Meaning 'My lips don't speak, my head won't ache'. "

But Ben still didn't get it. Gabriella went on. "It's been the attitude of Hungarian village people going way back to serfdom. If one didn't speak, didn't say anything, he wouldn't get into trouble. And none of them, I mean the villagers, want anything to do with the police. We didn't get anywhere with them. Nobody knew anything about anyone looking for, or actually buying, human manure. Nobody knew anything, and the forensic people said, even if they sampled every cesspool in Celldömölk, after all this time, the solidified excrement over Köröndi's body could no longer be identified." He then added, "Whoever it was, had to get Köröndi's body, or Köröndi still alive, to the old boxcar on the siding in Celldömölk, get him into the boxcar, bury him under a huge mound of fresh shit, leave a note, lock the boxcar, walk away, and yet nobody in a town of about eight thousand people saw, or heard anything."

"End of story?" Ben asked.

"End of story." She nodded in agreement. "We went through the usual routine, questioned what seemed like the whole town of Pápa and Celldömölk, and came up with nothing."

"In other words, I take it, you questioned people in Pápa because Köröndi had worked there at the time the Jews were taken away?"

"Yes. And because Köröndi lived in Pápa. He was put in prison after the war for his part in what was called 'crimes against humanity' and served six months, but still lived in Pápa supporting himself with whatever odd jobs he could get."

"In other words," Ben asked, "he had to be taken from Pápa to Selldo . . ." he still couldn't pronounce the name of the town, "and killed in Selldomuck, or do you think he was done in, in Pápa and was taken dead to Selldumack?"

"Either of those are possibilities. He wasn't a big guy, could easily have fitted into the trunk of even a small car. But like in Celldömölk, nobody knew anything in Pápa either. Nobody even admitted to knowing Mr. Köröndi beyond knowing him as someone who lived near by, or bought his groceries in a certain store. Nobody wanted to admit to any association with Mr. Köröndi for fear of being implicated with him, or his war . . ."

A quiet knock on the door's glass panel interrupted them again. Inspector Fredericks stuck his head into Ben's little office. "Could I speak with you a second?" He looked at Gabi. "Please excuse us a moment Captain," She nodded. Ben got up and as he went through the door, Fredericks closed the door behind him. He pulled Ben by the arm a few steps from the door. "Katz is pissed." He hissed. "He is gonna have your head. He wanted to talk with you before you discussed anything with the Hungarian captain, and waited till five thirty for you."

"Didn't you call him?" Ben asked.

"I called him, but he was in a meeting and I left a message for him. I guess he didn't get, or pick up the message." Ben was about to say something but Fredericks cut him off. "He wants you in his office first thing in the morning."

"First thing in the morning," Ben repeated.

"Yeah. First thing, and if you want to know what I think, I think he is going to have your head and hand it to you. The way he was shouting at me on the phone just now, I think you might as well kiss the captaincy good bye, and consider yourself lucky if he isn't going to bring you up on charges for insubordination." Ben didn't say anything. He just stood quietly and watched Fredericks walk away from him. A couple of seconds later he went back to his office.

"I am sorry to have kept you, Ben," Captain Kerek said pleasantly, "but I didn't realize how late it was. I hope I didn't cause any trouble."

"Not to worry." Ben said.

Outside his barred window the little patch of sky that was visible between the tall buildings that surrounded the precinct was pitch black, and the orange glow of the powerful mercury lights on Eighth Avenue reflected off some of the walls. "If you are hungry and don't have other plans," he turned to Gabi, "maybe we could grab a bit of something to eat."

"That would be nice," she agreed and stood up.

"We could go over to Sardi's. I know the headwaiter and we might get to see some Broadway stars, or," he said, noticing no interest in her expression, "we could get one of Gallagher's world class steaks. Do you eat steak, Captain?"

"Yes, I do. I love American steak."

"So, I guess Sardi's is out then?"

Gabriella nodded. "I am not a fan. I mean if I see a movie star, it's OK, but that's about it."

Ben liked the young woman. In fact he liked her more now than when they first met just a few hours ago at lunch. And it was now past his regular dinner time, and he didn't even notice how fast the time passed as he was listening to her beginning to lay out what he already thought was a fascinating, and challenging case. "All right then," he reached for his coat, "we'll go to Gallagher's and you'll have the best steak you've ever had."

Some time later they walked into Gallagher's on 52nd Street and Ben noticed the amazement on Gabriella's face as they walked past the glass paneled cooler with sides of beef hanging by the dozen. The Maitre d' smiled at Ben and grabbed a couple of menus.

"Good to see you, Ben." he greeted them. "I haven't seen you for some time and I thought you might have retired."

"No. Not yet." Ben winked at him," I am close to it, but not yet. This is Captain Kerek," he introduce Gabi, "she is visiting us all the way from Hungary on a case." The Maitre offered a hand. "Glad to meet you, Captain. How do you like America?" he asked as he was leading them to a table near the charcoal grills and chefs broiling steaks and chops behind the glass partition.

"Fine," Gabriella said. Since she arrived in New York, it was the first question everybody asked her when they first met and the other person found out that she was from abroad. "I like it a lot," she added.

The Maitre d' handed them the menus. "Enjoy your dinner." he said and winked at Ben. "It's on the house." He walked away even before Ben had a chance to thank him. A waiter was standing at the table. "Can I get your drink order?"

"Would you like a drink?" Ben looked at Gabi.

"I'll have a glass of Merlot."

Ben liked this gal. There was no pretension about her, she was direct and to the point. Yet she was pleasant and good to be with. He ordered a Jack Daniels on the rocks for himself and turned back to Gabi. "I hope," he referred to their lunch conversation, "that you are not going to tell me that steak is a Hungarian food."

"I won't," she laughed. "We don't have good beef in Hungary. There isn't anything that could even remotely compare with western beef production. We have a lot of dairy cattle, and work animals mostly on farms, but only the old ones get sold for beef. The calves are sold as soon as they can be weaned and the mother can produce milk. We eat a lot of veal, pork, geese, chickens, but I am afraid our beef is very second rate."

"Well," Ben said, pleased, "I hope you'll enjoy our beef. Do you know what you're going to have?"

"I'll have the 16 oz. Filet Mignon."

"That should be great rare." Ben suggested.

"I'm afraid I am not that American yet." Gabriella said quietly. "I grew up on well done meat, not even pink on the inside."

"That would be the surest way to ruin a good steak." Ben put down his menu. "Let me tell you something. I hope you'll take it from an old steak lover, the steak in this restaurant can be eaten raw. It will melt in your mouth, and if you overcook it, it will become dry, tough, tasteless, and inedible."

Gabi looked at Ben, obviously considering what he just told her. "OK," she said. "If you say so, Ben. I'll try it. How should I order it?"

"I am having mine, rare to medium rare," Ben said. "but considering what you just told me, to be on the safe side, why don't you order yours medium. And I would recommend," Ben added, "a real Idaho Spud. I don't know if you have ever had one, they are great."

"I love potatoes," she said sincerely.

Ben looked at her. "Potatoes? These are spuds, Idaho Spuds."

The drinks were brought to the table by the waiter. "To your health," Ben lifted his glass. "What do you say in Hungarian?"

"We say *'egészségére'*; to your health." They both sipped their drink. "Wonderful wine!" Gabriella said and took a second sip. "We used to make a very good red wine in Hungary, the Egri Bikavér, Bull's Blood," she translated, "but now the vineyards have been enlarged and they are selling the label. It's a famous wine, but not very good any more," she said sadly.

An hour and a half later they were topping off with some Napoleon brandy. "This was a wonderful experience," Gabriella said. It wasn't hard to see how much she enjoyed her meal and the evening. "The next time I'll have my Filet rare." She smiled at Ben. "Thank you Ben. This was a great evening, but I must go. I have to turn in early, I'll be catching American flight number 1 at 9:00 am to Los Angeles in the morning."

"I take it, it has to do with number 20?" Ben asked.

"Yes, sir. Our consulate made the arrangements with the LAPD. I'm being met at the airport in Los Angeles."

They were heading out of the restaurant. "I'll see you as soon as I get back to New York, Ben," Gabi said as they were shaking hands in front of the restaurant. She almost didn't hear Ben, and wasn't sure if Ben might have said, "If I don't see you before."

*   *   *

As soon as he was in his car, even before the car cleared the exit from the garage onto 54th Street, he called the police operator on his radio. "Get me Inspector Fredericks, please." The operator came back in few minutes: "Inspector Fredericks is not answering his call, Ben. Shall I keep trying?"

"Yeah. Keep trying him and if you can't get me, I'll probably be going through the tunnel, tell him that I have to talk with him. It's urgent."

"OK, Ben." The operator signed off.

He was thinking about his day and suddenly realized the change that had taken place in him since morning. He was not feeling the same as he had before lunch, or for that matter, for the past couple of months. He suddenly realized that in fact he was feeling the way he used to feel before his encounter with the druggy's ice pick, when he would start on a new case, full of anticipation and drive to get the job done. He felt like a new man, a condemned man who was suddenly given a new extension on life. He was back in the game and he knew it. He flashed his badge going through the toll booth at the Queens side of the Midtown Tunnel and headed east on the Long Island Expressway. His radio came alive with a crackle, it was Inspector Fredericks. "What's up, Ben? I hear you're looking for me."

"Yeah, Bill. I need a favor."

"Speak," Bill's voice came over the speaker under the dash. "What can I do for you?"

"I need you to call the . . ." he caught himself, realizing that they were on an open frequency, "call Commissioner Katz for me in the morning and please tell him that something came up and I won't be able to come to his office for a couple of days."

"You're not? Why not?" Fredericks' voice left no doubt he expected disaster. He repeated, "Why not Ben? Why can't you see him?"

"I'll be out of town for a couple of days, Bill. I'll call you and explain tomorrow."

"You'll be where out of town?" Fredericks' voice crackled. "What is this about?"

"Something came up suddenly, and," he paused a second, "could you telex an authorization to American Airlines for a round trip to Los Angeles, flight number 1 leaving at nine o'clock tomorrow morning with an open return, and a week's worth of vouchers, you know the usual stuff, hotel, meals, car, the works." He spoke into his mike. "Bill. You copy?"

There was no answer. Ben repeated: "Bill? Are you there?" Finally Bill's voice came back on. "Call me as soon as you get home." The characteristic click that followed told Ben that Inspector Fredericks had signed off. He turned his red flasher on, lowered the window and put the flasher on the roof of his car. He turned on his siren and floored the gas pedal.

* * *

The line was moving slowly. There were maybe a dozen people ahead of him going up to the ticket counter in the newly remodeled American Airlines building at Kennedy. He had time to think. He thought there were three possibilities. One; Fredericks would have a message waiting for him: "Get your ass in my office. No delay!" Two: "Take it up with the Commissioner. He is expecting you this morning." And Three, and very unlikely: "He would have no message but there would be a ticket and vouchers for him at the ticket counter." And there would be one more likely possibility, it occurred to Ben that none of the above might be waiting for him; there would be no message, no tickets, vouchers, or anything.

Ben considered other scenarios, but they really didn't matter; he either went, or he didn't. And he wanted to go. For the first time since he got out of the hospital, he felt like a cop again, having motives to figure out, clues to follow up, adding two and two together, and eventually chasing down a killer, solving the case. He also liked the young Hungarian cop, who, he sensed, genuinely wanted his help, but most of all this case promised to be a big one, perhaps the biggest he ever had, and he wanted it. Just on the basis of what took the entire afternoon and evening for Gabriella to describe, he figured he was going to need a dozen barf boxes, and he could tell that the leads were going to go beyond the boundaries of New York City, his hunting territory of a little under twenty-three years, and most likely even out of the country. And if he was going to be part of it, he had to get to Los Angeles now, get in on the investigation of murder number twenty, and then back off from there to number one, the "shit case," as Gabi called it, which kept him up most of the night. Mentally, he had a modus operandi figured out, a logical, step by step procedure to follow, then move onto case number two, three, four, and so on, to pick up the trail of The Rat and eventually catch him. He was on the case. He figured the Commissioner would be happy to hear it, and it made little difference if the big "C," Commissioner Katz, heard about it this morning, or a week from now. The next step was to get to LA.

He even had his credit card out of his wallet, just in case he was going to have to pay his own way, because in spite of Fredericks, or the Commissioner, he was going.

The young woman in the snappy uniform behind the counter punched some keys on her computer and looked at the screen with an expression that she tried to keep blank, but one, which she might have hoped elevated the importance of her job. It was obvious that there was something on the screen she didn't quite expect. She punched some more buttons and the printer came alive, spewing a couple of sheets of printout. She tore the sheets off when the printer stopped and handed them to Ben.

Ben smiled, as he read the note: "It's your ass. I hope you know what you're doing, though I know you don't. I'll call the big "C" this morning probably after ten, in order not to interfere with his early meetings." If Bill was standing next to him, Ben would have kissed him. He knew what was behind the sentence, "not to interfere with his early meetings until after ten." It meant that by ten o'clock he would most likely be over Pittsburgh, or Cleveland, on his way to the coast whether the big "C" liked it or not. It was obvious that Bill was still his partner, his back-up, and even the next sentence in the message didn't surprise him: "You and I might be retiring together, probably next week, demoted to patrolman. My regards to the Hungarian flatfoot, and have a good time in Tinsel Town. Orders and vouchers to follow via channels. B. F."

"Are you armed, Captain Chapman?" He heard the ticket agent ask him, and for a moment he was startled. He was too engrossed in his thoughts, and didn't expect the question, and wasn't used to the Captain before his name. He figured that his promotion, as far as Bill Fredericks was concerned was a done deal. "Yes," he answered her, "I have a standard issue, 38 caliber revolver on me."

I have to ask you to fill out some papers, and as long as your orders don't specify the necessity of remaining armed, I have to ask you to check your weapon with us." Ben nodded, and asked the young woman if a Captain Kerek had checked in yet. She punched her key-board, and without looking at Ben, obviously reading her computer screen, a moment later told Ben: "A Gabriella Kerek has checked in, but I don't see a Captain Kerek. Ben asked her if a seat next to Ms. Kerek might be open. The ticket agent went back to her computer. "There is a window seat next to Ms. Kerek." She said a moment later, "Would you like to have it?" Ben nodded. "Thank you very much," and waited for the agent to hand him his tickets and boarding pass. "Please follow me," she said and put a 'Next Agent' sign on the counter in front of her. Ben followed her to an office where she took a small lock-able metal case from one of the cabinets and handed Ben a couple of forms to fill out. Ben unsnapped his holster from his belt and put his gun in the metal box. The forms said nothing about any other weapon and he left his snub-nose 38 strapped to his ankle. "Do you think Ms. Kerek is armed?" the ticket agent asked him.

"I seriously doubt it." he said with a straight face, "as far as I know she seldom carries anything more than a small Billy club." The agent didn't ask any more questions.

*   *   *

Ben scanned the crowds as he went through security, but didn't see Gabi anywhere. His gate, 9A, was at the far end of the long walkway and just as he got closer he spotted Gabi, standing at the large glass panel looking out at the runways and the tarmac, watching the planes land or take off in the distance. He bought himself a paper at the news stand, not so much to read it, but to cover his face as he sat down in one of the furthest seats from the gate, keeping an eye on Gabi, and he was pleased to see Gabi was traveling alone.

Some time later, after the flight had been announced several times, just as the last of the passengers were about to go through the gate, Ben got up, pulled the rim of his hat down over his eyes, put on a pair of large dark glasses and turned the collar of his coat up. Gabi was settling into her seat as Ben came through the partition between the first class and the coach compartment. He put his suit-bag into the overhead compartment, and with newspaper in hand, held carefully to cover his face, sat down next to her. Her eyes were closed. She was sitting in Ben's assigned seat by the window, but Ben didn't say anything. He didn't want to risk waking her, just in case she was really dozing, though he sensed she wasn't. He had done the same thing many times when he was traveling on a case. It was easier to close his eyes as soon as he sat down and feign sleep, than to risk getting into a conversation with a talkative person sitting next to him. He smiled now, as he knew that she was probably doing the same thing, and sensed that he liked the young police officer even more than he did the day before.

Chapter 3

Case Number One.

. . . eleven years earlier in Celldömölk, Hungary . . .

Köröndi Pál sat on the buckboard of his cart, wondering how much longer he would have to wait. He got to the wire gate at the end of the siding, weeds growing in between the tar covered ties, with a lonely, old boxcar sitting on no longer used, rusty rails. The old boxcar's boards were rotted by the rain and years of neglect, and the metal roof and strapping that held the car together, were rusting away. He didn't know how much longer he was going to have to wait.

The envelope with a note, and 10.000 forints in cash, was stuck into his mail slot three days ago. He didn't know what to make of it at first, there was no return address, no signature, or any indication of who sent it. It only said to bring the load to this spot and wait. He was to get another ten-thousand forints when the wagon was at its destination and the manure was unloaded. Twenty thousand forints was a lot of money and he needed money badly. This was a large windfall, and he didn't care who it was from. Besides, his cesspool needed cleaning out anyhow. It was almost full to the top, and he thanked God for the timely note before he would have emptied the pool anyhow. Twenty-thousand forints was more money than he had seen in one sum since he was released from prison six years ago. He had no regular job and lived on whatever came his way, whenever anybody had something dirty to do that nobody else would touch. He was desperate and had no choice. His pension was taken away from him when he was sentenced for—what he still told himself—serving his country. He did what he was told, what he was ordered to do, and what he believed was in the best interest of his country. The Jews were bleeding the country, and when the opportunity came, he was happy to play his part in getting rid of them. He loved the service. After serving in the Gendarmerie for fifteen years, rising to the rank of Staff Sergeant, he enjoyed his position which put him above, and gave him power over, the average person in the territory he patrolled. He loved the Gendarmerie. He remembered being the sergeant in charge of the detachment that herded the Jews into the Ghetto in Pápa, and beating the crap out of some of them at the headquarters he commandeered for his unit, the former home of a wealthy Jew. Of course some of the Jews did come across with money and other valuables rather than risk being tortured, but most of the money was gone now, even the small amount he managed to hide before he was arrested.

The smell, coming from his cart behind him, was awful. It took him the better part of the afternoon the day before to bail out his cesspool and load it into his cart, but he wanted to get an early start to get to Celldömölk before evening. It wasn't that Celldömölk was so far, but his old horse, he knew, couldn't break into a trot even downhill. And as bad as the smell was, this time he was going to get money for what he had to do for nothing at least twice a year, once in the fall and once in the spring; cleaning out his overflowing cesspool under the outhouse. Moving the small outhouse was the easy part. He hitched his horse to the metal ring near the ground on one side, and dragged the small wooden shack over to the side, exposing the cracked, and crumbling cement pool under it. The smell of bailing the pool was the worst and even after he washed the sides of the pool down with lime, the smell lingered for days, usually until the first rain cleared the air.

He rolled a cigarette and wondered who wanted to buy the stinking shit and pay twenty-thousand forints for it. Whoever it was, was a godsend. He sat and waited. Occasionally somebody came by, but when they got in range of the smell they would cross over to the other side of the road and hurry away as fast as they could. It was getting late in the afternoon and he was hoping that whoever it was that sent him the note with the money would show up soon. He wanted to get rid of the manure, get the rest of the money, and get back on the road to Pápa before nightfall. He fished the note out of his pocket to make sure he was in the right place. Yes, the gate to the rail-yard was at his left, and almost directly across from the gate was the little grotto with the Madonna, just as the note said, accurate even to the peeling paint. He thought how sad it was that these little roadside places of prayer had fallen into neglect since the Russians came into the country and their local lackeys got into power. He was not a very religious man, but he sympathized with anything that fell into disfavor under the new regime.

He was getting hungry. The little canvas sack was next to his feet and he got off the cart, hoping to get away from the smell while he ate. He put a couple of handfuls of oats into the feed sack and hung it over his horses head, with the horse's snout in it. It was lunchtime for both of them. Some time later, after he finished his onion and his piece of bread, he wiped his pocket knife and looked around but saw no one in sight. He climbed back on his cart and waited. The flies were swarming on the straw that covered the load in the cart behind him and were getting his horse nervous. He noticed that the heaping load of dung he piled into his cart the day before, was now barely filling the bed and figured that the liquid part of the manure had dripped out through the cracks between the boards of his wagon, and the shaking and bumping over the rough road packed his load down into the bed. He hoped his contact was going to show soon, and he was going to accept what now looked only like half a load, so he could get on his way back to Pápa. Then he dozed off.

It was almost completely dark when he felt a hand shake him roughly. He woke with a start but couldn't see who was waking him. He could only make out the outline of a figure walking briskly away from him towards the old, wire gates. When the gate was open, he saw the silhouette wave his arm in a large sweeping motion, indicating the path he should take, driving into the yard. He made a clicking sound with his tongue, smacked the horse's rump with his whip and yanked the left reign hard. The horse responded slowly and the cart was going through the gates, just as the shadowy figure indicated. But the man didn't wait for him. He was already up ahead by the old box-car, and in the semi darkness he saw the man unlatch, and slide the door of the boxcar open. The door squealed, and the shadow jumped up into the car, leaning out of the door and signaling to Köröndi to hurry up and pull alongside the box-car. By the time the cart stopped at the boxcar, the man was inside the car, motioning him to get the load shoveled into the boxcar. Köröndi Pál grabbed a shovel off the back of the cart and within minutes was working hard, shoveling the manure into the box car. The other fellow stood quietly to one side, watching him. "What are you going to do with this stuff?" Köröndi asked, but the other fellow didn't answer. Köröndi asked again, but when he still didn't get a reply, he abandoned the issue and went on shoveling. The quicker he finished, the quicker he would get his money and get back home. The smell in the car was stifling. The other man had a handkerchief covering his mouth and nose, and Köröndi thought, that may have been why he didn't answer him.

Just as he was scraping the last of the dung into a heap: the other fellow held a white envelope towards him. He took the envelope and opened it. To his surprise and delight he counted 15.000 forints instead of the ten he expected and he figured the extra five was a bonus. He was elated. Though in reality, even this wasn't a great deal of money, it came to him unexpectedly, and to him, it was more than he could have made in four or five weeks doing odd jobs. He looked at the crisp new bills in the envelope again and was about to thank this stranger, when the stranger stepped forward, grabbed the back of Köröndi's neck and pressed a cloth over Köröndi's mouth and nose. Even with the stench of the manure in the car, Köröndi recognized the smell of ether. He struggled but didn't want to drop the envelope, and the stranger's grip was like a clamp of iron. Köröndi was not a young man any more. His energy was spent after bailing his cesspool most of yesterday, and now shoveling the dung into the railroad car had him winded. Within seconds he felt the strength ebb from his arms and legs and he sank to the floor. He was somewhat conscious but couldn't move, or say anything. What was this about? He was frightened. He knew he had lots of enemies. He mistreated lots of people while he was in the Gendarmerie, not just Jews, but others in the villages, most of the time for no other reason than for his own enjoyment and exercising the superiority of his position. More than a few people had gotten even with him after the war and he was beaten up a number of times, but this time, lying on the floorboards of the old boxcar next to a heap of stinking dung, he shuddered as the sudden realization came to him that this was going to be a lot worse than being beaten up. He could not make out the features of the tall silhouette. It was night and there was no light at all in the car. He felt his ankles being tied tightly, and his hands tied behind his back. Some cloth was stuffed into his mouth, and a kerchief wrapped around his face, holding the cloth tightly in his mouth. The dark figure went through Köröndi's pockets and removed the envelope with the note that directed Köröndi where to deliver the manure, as well as the envelope, which he handed Köröndi just a few minutes ago with the fifteen thousand forints. He then wrapped a thin rope around Köröndi's neck and made him stand up. Köröndi was gagging as the effect of the ether was slowly wearing off and he tried to scream, but the wrap around his mouth held fast and he was gagging on his own tongue. A savage kick to his groin sent him reeling, collapsing him onto the heap of manure. As he could only breath through his nose, the smell of the manure was penetrating his brain and his lungs, which were about to burst. The stranger picked up Köröndi's shovel and started digging the manure from under the gagged man. Very slowly, Köröndi was sinking into the manure heap, shaking his head side to side, trying to scream, but couldn't.

He was completely conscious now. The effect of the ether had worn off and horror was reflecting from his eyes. Beads of perspiration formed little rivulets running down the side of his face, as he heard the dark figure's words reverberate in the empty box car. "The last train of the evening is about to leave the station. Soon the lights will be turned off and all who work at the station will be going home. Even if you could spit out your gag, there will be no one within hearing to hear your cries. But unlike your unfortunate victims, Sergeant Köröndi, some of whom took ten days to die in a box car just like this one, you are very fortunate; you will be dead by the morning."

Finally, the stranger took a yellow sheet of paper from his pocket and read out loud:

"Dr. Goebbels called all Jews vermin, the worst of all 'Rats'. You Sergeant Köröndi repeated this statement to your men on many occasion, and encouraged and ordered them to treat Jews like vermin. You have been known to torture, rob, and murder Jews. It is appropriate that we commemorate this day, July 4, with your execution. It is the anniversary of July 4, 1944, when you ordered and supervised the process that jammed as many as a hundred people, the aged, the sick, and even babies into small box-cars just like this one, and sent over three thousand Jews from Pápa to their death at Auschwitz."

Köröndi tried to struggle, to free himself, but he couldn't. His ties held, and his feeble moans were lost in the small boxcar. His eyes burned with horror, as all his strength ebbed from his body and he listened for the rest of his sentence:

"To correct the miscarriage of justice," the stranger continued, *"that sentenced you for only six months in prison for your horrendous crimes, but allowed you to live; in the name of all your innocent victims I hereby sentence you to die in the manner you imposed on them. You will die slowly, suffocated by your own excrement. May you be confined to hell for all eternity.*

The Rat."

He covered Köröndi's face with the sheet of paper and slowly, but deliberately, shoveled more dung over him in a neat mound until none of Köröndi's body remained visible.

The train in the distance was leaving the station, the few arriving passengers were hurrying from the platform, and within minutes the station was empty. The black silhouette jumped from the boxcar, and as quietly as he could, slid the door shut. He led Köröndi's horse out of the yard, and closed the wire gates of the rail yard behind him.

Several days later the cart and the dead horse were found in the ditch alongside a seldom traveled secondary road between Celldömölk and Pápa, and because of the horse's decomposing condition and the smell of the cart, both were hauled to a nearby dump and incinerated. Nobody knew who the horse and the cart might have belonged to, and nobody cared.

Almost three months past before a railroad worker noticed a very large swarm of flies on the old boxcar and the body of Sergeant Köröndi Pál was discovered. It was encased in a mound of rock hard, baked dung inside the old box-car by the deadhead at the end of the siding.

Chapter 4

Going to Los Angeles.

The stewardesses were pulling and shoving the food carts up to the front of the coach compartment, and the aroma of baked lasagne and chicken on rice was filling up the cabin. Having lunch this early in the day was not Ben's idea of high living, but the airline operated by the dictates of the arrival time of the flights. Lunch, including clean-up, was figured to take between one and one and a half hours, give or take an extra twenty minutes, and when it ran over schedule, the crew had to hustle to start the movie, so it would be over before the plane touched down at LAX, Los Angeles International Airport. When the cart got to Ben's seat, the stewardess wanted to know if the Captain, pointing at Captain Kerek, wanted lunch. It was obvious that the flight crew had been briefed that there were two police officers on board, without any consideration given that one might not be an American. Ben said he didn't know and the stewardess gently touched Captain Kerek's shoulder. She woke up, taking a few seconds to realize where she was. Ben figured she must have really fallen asleep after first faking it. She sat up straight in her seat and when she recognized Ben, seemed startled. "How did you get . . . . . . what are you doing here?" She finally organized her words.

"I'm going to Los Angeles," Ben said.

"I didn't know . . ." She seemed flustered.

"You asked me to help you," Ben said quietly. "Did you not?"

"Oh, yes." She was collecting herself, "I did."

"Well. I am going to Los Angeles to help you."

She was sitting straight up now and Ben figured she must have been deeply asleep. Ben asked for the lasagne and she took the chicken on rice. "Your English is wonderful." Ben turned to her as they were having lunch. "Where did you learn English?"

"In school," she answered without elaborating.

"Amazing," Ben said with genuine amazement, "I took all sorts of languages when I was in school, Latin, Spanish, French; can't say boo in any of them." They talked for a while. "So, how did you get mixed up in this racket, the police, I mean?" Ben asked her.

"I took law at the University," she answered, "and when I finished the University, I had to go into the Army for one year."

"Why did you have to do that?" Ben asked.

"Everybody has to serve in the Army." she answered. "Male and female, everybody has to serve, it's compulsory. So, with my background in law I wound up in the Military Police, and I liked it."

"But wouldn't a practice of law been more lucrative?"

"Not really. Under a socialist system there is not much need for civil law. And what law there was, I didn't think was that interesting, or lucrative." Ben nodded. "And I liked police work. I went to the Police Institute and was given a Cadet Officer commission. It took me ten years to make captain, I was promoted just about six weeks ago, and here I am." She smiled at Ben.

She had a nice smile Ben thought. As a matter of fact, her whole attitude, everything about her was kind of appealing. "That's interesting." Ben said. "I guess over there going up the ladder is a little faster than with us, at least in New York. I was a lieutenant for twelve years, and if you hadn't come along I probably would have retired a lieutenant in about a month and a half."

"Why do you say if I hadn't come along?" She was looking for an explanation.

"I still don't know all the details," Ben explained, "but the Commissioner, Commissioner Katz in New York, wanted me to work with you."

"My ambassador asked Commissioner Katz for the help of his best detective," she offered an explanation. "This is a very difficult and a very involved case." She looked like she wanted to tell Ben about it all at once, but didn't know where to begin. Ben's look was asking for more. She felt encouraged and she continued. "We, the Hungarian police, think there might be some connection between these cases and someone living in the United States, probably in New York."

"What led you to that conclusion?"

"Well, it's not exactly a conclusion, but all the victims 'till now, had some part in the persecution of Jews." When Ben didn't offer any comments, she continued. "Those who survived the Holocaust, we think are too old to have murdered nineteen," she corrected herself, "twenty people."

"So?"

"So, we figure it might be a descendant of a Holocaust survivor."

"But what makes you think that the killer lives in New York?" Ben asked.

"We don't know if he does. We think he might."

Ben didn't comment. They sat quietly for a while. The lunch trays had been removed, and the movie started. They lowered their window shade though neither of them wanted to watch the movie. "Can you tell me anything about this new murder, number twenty," Ben asked her, "in L.A.?"

"The information that reached me so far," Gabriella started, "is that the victim is another figure who played a part during the Nazi era. He was an English teacher and a small time politician, who, at one time in the late thirties, ran for political office as a district representative of western Hungary, the district where the city of Pápa is located."

Ben looked up. "Pápa? You say, Pápa? He repeated.

"Yes." She nodded.

"Don't you think it's odd that the first case, the first murder, involved a victim from Pápa, and now, this newest case also involves a victim from the same city. Don't you think this is odd? Don't you think there is, or might be, a connection?"

"I do," she responded simply. "We think, I mean the police in Budapest believe there is a definite connection. You see," she added deliberately, "there were eight other cases involving people from Pápa." Ben let out a little whistle. She went on. "That's why we think there is only one perpetrator. And since most of the twenty-five victims were from Pápa . . ." she trailed off, ". . . and incidentally, the next five targets named by The Rat are also from Pápa." She added quietly, "We think the perpetrator is from, or related to someone from, Pápa." Ben let her talk. "Most of the survivors of the Holocaust from Pápa immigrated to other countries after the war. Some went to Israel, a few to various South American countries, some to Canada and Australia, but most of them came to the United States and the largest percentage of these settled in New York." She looked at Ben.

"Have you checked them, I mean the immigrants from Pápa, yet?"

"Not yet, Ben. That's one of the areas where we need your help."

"And the others?"

"The other what?" she asked.

"The other areas you need my help."

She smiled. "We need your help, your expertise and your legendary talents as a detective, Ben, in all aspects of this case."

Ben was floored. He never liked to be buttered up, played up to, and every time someone tried, it turned him off immediately. But he liked this woman. And the way she talked, in a sort of an informal manner, she didn't sound like she was buttering him up. Besides, Ben figured, she really had no reason to. She seemed to operate very capably on her own, and at this point in the game, Ben figured, he wasn't even supposed to be with her. He still had to have his talk with the big "C", as until the Commissioner confirmed him on this case and his promotion to captain became official, he was only along for the ride. But inwardly, his instincts that served him so well in the past, told him he was on the case. He didn't know why, but he figured for some unknown reason the Commissioner wanted him—and no one else—on this case, and his talk with the big "C" would reveal why.

"Well, now that we are on the way to tinsel town," he turned to Gabi, "maybe I should use a showbiz expression. I don't know if I'll be able to live up to that billing."

"What do you mean?" Gabi asked sincerely.

"I mean that crack," he was instantly sorry he used the word 'crack,' "my 'legendary talents' billing."

She remained serious. "We heard about you from Commissioner Katz. He told my Ambassador you were amongst the top detectives, perhaps the best on the force. It was he who described your talents as legendary. In fact," she added with a smile, "when Commissioner Katz heard about our perpetrator signing his notes, as The Rat, he told my ambassador if anyone could solve this case, 'The Rat Catcher' would, and that you were known as 'The Rat Catcher'." She paused and smiled. "Are you 'The Rat Catcher,' Ben?"

"A rose is a rose . . . it's a name that was somehow tagged on me. But I don't know if it means any more than my other nickname."

"Which is?" she asked with a smile.

Ben hesitated. He was not comfortable with this conversation but she seemed to be pleasant and he continued. "Doorknob." he said quietly, but she pursued the subject.

"Meaning what?"

"It's a reference to the size of my nose," he said sheepishly.

It took a few seconds for his explanation to sink in. As good as her English was, it didn't include some of the jargon of the private, in house humor of the New York Police Department. "Doorknob." She repeated and smiled. "But that has nothing to do with your police work. Does it?"

"No." Ben shook his head. He tried to explain. "In the department almost everybody has a nick name. Mine is 'Doorknob,' Sergeant Finnell is 'The Mick', even the Commissioner has a nick-name. Behind his back everybody calls him the big "C" that stands for the Big Cat."

"I know," she said. "But that's a translation of his name, right?"

Ben nodded. "Right. Katz, his name in English means Cat."

"That's a German name, right?" Gabi asked.

"It might be," Ben said. "He might be of German ancestry, but actually, I think his name is Jewish."

"You Americans have such interesting nicknames, like Doorknob, she added, "it's funny. Do you like it?"

"Not particularly. But I've learned to live with it, the way I learned to live with the size of my nose."

"I think your nose is very good looking," she stated flatly without any obvious secondary meaning. "It has a noble, a sort of a Roman quality to it," she added.

"Well. bless your heart." Ben felt a bit uncomfortable, but the unexpected remark flattered him. "Do you have nick names in Hungary?"

"Some, but mostly an affectionate abbreviation of one's name, like mine, for instance." She explained, "My name is Gabriella, but it's too long for everyday conversations and amongst friends. That's why I like Gabi."

"Would you like me to call you Gabi," he tried to pronounce the name as she did, "or would you prefer Gabriella?"

"I would like Gabi," she said simply and made no further comment.

Ben changed the subject. "Tell me more about the first murder, 'the shit case'," he added and looked around with an embarrassed smile. But the people behind and in front of them, were watching the movie with earphones on, and nobody seemed to hear.

"Aside from what you've already read in the report, I don't know if I can add much more." She shook her head. "I had to get special permission to go with the team to Celldömölk, but as a junior grade officer cadet, I didn't have much to say or do as the investigation was going on."

"But I know you dug into this case since," Ben remarked. "No pun intended, but that's what I think you told me, and I'd like to hear your observations, conclusions, guesses, everything you could tell me about the murder, and about the victim. For example, whom did Mr. Köröndi mistreat in the Ghetto who might have survived? Who found him in the box car after he was murdered? What happened when he was found? What sort of forensic work was done? Who did the forensics? And now that you are in charge of all The Rat murders, what are the similarities?"

"I understand, Ben. But that's a lot of questions. Let me see." She thought about Ben's questions. "First, I did dig into this murder," she smiled at Ben, "no pun intended, and every subsequent one. I do have a lot of observations and even more guesses and questions, but unfortunately, very few conclusions. Let me see." Her eyebrows came together in concentration. "The only thing we know about Sergeant Köröndi's role in the Ghetto is, he mistreated everybody he came in contact with. But he concentrated on the wealthier members of the Jewish community, mainly to extort money and valuables. Those who wouldn't cooperate were very badly mistreated, tortured, and in some cases killed. The cause of death in the official documents and on the death certificate, in all these cases was noted as 'Lock-jaw.'"

Ben looked at her. "Lock jaw?"

"Yes." She tried to clear it up, "Lock-jaw was a snide, sick, Gendarme humor, meaning the person who died was murdered when he didn't talk. The gendarmes used to joke about the 'lockjaw cases'. But," she went on, "less than four hundred people came back from the original population of 3000 Jews in Pápa and they could add very little to what was already known." She thought for a moment and added, "Those who came back to and remained in Pápa were appalled at the sentence of six months in prison and particularly after The Book was found, they all believed Sergeant Köröndi should have gotten the death sentence."

"What book?" Ben asked.

"It's mentioned in the report, but nobody knows who wrote it, or where it came from."

"But what is this book?" Ben's eyes searched her face in the light reflecting off the movie screen in the dark cabin.

"We refer to it as the 'Book,' though it is only a manuscript written by hand by one of the survivors who returned to Pápa, and has probably died since. The interesting thing about this book is that it lists twenty-five people, all of whom had something to do with the deportation and the murder of the Jews who were taken away from Pápa. And what's even more interesting," she paused for a moment, "is that this list of twenty-five are the people who became the targets and the victims of The Rat."

"But The Rat has only dispatched twenty of them," Ben said.

"So far," Gabriella said. "One of the two notes The Rat left just three days ago in Los Angeles, I understand names the remaining victims."

"Hum," Ben couldn't hide his interest. "Have those people been notified?"

"I don't know what my commander has done, or will do about it, but I suspect he will not notify them." Ben nodded and she went on. "I would prefer if they were not told. That way we could stake them out, and hope to catch The Rat when he strikes next. We know who they are, where they live, and know from The Book what crimes they are accused of. As the note said, they are the remaining five of the original twenty-five, and all live in Hungary." Then as an afterthought she added, "If we tell them, they'll scatter, we won't catch The Rat, but The Rat will surely pick them off one by one."

"What makes you so sure?"

"He hasn't had any problem finding and doing his victims in till now, in some cases, I might add, in the most ingenious ways. And the interesting thing is, since The Book was sent to us we have known who his victims would be. They were all listed in The Book."

"In other words," Ben was emphasizing his words, "after the first murder, the 'Shit case,' it was known who his next victims were going to be?"

"Not really. When Sergeant Köröndi's body was discovered, in spite of the unusual elements and characteristics of the murder and the note the murderer left covering Köröndi's face, it was classified as an ordinary murder. But after The Book was found, the Köröndi murder was reclassified because by then two others had been murdered in South America. One, as well as Köröndi, were named in The Book, but all had a note identifying them by The Rat."

"So, why weren't the others staked out?" Ben wanted to know.

Some were, but quite a few of them were not Hungarians. They didn't live in Hungary, and we could not have staked them out even if we knew who they were, because we had no resources outside of Hungary and had no jurisdiction. Besides," she added, "we assumed that some of the people on the list were deceased." She paused and added, "In all those cases—ones outside of Hungary—we cooperated and exchanged information with the local authorities. I am here in the United States now, because we believe that the perpetrator might be living in New York, and now also because the Los Angeles Police asked the Hungarian consulate for information about the victim. When the notes The Rat left were mentioned, we informed the LAPD about the other murders, and our interest in the case, they asked us to cooperate. We learned a lot from all the other investigations, I mean the ones outside of Hungary but, so far, it hasn't helped with catching The Rat."

"In other words, it's possible that besides the remaining five target subjects in Hungary, some other Nazis might still be alive elsewhere, and might still become The Rat's victims."

"It's possible, but at this point, I don't think so."

Why not?"

"The wording in The Rat's note in Los Angeles referred to his next five victims, as 'my last five targets'." She emphasized the 'last.'

"So, then . . ." Ben hesitated, "if all his next victims are now in Hungary, why do you want me to be involved?"

She answered with almost no hesitation. "First, like I said, we would appreciate your expertise, Ben, and second, even if we know where the victims are, we still don't know who, or where, The Rat is and we believe he might be an

American."

"Well, American or not, the guy certainly moves around," Ben remarked after a while.

"Indeed. And he is ingenious."

"Do you think," Ben asked, "you could get me a copy of that book, the one . . ."

She cut him off. "I've already ordered a copy for you, Ben. It should be in the next diplomatic pouch from Budapest and I could have it delivered to you in New York, or in Los Angeles."

"The sooner, the better," he then smiled at her. "I have to grab some zees." Ben tried to explain, "American slang. Catching 'zees' means taking a nap." He winked at her. "You just gave me an earful, and adding that to the stuff you told me yesterday, kept me up thinking most of the night. I need to get a little shut-eye." he explained, "a little sleep before we get to the City of Angels. Besides," he added, "I do my best work while I am asleep."

She seemed disappointed, "But I have to tell you about 'The Piranha case.'" She almost pleaded. "The Piranha case . . ." she trailed off seeing Ben close his eyes. ". . . in South America."

She looked at the screen blasting with spectacular images and blaring sounds of a movie, 'Streets of Fire'. A fierce fight between the head honcho of a motorcycle gang and the hero of the movie was about to start but she wasn't interested. She raised the shade over her window a bit. Bright daylight pierced the cabin and some of her neighbors threw scornful glances. Below, the snow covered peaks of the High Sierras were reaching for the belly of the plane, and she thought how majestic these mountains were. Yet, at their base, the vast California desert spread out to the horizon. She looked at her watch. There was almost another hour before landing in Los Angeles. She lowered the shade and closed her eyes.

*   *   *

A well dressed, good looking young man gave them a highly refined, broad hand gesture of welcome as they came out of the long jetway, into the terminal. "Welcome to Los Angeles Kapitan Kerek," he smiled at her. "I am Rózsa Gyuri," He introduced himself, "I am Rózsa Gyuri, he then re-stated his name for Ben's benefit, "George Rózsa, press attaché with the Hungarian Consulate here in L. A." He kissed Gabriella's hand in a grand European manner.

"May I introduce Captain Chapman of the New York Police." Captain Kerek said. "He has been assigned to this case at the request of Ambassador Csipö." The press officer shook hands with Ben, "It is an honor to have you with us on this very important case, Captain. We appreciate your involvement." He then pointed to two men standing to one side and slightly behind him. "May I introduce Lieutenant Hill and Sergeant Silver of the Los Angeles Police. They are in charge of this case and will be giving you the information and the assistance you'll need."

Around them, travelers were hurrying from the gate, families and friends were going through the usual greetings as they also started to walk slowly towards the baggage area. The Los Angeles Airport, LAX as it was known and referred to by all natives of Los Angeles, was immense and complex. It took them a long time walking through tunnels, down and up stairs, and standing on endless, slow moving conveyors with business travelers rushing by and passing them on and off the conveyor. The baggage area was crowded with a throng of people. Ben smiled as he recognized some of the people who had rushed passed them on the way to the baggage claim, but now had to wait for the luggage to arrive. Ben stood quietly letting the press officer talk with Gabi, and noticed that the two local police officers seemed to be uncomfortable. They were standing by themselves, probably thinking, Ben thought, of all the things active cops had to give up—as the cops in New York would say—to baby sit a bunch of "fucking non-combatants." He eased up to the two Los Angeles cops. "Beautiful day today." He nodded his head towards the huge glass walls looking out to the traffic and people on the outside of the building. He sort of sensed the looks the two cops gave him, but one of the two, the lieutenant, smiled at him and said: "It's like every day, Captain. That's why people love this city. The weather, it's always nice." They stood quietly a little bit longer. Ben broke the silence, "Did you guys get my authorization?"

"Yes, sir." Lieutenant Hill nodded to Ben. "Came in this morning. We could take you directly to the scene unless," he looked at Ben, "you'd prefer to check into your hotel first."

"I'll leave that up to Captain Kerek," Ben nodded towards Gabriella, who was in what seemed like a busy Hungarian conversation with the Consular Press Attaché.

"Actually," the lieutenant was a bit hesitant, "it would be nice if we could go to the scene. The body was moved to the morgue two days ago, but we would like to wind up the work at the scene and give the house back to the victim's widow and son."

Ben nodded in understanding. "Anything new in the case?" he asked, though he didn't really expect any revelations.

The claxon of the luggage carousel blasted as a red beacon came on and the stainless steel serpent of the carousel came to life. Within seconds, suitcases and other luggage were spewing from several feeders and impatient travelers were shoving to get to their luggage. The crowd around the carousel was thinning out as Ben spotted his suit-bag. Gabriella already had hers and they were on their way out of the terminal. There was a limousine with red, white and green flags attached to each of the front fenders, directly across from the exit with a black Chevrolet Caprice in front of it. The Chevy had a red rotating beacon on the roof.

Gabriella turned to Ben and the Los Angeles cops. "Mr. Rózsa asked me to ride in the Limo with him." She was apologetic. "I hope you don't mind. We'll follow you to the victim's house." The chauffeur held the door for her as she, followed by Rózsa, got into the car. "You'll ride with us then," Lieutenant Hill turned to Ben with an approving smile and all three of them got into the black Chevy. "First time in LA?" The lieutenant asked, looking back over his shoulder at Ben. "No," Ben replied slowly, "been here a couple of times before." Then he added. "Came out here about six years ago to pick up a young actor type. Killed his stepmother in New York after she took up with one of her neighbors and stopped banging him." The two LA cops snickered but made no comments.

Even though the traffic was very heavy, their car made good time as it was weaving in and out of lanes, with the red beacon going and turning the siren on now and then, heading north on the 405 Freeway. Ben turned around and saw the Limo right behind them. He marveled at how well the young sergeant was driving. These two, he thought with an inner smile, were different from New York cops. That was his first impression when they met at the airport just a short while ago, and he noticed the understated but stylish way these two were dressed. Both wore light weight jackets, knit shirts, and slacks. They were well groomed and if anything, Ben thought, looked more like young executives on vacation, than cops. New York cops, plain clothes people, somehow always managed to look like cops. They wore cheap clothes bought at Barney's, didn't always get a haircut when they should have, and usually wore shoes with "COP" written all over. He particularly noticed the shoes. These two had lightweight shoes with rubber soles, almost a cross between regular shoes and sneakers, though definitely not sneakers, but certainly not the heavy soled black shoes the New York cops favored. "How did you get assigned to this case, Captain?" Hill turned back to Ben. Ben didn't answer right away. "To tell you the truth, Lieutenant, I don't know." He felt his statement needed an explanation. "I was about to retire, six more weeks to go, but my buddy, my C. O. volunteered me to the Commissioner."

"That's a rough break," Hill offered sympathetically.

"Not really." Ben said. "I was going off my rocker with boredom when this came up. I think this is a real case," He said with emphasis. "What's your take on it?"

"I don't know," Hill started. "When I got called to this case four days ago, it sounded like just another blotched burglary and an old guy that kicked the bucket. Didn't think much of it at first, but than other things started turning up."

"The notes, you mean?" Ben asked.

"The notes and some other things." He turned to Ben. "What do you know about this case, Captain?"

"Not a hell of a lot more than what you know, except this guy was knocked off by a perp that also killed nineteen others all over the lot."

"We are getting the same info," Hill said. "But who is this guy? And why is he wasting all these people? You know anything about that, Captain?"

"He calls himself The Rat. That's all I know. Plus the fact he has a very unique, and interesting modus operandi, and all his victims were somehow involved with the Nazis in World War Two." He stopped and asked: "What was in the second note?" It was almost like getting a small electric shock when Lieutenant Hill answered. "We don't know yet. The notes are being translated now, as we speak, but we found them only late last night, so we don't know what they say."

Ben had that feeling many times during his years on the Force. It was like stepping into something he shouldn't have. Something that came his way unexpectedly, but without knowing what it really was. It was hearing something he sensed might be important, without knowing why it was important. He was glad to see that neither of the two LA cops noticed his reaction. Both of them were looking straight ahead, and when Ben didn't continue, Lieutenant Hill turned back to him. "All sorts of things didn't add up. I mean, at first, as I said, it was just another case of burglary and as a result an old guy kicking the bucket. Then it turned out that his wife, who, incidentally is older than he was, couldn't talk to us. She doesn't speak any English. We brought in an interpreter who found out they were Hungarian—actually she was German—but he was a Hungarian, and came to Los Angeles about ten years ago. They have one son, who works for Universal Tours, some sort of midlevel executive. But the old man didn't have a job, in fact he was confined to a wheel chair the last few years. We couldn't figure out what they lived on. She didn't work either, and the money their son makes could hardly pay for the house they occupy, in an expensive area. We started digging, and found out the old people had no Social Security numbers, and besides a small bank account in the son's name, no bank accounts or credit cards in the old folks names. Then we found a drawer full of cash, bundles of neatly stacked hundred and fifty dollar bills." He stopped to look at Ben. "Close to three-hundred thousand dollars." He paused a bit. "Then we found the note that threw us a curve. We didn't quite know what to make of it. This is the first case of this kind in LAPD history."

Ben listened quietly. They were in the hills now and the car was working over to the right of the road, as they came over the top of the hill, going slowly so as not to lose the limo. "We are going to pick up the 101 Freeway," Hill pointed to the large, green overhead signs, "and then it's only a couple of more minutes to the house." The traffic on the Ventura Freeway was worse than on the 405. Almost as he was reading Ben's mind, Lieutenant Hill turned back to face him again. "This is probably the worst freeway in Los Angeles. But it's only a few minutes more." The car got off at the Barham Boulevard off ramp, and in a couple of minutes they were curving up the steep hillside on a narrow local road and pulled up behind a patrol car in a private driveway. The uniformed officer stepped out of the car and smiled at them. "Like I said," Hill said to Ben, "there is not much to see here any more. The body is in the morgue, the rooms have been cleaned up, but I thought you and the Hungarian Lady would want to see the scene."

Ben looked up at the house above them on the hillside. It was a two story, Californianized Tudor type house, with a big brick balcony in front of large leaded windows and French doors. "We have a bunch of photographs," Hill told Gabi and Ben, "and it might be best if you could just look around, get the hang of the place, and tomorrow we can look at the pictures and go over the details." Both Gabriella and Ben nodded. The house struck Ben as dreary. He could almost smell death in the dark rooms, furnished with heavy, old fashioned furniture. He didn't know why, but the place was unnerving him. He had been at murder scenes before but this place was different. He tried to put his feelings out of his mind, and stepped through the large French doors onto the terrace. He took a deep breath, drawing in the marvelous scent of orange blossoms and looked out over the valley. From his vantage point on the steep hillside, he could see over the rooftops of the houses on the downhill side of the street, and the huge trees around the neighboring homes. In the distance he could make out the back gates to the immense Universal Studios back lot, and a little further down, some of the buildings of Warner Brothers Studios. He realized Gabi was standing next to him, and the others were also coming out of the house onto the terrace.

"I am going to have to check in at my office," Lieutenant Hill told them, "but if you'd like, we can meet later and go to the morgue, or go over the reports." When nobody answered right away, Hill seemed relieved, and continued. "Actually, all that is scheduled for tomorrow. By then we'll have this thing pretty much in one package, so why don't we take you to your hotel and let you rest up a bit from your trip. The hotel is just over the hill, it's the Universal Sheraton, and you are all checked in. All you have to do is get your keys at the front desk."

*   *   *

The valet parking attendants and the bellhops made a special play when the limo with the flags on the front fenders, following a police car with the red beacon, pulled up in front of the hotel. Ben watched with amusement again, as Attaché Rózsa kissed Captain Kerek's hand in a grand, old European manner. Lieutenant Hill extended his hand towards Ben. "Here is my card. Call me any time. I'll pick you up around nine, nine thirty." Ben shook hands and looked at the card. "These guys do believe in publicity out here," he thought. The card said: "HOLLYWOOD HOMICIDE" "Our day begins when your day ends." Lt. Craig W. Hill . . ." and telephone, pager and fax numbers. He shook his head in appreciation and followed Gabriella into the green marble and brass lobby to the front desk to pick up his key. "What room are you in?" Ben asked, then added, "In case I need to get a hold of you."

"I am in," she looked at her key, "973." Then, as an afterthought she added: "But Mr. Rózsa asked me to have dinner with him this evening." Ben thought she was blushing and was a bit self-conscious. "He wants to discuss the Molnár murder," she explained as they stepped into the elevator. "What is your room number?" she asked Ben, "in case I need to call you." Ben thought she blushed again. He looked at his key but didn't answer. The elevator stopped on the ninth floor. They both got out. "I guess," Ben said quietly, "I am your next door neighbor, 975." They both seemed to be a bit flustered. "You have any plans for the evening?" she asked him as they reached their doors. "No. No plans," Ben answered and looked at his watch. It was quarter of five. "I guess it's still a bit early for dinner here, although," he smiled, rubbing his stomach, "my stomach tells me it's past my regular dinner time. I guess I'll have a room-service hamburger, a bottle of Budweiser, and see if The Rat will let me sleep tonight." She seemed to be hesitating at her door, as if she were trying to say something, but Ben had his door open. "How 'bout breakfast around eight?" he asked. She nodded.

"I'll meet you in the coffee shop," Ben said, "and have a nice time with Mr. Rózsa."

"Thanks," she said quietly. "It's business, you know."

Ben looked at her and thought he saw her blush again in the subdued light of the corridor. He nodded and almost as if to himself said, "Whatever. Good night," and walked into his room.

He unpacked his suit-bag, turned on CNN, and laid down on his bed. Within seconds he was asleep. He didn't know why he woke up, except he was all keyed up, as some of the information Gabi had given him about The Rat murders was slowly coming into focus. He was restless. He was always restless when he was on a case, but he had to admit to himself that with all the murder cases he had ever investigated, he was never on the trail of anything even close to The Rat murders; and this case was growing by the minute. It wasn't just that a serial killer was on the loose; it was a combination of the cunning, and the daring of the murderer, and the sentences The Rat handed out in such incredible, unimaginable ways, to a bunch of murderers—the butchers of thousands of innocent people. He noticed in the lower left hand corner of the TV screen that the time was 8:55, EST and thought he must have been dozing for about an hour. It might be a good time to call Bill Fredericks; given the three hour difference, Bill would be at home by this time, possibly sitting down to, or having finished, his dinner. But he knew Bill never really minded whenever he called him. He picked up the phone, and looked at the long distance dialing instructions. He dialed 9-1-212 878-8888. An operator came on almost immediately. "Official 7611," Ben spoke into the phone. He heard some clicks and a dial tone came on. He dialed Bill's home number and after three rings he hung up. This was a pre-rehearsed routine Bill and he used to let the other guy know who was calling. Then he went through the same routine, dialing the phone again, and heard Fredericks' voice come on almost as soon as the phone finished its first ring. "How is sunny California?" Bill's voice came out of the ear piece. "Sunny," Ben answered, and they both laughed. "Thought I'd check in with you. What's new at Midtown?"

"The place is buzzing with the news you are staying on. The consensus is that you copped the biggest apple."

"Yeah. Right." Ben said, "It'll make me rich. Right?"

"Right. Rich and famous."

"No shit, Bill, did you talk with the big 'C'? "

"Yes, I did. After he busted me to patrolman duty on Staten Island, he told me to tell you, you are also busted."

"What else did he say?" Ben asked, ignoring Bill's cracks. "He wants to talk to you." His voice turned serious. "And this is no shit, Ben. He wants to see you as soon as you get back into town. He was screaming at me on the phone this morning. He said, and I quote, "you were chasing your own agenda, and he was sure you didn't know what you were doing."

"That's interesting." Ben said quietly, "I thought he recommended me as the best detective on the force. What else did he say?"

"That's about it. But if you ask me, he has something up his sleeve he doesn't want to give out to anybody but you."

"Sounds like it, what else did he say?"

Bill's tone turned lighter. "He said you were probably just chasing tail at departmental expense." There was silence at Bill's end, then Bill came on again. "Do you mind if I ask you a question, Ben?"

"Shoot."

"You're not chasing tail, Ben. Are you?"

There was more than a little indignation in Ben's voice. "You know me better than that, Bill!"

"Yes, that's why I'm asking. Are you chasing tail?"

"Of course I am," Ben laughed and heard Bill laugh out loud too.

"Well, have a good time, Ben. Enjoy the case, or retirement, or both." Fredericks hung up.

Almost as soon as Ben hung up, there was a knock at his door. He jumped off the bed and automatically reached for his holster. "Who is it?"

"Room Service."

"I didn't order room service," He mumbled, almost as if to himself," and walked to the door. Through the peephole he saw a uniformed waiter checking a card in his hand against the number on his door. Ben opened the door. The waiter pushed an elaborately set table into the room and hurriedly walked out. There was no bill to sign, and the waiter didn't hang around for a tip as room service waiters usually did. When the door closed, Ben noticed a single red rose attached with a ribbon to a small split bottle of Champagne, and a small envelope taped to the rose. He opened the envelope and looked at the card. "I am sorry, but I couldn't get real Budweiser. And I hope you'll enjoy a steak instead of a hamburger, though it may not be as good as Gallagher's. Gabi." There was a small P. S. "I am so glad you are with me on this case."

He lifted the metal cover from the plate. A beautiful steak was nicely arranged on the plate next to an immense Idaho spud. He took a sniff of the rose, and sat down to eat his dinner.

Chapter 5

Case Number Twenty.

. . . five days earlier in California . . .

She looked into the rear view mirror and adjusted her large, designer sunglasses. Renting the car was remarkably easy. But this was America and as long as the clerk behind the counter was satisfied that her driver's license was OK, and her credit card wasn't rejected by the computer, a midsize car was waiting and ready for her just minutes after the papers were signed. Her driver's license and her Social Security card, in the name of Cathy Tobias of Pasadena, California were the best forgeries, but her MasterCard was real. She was pleased. Her plane from Amsterdam landed just a short while ago at San Francisco International, and nobody paid much attention to the attractive, blond woman who got off the plane and boldly walked through the exit marked for 'US Citizens only.' She collected a small suitcase, extended the pull handle, and walked out of the building to the Budget Rent-a-Car courtesy van stop near the exit. The van picked her, and a bunch of other travelers up, and within minutes she was standing in line at the Budget Rent-a-Car counter.

Now, as the city of San Francisco was receding into the distance behind her, she was enjoying the view, the magnificent rock formations along the Pacific Coast Highway, and the endless ocean on her right. She acknowledged the friendly smiles of some men in passing cars, and she figured she would be in Los Angeles by about midnight, and at 1243 Hillcrest View Street shortly after. She looked, and felt, like a typical mid to late thirties Californian; attractive, well dressed, as Cathy Tobias was supposed to look and feel. She didn't think she would meet too many people, and even if she did, she didn't think any one would question who she really was. She slept most of the way from Amsterdam and aside from talking with the stewardess briefly, nobody tried to talk to her. She went over her plan again, as she had for what seemed like the hundredth time, and tried to imagine how Mr. Molnár, whom she was going to Los Angeles to see, was going to react to her. She knew that being an invalid, Mr. Molnár was going to be at home, and the only other persons in the house, were his 84 year old wife, and their Hungarian housekeeper, who also doubled as a practical nurse and was almost as old as either of the Molnárs. She didn't expect much trouble from any of them. As in the past, when she was getting close to any of her victims, she was anxious, but not worried. Her self confidence propelled her, and she never doubted that something she didn't anticipate would happen. Something she might not be able to cope with and handle.

Some Pelicans caught her attention, skimming the curl of the breaking waves, diving occasionally for their dinner. Seagulls circled overhead and the slowly setting sun was beginning to tint the water with an iridescent, golden sparkle. It was a beautiful sight. She had visualized, imagined would be a better word, the California coast, but as many pictures as she studied, as many documentary shows she could find about the California coast line, as much as she read about it, the real thing far surpassed her expectations. She was sorry she couldn't stop here and there, get out of the car and enjoy the magnificent views, but she was on a tight and well calculated schedule. Besides, she didn't want to risk some eager Romeo trying to pick her up, and create a problem for her. She had a schedule with checkpoints to reach, and it was important that she did not deviate from her plan. She didn't want to get to Los Angeles ahead of her schedule, but had to be there no later than one in the morning. She read that people went to bed early in Los Angeles, but also knew that some got up very early, and she wanted to be back on the road, going north before daylight.

She spotted the first of the 101 Freeway signs, and the large yellow arches of McDonalds just north of Ventura. She got off the freeway and pulled into the take out lane of McDonalds and ordered Chicken McNuggets, fries with extra ketchup, and a large soda. She loved American junk-food. It was tasty, and dishes like the Chicken McNuggets were easy to eat even as one was driving a car. And she loved American freedoms. One could go anywhere, any time, do anything, and as long as one didn't do anything outrageous or stupid, nobody was going to ask any questions.

The freeway on-ramp was less than a mile ahead, and she maneuvered her car onto the outside lane going south. Most of the traffic was going north, but the south lanes were in relatively good shape. Headlights were coming on as it was getting darker and the sun, a spectacular, huge red disk was sinking into the Pacific on her right. She had never seen a sunset as spectacular as this. It seemed as though the sun was diving into the ocean, disappearing from the horizon in a matter of seconds. Then it got dark and she turned on her headlights. The first sign of Los Angeles, a dark cloud of pollution over the valley, was already visible in the distance. The clock on the dash said 10:17 and she knew that barring the unforeseen, she was going to be on time, exactly as she scheduled it. Cars were zipping past her, but she was in no hurry. Her speedometer was indicating a mile or two over the 65 mile speed limit. Even with that, she had seen a show on television about California Highway Patrolmen occasionally stopping good looking females and trying to make dates with them. She didn't want to speed, or do anything for which she could be stopped. She carefully dusted the front of her blouse and skirt. She wasn't too concerned about leaving leftovers of her dinner in the car. The car would be washed and vacuumed as soon as she turned it in tomorrow morning, but she knew that Mr. Molnár's house was going to be gone over with a fine tooth comb in the days to come, and she didn't want any Chicken McNugget pieces left behind at the Molnár house.

Just a few minutes before one o'clock she turned the ignition off in the driveway of 1243 Hillcrest View Street. She didn't think it was a good idea to park in the driveway, although there wasn't much of a chance of her having to back out, to get away in a hurry, but she knew that parking in the street would have been more risky. It was frowned upon in some neighborhoods in Los Angeles, and the police would note and check cars left parked along the curbs of local streets particularly at night. Parking in the driveway of Mr. Molnár's house was safer. She stayed in the car for a few minutes. Nobody in the house must have noticed, or heard her, as no lights came on. She could make out the dim glow of night lights throughout the house, but otherwise the house was dark. She pulled a tight-fitting black hood over her head with only two slits for her eyes, and quietly opened the car door. The large bushes on both sides of the steep stairs going up to the house, and thick shrubbery all over the hillside and in between neighboring homes hid her from view. Some steps branched off to the side, going up to the front door, but she continued around the house at garage level to the back entrance. She extricated a set of passkeys—the type used by locksmiths—from a small bag she had hanging from her shoulder, and in a matter of seconds quietly pushed open the back door of the house. She listened intently but there were no sounds of any kind coming from the house. In a flash, with quick and deft motions she had a piece of duct tape pressed over the bolts of the door lock. She reached out to one of the bushes next to the door, and tore a small leaf from one of the branches and inserted it between the door and the door frame, as she pulled the door closed. Like a cat, she retreated to her car in the driveway, yanked the black hood from her head, and in a matter of seconds was backing out onto the street. At the bottom of the hill, she turned right onto Barham Boulevard and went over the hill all the way to the large, hanger-like buildings of the Warner Brothers Studios, and turned into the parking lot of the Copper Penny Restaurant diagonally across from the Studio. There were still some cars in the parking lot. She pulled into a slot away from the cars and turned off her headlights. The engine purred quietly as she pulled a small pair of binoculars from her bag. From her vantage point, she could see the entire hillside over Barham Boulevard, and immediately identified the purple-orange street light near the Molnár house on Hillcrest View Street. Through the binoculars she easily spotted 1243, the large, leaded glass French doors leading out onto the terrace, but the house remained dark. She sat for some time, looking at the house occasionally through the binoculars, but there was no change. The house remained dark, just as it was when she first saw it.

There were several possibilities: One, the house had no burglar alarm; Two, the house had a burglar alarm, but it was not activated, or did not go off; Three, the burglar alarm did go off, but there was no response yet; Four, the burglar alarm did go off, and the house was now crawling with armed security people, waiting in the dark for the burglar to return. Almost as soon as she thought of this scenario, she dismissed it. If the security people or the cops, who would have surely answered the call also, had found the tape over the slide bolt of the back door lock, they would have awakened the people in the house, would have turned lights on, and most importantly would have had their cars on the street in front of the house. But the street was empty, and the house remained dark. She waited some more and brought the binoculars up to her eyes, again and again, but there was no change at 1243 Hillcrest View Street. She backed out of her parking space and turned right towards Hillcrest View Street.

She knew that after the initial installation, very few people continued to use their burglar alarms. Most never really learned how to use it correctly, and after a while it would become an annoyance, as it would come on, wake up the neighborhood, and then one would have to deal with the security company and the police. Elderly people like the Molnárs and their housekeeper didn't like gadgets like burglar alarms, but would have it installed, if for no other reason but to reduce their home owner insurance premiums. Burglar alarms came with the houses at times, which could have been the case with the Molnár house, but the Molnárs probably figured no need for it. Of course, she thought with a smile, they were the ones who should have had a burglar alarm, and should have used it scrupulously. But the house gave no signs of the back door having been opened, as she eased into the driveway again, and turned off the engine. She pulled the black hood over her head, slipped out of the car and headed up the stairs towards the back door. The door was as she left it about forty-five minutes ago. The small leaf was still stuck between the door frame and the door near the bottom, as she gently pushed the door open and listened. The house, as before, was quiet and she figured, if there was a burglar alarm and it was armed, it should have gone off the first time she opened the door almost an hour ago.

She stepped into the house. Her guess was the Molnárs, being old and Mr. Molnár being an invalid, would probably be sleeping in separate rooms, and the housekeeper probably had her own room nearby. Indeed, she heard snoring coming from one room with the door slightly open, and as her vision slowly adjusted to the low light levels of the dim night lights, she could make out the face of a woman in bed through the slightly open door. She didn't know if she was the housekeeper/nurse, or Mrs. Molnár, but it really didn't make any difference. She pulled out a small, plastic, squeeze bottle and a white handkerchief from her shoulder bag and dropped a few drops of ether onto the handkerchief. The woman in the bed moaned slightly as she pressed the ether saturated kerchief over her mouth and nose, but went limp in a second. She bound her hands and feet with nylon packing tape, and put a piece of tape over her mouth. She unplugged the phone next to her bed from the wall, and quietly stepped out of the room. The purple-orange Mercury street light came through the large leaded French doors of the living room that lead out to a terrace and projected a beautiful pattern on a wide stairway that was leading up to the second floor, and, she figured, to the bedrooms. The stairs had thick carpeting and her steps were completely silent. She heard the heavy breathing of an elderly person who might have been asthmatic, or just couldn't breathe well due to age. It was Mr. Molnár. Mrs. Molnár was sleeping in the adjoining room with a night table light on, filling the room with a dim pink light coming from under a large, silk shade. She had the little bottle and the handkerchief in hand as the woman in the bed turned and opened her eyes. She was startled at first, then she panicked and wanted to scream, but the intruder's hand clamped the ether saturated cloth over her face, and like the housekeeper, Mrs. Molnár passed out quickly. In seconds she had Mrs. Molnár tied up, and had picked her up from the bed and thrown her over her shoulder like a rag doll. The Rat carried her into Mr. Molnár's room and dumped her into a large armchair. She didn't move.

She went to Mr. Molnár's bed. He was awake, his eyes wide open, paralyzed with fear. He tried to sit up, but couldn't. "Let me help you." The intruder said in a friendly voice, and helped Mr. Molnár sit up. "Perhaps you might be more comfortable in your wheelchair?" She asked pleasantly, and lifted Molnár effortlessly over to the wheelchair. "Now, if you promise you won't make a fuss," she continued, "I won't have to tape your mouth shut. And I don't want to tie you up or put you out, because I want to talk to you, and I want you to understand me." She paused for a beat. "Do you know who I am?" She asked Molnár. He shook his head. "I am The Rat." she said simply. "You have heard of me from some of your friends, and no doubt have realized, that most of them fell silent in the last ten years. You see, Mr. Molnár, they are dead. As you must have heard, they died for their horrible crimes at the hands of The Rat, me. I killed them! As compared to their crimes, even death was a light sentence. And to show you what a kind person your executioner is—not like you were when you and your friends organized the deportation of over three thousand people from the Ghetto in Pápa—I brought you a very special present Mr. Molnár. She pulled a tightly wrapped package from her shoulder bag. Would you mind if I called you István? Or maybe even Pista, as your friends called you in the good old days? Would you like that, Pista?" Molnár looked like he was trying to scream but couldn't. "I thought you might like to leave this earth, properly dressed in your favorite clothes, as in your glory days." She opened the package and pulled out a green, military style shirt. "Here. Let's put this on first, Pista." He tried feebly, but couldn't resist her, as she pulled the shirt over his head. "Now, that's nice. And your neck-tie. Your favorite neck-tie." She slipped a red necktie, already knotted, over his head and stuffed it under his collar. "And we mustn't forget your Sam Brown belt." She slapped a leather belt over his right shoulder and buckled the waist belt. "And now, the most important item of your uniform District Leader Molnár, your armband." She pulled a red armband from her side pack and wrapped it around Molnár's left arm just above his elbow. The six inch wide armband had a white field in a black circle, and in the middle of the circle was a green, four pointed cross, with arrowheads at the end of each section. "Well now! Don't we look nice, District Leader Molnár? Just like the glory days! When you join your friends in hell, they'll be sure to recognize you." The Rat took her time. Molnár was half dead already with fear. "And now, it's time to go Pista. Say good by to your dear wife. She is as guilty as you are, and it won't be long before she'll also be joining you in hell. But for now, she'll have the pleasure of watching you die. She is awake now, her eyes are open, and you can watch her, watching you die."

She paused again and pulled two yellow sheets of paper from her shoulder bag.

"Hear my verdict, District Leader Molnár. In the name of all the people you and your friends called 'The Rats,' over three thousand people from the city of Pápa, your district, whom you robbed of their worldly goods, and whom you sent off to be slaughtered, this Rat sentences you to die."

She pulled some wires attached to a small transformer and a battery. "Here, Pista." She wrapped the naked ends of the wires onto each index finger of Molnár's hands. "This device is not as strong as the ones you used on your victims, and by itself it is not going to kill you. But it will stop and disable your pacemaker, and without your pacemaker you will die slowly, and I hope, very painfully. Hell is waiting, Pista! Good bye." She twisted her end of the two wires together, and Molnár gave out a small cry and jerked back in his armchair. His eyes were wide open, he was grabbing at his chest, and was trying to catch his breath. The Rat gave him another jolt, and a few seconds later another. Molnár's head slumped forward, but he was still breathing heavily and irregularly. "One more for good measure," The Rat said. "I must go now, Pista. Rot in hell District Leader Molnár." She undid the wires from Molnár's fingers and put the little apparatus back into her shoulder bag. "But before I go," she turned to Mrs. Molnár, "I am sure you wouldn't mind helping out a bit with my expenses. Where do you keep the money?" The frightened woman nodded her head towards the dresser. She pulled out the top drawer. The entire drawer was filled with neatly stacked bundles of money. The Rat took some bundles and slipped them into her shoulder bag. "I would thank you, Mrs. Molnár, if I thought the money belonged to you. But I know it doesn't. Perhaps the people it was taken from will be happy to know their money is doing some good."

As quietly as she came no more than a half hour ago, she slipped out the back door, and pulled the door shut behind her. Her car started, but there was nobody around to hear it as she backed out of the driveway onto Hillcrest View Street and turned left towards the 170 Freeway at the bottom of the hill and at the end of Barham Boulevard. She took the 170, the Hollywood Freeway north, to pick up the 5 Freeway just past Burbank.

The 5 Freeway was almost devoid of cars and trucks. An occasional pair of headlights would show up in her rear view mirror, or on the other side of the wide freeway coming towards her. She opened her window and pulled the small squeeze bottle of ether from her shoulder bag. She carefully unscrewed the top and stuck her arm out of the car. She squeezed the bottle repeatedly, until it squirted no more liquid. She let the handkerchief unfurl in the slipstream of the car, and air out, until all traces of ether were gone. Next to her on the passenger seat, the remains of her dinner were sitting alongside her shoulder-bag. She took the lid off the large soda container and dumped the remaining soda onto the freeway. She carefully placed the small squeeze bottle and the handkerchief into the container, stuffed her black hood tightly over them, and replaced the lid with the straw still sticking out of it.

The numbers on the clock on the dash glowed brightly; it was 3:47 in the morning. About twenty minutes past the Bakersville Exit, and up ahead, just beyond an off-ramp, the huge, bright Exxon sign reminded her, it was time to fill up. She hit the brake, the cruise control clicked off and she slowed down just in time to take the off ramp. The gas station was brightly lit but there was no one around except for the attendant who was half asleep in the small booth. She pulled up alongside one of the pumps, and smiled as she inserted the MasterCard with Cathy Tobias' name on it. She fully expected the pump to reject it, and even set off an alarm in the booth, but much to her amazement the pump accepted the card and she set the nozzle to fill and shut off automatically. While the car was filling up she dumped the soda container in the trash barrel and went into the convenience store and the ladies' room. When she came out, the car was full, the pump shut down, and its sign flashing: "Receipt: Yes. No." She hit the 'No' button, took the gas nozzle out of the tank, and replaced the gas cap.

The Rat was pleased. Twenty down, five more to go. She no longer felt any pangs of conscience as one after the other these criminals that were marked for death in The Book, were dispatched. In fact, as she was approaching the end of the task, she wished it would be over, all murderers named in The Book having been dispatched, and she could look back on a job well done—and as they said in romantic novels—live happily ever after. But she also knew she couldn't relax her guard. She didn't find killing these horrible people a pleasure but it was something she wanted to do, as she felt it was her calling to do so. It was dangerous, and yet, flirting with danger and getting away with it, was one of the rewards. She knew that as carefully, and as thoroughly, as she prepared each and every case, the unforeseen element was always there, anything could go wrong, and she would be next in line to die. Even the slightest accidental slip-up could spell disaster, and she was angry for having taken such a stupid chance, by using the phony credit card that could have had her arrested at the pump.

Actually, she thought with a smile on her face, the credit card wasn't phony. It was completely legitimate. And she smiled even brighter as she recalled how easy it was to get it. She went to Vienna for the weekend to pick up the new papers her forger in Vienna had prepared. He was an artist of the highest abilities. There were no documents he couldn't forge, and do it so masterfully that detection would be very difficult even by experts. But his success was not based exclusively on artistic, and technical abilities. The documents were hard to disprove, because the people they represented were real. Cathy Tobias, whose name appeared on all her documents, was a real person. She was a teacher, who lived by herself in Pasadena, California, at 14 Motor Avenue, not far from the Huntington Library that she often visited. But she must have been a frugal person who seldom charged purchases against her card, which is what made her an ideal choice. Had she used her card more frequently, the master computer at the credit card company would have picked up the discrepancy, and therefore the use of a duplicate card would have been chancy. The Rat's other documents were also in Ms. Tobias' name. The only difference between them and the real counterparts was that The Rat's passport showed her own picture, the picture of an attractive blond. Her driver's license was likewise real, and probably would have stumped an employee of the

California Motor Vehicle Department.

She loved working with her forger, spending hours in his studio, where he also painted some very beautiful oil canvasses, some of which were frequently shown in several of Vienna's better galleries. He was an accomplished artist, and a very good one. He was also an interesting man, who probably made more money forging documents, than with his fine art. They had a good relationship. He never asked what she needed the forged documents for, and accepted, though never believed, her explanation that she worked for a motion picture company, which occasionally needed these kinds of documents for filming a movie.

But the one thing her forger couldn't, or wouldn't, do were credit cards. Credit cards, he explained, were constantly monitored by bigger, newer, and better computers, and even a first time use could be disastrous. But getting a legitimate credit card was easy. Just as he suggested, she walked into a police station in Vienna, and made a complaint about her purse having been taken on the subway. A bored police sergeant made out a report. She took the report and went to the local office of MasterCard just a few minutes before they were to close for the week-end, and after showing her police report and her American Passport, was issued a new MasterCard within minutes.

The card served her plans well. Actually the only thing she needed the card for was renting a car, as she knew that car rental companies wouldn't take cash. Anyone renting a car for cash could have sold the car within minutes after renting it, and could not have been traced. Next to having a valid driver's license, it was essential to have a credit card. The renting of the car was, in fact, the one really risky part of her entire mission. But even though she, as Cathy Tobias, vacationing in Vienna reported the card stolen, the new one was accepted without question at the Budget Rent-a-Car counter at the San Francisco International Airport. She couldn't help wondering what the real Cathy Tobias's reaction was going to be, when her card was rejected at a department store, or at a restaurant. But for The Rat, the card had fulfilled its purpose; it was not going to be used again.

It was half past four as The Rat pulled off the Freeway again and into the take-out lane of Burger King. She ordered the Giant Crossanwitch with two eggs, Canadian Bacon, Jack Cheese, and coffee. She was hungry and attacked the large sandwich as soon as she was back on the Freeway. It was still dark. She looked in the rear view mirror, looked towards the lanes to her sides, but didn't see any other cars. She slowed down, pulled the black blouse over her head and put on a light colored, short sleeve knit polo-shirt. Changing her black slacks to khakis was a bit more difficult in the moving car, but in a short time the shirt was tucked into the pants, and she laced a western type belt through the loops of her trousers. She kicked off her pumps, and slipped into a pair of Nikes. Her pumps fitted into the paper bag the Giant Crossanwich came in, and her blouse easily rolled into the coffee container. The first signs of daylight, a narrow strip of light blue sky over the horizon, was beginning to show just slightly behind her on her right. She looked into the rear view mirror and with a deliberate swing of her right hand ripped the blond wig from her head. A shock of dark brown hair, styled in the fashion of a middle aged yuppie, fell from under the wig, as the attractive blond woman,

Cathy Tobias of Pasadena, California was metamorphosing into a brand new person and was no more. The new person looked into the rear view mirror, and compared his mirror image to the photograph in Cathy Tobias' Passport. He ripped the photograph from the Passport page, tore it into small bits, and let the wind outside of the car take the small fragments. Likewise, tiny bits of Cathy Tobias' driver's license, and social security card, were scattered over miles of the 5 Freeway. The Rat stuffed the MasterCard into the empty McDonalds bag left over from the evening before, and rolled the bag shut. There was another gas station up ahead, and the new Rat, a totally different person, pulled off the Freeway and into the gas station. All the garbage from the car was swallowed up by the trash receptacle as he got back into the car and headed towards Budget Rent-a-Car at SF International.

His flight wasn't leaving till 8:57, and it was only seven thirty when the car pulled up and stopped behind another rental car being checked in. The loudspeakers kept repeating a loud message:

"Please leave your keys in the car, and check the trunk and the interior of your car for personal belongings. You may use The Budget Express Check-out, by entering the amount of gas indicated by the gas gauge, the time, and the mileage on the odometer, in the appropriate places on your rental contract. Drop your contract into the Express Check-out Box, and proceed to the courtesy bus in front of the rental office. Thank you for choosing Budget, and we look forward to serving you again in the future. Please leave your keys in the car, and check. . ."

The Rat filled in the contract, took the small carry-on suitcase from the trunk and pulled out a wallet from one of the top pockets. Won't Cathy Tobias be surprised when she gets her bill for car rental. The Rat smiled, dropped the rental contract into the Express Checkout Box and walked towards the courtesy bus in front of the rental office.

Chapter 6

Sunny California.

"The case of the Hillcrest View 'execution' murder continues to baffle the police. Lt. Craig W. Hill, in charge of the investigation for the Crime Unit of LAPD's Hollywood Homicide Division disclosed at yesterday's press briefing that the LAPD is no closer to solving this bizarre murder than they were four days ago when Mr. Molnár's body was found in his million dollar home on fashionable Hillcrest View Drive in the Hollywood Hills. According to Lt. Hill the only conclusion the investigation has produced so far is the motive for the killing of Mr. Molnár and the brutalizing of his wife and their housekeeper, a Mrs. Domonkos, who, like Mr. and Mrs. Molnár, is of Hungarian origin. Lt. Hill emphasized that the motive for the killing of Mr. Molnár had to be revenge, perhaps the settling of an old score, and that it was done with the precision of a professional hit-man of the highest caliber. All other motives were ruled out. None of the beautifully appointed home's furnishings were disturbed, nothing of value was taken, in fact a very large amount of cash was still in the unlocked top drawer of Mr. Molnár's chest of drawers in his bedroom, undisturbed. Lt. Hill pointed out, that the murderer had to be powerful enough to tie up both the housekeeper, Mrs. Domonkos, and Mrs. Molnár and carry Mrs. Molnár into her husband's bedroom. Mrs. Molnár witnessed the entire execution, but so far could only give fragmented information to the investigating team, as she is currently being treated at the Hollywood Good Samaritan Hospital for shock, dehydration, and minor scrapes and bruises. In the opinion of the medical examiner, both she and Mrs. Domonkos would have expired if it weren't for a Mr. Hissle, a sanitation worker with the North Hollywood Ash and Waste Disposal Company. It was Mr. Hissle's regular day to pick up garbage at the Molnár residence the morning after the murder, but according to Mr. Hissle, when he found no garbage at the usual site at the Molnár house and was about to ring the back door bell to find out if they had forgotten to put out the garbage, he noticed the back door was ajar and decided to investigate. He heard moans and noises coming from one of the downstairs bedrooms and found Mrs. Domonkos gagged and tied up. When they went upstairs to check on the Molnárs, Mr. Molnár was already dead on the floor, apparently having fallen out of his wheelchair. Mrs. Molnár was unconscious and had to be given oxygen when the paramedics arrived.

Had it not been for the tape found on the slide-bolts of the back entrance door to the house, had the murderer not tied up Mrs. Molnár and their house-keeper, the death of Mr. Molnár would have been classified as "due to natural causes." There were no signs of struggle, and no injuries to Mr. Molnár were detected, other than what was caused by his falling to the floor, and, in fact, the cause of death is still given, and entered into the death certificate, as 'congenital heart failure' due to Mr. Molnár's malfunctioning pacemaker. What could have contributed to his pacemaker's malfunctioning is at this point, unclear. One theory, according to Lt. Hill, is that a burglar might have been disturbed in the commission of a robbery attempt and fled. The sight of Mrs. Molnár, tied up and gagged, put an undue stress on Mr. Molnár's pacemaker, which in the end caused his heart to fail. This, of course is "a far fetched supposition," Lt. Hill emphasized, and told the press the investigation was continuing.

What makes this case so unusual, are the many, already discovered, highly unusual factors. The Molnárs came to Los Angeles roughly a decade ago from their native Hungary; it is assumed for political reasons. Accompanying Mr. and Mrs. Molnár was their longtime friend/house keeper, who also doubled as Mr. Molnár's nurse. Mr. Molnár, in his late seventies, was an invalid who needed round the clock help, though no medical supervision. He spoke English, in fact it was ascertained that he was an English teacher at a small, rural high-school in Hungary. Neither Mrs. Molnár nor Mrs. Domonkos spoke English. The Molnár's son, Beni, was out of town at the time of the murder and could not be reached by this reporter. The Molnárs had no visible source of income, which raises questions about the expensive home on Hillcrest View Drive and the large amount of cash, said to be in excess of a quarter of a million dollars, that was found in Mr. Molnár's dresser. One other baffling aspect of the murder was the garment Mr. Molnár was wearing, some sort of a pseudo military . . . "

"Good morning." Ben was interrupted by Gabi's friendly voice. "Am I disturbing?"

"No. No." Ben looked up at her cheerful face, "not at all. I was just reading about the Molnár case," he showed the paper to Gabi.

There were no others in the coffee shop, besides a couple of waiters lingering at one end near the large windows, which looked out onto the gardens of the Universal Sheraton Hotel. "May I join you?" Gabi asked.

"Of course," Ben stood up. "Please, have a seat." He went on to explain, "I woke up early, on New York time, and came down to have a cup of coffee and read the paper. This town runs on publicity," he said, indicating the paper with a nod of his head. "Lieutenant Hill and Sergeant Silver might be coming out of this with a commendation, maybe even a promotion." But she didn't seem very interested. It almost seemed to Ben, she might have been upset about something.

"I was up early too. My clock is off even more than yours." She explained and looked at her watch. "Right now it's four in the afternoon in Budapest." Then she added, "In a couple of hours I'll be ready to go to sleep." They both laughed.

"Yep. The world is getting smaller," Ben commented. "How was your evening with Mr. Rózsa?" he asked.

She turned serious again, Ben thought, with a disappointed expression on her face. "It was all right," she said without offering any more detail, and Ben didn't press. He looked at his watch. "Lieutenant Hill is picking us up in about an hour. How 'bout some breakfast? Incidentally," he added, "this is a very interesting article about the Molnár murder." She took the paper and looked at it. "How was your dinner?" she asked with a small, but almost mischievous smile.

"Oh," Ben lead on. "It was all right. Typical hotel cooking. You know, dry hamburger, soggy french fries. No salt and pepper on the tray, the usual."

Gaby was baffled. "You had a Hamburger last night?"

"Yes," he said, but couldn't contain himself any longer. He laughed lightly. "My dinner was wonderful. Some kind and generous soul treated me to a magnificent steak and the biggest Idaho Spud I've ever seen. I even loved the champagne," he stopped for a second, "and the rose was a very nice touch. Thanks Gabi. It was very nice of you."

She was pleased but a bit self conscious. "Did the champagne help you sleep?"

"It did, indeed. That, and the rose I put on my pillow."

She blushed. "Is Mr. Rózsa going to accompany us this morning?" Ben asked. "I don't think so," she said with a serious face, and Ben didn't pursue the subject. "I think I'll have some breakfast," he said and picked up the menu. "Me too." She also picked up a menu and the waiter came over to take their order.

*   *   *

Lieutenant Hill's office was nothing like Midtown North. It was in a brand new, modern building with large windows, lots of glass, fluorescent lights all over, and more space than, Ben thought, the police would need or should have. But just like Midtown North in New York, there was lots of activity, uniformed and plain-clothes people rushing around, telephones and faxes ringing and printers spewing sheet after sheet of interoffice communications. Ben noticed the sign overhead just as they entered: "HOLLYWOOD HOMICIDE" "Our day begins when your day ends."

"We have a team meeting scheduled in a few minutes," Hill looked at his watch, "You guys want some coffee?" Both Ben and Gabi shook their heads. "Just had breakfast. Thanks." Hill picked up some papers and glanced at each. "Did you see the piece in the paper this morning?"

"Yes," Ben replied, "very interesting."

"And that isn't the whole story," Hill commented. He picked up a bunch of papers from his desk along with a pad and a pen, and indicated the door. "Why don't we go into the briefing room? The others are probably already there."

The small conference room had about eight people around a large, Formica table. There was a white board with markers and eraser, a video monitor with VCR, and an overhead projector and a slide projector on a stand. Most of the people were nursing cups of coffee.

"Good morning, everybody." Hill opened up. "Meet Captain Gabriella Kerek of the Hungarian Security Agency, and Captain Benjamin Chapman of the second best police force in the USA, the NYPD." He smiled at Ben, as everyone else in the room smiled also. "Just a joke, Ben." Ben smiled. Hill turned to the room. "Who has the summation?" An attractive, though slightly overweight, red-head held up her hand. "I do."

"Roll it." Hill used a movie expression and leaned back in his chair.

The report went on and on, but there wasn't much new as far as Ben was concerned. Basically, as a murder, this was a very clear cut case. One guy was knocked off, nothing was taken, nothing was disturbed in the house, and no fingerprints were found. The murderer got away cleanly, leaving nothing behind that would have offered even a hope of a start. In another ten years, Ben thought, some new thing would come to the surface and blow the case wide open, or nothing would happen and the Molnár murder case, file number whatever it was, would be taken off the board. He looked at Gabi from the corner of his eyes. She sat without expression and Ben was wondering what she might be thinking. To the cops in the room, this was another case, just as it would have been in New York, another murder, another day, another dollar. These guys in the room, Ben looked around, were all paid to deal with these cases, whether they solved them or not. And tomorrow, or even before, the phone would ring on somebody's desk, and a hysterical voice would be talking about another stiff in the gutter, or in somebody's bedroom. But those would be the ordinary murders. This one here, Ben thought inwardly, was anything but ordinary. The report was simple. It pared the case down to its essentials, "nothing but the facts, Maam." Ben smiled, thinking about another Hollywood cop, Sergeant Friday, on television. If these guys in the room had any questions, and he figured they must have, they didn't show it, they just went on, going through the motions by the numbers, as it was laid out in the manuals, and as they learned to do at the Academy. But Ben had lots of questions.

The summation droned on. As the plump woman cop was reading the reports, Sergeant Silver was taping photographs to one of the long walls of the room. There were pictures of Mr. Molnár's dead body on the floor, Mrs. Molnár still tied up, the garbage man, Mr. Hissle, a drawer full of bundled hundred, and fifty dollar bills, the tape over the slide bolts of the back door, the yellow sheet of paper the murderer left behind, but it was clear to Ben, none of the people in the room had any more ideas about who the murderer might be than he or Gabriella. As the summation finished, Lieutenant Hill took the helm of the meeting. "A duplicate file has been made up for you Captain Kerek and Captain Chapman." He handed them a file folder and continued. "Because of the jurisdiction in this case, I ask that you not discuss any aspects of this case with any one." Ben and Gabriella nodded. Hill continued, "Anything you could add, or contribute to the case would be very greatly appreciated, and I, and my staff," he indicated the people in the room with a sweep of his arm, "are here to assist you, answer any questions you might have." He paused a second, and added, "I understand your involvement, and the importance of this case to your investigation." He looked at Captain Kerek and Ben. "Do you have any questions at this time?" Both Ben and Gabriella shook their heads. Hill looked around the room. "Who interviewed the neighbors?" A hand went up at the end of the table. "Yes, Jesse." Hill prompted. What did you find out?"

"Nothing. Zilch. Nada. I talked with the people in the houses on each side of the Molnár house, and the people in the houses on the other side of the street, opposite the Molnár house. Nobody heard, or saw anything. Some peeps, as usual, heard a dog bark, one guy heard coyotes, two people in the house across the street knew for sure it was the garbage man who done in Mr. Molnár." He stopped to look at Lieutenant Hill, "The garbage man, incidentally, the one who found the housekeeper and Mrs. Molnár, and the body, has an iron clad alibi. He had spent the night with two Sunset Boulevard hookers, both of whom independently corroborated his story."

"Go on, please." Hill prompted.

"There are no tire marks, and no sign of forced entry, therefore the conclusion is; the neighbors could not have heard anything."

"Did they tell you anything about the Molnárs? I mean, what kind of people they were? The usual?"

"Nobody, none of the neighbors knew the Molnárs. They hardly ever saw them, and nobody ever talked to them. One guy, a fellow across the street from the Molnár house, saw Mister Molnár sitting on the terrace in his wheelchair and he waved to Mr. Molnár who acted as if he didn't see him, and didn't wave back." Hill nodded. "One of the other neighbors remembers taking a cake over to the Molnárs when they first moved in, but saw only the housekeeper, Mrs. Domonkos, who couldn't talk to her and, she remembers, Mrs. Domonkos just took the cake and closed the door in her face. That's it so far. I'll be talking with them again this afternoon, just in case they remembered anything, but I don't expect much."

"Thanks, Jesse." Hill turned towards Gabriella. "We heard from Attaché Rózsa. He gave us some insight into the clothes Mr. Molnár was wearing. The photographs are in your folder." He nodded his head in the direction of the folder in front of Captain Kerek. "Could you give us your thoughts, anything you might be able to add. According to Attaché Rózsa, it is some sort of a Nazi uniform."

"It is," Gabriella nodded. "It was the uniform for the Hungarian Nazis. Very few ever wore it, except on special occasions, like when Mr. Molnár was campaigning for the District Leadership."

"Mr. Molnár was in politics?" Hill asked.

"Yes. He was an English teacher in the high school in a town called Pápa, in western Hungary. He also taught German occasionally, but mostly English, though his German was better than his English. He finished his education in Germany, and married his wife there. She is a German national whose father was one of the early members of the Nazi Party in Germany. The Molnárs returned to Hungary in the mid thirties and Mr. Molnár became one of the teachers at the high-school. He tried very hard to put together a Hungarian Nazi organization, but lost two elections and only became very active in the Hungarian Nazi party, which, incidentally, was called The Nyilas Keresztes Party, later. Their symbol was the green arrow cross with the arrowheads, like the one on the armband Mr. Molnár was wearing."

Hill smiled at her. "You know, if I didn't know any better, I would never have suspected you were not an American. Your English is perfect, no accent at all.

Where did you learn to speak English so well?"

"This may come as a surprise," she smiled, "I learned to speak English in high school, some of it in the same high school where Mr. Molnár taught."

Ben looked up. Indeed, this was a surprise, but he didn't say anything.

"So then, actually you've already briefed us that Mr. Molnár was one of those people who mistreated the local Jewish population and played a big part in their demise."

"That's correct," Gabriella replied. "We know this from our own investigation, from the notes The Rat, the murderer, left behind at all of the sites. And, incidentally, Mr. Molnár, as all the other victims of The Rat, is also described in a manuscript Attaché Rózsa briefed you about, which is being translated for you now."

"Of course," Hill broke in, "you understand that even with the larger aspect of the other murders, for us this is only a local investigation, and that we have no interest in this case beyond our jurisdiction."

"My department, The Hungarian Security Agency, is fully aware of that, Lieutenant Hill. And we very much appreciate your willingness to help our investigation and let us observe and be involved in your investigation. There are two aspects I might want to mention at this point. One, I ask that you do not release the contents of the second note The Rat left at the Molnár house. If the next victims, the future victims, The Rat has marked for murder and so boldly named, get hold of this information, we won't be able to stake them out and hopefully get The Rat. They'll go into hiding and we'll be back to where we are now. Secondly, although this is going to be handled through diplomatic channels, the large amount of money that was found at the Molnár house, and we believe that there is even more hidden somewhere in the residence or perhaps elsewhere, is going to be claimed by the Hungarian Government as belonging to the victims of Mr. Molnár and the Hungarian Arrow Cross Party.

"Yes. Well," Hill commented, "that might be, and whatever the diplomats will work out," he smiled at Captain Kerek, "will be all right with the LAPD. At this point the money is impounded in the Property Clerk's Office, pending the court's disposition." Captain Kerek nodded. "Do you have any questions for any of us?" Hill asked. "Not at this time," she answered. "I'll be going over the material in the folder, and if there are questions I'll be in touch," She added. "The translations, and copies of the originals of The Rat's notes, I take it, are in the folder?"

"Yes, they are. Everything we came up with so far is included, and anything we'll be coming up with will be forwarded to you, Captain Kerek." He turned to Ben. "How about you Ben? You have any questions?"

Ben smiled, "I'm just along for the ride, Craig. Actually, I am as new to this case as any of you guys. I know no more than you do at this point, but I'll be working with Captain Kerek, mainly on the New York angle, and if I come up with anything, I'll let you guys know."

"What exactly is the New York angle?" Hill asked.

"Captain Kerek believes," Ben turned toward Gabi, who cut in, "We believe that the murderer, The Rat, might be someone living in New York." Hill nodded his head.

Ben asked, "Do you or any of you guys have any theories, guesses?" He looked around the room, but nobody answered. Finally Hill commented. "It's too early in the game, but frankly, and between you and I and the lamp post, this case is closed. It's not going anywhere. We are stymied, nothing to go on."

Gabriella agreed, "I know what you mean. We have been feeling that way for the past ten years. Ten years of investigation and twenty murders later, beyond believing that all the killings were done by one person, we are still nowhere." There was silence in the room, then Hill spoke, "What makes you sure that the killings are the work of one person?"

"We are not sure. Of course we can't be, but everything we know points in that direction. One person can be as perfect as The Rat has been till now. Two people, an organization perhaps," she shook her head, "not possible. Something would get out, something would go wrong, something would break. My personal feeling is that it is definitely one person."

"What about you, Ben? What does your nose tell you?" Hill smiled at Ben.

Ben was a bit put off. The sudden unexpected reference to his nose so out of the blue threw him a bit. "What does my nose have to do with it?" He asked somewhat bewildered and a bit irritated.

"We checked you out, Ben," Hill smiled. "We were told you can smell a rat from a mile."

Ben shook his head and slid up on his chair. "By now this rat is a lot more than a mile from here."

"You know," Hill said, "when we first went to the house, I thought this was going to be an easy case. I mean, when I saw the tape on the slide bolt of the back door lock, I figured we were dealing with an amateur. When I saw the tape I thought here was a perpetrator who saw something on television and copy-cated it, put the tape on the lock, than panicked and fled, leaving the tape on the door." The room was quiet. Ben broke the silence, "Did you ever consider that The Rat might have left the tape on the door on purpose?"

"Yes," Hill replied. "About ten minutes after I came out of the house, after I found nothing, but a piece of tape." He thought for a while. "But I still don't know why he left it, or why he needed to put the tape on the door in the first place."

One of the plain clothes men spoke up, "Maybe he wanted an easy exit."

"That makes sense," Hill said, "but, if the perp had no problem opening the door without force from the outside, why could he not have opened it from the inside?"

"Or," Ben chimed in, "maybe he went into the house more than once and maybe he didn't want to bother opening the door twice in the dark, however easily he might have done it the first time."

Hill, the others in the room, including Gabi, looked at Ben. There was a long pause. Hill spoke up again. His face was somber as he asked Ben, "Why would he do that?"

Ben shook his head, "I don't know."

*   *   *

The Myako was a Los Angeles landmark. Ben and Gabi sat at a small table in one of the many oriental looking, open sided little pagodas, each having one table only, and each covered with climbing shrubs that emitted a sweet and marvelous scent that permeated the hillside. The Myako was one of Los Angeles' original Japanese restaurants built on the hilltop overlooking the city below, long before Japanese restaurants became the craze. And it was still one of the best. The old pagoda sat on the top of the hill, overlooking the little kiosks, with beautiful gardens and staircases winding up and down between the azaleas and other flowering shrubs and their rich scents. Waitresses, dressed in traditional garments, beautiful kimonos, wearing wigs, were waiting on tables as colorful lanterns illuminated the hillside in a pleasant, understated way and the strange, but peaceful pangs of samisen came over the loudspeakers.

"This is a beautiful place," Gabi commented. "How did you know about it?"

"Goldie, my wife," Ben replied, "had some relatives in Los Angeles. We came here on our honeymoon. She loved this place." He said sadly, with a smile. "We came here a lot."

"Can I ask you," Gabi turned to Ben after a while, "when did she die?"

"Little over a year ago." He shook his head side to side and looked around, as though bringing up old memories. "I miss her a lot," he said, and Gabi thought there might have been a tear in his eye.

"I am sorry Ben," she said simply.

"It's OK," Ben collected himself, "I don't mind." He looked out over the city, sparkling below them like a huge gem, with headlights and tail lights of cars winding through the distant streets, like so many gleaming necklaces of diamonds and rubies. They sat quietly. "She died unexpectedly, without warning." Gabi listened. "There was an autopsy . . ." Ben started with hesitation in his voice, "and we found out weeks after she died, her death was caused by something that happened to her in Auschwitz in 1944. She was a young child then, hardly more than a baby, and she must have been one of those kids who had been experimented on," his face was screwed up in pain and anger, "by those madmen who killed her." Gabi listened, as Ben went on. "All her folks were dead by then, they were killed almost as soon as they arrived in Auschwitz. She was the only one of her family who somehow survived and was brought to the US with a bunch of other kids. She had a number tattooed on her arm, and she was very self-conscious about it. Always wore long sleeves, and when we went to the beach, or once to Puerto Rico, she would put a band-aid over the numbers." He stopped talking and realized he had gotten carried away. "Sorry, Gabi," he forced a smile, "didn't mean to . . ." But she stopped him. She reached across the table and held Ben's hand in both of hers.

"Well." Ben tried to change the subject, "everybody has a story. What's yours?"

"My father was killed in the war . . ."now it was her face which showed pain, "and my mother was raped by the Russian soldiers when they came into the country."

Ben was sorry he asked. He squeezed her hands and said, "Enough. The war has been over for thirty years. He lifted his glass of plum wine, "to those who died, and to those who are alive." He emptied his glass and waved to one of the waitresses for another round. "Have you ever had Japanese food?" he asked Gabi.

"Yes," she said. "There is a Japanese restaurant now in Budapest, but it's not as good as the ones here in America."

"You like it? Japanese food, I mean?"

"Yes. I do. I didn't think I could eat sushi, raw fish, but when I finally tried it, I liked it."

"The sushi is the best in the world here," Ben said, "but if you like tempura, it's also the greatest here." The second round of plum wine arrived at the table.

"Ben . . ." she started with hesitation, "there is something, . . ." Ben looked up, and she seemed to think the better of it. "Nothing. Never mind. It's not something that couldn't wait." Ben didn't press. He picked up the ornate menu. "What are you going to have?" he asked.

"I think I'll have the sushi appetizer, and," she looked at Ben, "the shrimp and vegetable tempura."

"Why don't we do this?" Ben looked at her over the rim of his menu. "Let's get the boat. It might be a bit much for just the two of us, but it has a wonderful assortment of everything. Sushi, yakitori, tempura, steak, salads, the whole bowl of wax." He looked at her. "The whole bowl of wax, meaning everything."

"OK," she said. "I understand, but on one condition."

"Shoot."

"It's my treat."

"Vow! That makes it even better!" He put his menu down and added, "I didn't think Hungarian per diem was this good."

"I'll put in for entertaining the entire LAPD team." They both laughed. "And," she added, "I think we ought to have a bit of sake to celebrate a good murder, and a very pleasant evening."

"Gabi," Ben held his glass high, "I have heard Hungarian women were very special. I've heard they were very beautiful, marvelous company, generous, and it seems that you are proving everything I ever heard right."

She blushed. "Everything?" She asked with a shy smile.

Ben gave her a long look, but didn't say anything. He waved the waitress over and ordered the boat.

*   *   *

It was the second time this evening Ben was surprised. Though he didn't comment, ask questions, or make any kind of a remark, he was surprised to see the bundle of large bills she pulled out of her purse to pay the cabbie. She paid with cash at the restaurant also, and he noted the large tip she left. "You guys sure know how to travel and live well," he said as they got out of the cab, with one of the over anxious doormen holding the cab's door. "Oh, you mean the cash," She said lightly. "We get an allowance. The Agency doesn't encourage the use of credit cards." Ben looked at her questioningly as they entered the lobby. "Why is that?"

"Well. I think it has to do with foreign exchange; cuts down the paperwork, we can move faster, and best of all," she smiled at Ben, "we get to keep what we don't spend."

"The way you threw money around tonight," Ben wagged his head, "You ain't gonna keep a whole hell of a lot." He stopped in the middle of the lobby. "What say, I'll buy you a nightcap?"

"I am glad you asked. I am ready to wake up," she looked at her watch. "It's seven in the morning in Budapest and I am not going to sleep anyhow. Buy me a drink." She added with a smile.

They settled into the huge, soft, leather armchairs in the lounge. She ordered an Amaretto and Ben ordered a brandy. "What happens when you run out of money?" Ben asked.

"What?"

"When you run out of cash on a job, your cash allowance. What happens then?"

"Oh," she smiled, "I use my credit card."

The waiter came to their table. "We'll be closing up soon, if you'd like another drink." Ben nodded and a few minutes later the waiter brought another round.

"Thank God for the drinks. I don't think I would be able to sleep otherwise." She took a sip of her Amaretto and looked at Ben for a long time. "Ben," she finally started, "I must tell you something."

Ben looked at her with glazed over eyes and threw the entire snifter of his Napoleon Brandy down his throat. "Go ahead." He slurred his words a bit. "Speak."

Gabi looked at him. "Never mind. Some other time." She finished her drink and stood up. "It's time to go to bed." She threw a ten and a twenty dollar bill on the tray on top of the bill and started towards the elevators.

*   *   *

The pink message slip caught his eye as soon as he opened his door to his room. It was from Fredericks. "Call as soon as you can. Urgent." He didn't think he was in any shape to call and tossed the slip of paper onto his night table. Then he fell on his bed and fell asleep with his clothes on. He woke with a start and squinted his eyes in the bright lights of the room. He thought he heard knocking on his door. Sure enough, a few minutes later there was a quiet, discreet knock on his door again.

His head was spinning as he got off the bed and went to the door. Gabi was standing outside about to knock again as he opened the door. She looked at him sheepishly. "I couldn't sleep. Do you mind?" He stepped out of her way and she walked right in. "I have been up all this time, and I thought that you might also be up."

"Yes, I couldn't sleep either," he said, realizing how ridiculous this might have sounded in view of his wrinkled clothes and the rumpled cover on the bed. "What time is it?" he asked, though he thought he should have looked at the clock next to the bed, instead of asking.

"It's a little after four." She said.

He acknowledged her and pointed to one of the chairs in the room. "Please have a seat." She sat. "I hope you don't mind me breaking in on you like this," she started, "but I must tell you something."

"You don't think it could have waited till morning?" Ben asked and tried to suppress a yawn.

"It could have, Ben. In fact I wasn't going to tell you this for another couple of days, maybe even a week, but tonight, in the restaurant, when you told me about your wife, I mean how she died, . . ." she seemed flustered, looking for words.

"What about how she died?"

"You know. What you told me about the experiments on her at Auschwitz . . ." She stopped and looked at Ben painfully.

"Yes?" Ben didn't quite know what to make of this.

"The doctors who did those experiments . . ." She stopped again not knowing how to continue.

Ben was sobering up fast. "Please," he said. "Go on. Please."

She took a deep breath. "One of the doctors who did those experiments, and his assistant, were case number two." She waited for Ben to ask something, but Ben just looked at her. She went on. "These two were discovered living, hiding," she corrected herself "in Venezuela."

"Please," Ben sat down on the edge of the bed, "go on."

"I don't know where to start," Gabi was still flustered. "There is so much to tell."

"I'll listen to whatever you have to say," Ben encouraged her. "Please go on."

It took some time for Gabi to collect herself before she finally started talking. "We would have never known about these murders if one of our skydivers had not accidentally stumbled on them. He went to Venezuela with a group of European BASE jumpers, . . ." she stopped and looked at Ben. "Do you know what BASE jumpers are, Ben?" Ben nodded. "I think so. They are the crazies that jump off buildings, like the fellow who jumped off one of the World Trade Center towers. Right?"

She nodded her head. "Right. Anyway, one of our paratroopers from the Army—he was a member of one of these BASE jumping clubs—went to Venezuela with a bunch of other BASE jumpers from all over Europe to jump off Angel Falls in Venezuela. It is the world's highest waterfall and by this time it was one of the most desirable places to jump from, and BASE jumpers went there from all over the world. The Falls are deep in the interior of Venezuela, and until the BASE jumpers discovered the place, very few people ever went there. There was a small town; actually, it wasn't even a town, a place called Kaneima, with only a handful of Europeans living there amongst the native Indians. This was a very beautiful place, but it was so remote, it wasn't even on the map until the BASE jumpers discovered it. And getting to it was next to impossible. One could only get there by plane, but very few people ever needed to go to Kaneima. That might have been the reason the Europeans who lived there chose it, simply because it was so remote and hidden, nobody even knew the place existed. Anyway, it turned out; the BASE jumpers discovered that one couple, Alfred and Violetta Kuhle, who were supposed to have been Yugoslavian refugees, went to Venezuela after the war. At first he managed one of the best hotels, the Humboldt, in Caracas, then he gave up his job suddenly and both he and his wife disappeared, as though from the face of the earth. Another, younger man, Ferdie Witt, another blue eyed blond 'Yugoslavian'," Gabriella made quotation mark indications with her hands, "also lived at Kaneima with four of his native Indian women. There was a third, said to be an adventurer/diamond prospector, who was from Latvia and was married to a very beautiful, young woman, who, as rumors had it, was an Austrian countess. It was strange, as the BASE jumpers were finding out, that aside from the Latvian couple, none of the people had any stated reason for living in this remote corner of the jungle, and it was even stranger that all of them spoke nothing but German. Ferdie Witt occasionally guided people, photographers, explorers, on jungle trips, and became the favorite guide of the BASE jumpers. He was said to have had an eye for the ladies, and most of the female jumpers liked him. On occasions he took some of the jumpers on boat trips on the Churun and the Carrao rivers, to demonstrate the eating frenzy of Piranhas, the ferocious, flesh-eating small fish in some parts of those rivers. We would never have known about these people, and their murder, if it wasn't for a group of jumpers Ferdie took on one of these trips.

As we got the story, Ferdie left the group, presumably to chase some of the females while the other jumpers were picnicking, and when he didn't come back when he was supposed to, the group went looking for him along the edge of the river. They found Ferdie's aluminum outboard tied up to a tree along the river bank. Ferdie was half in, half out of the boat, as though he was trying to get into the boat from the water, both of his arms were in the boat, he was hanging onto the side of the boat by his armpits, but the bottom half of his torso was almost completely gone. It was eaten down to the bone by the Piranhas, some of which were still snapping at what ever parts of Ferdie they could reach. Ferdie was a skeleton from the waist on down. There was no one else in the boat with Ferdie when he was found, but it was presumed that if Ferdie had someone in the boat with him he, or she might have fallen in, and when Ferdie jumped in to help, both were attacked and killed by the Piranhas. He often took good looking young females, or groups of tourists, or anyone who paid him, to impress with his Piranha demonstration; dipping a hunk of meat on a wire into the water, and seeing how it was torn to shreds by the Piranhas. This could have happened, possibly after Ferdie demonstrated feeding the Piranhas, and the water was full of the fish. The group searched the river bank, but no one, and no remains of any one were found. Apparently this was the big, international jumping event of the year, with jumpers from all over the world, and most of the jumpers, even though they mingled with one another, didn't really know each other.

Ben was fully awake.

"Fortunately, some of the jumpers took photographs and got the boat and Ferdie's remains back to their base camp at Kaneima where a yellow sheet of paper was discovered, stuffed in Ferdie's mouth." Gabi stopped talking and looked at Ben. It was obvious to her that Ben wanted to hear the rest of the story.

"The note—you guessed it, Ben—was from The Rat. It identified Ferdie, as SS Hauptsharfuehrer Conrad Hagelhoff, a medical orderly in the SS, assigned to the medical experiments at Auschwitz." Her voice trembled and she noticed that Ben's head slumped forward. She stopped talking. "Are you all right, Ben?" she asked with concern in her voice. Ben lifted his head and nodded. "Go on," he said, "I want to hear the whole story."

"Are you sure?" Gabi asked.

Ben nodded again, "Please go on."

"Very well." She shifted in her chair and picked up the story.

"This incident was reported to the Venezuelan authorities, but not for some time, as there was, at that time, no communication between Kaneima and the rest of Venezuela, other than an unreliable radio, which sometimes worked, and sometimes didn't. Besides the nearest town with police was hundreds of miles away, and getting to Kaneima was difficult. When the jumpers left Kaneima, after their event was over, this incident somehow leaked to the press, which is how it finally got to us in Hungary. We wouldn't have had any interest in the case; it was just another murder somewhere in the world, if it weren't for the little yellow piece of paper, signed, 'The Rat.' We contacted the Venezuelan authorities and explained our interest in the case and with their help our team was flown to Kaneima. By this time the remains of Hauptscharfuehrer Conrad Hagelhoff, aka Ferdie Witt, had long been buried and no real clues could have been expected by questioning anyone who already had been questioned extensively by the Venezuelan police just after the murder. The Venezuelan police showed us The Rat's note and that is when the big surprise surfaced. It turned out the police first on the scene were from Ciudad Bolivar, the nearest big town; not a very sophisticated bunch, and their version of The Rat's note lost a lot in the translation. It was written in Hungarian, same as the one covering Mr. Köröndi's face under the dung in the box car, as well as all the other notes since. The note, as all the notes, was a death sentence, describing Hagelhoff's crimes. The note pointed out that Hagelhoff was to die, as his victims did, being dismembered. It was," she explained, "the conclusion of our team that the note found in Hagelhoff's mouth could only have been put there before his body was found and therefore, the killer, The Rat, had to be in his boat with him when he died. It was also surmised, that The Rat might have thrown Hagelhoff's camera, a Leica IIIC, in the shallow water, which might have been the reason for Hagelhoff to jump into the water to retrieve his expensive camera, or that Hagelhoff might have been pushed out of the boat with camera in hand. The water soaked camera was still in his hand as he tried to get back into the boat, but my team believes that The Rat held him by his neck in a way that prevented him from getting back into the rocking boat. The team figured that Hagelhoff might have been alive for some time after the Piranhas started ripping the flesh from his bones." She stopped and took a deep breath. "And the note also revealed that Hauptscharfuehrer Conrad Hagelhoff was not the only victim."

Ben looked up sharply.

"Violetta Kuhle was dead of Aids, and Alfred Kuhle was barely alive when our team arrived in Kaneima. He was on his last leg, and indeed, we learned that shortly after our team of investigators talked with him, he also died of Aids. He knew he was going to die; the investigators concluded when he volunteered another note from The Rat, which sentenced him to death, to die as his victims did, by having a disease administered to him that would slowly, and painfully kill him over a long period of time. There is a translation of The Rat's note in your file. The note, received by the Kuhles some time after the movie company left Kaneima, pointed out that the bottle of raspberry syrup Mrs. Kuhle was given by one of the movie people was laced with the aids virus. It was hoped, The Rat's note pointed out, that she would suffer a long and painful death, and that her husband would watch her die slowly, as the subjects of his experiments died in Auschwitz. The Rat's note also pointed out, it was hoped that all around her, her husband and the other Germans would all contract aids from her, and also die painfully over a long period of time. Unfortunately I couldn't go on this trip," Gabi added; "our agency didn't have the money, and I was still a junior officer."

Ben interrupted, "What did their death have to do with Haupt . . . something Hagel, what's-his-face's death?"

"That's what we found out when we got to look at The Rat's original note, and the note Kuhle had voluntarily given to our team. Alfred Kuhle, aka Dr. SS Sturmbannfuehrer Anatole Hubert, was a physician, self appointed scientist, who did experimentation . . ." she hesitated and looked at Ben with a miserable expression on her face. Ben looked at her, sensing her distress. He felt a certain affection towards her for sensing, respecting, and sharing his sorrow. "It's all right, love. I might as well hear the rest of it. Sooner or later you would have had to tell me anyhow."

"Yes," she said with hesitation, "he was as bad as Hagelhoff. Hagelhoff cut limbs, arms, legs, fingers, ears, noses off of living subjects, ostensibly as part of a study on how to deal with soldiers who lost a limb in combat. Dr. Hubert's experiments didn't have anything to do with soldiers, he . . ." she hesitated again, but Ben encouraged her with a smile and a nod of his head. "He . . ." she repeated, "experimented on children. Did unnecessary surgery without anesthetic, removed internal organs, and infected children with all sorts of terrible diseases, just to see the little kids suffer over a long period of time. . ." She looked like she was about to get sick.

"It's all right, Love." Ben pulled her to sit next to him on the bed. "You don't have to tell me any more."

"It's all right then? You don't mind me telling you about this?"

"No, Love." He thought for a while. "If you want to know the truth, hearing about this makes me feel a little better," he explained. "For the longest time I lived with suspicions of what might have happened to Goldie in the camp, but didn't question her, because I knew she didn't want to talk about it." He paused again. "Now the only thing I hope is that we catch The Rat."

Gabi gave him a puzzled look, "What do you mean?"

"I mean that I hope I'll be the one to catch The Rat, and when I do, I'll shake his hand, hug him and give him a kiss, and thank him for all he has done."

She laughed and hugged Ben. "You are . . ." she was looking for words, "so funny."

He smiled and remained silent for some time. "How did The Rat know about Dr. Hubert?" Ben asked.

"We don't know. Interpreting the clues from The Rat's note, we believe that The Rat went to Kaneima once before, about two years before Hagelhoff's murder, we figure, and this is only a guess, The Rat learned about Hubert from The Book, and went to kill him, and found out about Hagelhoff while he was at Kaneima. Of course we don't know how The Rat found Hubert, living in that place that wasn't even on the map, or how he managed to go there. We believe he went with a movie company that filmed at Kaneima, and we believe that while he was there, he some-how infected Mrs. Hubert with the aids virus. It was only a matter of time before Mr. Hubert was infected also. But we would never have known about the Huberts if the note left in Hagelhoff's mouth didn't tell us about them." She stopped talk-ing for a second, then finished the story. "When we found out about the note from the Venezuelan newspapers, and when we finally got to see the original, we com-pared it to the Köröndi note, and it became obvious that we had two murders by the same perpetrator. Then we got The Book and started asking the authorities of other countries in Europe if they had murders with similar notes left behind, and found four of them."

Ben looked up. "Who were they?"

"You've had enough for one day." She stood up and looked at her watch. "Well, it's almost time to go to bed." Ben looked at the clock on the night table. It was seven minutes to seven in the morning. "You mean in Budapest?"

"Anywhere," she said and quickly slipped out of her clothes. Before Ben realized it, she was in Ben's bed under the covers. Ben looked at her for a while, but her eyes were closed. Ben kicked his shoes off, got undressed and got into bed next to her.

*   *   *

The phone rang with a muted, but urgent ring. Ben's head was spinning, and at first he didn't know who the warm, soft body was next to him. The clock said quarter past eight. He was hurting as he sat up, trying to clear his throat, and focus his thoughts. Even before he could say hello, Fredericks' voice erupted from the handset like a volcano. "Thanks for returning my call Buddy Boy!" Ben looked over to Gabi, as if the voice could have wakened her. "Sorry, Bill," Ben started, "I thought it would have been too late to call you by the time I came in . . ." Freder-icks interrupted him. "Since when is 'too late,' too late to return a call when I said it was urgent?"

"Well," Ben started to explain, "with the time difference . . ."

"Never mind the crap." Fredericks was calming down. "I am doing double gainers to cover your ass with the big "C", but this is it. For your own good, you dumb bastard, you'd better get your ass on the next plane back to New York, or stay in California for what I care." Ben was listening but he figured he was going to let Fredericks run down a bit. "Here is the deal." Fredericks emphasized each word. "You'll be back in New York by Friday and in the Commissioner's office by ten, in the morning."

"Or else, what?" Ben mumbled.

Fredericks was stuttering, all boiled up. "Or else what?!?" He screamed. "What the hell do you mean or else what? Are you crazy? You have the Commissioner. . ." but he couldn't find the words to finish.

"OK, Bill," Ben said calmly. "I'll be in the big 'C's' office by ten Friday morning."

"You goddamn well better be." Fredericks slammed the phone down.

"He is pretty mad, isn't he?" Gabi said quietly.

Ben looked at her. Her eyes were closed; she was curled up like a kitten, and Ben realized how very, very beautiful she looked. Ben got back under the covers, felt the heat of her body, and they made love.

Chapter 7

Meeting the Big Cat

The Red Eye touched down with a thump, a couple of small bounces and the squeal of the tires. Ben's eyes popped wide open, as he realized that the plane had landed, and that he was back in New York. He couldn't sleep on the plane, though he tried as hard as he could, and although he was exhausted, his eyes didn't close till just before the plane started its descent for New York's Kennedy Airport. He wasn't looking forward to this day, to the meeting with Commissioner Katz, who was mad as hell at him, but inwardly he thought that he was going to be able to square things with the Commissioner and with Bill. He couldn't imagine why the Commissioner was so bent on having a meeting with him, and what he might have up his sleeve that would be so important that the meeting could not have waited till Monday. He sort of sensed that at this point, as important as the meeting might have been in the first place, the meeting this morning would probably be more an exercise of authority—an ego trip—than anything that might have to do with The Rat murders.

He smiled walking toward the airport exit, dragging his small carry-on, remembering yesterday, and it finally dawned on him that he was in love. There weren't too many passengers this early and he hopped into the first cab in line. The driver with a purple turban and thin beard looked at him from the rear view mirror. Ben gave him the address, 306 West 54th Street, and settled back into his seat. It took some seconds before Ben realized that the cab hadn't moved. He thought the cabby didn't understand him, and he repeated: "306 West Fifty-Fourth Street, between Eighth and Ninth. Please." But the cab still didn't move. The Pakistani driver kept looking at him in the mirror. "What's happening?" Ben asked the man. He could hardly understand the driver, who spoke very quietly and with a heavy accent. "I want to pick more passengers." Ben got pissed. "Look, you clown," he leaned forward and flashed his badge, "I am a cop. You wanna play your fucking games, or take me where I told you? Understand me? Get going." The cab started with a lurch, throwing Ben back into the seat. The cabby kept throwing nervous glances at him from the mirror, but in seconds they were out of the airport, on the Van Wyck Expressway, past La Guardia on the right, and over the Triborough Bridge into Manhattan. Ben was wondering why they didn't go through the tunnel, or the 59th Street Bridge, and was about to ask the driver when he turned and spoke to Ben: "Where did you say to go?" Ben was about to jump into the front seat to strangle the guy. This was an old cabby trick. Take the passenger the long way around, rack up a large charge on the taxi-meter, and then ask the passenger where he wanted to go. An honest mistake, particularly by someone who didn't speak the language well. He screamed at the frightened driver, "Stop the meter now, or you're going to jail! Capisce? The cabby straightened up the flag. "Sorry," He said. "Mistake. Where you go?" Ben was trying to calm himself. He realized he was tired, anxious about the meeting with the big Cat, and exhausted by an all day lovemaking session with Gabi in LA. "Go to 54th Street, between Eighth and Ninth Avenue, on the right. Understand?" The cabby nodded.

Ben asked the driver for a receipt, and the driver handed him a blank slip of paper. "You fill in," he said with a confidential wink, as if saying; "You could make money on this deal." Ben tossed the paper back at the cabby. "What's the matter? Can you write?" He knew the cabby was in trouble. Unless he owned the cab, which Ben knew he didn't, he was going to have to account for the extra mileage that wouldn't tally with the fare. The cabby was about to explain something, but Ben didn't give him any room. "Pull over there," he yelled at the Pakistani, and pointed to the no parking zone directly in front of the Precinct. "Start writing, clown." The cabby filled out the receipt. Ben looked at it and tossed him a twenty dollar bill, though the receipt was for twenty-eight dollars. "Keep the change," Ben said, and got out of the cab. He heard the spinning tires scream as the driver burned rubber, getting away.

The night duty sergeant was cleaning up his desk, getting it ready to turn over to Sergeant Finnell who was standing behind him with a cup of coffee in hand. He smiled, "Well. The prodigal son has returned." He was about to say something else, but Ben stopped him. "Careful with the words, Mick. You are talking to a captain." Finnell just smiled, "Yes sir."

"Is Inspector Fredericks in yet?" Both sergeants shook their heads. Ben walked away, but Finnell's voice stopped him: "Captain Doorknob, Sir!" He didn't give Ben time to answer. "The Precinct Commander, Inspector Fredericks, told me to tell you that he wants to see you after," he emphasized the 'after,' "you've had your meeting with Commissioner Katz." Ben was put out once again this morning and he went back to the desk and Finnell. "Now, you listen to me you Irish flatfoot. I've just about had enough of your Doorknob shit. From now on you show me the proper respect my rank demands. That's an order." He turned and walked away wishing he hadn't done that, particularly as he heard Finnell say, "Yes, Sir." without any sarcasm in his voice.

He thought his office smelled. He looked around the dimly lit, harsh green and vomit yellow oil painted room, his bulletin board, the clutter, and thought about the years he spent in this rat-hole, and couldn't help but envy his counterparts in the cheery, brightly lit offices in California. But he was fond of this place. This is where he spent most of his later years, and he thought of his little office as a worn, but comfortable old sweatshirt with fraying cuffs that had stretched out of shape long ago; easy to get into without fear of somehow damaging it. He decided against getting a cup of coffee that might make him more edgy, and instead thought of trying to catch a few moments of sleep before leaving for the Commissioner's office downtown. He leaned back in his chair and closed his eyes, but didn't think he would be able to fall asleep. He thought of Gabi, and was wondering when he was going to hear from her. He hoped his meeting with the Big Cat was going to go all right. He wanted to stay on the case. One way or the other, Commissioner or not, he knew that Gabi was in his life to stay. The story of the two SS thugs and their murder in the Venezuelan jungle kept coming back to him, and as hard as he tried, he couldn't shake the images Gabi's descriptions conjured up in his mind. Little children being cut up, experimented on, poisoned by these two bastards, murdered in the most unimaginable, horrible ways. The images upset him, and he tried very hard to put the thoughts about Goldie being experimented on as a child, possibly by these same thugs, out of his mind. But he couldn't. He knew that Goldie couldn't have children. He always wanted children but it just didn't happen. Now, here he was being asked, directed, actually ordered to help hunt down whoever was dispatching these criminals; all of whom, he thought, should have been on the gallows long ago. But some were still alive, hiding in the jungle, or others like Molnár, living in a million dollar home with a quarter of a million dollars cash in a drawer. "Thank God for The Rat," he said to himself, and couldn't understand why a country like Hungary or Germany didn't arrest and execute these terrible people, some of whom cut limbs off of little children, just for fun.

He knew he was very tired, upset, and at the same time deliriously happy. He must have fallen asleep as a hand was shaking his shoulder. It was Bill Fredericks waking him. "Boy, you must have really worked hard in Los Angeles." He wasn't smiling, but Ben thought he wasn't angry either. "Better get going. The Commissioner wants you in his office by ten." Ben looked at his watch. It was nine-thirty. He got up quickly and straightened his tie. "I better go," he said. "You better," Bill agreed, "but from the looks of it, I better drive you, or you won't make it."

Bill turned on his siren and put the beacon on top of his car. The traffic going downtown on Broadway was heavy, but the cars got out of their way and in minutes they blew past the old Times Building at 42nd street. Ben was wondering why Bill didn't say anything, or ask questions about Los Angeles, The Rat murders, but thought that he was concentrating on the driving, zipping in and out of lanes, trying to get him to One Police Plaza and the Commissioner's office on time. Finally, Bill spoke up as they got below 14th street and the traffic thinned out: "Where is your car?" he asked Ben.

"Holly shit!" Ben sat up straight. "I forgot I left the goddamned car in the police lot at Kennedy."

Bill gave him a look. "Boy! You must have had some trip. You look like a squeezed-out, worn-out hospital mop."

"Thanks, Bill." Ben agreed, "I feel like one."

"What happened to you out there?" Bill asked. "Did you fall in love?"

"Yes," Ben said simply.

"Yes, what?"

"Yes, Sir."

"I don't mean that crap! You really fell in love?"

"I did, Bill." Ben nodded his head for emphasis. "Truly and deeply."

"Well." Bill looked straight ahead, still not convinced that Ben was serious—they played these games, putting each other on for years—"the next thing you'll be telling me is that you are moving to Hungary, and that you are joining the Hungarian Security Agency."

"That I doubt," Ben said, "but unless the Commissioner takes me off this case, or even if he does, I will be going to Hungary."

Bill turned serious. "Well. I hope he doesn't take you off the case, but one word of advice," Ben looked at Bill, "Watch your temper, and don't step on his toes."

Ben nodded, "Thanks Bill."

The car turned off Park Row and pulled into the Circle in front of One Police Plaza next to the Manhattan end of the Brooklyn Bridge. Fredericks looked at his watch. "You have just four minutes to make it to the 14th floor. I know he is chewing on his finger nails. You better go." Ben got out of the car and Bill called after him. "I'll wait for you in the lobby. Some people might come by I could shake hands with. I might need their support." Ben smiled and waved, and walked into the large red brick building.

*　*　*

"Ah, Lieut, . . . I beg your Pardon, Captain Chapman." The female sergeant in the outer office greeted him. She looked at her watch and smiled. "Right on time. I'll tell the Commissioner you are here." She pointed to one of the red leather armchairs along the wall and picked up the phone. Ben figured that being addressed as 'Captain' by one of the Commissioner's people might be a good sign. But just as he was about to sit, the sergeant behind the desk called out to him, "I guess Commissioner Katz is ready for you." She pointed at the doors on the side wall. "Go right in."

"Well, at least you are on time this morning. Come on in, Chapman." The Commissioner pointed to a chair opposite his desk. Ben sat and felt very uncomfortable. The office was large, with large leather sofas, end-tables and lights, coffee tables, oil paintings on the walls along with the obligatory photographs of Commissioner Katz shaking hands with various dignitaries. Ben could see most of downtown through the large windows, the World Trade Center Towers in the distance, and the Brooklyn Bridge almost directly under the corner windows of the office. He thought he might be in for a chewing out, but didn't expect the Commissioner's opening line.

"First of all, I want to point out that this meeting never happened. Nothing that I am about to tell you may ever be repeated to friends, family, or any one. The only thing you are empowered to disclose is that I, and the entire department are behind this case, and we will not rest until it has been satisfactorily concluded. You get my meaning, Lieutenant?" Ben really didn't, but nodded his head and said, "Yes." He was wondering what this was about, and he didn't like the Commissioner referring to him as Lieutenant. He didn't think it was a good sign. The

Commissioner continued, "This case fell into my lap, not that I really wanted to get involved in it, but the word came from Washington. I thought it might be some political garbage, something I couldn't have given a good crap about, but I didn't think it would be a good idea to say no. Besides it was as easy to go along with it, as not." He continued looking at Ben with piercing eyes. "That's why I wanted to have a talk with you before you got started." Ben sat quietly, knowing that the real tirade hadn't started yet. "Bill Fredericks told me some time ago that you were retiring. I wanted you for something special, I don't remember what, but when I heard that you were leaving the force, I gave the case to someone else." He reached for his coffee cup. "You want some coffee, Chapman?" Ben thought some coffee would help him stay alert and nodded his head. The Commissioner looked as though he didn't really mean to offer the coffee, but now that he had, he picked up his phone. "How do you want it?" "Black, please." Ben looked grateful. The Commissioner ordered the coffee, put down the phone and continued, "Let's see, where was I? Ah, yes. Like I said, I didn't want this case and figured that as long as you were retiring and probably had nothing important to work on, I might as well throw it your way, let you go through the motions, stroke a few Hungarians, make them feel good, and retire when your time comes." He looked at Ben questioningly. "You get my meaning. Lieutenant?"

"I think I so." Ben said hesitantly and added. "In other words, I am not here to do a job, I am here to act a part!?"

"Whatever," the Commissioner said tersely. "If you catch The Rat, or whomever, the more power to you. I will personally present you with a commendation and the Hungarians will probably give you a medal. I figure, now that you are retiring anyhow, it wouldn't make a lot of difference to you how this case comes out."

"Well, Sir," Ben started quietly, "that's not entirely true. This case is very special to me."

The Commissioner cut him off, "What!? A murder, a bunch of murders? What the hell is so special?" Ben was about to explain, but the Commissioner held up his hands. "Do you know how many murders there are per year just in New York City?"

"I think so. According to the FBI crime statistics, last year . . . "

"Never mind that," the Commissioner seemed put out, and cut him off again. "I am quiet familiar with the FBI statistics, thank you. There were 1017 murders in New York City last year. That's 3.16 murders per day. We treated all of them alike. A murder is a murder. Wouldn't you agree, Lieutenant Chapman?

Ben was about to answer but the Commissioner wouldn't let him. "Well, that's not entirely correct. When you murder the Queen of England, or the President of the United States, or a millionaire philanthropist, a great scientist, a famous athlete or a movie star, it's not the same as killing a drug-dealer, a rapist, a cop killer, and so on. I personally wouldn't give a rat's ass if all the drug-dealers in the City bumped each other off. You get my meaning, Lieutenant?" Ben was about to answer, but the Commissioner held up his hands again. "It is my information that the victims of this assassin, The Rat, or whatever the hell he calls himself, were all ex-Nazis and the like. Not too long ago we trained hundreds of thousands of our young men to kill those bastards. And the more of them we killed, the more medals we got. I know; I was there. I saw the walking skin and bones skeletons at Buchenwald, the thousands of starved-to-death-corpses piled into and rotting in open boxcars. I personally think it's despicable that the Hungarian government and the Hungarian people are still protecting the worst of their recent past. So I am not altogether distraught over whoever is knocking off these bastards. Who knows how many in my distant family were butchered by these sons-of-bitches. So, help them as much, or as little as you can or care to. It will look good on your record, and won't hurt me politically. But I don't think," he added, "that I'll lose any sleep over those miserable bastards being rubbed out, or if their executioner is ever going to be found or not."

Ben didn't expect this. He had no idea that this was what the Commissioner was so bent out of shape to talk to him about. The realization came to him like a light bulb coming on the top of his childhood cartoon character's head, that the Commissioner apparently felt the same as he did about this case. He was pleased inwardly and held up his hand, asking to speak. But the Commissioner kept on raving, "It seems the Hungarian Police and the Hungarian Government are still protecting their murderers. And when you catch the executioner of these murderers, the remaining murderers will go free. I'll get some handshakes, a few congratulatory letters, maybe even an autographed photograph from the President of Hungary for the outer office, and you'll retire, and everybody lives happily ever after, except the ones The Rat will hopefully catch up with in the meantime."

Ben cut in, "May I say something, Sir?"

"I don't think so," the Commissioner ranted on, "You are here to listen . . ."

Ben felt the hairs standing up on the back of his neck: "You are going to listen to me whether you like it or not, Sir." he said. He wasn't talking loud, he didn't sound angry, but his voice was forceful and full of authority. The Commissioner looked at him with a surprised expression. He obviously didn't expect this. Ben went on, "I want to tell you, Commissioner that I completely agree with you." The Commissioner's face, though still angry, showed interest. "In fact, I couldn't agree with you more," Ben continued. "I have been on this case for less than a week, but what I have learned already would astonish you. And I haven't even scratched the surface. The one thing I did find out, that one of The Rat's victims was a Dr. Hubert, an SS doctor, who experimented on children at Auschwitz, and I wouldn't be surprised if he might have done something to my wife, Goldie, which eventually killed her." The Commissioner clamped a hand over his mouth in astonishment. "Another son-of-a-bitch The Rat disposed of," Ben continued, "worked with this Dr. Hubert at Auschwitz. He cut arms and legs off little kids, when they were conscious, just for the fun of it. The bastard that was killed in Los Angeles last week, who almost single handedly sent three thousand people to their deaths, lived in a million dollar house with a quarter of a million dollars in cash in his dresser drawer." He paused for a second. The Commissioner was white as a sheet. Ben lowered his voice a bit and went on, "So you see, Sir, I do agree with you about the Hungarians," he quoted the Commissioner, "still protecting the criminals of their recent past. But I also suspect, I feel it in my bones, there is some force I can't put my finger on just yet, that is at play here. You see, The Rat has announced almost every move he has made in advance, identified the victims by name and by their crimes, and he is still at large, and the Hungarian Police are unable, or," he let it hang for a beat, "possibly unwilling to apprehend him. I don't know if they are protecting The Rat, or just letting him do the work the Hungarian courts and the police should have done years ago."

"I'll be a monkey's uncle," the Commissioner broke in, "so what are you proposing, Lieutenant?" His voice was no longer angry.

"At this point I have no recommendations, Sir. As a cop, I want to dig into this case and go after it like any other murder. Just as you said, "A murder is a murder." he quoted the Commissioner again, "but as a man, the husband of a woman who was unbelievably mistreated by these bastards, and whose entire family was wiped out, I don't know; I wouldn't be at all disappointed if this case got away from me, and neither I, nor the Hungarians would ever catch The Rat."

"Well, I'll be a son of . . ." the Commissioner leaned forward in his chair with a much relieved expression. "Why, that's what I was hoping to tell you!" He seemed much relieved and leaned back in his chair. "I'll be." He repeated, "I thought you were gonna give me some gung-ho police crap, maybe even go to the papers . . ." He trailed off and shook his head in disbelief. "I'll be."

They both sat quietly. There was a knock on the door. "Come in," the Commissioner called out. The front-desk sergeant opened the door and stuck her head in, "I didn't want to interrupt," she said apologetically. She had a tray with a cup and a pot of coffee. She poured Ben a cup and refreshed the Commissioner's cup. Ben seemed as relieved as the Commissioner. "So where do we go from here?" the Commissioner asked.

"The first step is," Ben started quietly, "that I get to the point where I can make up my mind what this case is about. Ordinary police work. We already know a lot about The Rat's," he explained, "the murderer's MO, his motivation. The Hungarians think he might be living in the New York area. Possibly, though I doubt it, but have to run it down. I have to start filling my barf box, put the pieces on my barf board, . . ." The Commissioner cut in. "Your barf box, barf board?" He looked at Ben. "What the hell are you talking about?" Ben explained quickly and they both laughed. The Commissioner seemed more and more removed from the conversation; it almost seemed he was thinking about something other than what Ben was telling him. "This case is bigger than I thought it would be," the Commissioner said finally. "It's an international case. You will need a little back-up, won't you,` Ben?" He called him by his first name and looked around his large office as in deep thought. "You will need a large enough office, ... and a staff." The Commissioner was thinking out loud, and Ben listened in amazement. "Maybe five, six, younger guys to do research, chase things down for you. What do you think, Ben?" Ben nodded, but before he could say anything, the Commissioner went on: "And we should probably extend a courtesy office privilege to the Hungarian Captain. It would look good in way of international cooperation. Do you think that might be a good idea, Ben?"

"That would be very nice, Sir." Ben answered.

"What do you think of her, Ben? I mean the Hungarian lady captain?"

"She is very professional and very able. I like her a lot."

But he didn't think the Commissioner even heard him. "This is an international case with some very interesting aspects" the Commissioner continued thinking out loud, and seemed to smile as if to himself. "Yes." He leaned forward and slapped his desk. His mood was now a hundred and eighty degrees from what it was when Ben walked into his office and Ben felt much relieved. Things were playing into his hands and he was delighted with the way this meeting was turning out. "Yes," the Commissioner repeated, "I'll see to it that you'll get a large enough office with a staff, probably on the third or the fourth floor, and . . ." he seemed to be formulating a plan in his mind, "get the necessary clearances, authorizations, the works." He looked at Ben. "You'll be reporting to me directly, Lieutenant." He stood up and added, "I am glad we had a chance to talk before you got started. Let me know if there is anything else I can do for you." He extended a hand over the desk and smiled at Ben. Ben stood also. He knew the interview was over, but he had unfinished business on his mind. "It was my understanding, Sir, that a captaincy was to go with this assignment."

"Ah, yes," the Commissioner said imperiously as he ushered Ben towards the door. Once they were in the outer office he turned to face Ben well within earshot of the sergeant. "Of course. Please forgive me for calling you Lieutenant. The captaincy is in effect. The papers are in the mill, but I will personally see to it that they won't get bogged down." He turned to the sergeant: "Sergeant Miller, please assign someone to see to Lieu . . ." he corrected himself, "Captain Chapman's immediate needs." He explained, "Captain Chapman will be reporting here in the next couple of days to pick an office. His office is to be fully staffed and equipped per Captain Chapman's needs and a parking place will need to be assigned to him." He turned back to Ben. "Good luck, Captain, with this international case. I'll be following your progress." He shook hands with Ben. "And please give my regards to Bill Fredericks and thank him for me for his help."

"Yes, Sir. I will. Thank you, Sir." He was a bit bewildered by the turn of events, as he walked out of the Commissioner's office. Although he could have been fired, he didn't think that would happen when he came in, but he certainly didn't expect the way things turned out. He got into the elevator to go downstairs and tell Bill what happened.

A few minutes later he and Bill were sitting at one of the second floor windows of the Wang Palace, picking Dim Sum from the carts that never stopped circulating between the tables, and looking down at the snarled traffic on the Bowery and going up on the Williamsburg Bridge from Canal Street. "Commissioner Katz sends regards and asked me to thank you for your help with this case. I am under strict orders not to discuss this with anyone," Ben started, "but," he shrugged his shoulders and rolled his eyes, "you being my boss, I think . . ." and he filled Bill in about most of what had taken place in the Commissioner's office.

*   *   *

Bill insisted on driving Ben to get his car from the police lot at Kennedy.

Though Ben hoped Bill wasn't going to question him too much about what went on in California, he was grateful for Bill's offer to take him to the airport. He was tired and sleepy, and he didn't much feel like wrestling with another Pakistani cab driver. One Pakistani cabby a day was enough. But as they were coming out of the Brooklyn end of the tunnel, he could no longer hold it in; he had to tell Bill something about his trip to Los Angeles and explain why he didn't get back to him the night before last. He kept talking all the way to the police lot at Kennedy. Bill kept nodding his head, but when they pulled into the lot, Ben had no idea what he told Bill, and what he didn't. His car started up and within minutes he was out of the airport on the Van Wyck Expressway for the second time the same day, on his way to his home just two blocks in from Queens Boulevard in Forest Hills.

He went to the phone and dialed the Universal Sheraton in Los Angeles. He didn't expect Gabi to be in but he wanted to leave a message for her to call him at home. Then he lay down on his sofa and within seconds was dead to the world. It was pitch dark outside his window, nine o'clock according to his wrist watch, when he woke. He sat up, rubbed his eyes and hit the play button on his answering machine. One message was from Bill, but it turned out to be from the day before, and there were several hang-ups, as usual. He looked at his watch again. It was now a few minutes past nine and he figured that in California it was just six in the evening, and decided to try Gabi again. He asked the operator for room 973, but there was no answer and he left a message. He figured she might still be out working on the Molnár case, or having dinner. He didn't like the idea that she might be having dinner with that Hungarian ass hole of a clown, the Press Attaché with the Hungarian Consulate in Los Angels, and realized that he was jealous. He sensed that something didn't go right when Gabi had dinner with Mr. Rózsa the first night in Los Angeles, but he didn't ask any questions, as he didn't think it was any of his business. He didn't like Mr. Rózsa. He thought that Mr. Rózsa was over the top, too pompous, overly attentive, overly helpful, full of shit. But now, he definitely didn't like the idea, the possibility of Gabi having dinner with Mr. Rózsa again, but put the thought out of his mind and decided to call the Chinese take-out for some dinner. He had Chinese for lunch, but it was either Chinese or Pizza, and he decided that Chinese would be a little easier on his stomach. He took a bottle of beer from the fridge, and smiled as he noticed that it was Budweiser. He was about to pick up the phone again, but it was only quarter past nine and he decided to wait.

He couldn't get her out of his mind. He imagined her intelligent, sensitive face, and could hear her positive, yet very feminine voice ringing in his ear. He felt the closeness of her sweat covered body, and the passion she rang out of every second of their lovemaking. He missed her, and he didn't want to be without her ever again. He pondered the future trying to figure out how their lives would work out in the next couple of days, weeks, and months. He was sure she would have to go back to Hungary and he couldn't imagine how he was going to survive without her. He tried to think of tomorrow, the next day, of his own activities; starting to put together his team, and the pieces of the puzzle of The Rat murders, and The Rat. He jumped as the phone rang, but it was the Chinese take out place telling him they lost his address. He cancelled his order and called the Pizza place. He was two beers down when the Pizza arrived and he no longer felt very hungry. He ate two slices, and carefully put the remainder into his refrigerator, knowing that he would be throwing it out in a couple of days. It was almost ten o'clock, close to seven in Los Angeles, and he dialed the Sheraton. "Room 973 is not picking up," the operator said sweetly, "Would you care to leave a message?" He left another short message, "Hi, Love. Please call when you pick up this message. Doorknob." He didn't know why he signed off as Doorknob, but somehow he felt it was funny, and thought she would get a kick out of it. He watched television for a while but couldn't concentrate on anything that was on the tube. He decided to go to bed. He gave the Universal Sheraton one more call, but room 973 still didn't answer, and he went to bed. He didn't fully realize how tired he was. Even after his long afternoon nap, he fell asleep almost as soon as his head hit the pillow and didn't wake till about six, his usual time. His hand reached out for the phone on his night table. He dialed the Universal and asked for Gabi's room. There was no answer. When the operator, a man with the voice of an advanced gay person, came back on line again after a very long time, asking if he wanted to leave a message, Ben asked the operator if Miss Kerek had picked up her messages. "I have no way of knowing that," the operator whined, irritating the hell out of Ben, and asked, "would you like to be connected to the front desk?" He said no, and hung up. He couldn't imagine what had happened to Gabi; why she didn't call, or return his calls. He told himself all kinds of scenarios that could have prevented her from calling, but none of them made any sense and the more he thought about it the more upset he became.

He took a quick shower, got dressed and headed for the Landmark Diner on Queens Boulevard for his usual breakfast. Louise, an elderly waitress greeted him, "You been away for a couple of days?" She handed Ben The New York Times. "You're famous, hey, Ben?" She opened the paper to one of the back pages. Ben's picture was right next to Police Commissioner Katz's picture. The headline declared, "NYPD Goes International." He scanned the article:

> *"The world is shrinking and the world's most famous police department, the NYPD is reaching out towards new horizons. The five Boroughs of New York City are no longer the limit, as cases go international." Commissioner Katz elaborated on crime no longer being restricted to a local police jurisdiction, and with quick, international travel and communications, an interplay and close collaboration between the police forces of cities and countries of the world, is now a primary consideration of the NYPD. The Commissioner cited the recent establishment of an International Crime Unit under the command of highly decorated, veteran New York City Detective, Captain Benjamin Chapman, known affectionately by his closest friends, as 'The Rat Catcher.' The Commissioner did not detail any of the International Crime Unit's present functions or involvement, other than to say that this new agency is going to be instrumental in curbing the rising crime rate amongst the drove of illegal immigrants entering the country. "Captain Chapman," the Com-*

missioner concluded his statement, "was hand picked for his bravery and effectiveness in dealing with crime. He is certainly one of New York's Finest!"

Ben put down the paper. He was confused. What was this shit about? What did his work have to do with illegal immigrants, and international crime? He was assigned to one single case of helping to find a serial killer, who, at this time he didn't think he wanted to find. It was amazing how a politician could twist a simple case into personal advantage, even when the case should have been very personal to someone like the Commissioner, who, just yesterday morning talked about how some of his distant family might have been killed by The Rat's victims. And now, a day later, actually, considering the time of the Commissioner's impromptu news conference yesterday afternoon, less then half a day later, went completely against his principles. "If he ever had any," Ben thought to himself, "and turned this whole case into a political game for his own benefit." Ben regretted accepting this assignment. He could have retired in five weeks and lived happily ever after. But if he had turned the case down, he wouldn't have met Gabi, and at this point she was foremost in his mind. Nothing else seemed important except the love he felt for her, and his bewilderment at not having heard from her. He tried to come up with all sorts of explanations as he turned onto the Long Island Expressway, on his way to the Midtown Tunnel and the Midtown North Precinct.

Finnell acknowledged his good morning at the front desk with a smile, but just shook his head when Ben asked if he had any messages. Ben didn't even bother to take his coat off in his office before he reached for the telephone and dialed the Universal Sheraton Hotel in Los Angeles. The same fag he talked with when he woke this morning, came on line again. He asked for 973 and let the phone ring, but there was no answer. When the operator came back on, his voice whining, Ben asked to be connected to the front desk and explained who he was, and that he had been trying to talk with a Ms. Gabriella Kerek in 973, who hadn't returned his calls. "Let me check," the desk clerk said, and put Ben on hold. An eternity later Gabi's sleepy voice cracked through the phone. Like a burst balloon, all of Ben's anxieties evaporated on hearing her voice. "I was worried about you, Love. I didn't know what had happened to you. Did you get my messages?"

"No," she said, sounding like she was waking up, but would rather go back to sleep. "You didn't?" Ben felt like he could have strangled that fag son-of-a-bitch of a phone operator. "I left three messages for you." "I didn't get them," Gabi sounded as if she was only half awake. She asked Ben. "Could I call you a little later?" Ben was flustered. He expected a much broader reaction from Gabi. He thought that she would be happy to hear from him. "Sure Love," he said quietly, "Go back to sleep. Call me when you get up." "Thanks," Ben heard her say and the phone clicked off.

What was this about? He felt as if someone had thrown a bucket of ice water over his head, and wondered if she felt the same way about him as he felt about her. He was convinced that she was in love with him, but now she sounded like she couldn't have been less interested. He was confused. Wild thoughts were racing in his mind; could he have been a one night stand for her? And even though it was not even seven o'clock in California, how sleepy could she be not wanting to talk with him? Or, a thought slowly crept into his mind, was there somebody in her room, somebody in bed with her. He tried to put this thought out of his mind, but the image of her in bed with somebody else wouldn't go away. He remembered how quickly she slipped into his bed, without invitation, and the more he thought about it, the harder it became to put the idea out of his mind. He got up from his desk and took his coat off. He was in a daze, trying to collect himself and was angry with himself for behaving so stupidly about this whole incident. Maybe he miscalculated this whole thing with Gabi. What if she was in bed with somebody? Even with that pompous gigolo, Rózsa? She was a single, unattached, attractive young woman who liked sex and took it as, and when, the opportunity came her way. No more, no less. As lovely and likeable as she was, thinking back on their couple of days together, she really didn't give him any reason to believe that she was in love with him, aside from being charming and pleasant, and sympathetic as he told her about his wife, Goldie. He had to come to turns with the possibility that he might have grossly misunderstood their relationship, and that it was not what he, in fact, talked himself into believing. He was devastated. His world seemed to crumble, but he had to pull himself together, and the best thing he thought he could do at the moment was to start working, and try to get her out of his mind. He thought of resigning from The Rat Case, The International Crime Unit; chuck everything, and in five weeks retire as Lieutenant Chapman with 23 years of service, several medals and commendations, and the three holes the ice pick of the druggy left him with, in his chest,. But retiring now was ridiculous. He put the thought out of his mind and started going through the papers on his desk. He was going ahead with the new job. Political or not, it was a step up, a large step with a pleasant new office, a staff to do his bidding, his own assigned parking space, and all the perks his new position and rank was going to give him. "You played the dedicated, dumb cop routine," he told himself, "and the only thing you have to show for it is having made it to lieutenant, and a permanent disability pay the druggy's ice pick earned you, attached to a mediocre retirement in solitude. Not good enough! Pull yourself together," he told himself, "and make something out of this opportunity. Take the promotion, get the extra money and perks," but the most convincing thought that came into his mind was, the real opportunity this new assignment was going to give him; to get even with the miserable bastards that inflicted so much pain and sorrow on his wife and her family. That was it. That had to be the main objective which, even by itself, made this new job worthwhile. His head was clearing up. Besides, his thoughts drifted back to Gabi, it probably wouldn't have worked anyhow. He figured she had to be at least seven, eight, maybe even nine or ten years younger than he was; in the middle of her career in a foreign country on the other side of the world, just as he was about to retire. His rationale was reasonable, it made sense, but it still hurt.

He started separating and grouping the information given him by Gabriella, and Lieutenant Hill. The "Shit Case," the Molnár murder, the killing of the SS doctor and his assistant in the jungle in Venezuela already added up to an enormous amount of material to deal with, and, he realized, it was only the tip of the iceberg.

There were seventeen other murders he had not gotten much, or any, information on, and the five targeted victims in Hungary made this case the most unusual he ever had to deal with; in fact, the idea occurred to him, it was probably the single most complicated and interesting case he, or anyone in police work, had possibly ever heard of. But what was his part in it all? Gabi said that the perpetrator might be living in the United States, most probably in New York, and he decided that this was the aspect of this unbelievable case he had to get involved in. It was to be his starting point. But how? How was he going to find a single perp, in a city the size of New York City, or possibly somewhere else in the United States if, indeed, the perp lived anywhere in the United States? This was the proverbial, classic 'needle in the haystack' case, if ever there was one. But the pieces of the puzzle, the 'barf' as he called it, was beginning to come up. The name of the small city in Hungary, Pápa, was reverberating in his mind, and his instinct told him, that the beginning of his journey, the path that would eventually lead him to the identity of The Rat, started somewhere in Pápa.

*   *   *

Bill stuck his head into his office. "Working already!" He smiled and tossed a copy of The New York Times on Ben's desk. "Congratulations. Welcome to the club."

"What club?"

"The Club of Political Bullshit."

Ben laughed. "Yeah. I read the piece. I have no idea what it's about."

"I do," Bill said. "It takes one to know one." He looked at his watch. "What say, you'll let me give you an introduction to the world of politics in the NYPD? Why not listen to an old hand at this, an expert, I might add," he tapped his chest with his thumb, "me." He smiled at Ben. "Meet at the Greeks at noon?" Ben nodded his head. "I missed their slop anyhow. I'll meet you at noon," Bill closed the door and Ben's hand reached for the phone. He picked up the phone but didn't dial. He hung up, and picked up a copy of The Rat's second note the LAPD guys found at the Molnár house. He looked at the original and compared it to the translation, but of course he couldn't understand the original. He was wondering how good the translation was, and if it gave an insight into The Rat's mind, or if it might have covered up those nuances a police investigator could hang his hat on. Was anything lost in the translation? Was there a clue, or clues hidden somewhere in the text. Ben always thought of himself as a logical, cool headed, smart investigator who could see clues where others could not, who could put two and two together, and when necessary, outsmart and trap even the smartest perpetrator. It was his credo to automatically assume at the start of every investigation that the perp was very smart, and that he had to be smarter. It was the best way to start, because it was always easier to back down, than to realize too late that he underestimated a perp. And this perp, he smiled inwardly, The Rat, was the smartest of them all. He had to get into The Rat's mind from day one on, and into the minds of the Hungarian investigators, who, in spite of all the clues left by The Rat, were as far from apprehending him after ten years and twenty murders, than they were after the first one. This was going to be one hell of a big job, and he was beginning to look forward to the challenge.

He looked at the large clock over his bulletin board. It was twelve minutes past twelve. He fought himself but his hand reached for the phone and he dialed Gabi. A new operator came on and Ben asked for 973. After only a few rings the operator came back. "973 is vacant sir," She told Ben. "Are you sure?" Ben was astonished, but the operator insisted and Ben hung up.

*   *   *

Bill started his routine with the waiter who had a pained expression on his face. "What's the special today?" But the waiter just pointed at the menu. "No specials." "That's what I thought," Bill said, and looked at Ben, but it was obvious that Ben wasn't going to play. "I'll have the moussaka." Bill handed the menu to the waiter. "Me too." Ben also handed over his menu.

Bill could tell that there was something on Ben's mind. He gave a small laugh. "The first thing you'll have to learn is that the political world of the NYPD spins on bullshit. The Commissioner has to shine, and he expects you to shine also." Ben was quiet; his mind was far away. "Every now and then he'll parade you around, until this thing wears out, and he can no longer milk it, but by then he'll find something else to grab headlines with, and he'll leave you alone." He added, "Except, of course, if you fuck up, in which case he will act like he didn't know you, but if you score big, he'll be right there to take the credit. All you'll get is a commendation and maybe even your picture in the paper." He paused and looked at Ben. "What's going on, friend? You seem to be floating. What gives?"

"Oh, nothing." Ben shook his head. "This is turning into a monstrous mess." He started filling Bill in on the case, described the murder in Los Angeles, told him about the Venezuelan jungle murders, but said nothing about Gabi. "So, what do you hear from the Hungarian lady sleuth?"

"We didn't talk today." From the sound of it, the way Ben said it, Bill knew immediately that this was where the road was washed out, and he asked no more questions. The moussaka came; they ate it in almost complete silence, and headed back to the precinct.

"I'll be moving into a new office." Ben mentioned as they were going up the steps to the entrance of Midtown North. "I'll be sorry to leave this place." Bill nodded but didn't comment. Finnell handed Ben a pink message slip. It was from Lieutenant Hill in Los Angeles. "Please call as soon as convenient. Hill" the message said and Ben dialed the number even before he sat down at his desk.

"Hill." He heard Craig's voice. "This is Ben Chapman in New York. How are you, Craig?"

"Fine, Ben. Fine. And you?"

"I'm good," Ben said. What's up?"

"Nothing terribly important. Nothing that I think would help you, but I thought you'd want to know that the Molnár house was hit again last night."

"No shit." Ben perked up. "Was anybody else killed?"

"No. Nothing like that. It was a plain burglary. Nobody hurt."

"Can you give me details?"

"Yes. It was a completely botched amateur job. We sort of expected it. We have 86 thousand gang members in LA, and every time there is something in the paper about somebody's home with money in it, it's almost a sure bet that it will be broken into. These people all think that if money is discovered in one part of the house, there will be more somewhere else."

"Was there more money?"

"No," Hill answered, "no money, in fact as much as we could figure it, nothing was taken. Beni, Molnár's son, told us that he knew of nothing that was taken from the house, but the place was wrecked. The perp tore the place apart. Absolutely trashed it; ripped open the mattresses, cut the upholstery, pulled everything out of the closets, dumped the drawers, turned the place upside down from the basement to the attic, but didn't take anything."

"Well. That's interesting," Ben commented.

"Yes," Hill continued. "The house was such an unbelievable mess that we figure there might have been two, or even more people involved. We expected this, as I said, we even posted a patrol car for a couple of days after the murder and increased the drive-by checks, but this perp didn't go in from the street side. He came down the hill behind the house, through the yard of the house above the Molnár house, tore the phone line right out of the wall, broke a back window, and must have left the same way, up the hill."

"That's interesting," Ben repeated. "Say, have you heard from Captain Kerek?"

"I'll be seeing her later this afternoon."

Ben thought for a second. Maybe it was Lieutenant Hill she spent the night with. "Would you ask her to call me, Craig?"

"I will." He asked, "Anything new at your end?"

"No. I just started this morning, but there is nothing new at this end."

"By the way," Hill cut in, "Congratulations! We saw the piece in The New York Times this morning."

"Ah. Yes," Ben tried to minimize the Times article. "Commissioner Katz believes in publicity."

"You know what they say in this town," Hill broke in. "There are only two kinds of publicity: 'good,' and 'better.' Yours, incidentally," he added, "was great. Good luck with the job."

"Thanks, Craig. Thanks for the info. Take care."

"Yeah. You too, Ben." He hung up.

Ben went back to his work, but couldn't concentrate. He decided to go downtown to work on setting up his new office. The civilian attendant surprised him as he pulled into the garage under One Police Plaza: "Yes Captain Chapman," he leafed through some papers on a clipboard, "you are assigned Stall 81 on the third level." Ben was surprised, but didn't want to show it. He smiled at the attendant and said, "Thanks," and drove away. The attendant called after him, "Keep your keys in the ignition, and good luck with the job." Ben waved in the rear view mirror. He had no intention of keeping his key in the ignition, and locked the car with the burglar alarm remote as he got out. The elevator was only a few stalls from 81. He went up to the 14th floor and walked into the Commissioner's outer office. Sergeant Miller greeted him with a smile and handed him a fat file pouch. "Everything you need to know is in here. But," she added with a friendly laugh, "if it isn't, please call me and I'll take care of it for you." She extended a hand towards Ben. "I am Sergeant Eileen Miller. We didn't get a chance to meet formally yesterday."

"Ben Chapman," he said simply, and shook her hand.

"Your office number is 610. I hope you'll like it."

Ben took the elevator down to six. 610 had nice double, wood doors with his name, Captain Benjamin Chapman, in a brass frame under the brass numbers. Another sign that could be easily replaced, he thought with an inward smile, and wondered who the office might have belonged to before yesterday. The office was beautiful. Just like the Commissioner's, though not as big. It had an outer office, and through the doors leading into what he believed to be his office, he could see the furniture in the middle of both rooms under tarps, and painters working, putting up new wallpaper. He walked into his office. Like the Commissioner's, it was in the corner of the building but the view from this floor was more limited than the Commissioner's. He could see the entire span of the Brooklyn Bridge, a good section of the East River Drive, and most of the buildings in front of One Police Plaza.

On top of the tarp covered furniture in the middle of the room was a large bouquet of flowers in a basket with a small envelope pinned to the plastic wrap. He took out the card and felt faint: "With my best wishes for the new job, and with all my love, Gabi." He would have liked to sit down, but there were no chairs.

"Should I put them in a vase for you?" He heard a voice from behind him. He turned around. A young, uniformed cop held out his hand: "I'm Frank Campanelli, Sir, assigned to the unit as your secretary/clerk."

Things were progressing a bit too fast for Ben. For almost the entire past year, he had had very little going on around him, and now he felt, he couldn't catch up with all that was happening. Almost absent mindedly, or maybe because he felt a little shell-shocked by the unexpected flowers and message from Gabi, he shook Campanelli's hand and heard himself say, "Welcome aboard." As if from a distance, he heard Campanelli ask him again about putting the flowers in a vase, but he just shook his head. "No thanks. I'll be taking them with me."

"So far," Campanelli explained, "it's only me, and even I am only temporary. But there is a list of recommendations in your folder, with resumes. I will contact whoever you might want to interview and set up appointments. You might want to add your own choices to the list, or go entirely with them. I'll be available 24 hours a day. Please don't hesitate to call me at any time." Ben liked the young guy. All of a sudden, it seemed that everything was falling into place, all was working out, and he felt it difficult to contain himself. "When is this place going to be livable?" he asked Campanelli.

"The painting and wallpapering is supposed to be done by tomorrow afternoon, the clean–up by tomorrow evening, and even though the place will smell of fresh paint for a while, you could probably move in the day after tomorrow."

"OK," Ben faced Campanelli, "Is your number in the pouch?"

"Yes, Sir. Also my home number and my pager."

"OK," Ben said, and he felt like he was on cloud 9. "Unless you hear from me otherwise, I'll see you here the day-after-tomorrow at nine o'clock."

"Yes sir."

Ben put the flowers very carefully in the backseat of his car, got behind the wheel, and looked at Gabi's card again. He almost screamed with joy and relief as he re-read the card: "With my best wishes for the new job, and with all my love, Gabi." Suddenly his eyes caught a small word in the lower right corner of the card: "Over." He turned the card over. "I'm coming into Kennedy airport on American Flight 10, arriving at 11:00 this evening. If it wouldn't be too much to ask, it would be so nice if you could meet me. G." Ben leaned back in his seat and took a deep breath. Then he looked at his watch, but it was only 3:22. He turned the key in the ignition, backed out of his stall, and drove out of the garage and up on the Brooklyn Bridge. This had to be one of the great, if not the greatest, days in his life.

* * *

Flight 10 from Los Angeles was exactly on time. Ben watched the huge 747 ease up to the gate, and watched as the jet-way connected to the plane. He scanned the passengers getting off and spotted Gabi before she saw him, way down in the jet-way. He moved closer to the gate. Her face showed, Ben thought, apprehension, and relief as she spotted him. She almost ran to him and threw both her arms around him. "I'm so glad you could come," she said and choked a little on her words. "I didn't know if you'd come."

"Why would I not come?" Ben asked.

"I don't know, Love. I just wasn't sure."

"But I am here," Ben said cheerfully, "and I brought you something." He handed her a single, long stem, red rose, attached to a split bottle of Chandon. Her face showed that she was relieved and delighted. Ben took her carry-on and they started walking towards the exit. "I have to get the rest of my luggage," she said as she steered Ben towards the down escalator with a baggage pickup sign overhead.

"I thought all you had was this," Ben indicated the carry-on, but she shook her head. "No. I checked two more pieces." "Isn't that funny," Ben smiled, "I thought I remembered you traveling with only this one," he pointed again at the carry-on. "Yes," she explained. "When we went to Los Angeles. The others were delivered to me from the consulate. They came by diplomatic pouch."

There was a large crowd around the carousel, and, as usual it took some time before the claxon blared and the flashing red light indicated that the luggage was about to be delivered. The metal belt of the carousel started moving and soon luggage was spewing out. "Those two are mine," she pointed at two midsize identical suitcases that looked brand new and helped Ben grab them off the carousel. Ben left her with the luggage and came back with a Dollar Rent-a-Cart. "You know, I could take a cab," she said hesitantly. Ben didn't understand. "A Cab?"

"Yes. So you wouldn't have to drive all the way into the city."

"But, I thought . . ." Ben hesitated, "you'd be coming with me to my place."

A big smile broke out on her face and she threw her arms around Ben.

The traffic on the Van Wyck Expressway seemed to be easing up for the night. Ben could have put his beacon and his siren on, but this was no chase; this was a pleasure ride and he wanted to enjoy every moment of it.

"I didn't know if you would be happy to see me," she blurted out after a long silence. "I was so hoping you would have called me last night."

Ben didn't understand. "But I did call you, and left messages for you." They looked at each other, with confused expressions on both faces.

"I didn't get any messages," she said quietly.

Ben lifted both hands from the steering wheel, palms facing up, and cocked his head slightly and repeated: "I left no less than three messages for you, and called at least six times, but the only time I got you was when you did answer, but you were too sleepy to talk."

"I am sorry, Darling, but I was so sleepy. I was very tired because, I think the jet-lag caught up with me, and because," she smiled, "I didn't sleep much the night before." She continued, "I didn't even eat dinner I was so tired, and when I went to bed, I couldn't sleep because the disco at the hotel was directly under my room and the music and the drums kept me up." Ben listened to her, but tried to remember if he had heard drums the night before last while they were in his room, but dismissed his thoughts with the mental explanation that he was too occupied with things, other than listening for music. She went on, "I got dressed and went downstairs and sat in the garden thinking of you, and wanted to call you, but I thought that you must be tired, and I didn't call. You must have called me while I was downstairs."

"Actually," Ben explained, "I couldn't sleep either. I called several times, and left messages when I was told that your room didn't answer."

"Yes," she nodded her head, "you see the music was still very loud when I went back up to my room, and around three o'clock I asked the front desk to change my room. I was in 1405. Didn't they tell you? That's why I was so sleepy when you called."

Ben remembered the fag phone operator. "But you didn't get any of my messages? Even this morning?"

"I didn't get a single message." She seemed upset. "It's like that in most hotels now, even in Budapest. They ring the wrong rooms when the calls come in, don't take messages right, or don't give them to you when they do." She patted Ben's hand and kissed his cheek. "I am so sorry, my darling. I should have called you when I didn't hear from you. I will always call you from now on."

* * *

Ben woke to a strong smell of fresh brewed coffee and frying bacon. When he collected his thoughts he realized that she was not in bed next to him. He heard the noises coming from the kitchen and hopped out of bed. The night's lovemaking was better than in Los Angeles, if that was possible, and he was exhausted and at the same time rejuvenated. He felt younger, and very happy. He slipped into his bathrobe, put on his slippers and headed for the kitchen. Gabi was serving the eggs and bacon, the toast was wrapped in paper napkins, and the orange juice frosted the glasses. Her hair was done up in a red kerchief, and she looked kind of funny in Ben's pajamas. But even the oversized pajamas accentuated her sensuality, and when she kissed him, Ben didn't want to let go of her. "Are you going to be late for work?" she asked and Ben looked at the clock above the refrigerator. It was almost eight o'clock. "No," Ben replied, "I am my own boss now. I come and go as I please."

She had one of her new suitcases half open on the floor in one of the corners of the kitchen. "I have something for you." She pulled a large, yellow manila envelope from the top pocket of the suitcase and handed it to Ben. "The translation of The Book. It came in by diplomatic pouch the day you left LA. Ben took the envelope but seemed to be concentrating on the suitcase. "It's amazing how the world is shrinking. I didn't think you could buy those in Hungary," Ben indicated the suitcase.

"Oh, yes," she explained, "you can't buy them in a store but a friend of mine at the American Embassy in Budapest got them for me. They have a catalog for embassy personnel; they can get anything American made and for less money than it would cost here in the States. No taxes." She added and went on, "When I found out that I'd be coming to America, I had my friend buy two of them for me." Ben listened to her, but kept looking at the suitcase. He didn't know why, but once again he had that certain feeling he used to get when something didn't add up, and he didn't know why. But Gabi's story made sense, particularly as she went on explaining she didn't know how long she was to stay in America, and she brought both winter and summer clothes with her. "Could I keep them with you?" she asked Ben, indicating the suitcase. "Of course, my Love," he said as he finished his breakfast and patted his stomach. "Boy, this was good. I haven't had a breakfast this good in years. He made love to her on the kitchen counter and they went back to bed.

*   *   *

"The city can be particularly beautiful on an overcast day like this." Ben's car curled up with the traffic onto the Kosciuszko Bridge, with the glass towers of Manhattan glistening in the distance across the East River. "I've seen this skyline a thousand times," Ben told her, "and it's never the same. Always beautiful, but never the same." Indeed, the UN building reflected bright flashes of sunshine, interrupted and flickered by the steel girders of the bridge, and the other skyscrapers seemed to be changing colors as his car drove off the bridge onto the Brooklyn-Queens Expressway. Soon the skyscrapers of lower Manhattan, from the Twin Towers of the World Trade Center to the uptown business district seemed to be close enough to touch, and the magnificent sight opened up as he turned onto the ramp of the Brooklyn Bridge. "It is so beautiful," she sighed.

"And that's your office," Ben pointed to the tall red brick building at the Manhattan end of the bridge.

"My office?" She asked.

"Yes my love." Ben explained, "Commissioner Katz thought it would be a nice touch to extend courtesy office privileges while you are in New York." Then, as an afterthought, he asked, "How long do you expect to be in New York,

Love?"

"Actually," she lowered her head, "I'll be going back to Budapest in about three days."

"Three days?" Ben's voice was pained.

"Yes, my Darling. I have to. I have to go back to report, and catch up on what's happening with the five targeted victims." Then, she straightened up and asked Ben with a smile, "What will you do without me?"

Ben thought for quite a while. "I don't know," he said as his car pulled along the guard post at the bottom of the garage ramp of One Police Plaza. The civilian attendant waved Ben through with a broad smile, and called after him, "Don't forget to leave your keys in the ignition." Ben waived at him in the rear view mirror. He pulled into Slot 81 and helped her get out of the car. He then slammed the door, pushed the button on his alarm on his key chain to lock the car and motioned towards the elevator.

Frank Campanelli greeted them with a friendly smile. Ben introduced Gabi. "How is the work coming?"

"Should be able to move in tomorrow morning."

"That's great." He turned back to Frank, "I haven't had a chance to make up a list for you yet, but we'll work on that first thing in the morning." Frank nodded. "And, Frank," Ben continued, "could you see if Commissioner Katz would have a moment? Tell Eileen I'd like to introduce Captain Kerek."

"Right away, Sir." Frank reached for the telephone as Ben and Gabi walked into Ben's new office. The painters were gone, and some other workmen were installing telephone lines, cleaning up the bathroom, and setting furniture up in the conference room. "Nice little pad, eh Gabi?" Ben looked around with satisfaction, thinking about his old office, that dreary, smelly little cubbyhole at Midtown North, his home for all those years. This, he thought to himself, was the lap of luxury. "It is very nice," he heard Gabi, as if from a distance.

"That will be your hang-out," he pointed at a small office to one side. "Whenever you're in town, the place is yours." Gabi was about to kiss him as Frank stuck his head into the office. "The Commissioner apologizes, but he has a very important lunch date uptown, but should be back by 2:30. If you are still around and it wouldn't be inconvenient, he could see you as soon as he returns. Eileen will let me know."

"Thanks, Frank."

"Not at all. Incidentally, the commissary is just one flight up, they have great sandwiches."

Ben liked Frank. He seemed like a can-do guy without hang-ups, and had a very nice, accommodating way about him. "Thanks, Frank." Ben said again and looked at his watch. It was twelve o'clock on the nose.

"What would you want to do?" He turned to Gabi. "The commissary, or Chinatown?"

"Chinatown," she said in her direct, immediate, and almost naïve way.

* * *

Frank hung up the phone as they came back into the office. "Good timing."

He smiled. "This was Sergeant Miller. The Commissioner just came back and was asking for you." Ben looked at his watch; it was 2:30 on the nose. "She said," Frank continued, "to come right up."

The Commissioner must have heard them. He came out of his office to greet them. As he ushered them into his office, he waved to another uniformed officer to follow. The officer picked up a camera case and followed them into the office.

"You have the best of the best," the Commissioner indicated Ben, smiling at Gabi as the picture taking was finished and the photographer left. "If anybody can help you, Captain Kerek, Ben here is the one. The rest of the time with the Commissioner was small talk, and a few minutes later they were driving North on the East River Drive. "I want you to see some of this town," Ben told Gabi, as he pointed out some of the sights all the way up to and across the Triborough Bridge, then heading south on the Grand Central Parkway to Queens Boulevard, Forest Hills, his house, and right into his bedroom.

When they woke up around nine in the evening, he asked her, "What would you like for dinner, Love?"

"You," she said with a coy smile.

"That's dessert," he said, but she corrected him.

"It's the main course and dessert for me."

They made love again and afterwards he went into the kitchen to get the cold, leftover Pizza and two Budweisers from the fridge.

*   *   *

She was sleeping deeply. He could hear her even breathing, and marveled at her beautifully proportioned, athletic body. She was hard as a rock, yet soft as a feather pillow as he hugged her. She was gentle as a baby, sweet and delicious, or wild as an animal, as they made love. Ben sat down at the kitchen table and smiled, as he thought of how winded he was and that Gabi was wearing him down. Yet, at the same time he felt his vigor returning, replacing the stagnation that took over and dominated his life since Goldie died and the ice-pick incident. He loved the feeling, and the affection and the love he felt for Gabi overwhelmed him. He closed the door and made a cup of tea, being very careful not to make noise and not letting the kettle whistle. He opened the fat yellow envelope and pulled out the copy of The Book Gabi had brought him.

It wasn't really a book. It had no cover page, no author's name; it was a small bunch of photocopies of typed pages, the English translation of the original, handwritten manuscript, a copy of which was also enclosed. But it was there for look-see only, as he didn't understand the Hungarian language, and even if he did, he would have had a hard time deciphering the faded, scribbled handwriting. He took a sip of his tea, took a bite of the cold pizza crust, picked up the translation and started to read.

Chapter 8

The Book

There were scores of people responsible for our misery and for my family's unbelievably cruel end. It would be impossible to catch up to all those who were responsible, in hopes that justice could be served, and punishment meted out. There would, of course, be no punishment that could be equal to, or even come close to the terrible cruelty, these sadistic, vicious torturers and murderers inflicted on my family amongst so many others. Twenty-five of my close family perished at their hands, and it has since been my most fervent hope, that twenty-five of those who inflicted pain, terror, and torture, who were directly, or indirectly, involved in the suffering and death of my family could die at my hands. But as time goes by, and as I get older and meeker, I now know that this will not be, unless another rat, younger than I, or the offspring of a rat will find this account, and take it upon himself to fulfill my fervent wish to honor the memory of those who perished at the hands of these torturers and murderers, and bring them to their just deserves. The guilty will go on living, unless an Avenging Angel will take up the sword, and deal out just measures of punishments. I hope their suffering shall be long and painful.

Although the hardships of my people started long before, the real suffering, the humiliation and the tortures really began the day after the German Army occupied Hungary, and we were forced to give up all of our worldly possessions and move into wretched conditions in a so called Ghetto. For weeks, the Gendarmerie inflicted torture, beatings, and in some cases death to those whom they "interrogated" in hopes of extorting money and other valuables. The conditions of our life in the Ghetto sank below that of animals. We had no food, no medicine, no sanitation, and with every passing day, less and less hope of survival. But the worse was yet to come.

Sergeant Köröndi in charge of the Gendarme detachment that controlled all aspects of life in the Ghetto, was perhaps the worse, though if one considers the horror inflicted by others as well, it would be very hard to establish priorities. How far could one go beyond torture and murder? Sergeant Köröndi proudly quoted Dr. Joseph Goebbels, calling us rats, telling us again and again, we were the worst of all vermin. As I heard this over and over again, I was beginning to feel like a rat. Scrambling for food, hiding when possible, and becoming cunning just to stay alive. I, and my family, and three thousand other rats lived in our bur-row, at the whim of Sergeant Köröndi, who showed us no mercy. He had us locked in, starved, humiliated, beaten and eventually stuffed into boxcars. He took the one bucket of water, for almost a hundred people to drink, as well as the one bucket put in for sanitation, from our boxcar, and he told us laughing that he hoped we would die slowly, suffocated by our own waste. He was right. Many of us in the car died, as he predicted, lying in our own excrement by the time the transport reached Auschwitz. It is my most fervent hope that one of The Rats will deal with Sergeant Köröndi in a like manner.

I place Sergeant Köröndi's name at the top of my list, as one of the twenty-five I condemn to die. It is my sentence, in the name of all his victims, that he should suffer the dread of dying as we did. He should die as many of us died, covered with shit, urine, and flies. His cries for mercy should not be heard, and his coffin should be a boxcar, like the one in which my loved ones died. His crime, his execution at the hands of a Rat, should be known to all, and it should be a warning to those who will follow him.

But Sergeant Köröndi was not by any means alone, and he, and his part-ners in crime could not ever have reached the position of power they attained, if it weren't for people like District Leader Molnár — Molnár István — whose guilt surpasses all imagination and human comprehension. Without the likes of him, there would have been no Sergeant Köröndi, and others who will follow in this chronicle. District Leader Molnár was a young opportunist, who, like so many others of his ilk, saw an opportunity of easy wealth, prominence and power in the Nazi ideologies. While a student in Germany in the early thirties, he met and married the daughter of a German Nazi official, who became his idol and men-tor. When he returned to Pápa, and found employment in the Reformed Church School, the famous old Pápai Református Kollegium, he implemented his political ambitions by forming a local Nazi organization, which later became part of the Hungarian National Nazi Organization, the Nyilas Keresztes Party. His early attempts for elected political positions failed. This might have fueled his thirst and desperation for power, and he became the leader of the local Nazi organiza-tion, which at that time had no political position or power, but was much feared and resented, as it foretold the terrible events to come, such as the ones already playing out in Germany. The number one objective on Molnár István's agenda was the elimination of Jews by any means, and as quickly as possible. He fol-lowed the example of his German counterparts, and his speeches—some of which were printed in the local newspaper—were almost word-for-word identical to the speeches we heard on the radio from the Reichstag in Germany. He did not refrain from quoting Dr. Goebbel's references to Jews being worse than rats in his class-room; mad philosophies, which were taken up by his students, and the youth of Pápa, and later by Sergeant Köröndi and his thugs. He did not hesitate to wear the uniform of the Nyilas Keresztes Party to his classrooms, and as often as the opportunity presented itself, click his heels and give the outstretched arm Nazi salute. He did this so often that eventually some of the students imitated him and started wearing little red and green Arrow Cross symbol pins on their lapels. But the real Molnár István didn't come into focus until sometime later when, as District Leader, Molnár was instrumental in confiscating most of the larger business enterprises—mine included—that until then belonged to the wealthiest strata of the local Jewish population, and assigned some of the more important and profitable businesses to himself and his cohorts. The huge textile factory just outside of Pápa became part of the Molnár Empire, and through his father-in-law's connections he immediately landed a very large order for fabrics for German Army uniforms. Some of his very large profits went into bribes for his contacts, but I am certain most ended up in numbered bank accounts in Switzerland, and in other banks around the world. The previous owners of the factory disappeared almost to a man, and those who remained were later murdered in Auschwitz. District Leader Molnár also played a very important part in the organization of the ghetto in Pápa, and in the eventual deportation of more than three thousand people, of which only a fraction returned.

There is no need to go further into the deeds of District Leader Molnár. It would take the better part of this account, besides his crimes are well known, and clearly warrant his punishment. It is my sentence that Mister Molnár dies, as he lived. He is to be deprived of his worldly possessions, and that he should meet his maker in the full regalia of his Nyilas Keresztes Party uniform. His death is to be witnessed by his wife, who was, in many ways, as guilty as he was.

Ben leaned back in his chair. He stared at the pages in front of him in disbelief and took the last sip of his cold tea. He thought of making another cup, but remained in his chair listening to Gabi's even breathing from the room behind him and smiled, thinking about the changes she brought into his life. Until less than a week ago, he was spending most of his days in his dingy old office, having little more to do than think about his retirement, and realizing he was floundering. He had no idea what his life was going to be like, or what he was going to do after retirement. As he sat in his office, having nothing to do but look at the ceiling, he thought that in some ways his entire life was wasted. His years in the NYPD, and his disability benefits were giving him a more or less worry-free retirement, but other than that, and the three holes left by the ice-pick, he had very little to show for his life. His wife, the love of his life, was gone for more than a year now. He regretted having no children and envied his friends on the force, as he went with them occasionally and watched their kids play Little League baseball on some Saturday mornings. Goldie and he often talked about adopting kids, but it never happened. They suddenly realized that time had gotten away from them and it was too late to have a family. He smiled sadly, as he thought about Goldie and their life together. She was a caring, gentle, and quiet person. She went along with everything he wanted to do, never complained, though Ben could sense when she didn't really want to do some of the things he wanted to do. Their life boiled down to a simple life without much of the frills his buddies' lives seemed to center around. They seldom went to parties, never entertained, didn't travel, went to the movies occasionally and once every two weeks went to a little restaurant on Queens Boulevard. He took a slow look around his kitchen and suddenly realized how old, outdated, almost dingy, his kitchen and the rest of his apartment had become since Goldie died. He spent most of his time at the precinct, or out on a case somewhere, and it seemed that he came back to his apartment only to spend the night and change his clothes. At times he would even go into the precinct on his days off, to catch up on things, because staying in his apartment was lonely and boring without anything to do.

But now, he smiled once again, things had turned one-hundred-and-eighty degrees, and everything in his life had changed. He was on what might turn out to be the biggest and most interesting case of his entire career; a case promising to be full of excitement and interest, and best of all, behind him in his small bedroom, asleep in his bed was the woman of his dreams, offering joy and fulfillment to his life. Yes, he thought inwardly, at this moment life could not have been better. He looked at the old kitchen clock; it was ten minutes past four. He listened to Gabi's breathing for a while, put a paper napkin in between the pages and closed The Book. As quietly as he could, he went back into his bedroom and got in bed next to Gabi.

*   *   *

But he couldn't fall asleep. Though by now he had heard all the details of the Köröndi murder from Gabi and knew as much as there was to know about the Molnár murder, he thought the description of these two people in the account of the anonymous author of The Book made him understand the cases better, and gave a strong motivation for The Rat's actions. He also felt that the descriptions in The Book were full of clues, though he couldn't put his finger on them at this point. But the more he read, the more he reinforced his earlier thinking, that the path to The Rat's door started in the town of Pápa, and the first step on that path might be finding out where the "Book" came from, who wrote it, and who found it.

He was very tired. The events of the past few days, followed by the half night of almost continuous love making with Gabi exhausted him. He didn't know when he fell asleep. He woke slowly, as he felt her body on top of him, and he wasn't quite sure if he was going to be able to cope with Gabi's lust for love. But she was gently chewing on his ear and on his lips, kissing his neck, and her warm thighs were wrapping around his legs, ready to start the new day with a bang.

Almost as soon as they finished, he fell deeply asleep again, but woke what seemed like only minutes later. Gabi was not in bed. He heard her talking on the phone in hushed tones, apparently in Hungarian. He hoped that she wasn't talking with Mister Rózsa, the slick Hungarian Consulate official in Los Angeles. She was on the phone for what seemed like a very long time. He got out of bed slowly and headed for the bathroom. The shower hit him with full force and he didn't hear the bathroom door open and Gabi getting into the tub behind him. He felt her hands explore his soap-covered body, and he thought with a smile, if he was to die as a result of her insatiable appetite for love, this was definitely the way to go. She dried him off with a huge towel. He watched her put her hair up in another towel, and go into the kitchen and start making breakfast.

"I have some bad news for you," she started. Ben didn't ask what. "I just talked with my boss in Budapest; he wants me to come home as soon as I can. There seems to be a new development in The Rat case." But Ben almost didn't hear anything she said, other than realizing that she wasn't talking with Rózsa in Los Angeles and he felt relived. He asked after a short pause. "You said there is a new development. What development?"

"I don't know exactly. It might have something to do with the next five victims."

"I see." Ben seemed deep in thought. "When do you think you might leave?"

"I'll see if I can get on a flight this evening."

"That soon?" Ben seemed disappointed.

"Yes, Darling. I must go." She quickly added, "But I'll be back very soon. I promise." She continued frying the eggs in bacon fat. Ben remained silent. "I thought" he finally said "I'd go to Hungary also. I think I would like to visit some of the locations and get a handle on The Rat."

"Oh. That's great." She squealed delightedly. "When will you come?" She asked anxiously.

"I don't know. I started reading The Book this morning, and as soon as I finish it, and get to know as much as I can about the others The Rat put away, I'd like to start looking around in Pápa, talk to some of the people, ask a few questions, you know, the usual routine; get started with this case." Then, seeing the concerned look on her face, he added: "Incidentally, why do they call that town Pápa? I mean is there another town maybe called Mama?"

She laughed. Ben just loved her laugh. It was full hearted, innocent like a child's, and sweet, just like she was. "No," she said. "There is no Mama. I've heard, when missionaries came from the Vatican to convert the Hungarian tribes to Christianity, they settled where the town of Pápa is today and named their settlement after the Pope, Pápa. But there is no Mama." She smiled and hopped over to him and sat on his lap with her arms around his neck. "When can you come to Pápa, Love?"

"I'll look into it." Ben said, and explained, "I'll have to find out what the routine is going to be. I mean who I am gonna have to kiss to approve the trip, get the tickets, the usual bull sh . . .." He stopped himself. She said nothing, but kissed him. "I hope you'll come soon."

They finished breakfast in silence and Ben reached for the phone and dialed. This was the first time Ben called his new office and was a bit startled by Frank's greeting: "Captain Chapman's Office, Patrolman Campanelli speaking."

"Oh, hello, Frank. How are things going?" And even before he could identify himself, Campanelli answered him: "Great, Captain. Everything is falling into place. I hope you don't mind, I called some of the people Commissioner Katz recommended meeting with you, subject to your schedule tomorrow morning. I'll also schedule a meeting with your people as soon as you give me your list to contact."

"That's fine, Frank. I'll work up a list this afternoon. In the meantime, find out for me who I have to stroke," he caught himself, "what the procedure is to set up some overseas trips for me in connection with The Rat murders." He looked at Gabi and continued, "I'll be working from home most of the morning, in case something comes up. You can call me at . . ."But Frank cut in, "I have your number Sir. One other thing, Sir, should I advise the Commissioner of your plans to travel abroad?"

"No," Ben said hesitantly, "not just yet."

"Very good, Sir." Frank changed his tone. "Inspector Fredericks asked that you call him at your convenience, nothing important, he just wanted to know if he could assign your old office, and wanted to know if you could have lunch with him."

"Great, Frank. I'll call him. Anything else?"

"Yes Sir. Several people called, wanted to talk with you. I think they just want to know if you might have a position for them."

"I'll call them back this afternoon. Anything else?"

"One more thing, Sir. The building administrator wants to know if you want brown, gold, or maroon carpeting for your office."

"What color are the walls?" Ben asked, suddenly realizing that he had no idea what color the walls were in his office.

"The walls are a medium gold, Sir," Frank answered without hesitation.

"Well," Ben thought for a moment, "why don't you pick the carpeting Frank. Would you do that for me?"

"As good as done, Sir." Frank replied.

"I'll see you after lunch, Frank." Ben hung up.

"This guy is a gem." He turned to Gabi, who was doing the dishes. "Why don't we go in this afternoon, Love?" He was thinking out loud, "I'll have to make up a T.O. for Frank, and" he laughed, "maybe you can help me pick the carpet." But Gabi was serious, "What's a T. O.?"

"T. O. means 'Table of Organization.' You know, Hon, a list of people who will be working for me, and what their job is going to be."

Gabi remained quiet, seemed to be in thought. "But I thought it was only going to be you." He sensed her concern. "Don't worry, Love. It's only going to be me." She went on doing the dishes. "Would you mind if I didn't go with you this afternoon? I'll have to see if I can get on tonight's flight to Budapest."

"It's OK, Love." Ben kissed her again, "I'll come back early and take you to the airport." She didn't answer and Ben kissed the back of her neck again. "Can I help with the dishes?"

"They're almost done," she said. "Why don't you work on your T. O. and I'll call the airline."

* * *

The carpeting looked great! Ben thought it was a perfect match to the wall colors and everything else in his office. The big red leather desk-chair was comfortable and Ben smiled thinking about his old office with the rickety chrome and green naugahide desk chair, with sticking casters. This case, The Rat murders, was a miracle. After years of pounding the pavement, doing routine, dirty, miserable cases, this thing fell into his lap and he was sitting in his own spacious office, looking out over lower Manhattan through large plate glass windows, with a secretary in his outer office, a staff of people yet to be selected to do his bidding, but, he suddenly realized, he had not a clue as to what he was supposed to do, where, when, and how. When Bill Fredericks first told him about the possibility of this assignment, he was about to turn it down. And he reflected, if he had, he wouldn't be sitting in this office, wouldn't be on the case, and most importantly, and foremost, he couldn't be thanking Bill, the Commissioner, and God, for sending Gabi his way. He picked up his fancy desk phone, punched a button and was about to dial. Then, he thought about it and stopped dialing. Instead, he hit the intercom and Frank came on almost immediately, "Yes, Sir?"

See if you can get me my house, Frank . . ." Then, suddenly he changed his mind again. Maybe it wasn't such a good idea to show off to Gabi, having his secretary call her, and let Frank know that she was at his house. "Never mind, Frank," he said and hung up. He dialed his number himself and Gabi answered on the first ring. She sounded a bit drowsy, but perked up as she heard Ben's voice. "I hope I didn't wake you," Ben said sincerely. "No, Love. I was just dozing a bit. It's all right."

"Did you get reservations?" Ben asked.

"I am standby on the 11:00 P. M. flight to Budapest on MALEV, that's the Hungarian Airline" she explained, "and when I gave them my priority authorization, they promised me the first seat, if one became available."

"I am sincerely sorry to hear that." Ben said.

"Me too, Darling." Gabi answered "but I have to go. When will you get home?"

"I have a few more things I want to get done," Ben said, "and will leave here shortly. Why don't you catch some 'Z's?" he asked her, knowing that she loved to use the expression ever since she first heard him use it on the flight to Los Angeles, which now seemed ages ago. "I'll call you as soon as I'm ready to leave here." He blew some kisses into the phone and hoped that Frank didn't hear him.

He quickly drew up a list of old cronies from which to pick his staff. The Commissioner suggested six people, and he wasn't sure he wanted that many, or any of the Commissioner's choices. Then he thought, maybe he shouldn't go with old buddies either. The Commissioner suggested young people to chase things down for him, and he allowed that he might, indeed, need some younger people to do research, dig up records, interview people, do the shit details his old buddies might resent doing. He picked up the phone and pushed the intercom button again. "Could you come in, Frank?" Almost before he hung up, Frank was in the room with clipboard and pencil in hand. "I was thinking," Ben motioned to Frank to take a seat, "that some of my old contacts may not be right for this job." Frank nodded. "I mean," Ben explained, "this job is going to call for a lot of digging, running around, and the older guys may not be up to it. Besides," he was almost explaining to himself, justifying his thinking, "I think some younger guys, like yourself," he nodded towards Frank, "might like this job." Frank nodded. Ben continued, "Do you by any chance know five, maybe six young guys, like yourself," he repeated, "who might like this job, and be smart enough for it?"

"I think I could call a bunch of guys for you to talk with, Sir. When would you like to see them?"

"How 'bout in the morning?" Ben suggested.

"Very well, Sir. I'll have them in, ten o'clock be all right?"

"Ten would be fine," Ben nodded and Frank got up and left the office.

In a couple of seconds Ben heard him talk in hushed tones on the phone, no doubt lining up his crew. Frank was a super efficient young officer, Ben thought, and as he thought about it, an idea crept into his mind: Was Frank one of the big Cat's plants? Sitting in his outer office, doing his bidding, knowing all he was doing, and reporting to the Commissioner. He shook the thought out of his head. Even if Frank was a plant, which of course he couldn't be certain about, there was nothing he could have done at this point. Besides, Frank being a plant was academic anyhow. He had nothing to report on. Ben stood up and went to the window. The traffic on the Brooklyn Bridge was endless. Cars, trucks, people were crossing the bridge in both directions in an uninterrupted chain, doing their jobs, chasing their dreams, or just trying to keep their heads above water and survive in the jungle of New York City. How lucky he was, Ben thought again, looking around his office and thinking about Gabi. Strangely, he wasn't terribly anxious to get home. He needed a little rest and he figured he would be back in ample time for one more round of love-making before he was going to take her to the airport. But he wanted to hear her sweet, resonant voice, with the slightest little accent and reached for the phone. The phone rang, but she didn't answer. She might be in the bathroom, or out to get a breath of fresh air, or possibly taking a nap, Ben thought, and hung up. The beautiful, shiny brass clock on his desk said ten minutes past four, and he decided it was time to go home. He had nothing else to do for the rest of the day, and he was anxious to see Gabi.

"See you in the morning, Frank." He smiled at Frank, who stood up as he went through the doors, heading for the elevators.

As usual the traffic was bumper to bumper on the B.Q.E. Ben pulled up on the shoulder, and with his siren wailing, and his red beacon on the top of the car, he went ripping past the traffic that was almost at a standstill.

There weren't any lights on in his apartment as he opened the door and his first thought was that Gabi was probably asleep. But she wasn't in the bedroom. When he went into the kitchen and turned the light on, a yellow note pad, resting on the table propped up against a pitcher caught his eyes. He picked up the note:

I am so sorry I couldn't call you, Darling, but the airline called just a few minutes ago. A seat became vacant on the 6:10 from Kennedy to Amsterdam. I know there are many flights from Amsterdam to Budapest, even in the middle of the night, and I won't have a problem getting one. I didn't want to take a chance on not getting a seat on the later flight. I called a cab, which just got here. I hope you won't mind, I left one of my suitcases in the bedroom. It has clothes I won't need for a while, and I'll pick it up the next time I come to New York. I hope it's not an inconvenience. Thank you my love. I must rush, but will try to call you from the airport if there is time. If not, I'll call you from Budapest tomorrow. I will miss you, and I love you more than anything in the world. G.

P. S. I didn't have time to do my laundry. I left it by the washing machine in my laundry bag. I would very much appreciate if you could do it for me and just put it in the top pocket of the suitcase.

Ben re-read the note, again and again, and shook his head in disbelief. "To put it mildly," he said to himself, "Gabi was a rollercoaster ride." She was unpredictable, which, in a way, he had to admit, made her even more desirable. But he missed her already and there was a tug in his chest wishing that she didn't have to go. But he understood. She was a police officer, and in police work one's time wasn't one's own. He re-read her note again, and it filled his heart with joy to know that she missed him also and that she loved him. He thought of rushing out to the Airport, hoping to catch her, but he didn't think he could get there in time in the rush hour traffic, and he didn't want to chance missing her call, in case she could call. He took off his coat and looked around for something to eat, but the refrigerator was empty. He didn't feel like going out. He called the Chinese take out place and repeated his address twice. He then poured a generous portion of Jack Daniels and looked at his watch thinking about how long it would take for his food to get there, and if Gabi would call before she got on the plane.

Gabi's laundry bag was on the washer. It was a medium sized, white linen bag with a drawstring, and as he opened it, he noticed three large, faded letters 'PEA' on the bag. The letters were obviously not her initials and Ben was trying to figure out what they might have meant. He figured they might be some police issue symbols, or the mark of the bag's manufacturer, and gave up guessing about the letters and emptied the bag's contents into the machine. Goldie never let him do the wash, and now here was this young woman asking him to do her laundry. It was mostly frilly underwear, and Ben thought of how much fun it was to be in bed with Gabi, and how incredible it was to have sex with her. He couldn't remember when he enjoyed sex as much before, and recalled his buddies talking about having sex with women, other than their wives, as they put it: "Sin was more fun than marital bliss." The phone rang and he jumped to get it, but it was the Chinese take-out place, telling him they lost his address. He was disappointed it wasn't Gabi, and pissed beyond description at the stupidity of these people who couldn't ever get his address right. He gave his address, slowly and deliberately, and when the man at the other end said he had it, Ben made him read it back and told him if the food wasn't there in fifteen minutes, or if it arrived cold, he was going to come down and close the place down for sanitary violations. He was still on the phone, when there was a knock on his door. It was the Chinese delivery man with his food, with the right address tagged to one of the bags. He ate his food, an Egg Roll, Young Chow Rice and Orange Beef that was his favorite. He always ordered the same and very seldom experimented with other foods. Whenever he did, he usually didn't like what he experimented with. The washer was on the last spin, shaking the floor a little in the kitchen, and when it stopped, Ben transferred the clothes to the dryer and set the knob to "high" heat and "extra dry." He thought he would read a little and reached for The Book, but after a few minutes he realized how tired he was, and he couldn't concentrate. He finished his Jack Daniels, and went to bed.

§

Book Two

Chapter 9

Pápa

His eyes were closed, but he wasn't asleep. He would have liked to sleep as he was very tired, but his mind was full of growing, disturbing thoughts and the last three nights he could only fall asleep now and then, and only for very short periods of time. Time and again he would get out of bed, walk around in his apartment hoping to figure out, or at least come to turns with, some of the things that were bothering him. But he couldn't. Now, that the drone of the plane's engines were slowly numbing his brain, pushing him deeper and deeper in the direction of sleep, he was hoping he would fall asleep but then something would pop up in his mind and he would wake with a start. One thing he was pleased about; he was finally on his way to Hungary and he was looking forward to catching up with Gabi. Outside the plane, as much as the small window allowed him to see, the last vestiges of daylight were quickly giving way to a rich, deep blue sky, the edge of which was already pitch black. Time was passing fast flying east. He pulled his shade down and closed his eyes again but it wasn't long before his eyes opened, and he was staring at the ceiling again. He rubbed his eyes, pulled his seat-back straight up and pulled the crumpled manila envelope from his large shoulder-bag next to his feet. He pulled the table from the armrest, and turned the overhead light on. Fortunately there was no one sitting next to him he would be disturbing, or one who might ask stupid questions about what he was reading, or just trying to make small talk. He pulled a yellow pad and a chewed up pencil from the envelope and put the pencil in his mouth. As he flipped the pages, he made a mark or a note here and there on a page, and mark cross references to other notes on other pages on the pad. He leafed through the wrinkled up pages of The Book and tried to find other references, which he then also marked down in his pad. It was obvious that some of the things that didn't add up, or he could find no reasonable explanation for, disturbed him. Now and then as he read, his face would show puzzlement, anger, surprise, fear, and concern. The margins were now full of notes; text was underlined with asterisks next to them, with the appropriate references in his note book. At times he shook his head, as some of the things had no satisfactory explanations. What bothered him was, that the deeper he got into The Rat case and the more he learned, the more questions he had, and even now as he was trying to add two and two together, his questions multiplied, but he still had no answers. Yet, the case appeared to be almost too simple. It was too logical. Everything fitted neatly and reasonably in place, but in the end, the big questions: "Who The Rat was?" "Where he was?" "When and where and how he would strike next," still remained a mystery. He had no doubt, sooner or later he would get answers to his questions, as he had with all his other cases in the past, but, at this point, more and more doubts kept building in his mind, and they bothered him. He didn't doubt that there would be reasonable explanations for his doubts at one point, but until those explanations surfaced, he was very disturbed by some of them.

He looked at his list of questions and smiled as he once again noticed the heading on the page he wrote when he started to organize the beginning of his investigation. The heading at the top of the page simply said, "Ask," and there was a blacked out rectangle, blocking out Gabi, and the heading continued: "Captain Kerek." He remembered blocking out "Gabi," thinking the heading might be noticed at a meeting and he figured it would be better if the heading was more professional than personal. He looked at the list and the pleasant smile on his face was slowly replaced by a frown. This was the page that gave him the most concern, the one that disturbed him the most, though he still couldn't put his finger on why. Some of his questions were already answered and were already crossed off, and some had a note of explanation next to them. For instance, Gabi explained to him how she knew that The Rat's note covered Sergeant Köröndi's face when none of the reports, descriptions, or summations made mention of this possibly significant factor, other than stating that the note was found with Köröndi's corpse in the boxcar. He asked Gabi about this though he didn't know why this possibly significant, or insignificant, detail kept popping to the surface in his mind. Gabi's explanation was simple and to the point. The note covering Sergeant Köröndi's face was mentioned many times in connection with analysis and discussion of the case, but where it was found, was never assigned any special significance and didn't get into the final reports. For some reason Ben thought this little detail was, in fact, very significant, and although he crossed out the question after Gabi explained it, he maintained the question on another sheet on his pad, under the heading of "'Barf?!?!?!.'

He put the note pad on the little table in front of him and leaned his head back against the headrest. What bothered him was that there were too many other questions he thought only Gabi could answer. One of these he considered very significant 'barf,' had to do with the second note found at the Molnár house. Gabi told him about the second note, in fact gave him details of the note's contents on the plane to Los Angeles, but the summation issued by the Hollywood Homicide Division of the LAPD clearly indicated that the note, which must have fallen when Mr. Molnár fell to the floor from his armchair, somehow drifted under the bed and was not found until some time after the first note was found. But Gabi's explanation was immediate and direct, pointing out that the LAPD contacted the Hungarian Consulate about the notes, and that it was Attaché Rózsa who translated the notes first, and gave Gabi the information about the note and its content. But as logical and reasonable as this explanation was, the same as Gabi's explanation of the Köröndi note, it didn't clear his mind, and for some reason, it still puzzled him. It was 'barf' in his barf-box, ready to be sorted out, put in sequence on his 'barf-board,' and assembled as part of the overall puzzle. There were many, seemingly small and insignificant little details, questions surfacing in his mind, more and more in fact every day and every time he re-read The Book, but whenever he discussed these concerns with Gabi, her explanations quickly and logically cleared up matters. Yet, that gnawing feeling he had had so many times during an investigation, the questions that were explained but didn't go away, bothered him.

But the biggest, the most puzzling thing that weighed heavily on his mind, one that he considered most significant, one that he could not clear from his mind in spite of Gabi's very logical explanation, was how to handle the seventeen-thousand dollars he accidentally stumbled upon in Gabi's suitcase.

He clearly recalled coming home from his new office the day after Gabi left, and noticing the small red pilot light on the clothes dryer, indicating that the cycle was over and the dryer turned itself off. He suddenly remembered doing Gabi's laundry the night before but forgetting to take the laundry out of the dryer before going to bed. He smiled as he remembered trying to figure out how to fold the delicate, frilly, lady's underwear and how it reminded him of Gabi, his love for her and the wonderful couple of days they spent together. When he finished folding the laundry, he remembered Gabi's note asking him to put the underwear into the top pocket of her suitcase, but when he tried to put the laundry into the small pocket, it wrinkled the delicate garments and he decided to put them into the main compartment of the suitcase. The zipper was not locked and there was a winter parka with a fur trimmed hood in the suitcase. As he was arranging the underwear on top of the parka, he noticed—at first he wasn't sure—what looked like bundles of money under the parka. Although he thought it was none of his business, and he didn't think it was right, his curiosity got the better of him and he looked under the parka. He couldn't believe his eyes seeing neatly bundled fifty and hundred dollar bills. He emptied the suitcase and counted seventeen thousand dollars, almost all in new bills. He recalled Gabi paying the bill at Myakos in Los Angeles with large bills, and leaving a ten and a twenty-dollar bill on the table in the lounge at the hotel, and her explanation about operating with a cash allowance, rather then charging expenses and putting in for it later. At the time, this made sense, but carrying seventeen thousand dollars around in cash, in an unlocked suitcase, was a bit hard to comprehend. He called Lieutenant Hill in Los Angeles on a hunch, but when he asked Hill about the detail of the second burglary of the Molnár house, Hill confirmed again that the house was completely trashed, almost everything in the house was destroyed, but told Ben again that according to Beni Molnár, nothing of value was taken from the house. When Ben kept digging, he thought it was interesting and important, that Hill mentioned a small safe that was found empty, hidden behind a false bookcase. The safe, Hill explained, was not mentioned in the first report, because it wasn't found right away, and when it was found, it turned out to be empty.

Ben didn't know at first how to ask Gabi about the money, or even if he should tell her that he had found it, or tell her that he had counted it. Instead, when Gabi called the day after she left, Ben told her, he did her laundry and put it into the main compartment of her suitcase. It was a tremendous surprise and relief for Ben, though he still didn't know why, when without him asking, Gabi brought up the subject of the money in her suitcase. She explained that it was the remainder of her twenty-one-thousand dollar yearly allotment and simply asked Ben if he could deposit the money in a bank account for her. When Ben explained that according to American banking law, depositing amounts above five thousand dollars in cash called for a procedure that required the owner of the money to declare it's origin in writing, Gabi didn't think this would be a problem when she came to America next, and suggested Ben put the money in a safe deposit box in his own name until then. The following morning Ben signed a contract for a safe deposit box at his bank, and placed ten thousand dollars in the box. A day later he deposited the rest of the money, only to go back to the bank later on in the afternoon, and take out the second deposit, seven thousand dollars, which Gabi asked him to bring to her in Hungary the following day. Almost unconsciously he opened the zipper on his oversized shoulder bag next to his leg and even in the dim light of the cabin he saw the bundles of hundred dollar bills under his paperwork. He never traveled with this much money, in fact he never had an occasion to have this much money in cash. He thought it was strange how people operated in other parts of the world. But things were the way they were. He carefully put The Book back into the manila envelope, which was now covered with scribbled notes, took the chewed up pencil from his mouth and put it with his note pad in his shoulder bag.

The stewardess came over and asked him if he wanted anything, but he just shook his head and leaned the back rest of the comfortable, large, black leather chair in the first class compartment of the MALEV-Delta plane way back, and looked at his watch. He was going to be in Budapest in three and a half hours. He closed his eyes. The one question he still wanted an answer for from Gabi was the meaning of the three large letters: 'PEA' on her laundry bag.

*   *   *

He envied people who could sleep on a plane and arrive at their destination as fresh as if they had just gotten out of bed after a restful night's sleep. He felt wrinkled; his hair messed up, his eyelids burning, and his mouth tasting like he hadn't brushed his teeth in a week. In spite of all that, he thought the flight was a good experience. He was surprised and pleased when at the check-in counter the night before he was told that he was upgraded to "First Class," and his ticket was stamped "VIP." He didn't know why, but didn't ask any questions. This was the first time in his life he flew first class, and he loved it the moment he stepped into the cabin. There were only about eight large seats in the first class compartment, soft leather chairs with armrests and plenty of leg room between seats. The stewardess was an attractive young woman who helped him settle in, offered him drinks as soon as he was seated and told him not to hesitate to ask if he needed anything. Soft and mellow Gypsy music emanated from the speakers and dinner was served almost as soon as the plane took off and reached its cruising altitude. The food was good, and he could have had all the free booze, but he had only a glass of champagne, because it reminded him of Gabi.

    The airport, as much as he could see of it, looked pretty much like all other airports he had seen, except that there were some armed guards, soldiers with rifles surrounding the plane as it taxied to the terminal building. The stewardess brought him his coat and wished him a nice stay in Hungary. He was wondering how long it was going to take him to go through customs and if the telex he received from the Hungarian Security Agency would explain and permit him to hold onto his service revolver. Above all, he was looking forward to seeing Gabi, and even though he had seen her only four days ago, he was wondering how she was going to look, and if she was going to be happy to see him. But as hard as he searched the crowd when he came into the baggage area, she was not there. She would probably be waiting for him when he went through customs he thought, and went looking for his luggage. He didn't notice the two men who followed him, until one of them tapped him on the shoulder and bowed to him as he turned around. The man held out a hand and introduced himself in acceptable, but very heavily accented English as Inspector Hegedüs, and introduced the other civilian, a very young looking man, as Cadet Officer Mohácsi. Inspector Hegedüs explained that Captain Kerek asked to be excused, she had to go out of town for a couple of days and asked Inspector Hegedüs to take Ben to his hotel. Captain Kerek would contact him there. Ben was very disappointed. Hegedüs asked him for his passport and handed it to the younger officer who hurried away with it. Hegedüs asked the usual questions; if the trip and the accommodations were all right, and if Captain Chapman needed or wanted anything. Soon the suitcases were arriving, Ben lifted his off the carousel, but the younger officer took it from him, and handed Hegedüs Ben's passport with some papers in between the pages. Hegedüs led the way through the exit door and explained that the customs formalities had been taken care of and they would be going directly to Ben's hotel. The ride to the hotel in the small police car was not very comfortable, but the young officer drove well and in a short time they were riding along the Danube. Ben asked about the immense building across the river, and Hegedüs explained that it was, at onetime, the Royal Palace, now a museum. He also pointed out the beautiful bridges that spanned the river were all blown up by the German Army during the war and rebuilt since, exactly as they had been before the war. The hotel was right along the river and the doorman eagerly jumped to open the door, just as the other doorman had at the Sheraton in Hollywood when the un-marked LAPD car pulled up to its entrance. Hegedüs stepped out and the young officer handed the doorman Ben's suitcase. The doorman waved imperiously at one of the bellhops who came running with a small cart. Hegedüs explained again that Captain Kerek would be in touch and he hoped Captain Chapman would be comfortable, and that Captain Chapman was to sign for everything in the hotel and that all his hotel expenses were to be taken care of by The Hungarian Security Agency. He then ushered Ben into the spacious and beautiful hotel lobby, handed some of the papers to the desk clerk, who immediately handed Ben a key and his card, and told Ben to contact him at any time if he needed anything.

    Ben was amazed at how small the world was. Just a little over a week ago the same scene—more or less—played out in Los Angeles, and now, almost seven thousand miles from the lobby of the Universal Sheraton in Hollywood, the same scene was being repeated in the lobby of the Forum hotel in Budapest. Ben felt very tired and followed the bellhop to the elevators. His room was on the fifth floor and the bellhop ushered him out of the elevator with hand gestures and much bowing, and opened the door to Ben's room. Ben couldn't believe his eyes. Instead of a standard hotel room, he was in a two room suite with the bedroom off to one side. The window looked out over the river onto the ornate Chain Bridge and the Vár, the old Royal Palace, across the river. He tipped the Bellhop a dollar and was surprised to see how pleased the bellhop was to get an American dollar. The first thing he noticed, as he was approaching his bedroom was a small bottle of Champagne with a long stem red rose attached on the little table in front of the window. But what really stopped him in his track was the unmade bed, with Gabi in it.

"What . . . are . . . you doing here?" He stuttered, but before he could say anything else, she pressed her forefinger to her lips and smiled at Ben. "Pssst," she whispered, "first things first." And she motioned to him to get into bed.

*   *   *

Vásárhelyi Ferenc stared at the yellow sheet of paper he took out of the envelope that came in his mail this morning. He must have read and re-read the note a hundred times, and every time he did, he got more and more frightened. By this time he knew about The Rat, most of The Rat murders were written up in the newspapers, and occasionally the Budapest, or the Vienna television stations would show a piece about The Rat's latest victims. He knew for some time that his name was on the list. He knew that the other four members of The Ring were also on The Rat's list, all of them marked for death. One of the Hungarian papers picked up a news-release from an American news service describing the Molnár murder, and gave a vivid description of how Mr. Molnár was marked for death and executed by The Rat. The same newspaper article printed The Rat's notes, the one The Rat left at the Molnár house, and others discovered at the site of his other executions. All the notes were similar, yellow slips of paper, just like the one he was now holding in his hand. All through the years he read accounts of The Rat murders, and saw his old cohorts disappear one by one—murdered by The Rat—and he knew inwardly it was only a matter of time before his time came.

And now his time was at hand. The yellow sheet listed his crimes, things that happened so long ago, and things he used to talk about with pride with the other four members of The Ring. He remembered Hunter, his large German Shepherd dog he so meticulously trained to attack on his command, to rip chunks of flesh from the legs and arms of his defenseless, old and feeble victims, the people in the Ghetto, and some of whom were too young to know what had happened to them when the dog attacked. But those incidents were long ago, and after the war he and his friends paid a terrible price, being imprisoned for months at a time, for what the new regime called war crimes. How could this world have gone so completely wrong? It was such a wonderful world when he first volunteered for the Gendarmerie, and it was the happiest day of his life when the notification came that he was accepted just as he was graduating from high school. The

Gendarmerie was wonderful to him. Within two years he was commissioned as a Standard Bearer, the lowest commissioned rank in the Gendarmerie, but he was given a sword, a silver star in a gold field on his tunic collar, and a snappy little black bowler hat with a rooster tail stuck in the band on the left hand side. Four years later he was promoted to Captain and became Legion Commander with one of the largest territories in the Gendarmerie, covering the entire expanse of the Lowlands with all the cities, villages, and settlements within it. It was a large area to patrol, but after a while he was able to get bicycles for his men, the ones who had the greatest distances to cover, which until this time they patrolled on foot. He was proud of his men. He demanded a lot from them, but they were a proud bunch who didn't let him down. He encouraged them to act on their own, praised and rewarded them when they did their jobs the way he wanted it done, and promoted the ones who went out of their way to please him. Private Köröndi was one of his favorites. Köröndi enforced Captain Vásárhelyi's edicts to the letter, even if it meant beating the crap out of half of the young men during a visit to a village. Captain Vásárhelyi advanced him rapidly in the ranks. By the time he put Köröndi in charge of the Pápa Ghetto, Köröndi was a Staff Sergeant, and just as Vásárhelyi, a Lieutenant Colonel by this time, expected it, he ran the Ghetto with an iron hand. Vásárhelyi gave Sergeant Köröndi complete authority and never interfered with the running of the Ghetto, even when he went to the Ghetto headquarters and watched Sergeant Köröndi interrogate people. He encouraged Köröndi's extorting money and valuables from the people he brought in for interrogation. He knew the more Köröndi got away with, the more emboldened he became, and the more he got out of his next subjects. And the more Köröndi got, the bigger his share became. On the few occasions when he inspected the Ghetto at Pápa, he usually made a short speech to Köröndi 's detachment, and told them how pleased he was with the way they did their duty, and how proud the country was of them for doing such an outstanding job. He let the detachment watch as he released Hunter, and laughed with them as his dog attacked people who couldn't run away.

Vásárhelyi smiled, as he thought about the good days; but the élan, the swagger, was not in his steps as he stood to go inside his house. He knew that Köröndi, his favorite henchman was gone, and he knew how Köröndi had died at the hand of a killer who called himself The Rat. He wondered how he was going to die.

* * *

Lt. Colonel Vida Zoltán, was a career police officer, one of three sons of a prosperous farmer, but unlike Colonel Vásárhelyi of the nationwide Gendarmerie, his jurisdiction was the City of Pápa only. His small police force of 22 uniformed officers, three plainclothes detectives, and clerical staff were headquartered in an attractive, new building in the North District of the City, and he loved the way the walls of his building sparkled on sunny mornings, as he walked up the steps into the building. The walls sparkled because when the building was built, he agreed to have the outside walls finished with yellow colored stucco that had ground up glass mixed into it, which, on sunny days made the walls sparkle. Colonel Vida was not a complicated man. His only interest was to rise in the ranks and the hierarchy of the police, and in the political scene of the City of Pápa. He was careful not to go too far in any direction of an issue as he rose in the ranks, and joined the higher levels of the town's society. Some claimed he was a fence sitter, and even accused him of being on both sides of the fence at the same time when it came to some issues, but he somehow managed to end up on the right side, the side that survived the political infighting. He swam with the tide, with the popular and winning side, not out of conviction, but because of personal convenience and advantage. Though he remained the titular head of the Pápa Police under the Nyilas Keresztes rule of Hungary, he didn't object, or in any way try to oppose Dr. Horváth Gyula, and Lodz Imre from taking over the day-to-day running of the police. Dr. Horváth was a good friend. He was a teacher in the Reformed Church School for Girls, and a good friend of Dr. Molnár István, the English teacher at the boy's school of the Reformed Church, who became District Leader of the National Nazi Party. With his help, Dr. Horváth became the Political head of the Pápa Police with far reaching powers, but as long as Colonel Vida could keep his office, his uniform and sword, he did not oppose Dr. Horváth, nor his henchman Lodz Imre. In fact, as the Hungarian Nazi Regime took control of the country, he willingly became the titular head of all police activity and did the dirty work for Horváth and Lodz with zeal and without hesitation. He became part of The Ring, one of five murderers who operated from his building, used the building for their personal agenda of torture and executions whenever the mood struck them. They appointed Lt. Colonel Vida to oversee the enforcement of listing the Jewish population of Pápa, the confiscation of all personal property, the eviction of Jews from their homes and herding them into the Ghetto under the control of Colonel Vásárhelyi and Sergeant Köröndi. As a reward, Lt. Colonel Vida was given the old Landau house on Eszterházy Street, a beautiful large home with a turreted tower on nicely landscaped grounds with outbuildings, stables and a carriage house in the back of the property.

Lt. Colonel Vida was sentenced to two years at hard labor for his crimes as the head of the Pápa police under the Nazi Regime, and secretly he was bitter about the others, Dr. Horváth and Lodz Imre for instance, who served less than a year in prison for the things they did that were attributed to him. But the five members of The Ring swore to uphold The Ring till death and hold together no matter what. They did. Through the hard times after the new regime arrested them, during the trials and in prison, they never testified against one another and held to their oath of eternal solidarity and secrecy. And now that the end was near, he wondered if it was all worth it. He held The Rat's note in his hand, and he knew he was going to die. In a way he was relieved. The last decade of his life was nothing but misery, living in the hovel of a dirty little room in the back and below Dr. Horváth's house on Jókai Street, subsisting on what little food his distant relatives provided him with, wearing their old hand-me-down clothes, and trying to stay warm by burning other people's trash in his broken down little wood stove during the cold winter months. But he was grateful to Dr. Horváth for letting him live in the dingy little subterranean dungeon, for his family's landholdings had been confiscated and he would have had no other place to live.

He straightened his frayed jacket and decided to go to see Gyula. As grateful as he was, he was envious of Dr. Horváth who lived in his old house, apparently wanting for nothing, and he was wondering how Dr. Horváth was able to maintain a lifestyle, more or less like in the old days and where the money came from that allowed him the luxuries of a big house, a housekeeper, new clothes, and all the foods and wine he wanted.

Gyula was on the telephone as he entered the main section of the house. He seemed calm, in fact almost smiling into the phone. But Vida had seen that smile many times before when Dr. Horváth was charming or conning someone. As he listened to Horváth's end of the conversation, it became obvious that Dr. Horváth was talking with Rátz Joseph. "Yes, Jóska," Vida heard Dr. Horváth laugh into the phone, "I got your notice by mistake." He gave another forced laugh and continued, "You and all of us are sentenced to death." He laughed again as if this whole thing was nothing more than a stupid joke, something that wasn't supposed to be taken too much to heart, but at the same time should not be dismissed. "What did my note say?" he asked Rátz. Vida watched Dr. Horváth's face turn red and angry, even frightened, as he listened, but his voice did not betray him. "Not to worry, my friend," he said reassuringly, "The Rat will not get us! We will get him! Come to the vineyard this evening. I will call the others, and all of us will stay there together until The Rat shows up, and when he does, we'll get him." He listened for a while and asked, "Do you still have your garrote?" He listened. "It's all right, make one quickly, it doesn't have to be as nice as your old one, and be sure to bring it with you." He hung up the phone.

"There is a traitor in The Ring, Zoltán," Dr. Horváth turned to Vida.

Vida was wondering what this was about? Who was the traitor in The Ring? He knew it wasn't him, it couldn't have been Dr. Horváth, and he didn't think it could have been Lodz Imre. That left only Colonel Vásárhelyi, or Rátz Jóska, and if he had any money, he would have bet it was Rátz József. He never liked Rátz whom he considered a drifter, an unreliable, irresponsible opportunist, and a lowlife; a man without any education or background. But he understood Dr. Horváth's and Lodz Imre's infatuation with Rátz, who was a willing henchman who didn't pull back from doing any of the others' dirty work. He was known as the "garrotter." He frequently showed off his fancy, home-made garrote with the thin, but super strong silken parachute cord, and the wooden hand holds he carefully carved out of maple wood, with notches for each person he strangled to death. Whenever anyone showed interest, he would demonstrate his technique and explain the function of the handles that would lock the cord around his victim's neck and he would proudly describe how he would at times release the pressure for a few moments for the victim to regain some breath, and tighten the rope again until the victim was slowly strangled to death.

Colonel Vida felt Dr. Horváth's eyes focus on him. "I see you got your notice also." He pointed at the yellow slip of paper in Vida's hands. "I also got mine." He picked up and waved another yellow sheet of paper. "But it's not going to happen, Zoltán," he thundered reassuringly at Colonel Vida, who felt a moment of relief and hope for the first time since he opened his envelope a little while ago and read his death sentence from The Rat. Dr. Horváth was always the leader of the group, a hard willed and strong person who never caved in, never hesitated, and now as he looked at him and told him that the death sentence was not going to happen,

Colonel Vida felt relieved.

"No. Zoli," Dr. Horváth continued, "The Rat has done in some of our friends, but he is not going to get the better of us. The Ring will stand united against him and we will get him, before he can get us!" He slammed his fist on the table for emphasis.

Colonel Vida looked at Dr. Horváth silently and didn't want to interrupt him as he continued, "We will all unite and stay in my house at the vineyard on Kishegy. It's a small place, and all of us will sleep in the same room. One of us will always be on guard, and when The Rat comes, the four of us will overpower him and kill him." He looked at Vida with piercing eyes. "I say four of us Zoltán, because one of us will be dead by the morning. One of us is a traitor and I know who he is, and he will die." Colonel Vida didn't know what to say but Dr. Horváth handed him his yellow slip from The Rat. "What do you make of this, Zoltán?" he asked.

Colonel Vida took the slip and looked at it. He couldn't understand the heading at first, but the meaning of the note became clear as he read it:

> *To Rátz József,*
>
> *It is my sad duty to inform you that your death sentence is hereby lifted. I would have liked to execute you, as I have executed twenty other murderers who were named in The Book, and whose executions I accept responsibility for. Their crimes, as your horrendous crimes, would have dictated the death sentence in any court of the world, but not in Hungary, a morally bankrupt, sad little country that never lived up to its responsibility of protecting its innocent, or punishing its guilty. You and your partners in crime should have been dealt a just punishment long ago, but instead you were let off with ridiculous, token sentences, no more than a slap on the wrist that allowed you to live. Though it is not in my power to absolve you, I now must lift your sentence of execution, in hopes the Almighty God will take care of your just punishment. I, The Rat, executioner of the guilty, hereby lift your death sentence in exchange for your cooperation and help, in identifying and locating Dr. Horváth Gyula, Colonel Vásárhelyi Ferenc, Lodz Imre, and Lt. Colonel Vida Zoltán. Their death sentences will be carried out, one by one at my convenience and at a place of my choosing.*
>
> *Regretfully,*
> *The Rat.*

Colonel Vida couldn't believe his eyes. There was no mistake about it; Rátz, that no account little worm, sold them out to save his miserable soul. He shook his head and handed the note back to Dr. Horváth. "What now?" the look in his eyes asked Dr. Horváth.

"First," Dr. Horváth thought out loud, "we have to find out if Feri also got a note from The Rat." He turned to Vida. "Why don't you take my bicycle and go over to Tapolcafő and find out if Feri got his notice; I'd be surprised if he didn't," he said almost as if to himself. "Tell him to get over to my vineyard as soon as he can. Don't tell him about Rátz but insist that he go immediately, ready to stay for a long time, and to bring food and whatever weapons he can get his hands on, even if they are no more than kitchen knives or hatchets." He nodded his head towards Vida to go.

"But how are we going to get Rátz?" Vida asked, his voice reflecting fear and uncertainty.

"I asked the little bastard to meet us at my house on Kishegy tonight," Dr. Horváth replied, and as Vida looked like he didn't understand, Horváth explained. "He doesn't know that The Rat is going to let him off." Horváth picked up the yellow sheet of paper. "This notice wasn't supposed to come to me. As I figure it, The Rat made a mistake. He sent Rátz's note to me, and I know Rátz got my note instead. He called me this morning as soon as he found my note in his mail. As I figure, he believes his note that came to me, was a similar death sentence to mine. He doesn't know that The Rat promised to let him off. I know this is true because that's what he told me and because he called Lodz Imre and told him the same thing." He paused for a second. "As you must have heard, I told him I got his death sentence by mistake, and told him to meet us at the Vineyard."

* * *

The little black Lada purred along steadily on the Vienna — Budapest Expressway. It was the smallest car Ben ever rode in, yet it was surprisingly comfortable with two bucket seats up front, and a small fold-down seat in the back. His suitcase was in the back alongside Gabi's, who expertly maneuvered the little car around big eighteen-wheelers, most of which, to Ben's amazement had large signs in English declaring them 'Long Loads.'

"Why are these signs in English?" he asked Gabi.

"Didn't you hear?" Gabi smiled. "Hungary is joining the United States of America. You'll have to put an extra star on your flag."

"You mean. . ." Ben tried to make a funny, "I'll be a captain in the Hungarian Security Agency?"

"Not quite," Gabi threw a sideways glance at Ben, "but I might try for the NYPD."

Ben smiled and they rode along without speaking for a long stretch. "How far is Pápa from here?" Ben asked.

"Oh, another 100 or so kilometers, but in about half an hour we'll be getting off this road at Györ, and taking the country roads from there."

Ben nodded. He was still a little jet-lagged and the last three nights were not exactly restful. He had to admit though that the days were interesting. His briefing in the large, new building of the Hungarian Security Agency on Üllői Út was an interesting insight into how a police organization in an other part of the world functioned. But it was also obvious to him that just like in New York, a lot of the time was taken up with politicing, and police work almost appeared secondary. He met a lot of people, all of whom seemed to be concerned with his comfort, all of whom offered help, but the bottom line was, with all the day long meetings, he was no closer to The Rat than he was when he got on the plane in New York. He compared the personal and physical profiling with those made by the Hungarian Security Agency, the Polish National Police, and the Austrian and German counterparts. All were interesting fantasies, and he thought with a smile they would have made interesting chapters in a book, a police thriller, and he had to admit, some of them even had interesting and thought provoking suppositions. But in the end not one of them offered him anything he didn't already know, or guess.

The Rat was still out there, his intended victims clearly identified and waiting to be massacred. But he enjoyed Budapest. It was an interesting and beautiful city, in spite of the marks left behind and still visible after all these years by World War II and the 1956 uprising. He felt Gabi was uncomfortable talking about Hungary's role in the war and Ben sensed that she definitely did not want to talk about 1956, or anything political. Ben's second sense told him most of Gabi's colleagues knew, or at least suspected, the relationship between him and Gabi, and was convinced Gabi knew also, but didn't care. Their time after hours was almost like being on a honeymoon. They ate in the best restaurants in and around Budapest, listened to Gypsy music, and visited some of the interesting sites in the city, some of which went back to the Turks, and to the Romans. Gabi showed Ben the Royal Hungarian jewels, the crown, the scepter, and the orb, and told him that they were kept safe in the USA after the war.

Now, as the little car was rolling up the miles, it suddenly occurred to Ben that he didn't know what he was doing in Hungary; why exactly was he going to Pápa, and what was his role in this mess. Back in New York six young police officers were digging into the emigration records, going back to 1946, hoping to come up with someone who was Jewish, or possibly Christian, an ex-concentration camp inmate or a descendant of one, one with origins in or near Pápa or as a worse case scenario, from elsewhere in Hungary, or Austria, or Germany, or Poland, Czechoslovakia, Rumania, Yugoslavia and so on, now living in New York City or New York State, or somewhere in the United States of America. Failing all that, other countries of the Western Hemisphere would have to be considered, reaching out from there into South America, Australia and beyond; and from Ben's perspective the whole investigation boiled down to being ridiculous. He didn't believe The Rat was living in the US, and what puzzled him even more was the impotence the Hungarian Police exhibited in their investigation that had been going on over ten years with nothing but corpses to show for it. He recalled the sniveling complaint of the Superintendent of The Hungarian Security Agency, who just two days ago cornered him after the first briefing, whining and complaining about The Rat, whom he described as the worse nightmare of the Agency. The Rat, he told Ben knew everything the Agency knew, would consistently and successfully second guess the Agency's plans and actions, and had stayed at least one step ahead of the Agency for more than ten years.

But what was crystal clear in Ben's mind was that if The Rat was going ahead with his plans—and he had no reason to believe he was not—to kill the five remaining people on his list, he would now have to be in Hungary regardless where he was living. And since all five of his intended victims lived in, or near, Pápa it was logical to assume that The Rat was already in Pápa, or if not, he would be in Pápa before long.

He noticed more and more, young women along the road at the off ramps, and at exits into rest areas; blond wigs, painted faces, miniscule miniskirts, smiling and waving at the trucks, plying their trade just like in New York at College Point, and at the approaches to the Holland Tunnel. He was about to comment, but Gabi pointed to one of the off ramps and the big green sign over it with a curved arrow and the word: Pápa. "We'll be getting off here," Gabi said, "and will be in

Pápa in less than an hour." Ben looked at the countryside. It was very pretty. Lush green fields, trees and flowers everywhere, but the road narrowed to two lanes as they left the expressway. "I hope there won't be much traffic," Gabi commented. But Ben didn't see any traffic and didn't understand. Gabi explained, "Sometimes a hay wagon pulled by a couple of oxen takes up most of the road and it's almost impossible to pass, or a flock of sheep and the shepherd will do everything not to let you pass. "You have a siren?" Ben asked. "No," she smiled at him, "we're not allowed to have sirens, or radios, or beacons in private cars, but" she added, "if we come in a police car from the Agency, Pápa will close up tighter then a drum."

Ben marveled at Gabi's proficiency in the English language. He didn't think "tighter than a drum" was an expression one learned in English class in a Hungarian high-school, but he let it go. As the little car was winding through the villages, old women and children waved to them. They passed some horse drawn wagons, and small, long haired black dogs chased the car.

In the distance two tall spires of a church came into view. "That's Pápa," Gabi pointed ahead. "In a few minutes you'll be where the path to The Rat's door starts." Ben felt a little jolt again. The same feeling he had every time Gabi said something that somehow set him off, something that rang a bell, something that was unexpected, or something he didn't understand. He recalled thinking about a path starting in Pápa that would lead to The Rat, but he didn't think, at least at this point couldn't remember, mentioning it to Gabi. Maybe, it occurred to him, he might have been talking in his sleep, and said something about the path starting in Pápa. "What makes you think the path to The Rat starts in Pápa?" he asked her.

"I always thought it did," she answered immediately, keeping her eyes on the road, "and I thought you thought so also." Ben didn't comment. "Would you mind," she continued, "if I swing by a couple of the places you should see on the way to the hotel?"

Ben shook his head, "No. That would be fine."

In a short time the car was passing the old Calvary Cemetery with the roadside stations of the cross, and life size Roman soldiers mistreating Jesus under the weight of the cross. "This is Eszterházy Street," Gabi pointed to the right and turned the car into a wide, tree lined street of once beautiful private homes, some of which showed signs of neglect and disrepair. She slowed down and pointed at a house with a tower at one corner, "This is the old Landau house. Colonel Vida Zoltán lived here after he evicted the Landaus and expropriated the house."

"Where is he living now?" Ben asked.

"We believe," Ben thought it was interesting that she always used "we" when she referred to the Security Agency, "that he still lives somewhere in Pápa, or around Pápa, but it's not clear where."

"Could you tap his telephone?"

"This is Hungary, Ben," Gabi smiled at him, "the middle ages. He has no telephone."

Ben didn't comment, "Where next?" he asked.

"We'll swing by the house where the Landaus lived in the Ghetto for a short time before they were taken away."

Ben nodded. He looked around as the car wound through the curving, narrow, medieval streets and came to a stop in front of a small house with two storefronts and a massive, double wooden gate. "Let's go in," Gabi turned off the engine and got out of the car. As Ben got out, Gabi swept her arm to indicate the rest of the street. "This was the center of the Ghetto in 1944. The Gendarmerie's Headquarters were in that house," she pointed to a house, larger than most, at the end of the street, "and right next to the house the Ghetto was closed off with a high fence and gates. There were over three thousand Jews living in this area that normally had no more than about four hundred people." Ben looked around the quiet street, with hardly any one on it. "And this is where the entire Landau family lived," she pointed at the small house with the two storefronts. "The stores are recent." Gabi continued, "no more than a couple of years old and the people who own them live in the back of the house."

The house was interesting looking, Ben thought. It didn't look anything like any house in the States, but it fit perfectly with the other houses on the street. Ben felt a surging of his blood in the back of his neck, as he felt so many times in his years on the force when something he came face to face with had a particular meaning, part of a puzzle of a case he was working on. "Let's go in," Gabi suggested. "I know the people. I'm sure they'll let me show you around." Ben followed her into the little convenience store. Gabi greeted the young woman behind the small counter, who seemed to be happy to see Gabi, yet at the same time Ben sensed that Gabi's sudden presence, and introducing someone from America, made the woman behind the counter, tense. There was quite a bit of conversation in Hungarian, a strange sounding language, as the young woman indicated with her arm to come around the counter and into the rest of the house behind the store.

"Twenty-six of the Landau family lived in these rooms," Gabi said in English, but I wanted you to see this house, as it is typical of most of the houses in this part of the town and will give you an idea of how the people in the Ghetto lived. "It gives a very good flavor of life in the Ghetto, even a bit of history that goes back to the fourteen hundreds and the Turkish occupation of the country." They were walking out of the house and into the large garden behind the house. There were some sheds, and a tall fence at the far end of the garden. "That's part of the original fortifications of the city," Gabi pointed at the tall fence. "If we could climb up on it, it is ten feet thick at the top. On the other side, about sixty feet down is the old moat that at one time surrounded the city." Ben was getting quite a history lesson, but he sensed there was something more behind this visit than sightseeing, and that strange, unexplainable feeling was still raising the hair on the back of his neck. Something was missing. As they were walking quietly towards the front of the house he reached for Gabi's arm and stopped her. "How does this place fit into the big picture?" He looked intently at Gabi. Gabi's answer came like a bolt out of the blue: "This is where The Book was found." Her voice was without emphasis, matter of fact, but it froze Ben's feet to the ground. He couldn't move for a second. His eyes were riveted on Gabi, wanting to hear more. But Gabi was silent. "I thought," Ben started with hesitation, "you told me, you didn't know where The Book came from." Again, her answer was immediate and positive.

"We didn't know at first. It came to the Agency by mail. The only thing we knew was that it came from Pápa, it was postmarked in Pápa, but we didn't know who wrote The Book, or who sent it, and why."

"Who found it?" Ben asked, though he knew as soon as he asked, that there would be no meaningful answer to his question.

Gabi looked towards the front of the house. It was found when the house was renovated, when the local authorities were cleaning up after the war, and homes were desperately needed. "We questioned the workmen, the local police, the people who were to move into the house, and everyone else we could think of, but nobody knew or owned up to anything."

"Are any of the Landau family alive?"

"We believe several older people, and one young man came back. He went to live in Budapest, and worked for one of the motion picture studios. But the old folks passed away shortly after they came back."

"What happened to the young fellow who worked at the movie studios in Budapest?"

"We don't know. He, like so many others after the war, just disappeared. Evaporated, left the country illegally, and wherever they ended up, they would take on new names." She paused for a bit. "We believe that the young Landau ended up in New York."

The circuits were clicking in Ben's mind. "Barf" was coming up and as so many times in the past, "barf" was trying to click into place; one puzzle piece trying to mate with another. The house disappeared around him, and time seemed to stand still. It was only the puzzle pieces that were before his mental vision, and he felt he was standing on the doorstep, the beginning of the path, leading him to the identity of The Rat.

*   *   *

"There is one other place, I want to show you," Gabi said as they were about to get into the car, "my school. It has nothing to do with The Rat case," she explained, "but it might be interesting for you to see one of the oldest and best schools in the country."

They parked at a three story building, an imposing structure that took up the entire block. It was in bad repair, stucco was peeling here and there from the walls, and the large, red marble steps leading up into the building were crumbling. "The school was used as a military hospital during the war," Gabi explained, as they were entering the building, "and the state took it over from the church after the war, but doesn't have the money for repairs." The building seemed abandoned, there were no students anywhere, but it was after hours, as Gabi explained and pointed out the various areas in the building. "That was my favorite place," she pointed at a large doorway a few steps down, "the gymnasium." She grabbed Ben's arm and pulled him towards the doors. The walls in the large area in front of the doors were covered with photographs. Gabi pointed to one with a laugh: "This is me." Ben looked at the picture. There were three girls and one boy in standard karate uniforms. Ben recognized Gabi, as a young girl in the center of the group. "What does this mean?" he asked, pointing at the inscription below the photograph. "The winning Karate team – 1956" "I was the first student with a third degree black belt in the country," Gabi said with pride in her voice and an ear to ear smile on her face.

But 'barf' was coming up again, faster and faster since they got to Pápa. Ben didn't know what it was, but images he conjured up about The Rat murders were floating to the surface. Sentences from the reports were drifting before his eyes, and just now, as he was looking at the photograph of the young karate champs, it seemed to him that the report of the Köröndi murder indicated that Köröndi's testicles were crushed by what might have been a powerful kick to his groin. He almost didn't hear Gabi's descriptions of the various parts of the school, her class room, the library with ancient volumes, the Egyptian Mummy in the school's museum. His head was still spinning when they pulled up in front of the hotel, The Golden Griffin, just across from the big church on the main square of town.

"I have two rooms reserved," Gabi confided to Ben, "but they should be side-by-side."

Ben understood, but he was disturbed by the developments of the afternoon, which he didn't understand, or which he didn't want to come to terms with. All sorts of crazy ideas were floating around in his brain, most of which made sense, logical or intuitive, but none were pleasant. He hoped that, as in the past, they would have logical and reassuring explanations. Standing at the spot where The Book came from, finding out about Gabi being a blackbelt in karate, he told himself were all circumstantial and misleading, but his instincts found them disturbing and upsetting.

He decided to take a shower and was standing in front of the bathtub without shower curtains with only a hand held shower nozzle, when there was a knock on his door. Just as he had hoped, it was Gabi. She came into his room as he stood completely naked by the door. She had a sheet of paper in her hand. "It's in Hungarian," she said. She seemed excited, even a bit out of breath. "We had Dr. Horváth's telephone tapped—he does have a phone—and intercepted several of his conversations with two others of the 'ring'." As she spoke Ben tried to collate the information; mentally going back to The Book and trying to recall who, and what, Dr. Horváth was, and at the same time listen to Gabi excitedly explain the latest developments. "All five of them are retreating to Dr. Horváth's cottage at his vineyard tonight, apparently expecting an attack by The Rat."

He didn't know why, but Ben felt suddenly relieved. "I was about to take a shower, but haven't quite figured out how."

"Let me show you." Gabi pulled Ben into the bathroom but did not get undressed as Ben expected. She explained the function of the hand nozzle, and told Ben not to worry about water getting on the floor, which had a drain in the middle of it.

"Two of my associates are coming from Budapest, and the local police offered a constable to help us stake out the cottage." She stopped and helped Ben soap up his back. "I might have to be out for a bit," she said excitedly, "but have dinner downstairs, and I'll call you as soon as I get back." She was out of the bathroom before Ben could say anything, and Ben heard the door to his room close with a loud click.

Chapter 10

The Ring

"Why four?" Vásárhelyi asked.

"Because one of us will always be on lookout," Horváth explained. They all nodded in understanding. "There will be a sentry at all times, under the steps in the corner that is always dark. If anyone approaches the house, the sentry will tug on this string," he produced a small ball of string, one end of which divided into four branches, "that will be tied to every one of our wrists." The others showed interest and relief. Dr. Horváth was living up to his well earned reputation as a leader. "We will fix our bunks later," Horváth continued, "for now let's see what we have in way of food and weapons." The others opened their packs and in a minute the top of the table was covered with bacon, hams, sausage, canned food, and with knives, one meat-cleaver, some lead pipes and clubs, some even with nails in them. Dr. Horváth pulled a revolver from his pocket and put a box of shells next to it. "Where did you get that?" Lodz Imre asked with admiration in his voice. "I always had it," Horváth smiled, "I had it even when I was sent to prison. It was hidden in my attic. You fellows should remember it. You gave it to me in the good old days." He showed the inscription on the barrel: "To Doktor Horváth Gyula—From his faithful friends."

The others had to admit that Dr. Horváth was an able leader and a very clever man. All of them were sent to prison. Vásárhelyi served sixteen months, Lodz Imre served two years, Vida Zoltán served two years, Rátz served eighteen months, but Dr. Horváth served only four months, even though his sentence was for four years at hard labor. There was a lot of speculation he bought his way out. Nobody knew where the money came from, but everybody suspected he had to have lots of money stashed away somewhere. He lived in his old house, had all his old furniture and some he collected in the good old days. The paintings—some suspected—at one time belonged to Landau Miklós, a highly decorated wounded veteran of World War One, were still hanging in his rooms; and china, silver and crystal were all over his place. Nobody ever wanted, or had the guts, to question him about it. He took frequent trips to Italy and Switzerland, and it was suspected that some of his money was in secret accounts in Swiss banks. When he came back from one of those trips in a new Mercedes, there was some speculation about big payoffs to party functionaries who protected him, but that's as far as the speculation went, because the others of The Ring knew they needed him, and were dependent on him in many ways. He was good to all in The Ring. Vida Zoltán lived rent-free in his house on Jókai Street, though not at all like Dr. Horváth. Vida had one small room at the back end, and under the house. The walls were the rock foundation of the house that seemed to sweat, and were covered with moisture all the time and the dirt floor of the room was also wet and slippery on most days, particularly when it rained, or snow was melting outside the house. There was a small cot along one of the inside walls that was the driest, with a straw filled mattress and torn blankets. And there was a small cast iron stove in one of the corners with its pipe going through a pane of the casement window near the ceiling, just above ground level on the outside of the house.

Lodz, Vásárhelyi and Rátz, all got small amounts of money now and then from Dr. Horváth, and they knew they could go to Dr. Horváth for help any time they needed it. They envied, though secretly resented, the good life Dr. Horváth apparently enjoyed, but they couldn't afford to antagonize him and possibly lose his friendship.

Horváth picked up the revolver and slowly, with deliberate motions, loaded the chambers. "This weapon will be the last, or the first, line of defense against The Rat." He held up the gun and explained, "It will always be at that end of the room," he pointed at the far wall, "the furthest from the door. Even if The Rat surprises us, he will have at least two of us to fight him by the door, and one of the others at the far end will have the weapon to kill him." The others approved of the plan. Their faces showed the approval and the relief to know they had a powerful firearm all of them knew how to use. "Now," Horváth looked at them, "let's see what you fellows brought." Vásárhelyi picked up a good size meat-cleaver. Horváth took it. "This will be the sentry's weapon," he declared. "It's a great weapon at close range, and as The Rat will have to get by the sentry whom he will not see, one blow will part his hair right in the middle, down to his nuts." All of them laughed, as he swung the meat-cleaver in a swift, downward motion. "And you, Jóska," Horváth turned to Rátz, "did you bring your garrote?"

"I did, Gyula." Rátz pulled the short piece of rope attached to two wooden handles from his belt behind his back.

Horváth stepped to the vividly painted, baked clay head of Jesus with droplets of blood under the crown of thorns, and took it off the wall. He pointed at the nail, "The garrote will hang from this nail. If The Rat should enter this room, one of us near the door shall garrote him from behind. He handed the rope back to Rátz. "Now, Jóskam," he used the familiar, endearing way of addressing Rátz, "would you demonstrate for us how to handle this formidable weapon of yours?" He added with a laugh, "I'll be The Rat."

Rátz was pleased at being the center of attention. He stepped behind Horváth and with an incredibly fast move had the rope around Horváth's neck. "It is important," he explained to the others "that the rope is against the skin, and not on the collar. The left handle should be pulled away from the neck, and the right handle's tip, the top end, should be hooked under the rope as close to the person's neck as possible. That way," he demonstrated and Horváth felt the rope tighten against his neck, "the right handle will have a lot of leverage when one twists it by the bottom portion of the handle."

Horváth held up his arms in surrender and all of them laughed. It was great to have all of them together. The old camaraderie gave them strength and confidence, and a hope of ridding themselves of the danger—the dread of expecting death at the hands of The Rat that had haunted them for ten years now. Horváth was right. Together they would defeat The Rat, knowing that alone they could not. "All right," Horváth said as he helped Rátz remove the rope from around his neck. "Who will try first?" He pointed to Vida. "How about you, Zoli? Why don't you be The Rat; and, Feri," he pointed to Vásárhelyi, "you be the garroter."

Vida seemed to have fear showing in his eyes, but in the dim light of the kerosene lamp only Horváth noticed. He eased the situation with a joke: "Now Colonel Vásárhelyi, I hope you won't take this too seriously." He motioned to Vida to step out of the room, and placed Vásárhelyi to one side of the door inside the room. "Now, when The Rat," he pointed at Vida, "comes into the room," he faced Vásárhelyi, "I want you to step behind him, and before he has a chance to turn around, you must put the rope around his neck." He looked at the others. "One of you fellows should jump at The Rat, divert his attention from Feri, and hold his feet, or arms, and the furthest one in the room should get the revolver but don't shoot until a clear shot can be taken. Is everybody ready?" He looked around the room and motioned Vida to enter. Vida stepped into the room, hunched over, playing the role of The Rat, and as he did, Vásárhelyi stepped up behind him and twisted the rope around Vida's neck. Lodz lounged at Vida's feet, and Rátz instructed Vásárhelyi at the proper technique of tightening the rope. One by one, all of them took the garrote and tested their skill against another of The Ring. "All right now." Horváth took the rope and pointed to Rátz. "Why don't you be The Rat, Jóskam," he used the endearing name for Rátz again, "and let me get even with you." Everybody laughed, Rátz perhaps the loudest, but his laugh quickly turned into amazement, puzzlement and horror, as Horváth expertly tightened the rope, just as Rátz demonstrated it a few minutes ago. Vida was at Rátz's legs, holding them tightly together, as Lodz held Rátz's arms. Vásárhelyi had a benign smile on his face. He didn't understand and couldn't figure out the situation. He didn't know if this was some kind of joke, the members of The Ring having fun with one another, but Rátz's face was turning purple, his eyes were bugging out and the tip of his tongue was sticking out of his mouth. Finally, Horváth released his pressure and the rope eased a bit around Rátz's neck. "Now, Jóska," Horváth yelled into Rátz's ear, "Do you want to tell us why you sold out your friends? Why you agreed to help The Rat kill us, so you can save your miserable skin?" Rátz shook his head side to side, trying to talk, but all he could do was cough and gag. Horváth turned to Vásárhelyi, "Reach into my pack, Feri, there is a yellow sheet of paper, just like the one you got from The Rat, and I want you to read it to our good friend Rátz József." He gave the rope a yank. The strength was going out of Rátz's arms and legs. Vásárhelyi had the yellow sheet of paper in his hand and read it to himself at first, than, at Horváth's insistence, read it out loud:

> *To Rátz József:*
> *It is my sad duty to inform you that your death sentence is hereby lifted. I*

would have liked to execute you, as I have executed twenty other murderers who were named in The Book, and whose execution I accepted the responsibility for. Their crimes, as your horrendous crimes, would have dictated the death sentence in any court of the world, but not in Hungary, a morally bankrupt, sad little country that never lived up to its responsibility of protecting its innocent, or punishing its guilty. You and your partners in crime should have been dealt a just punishment long ago, but instead you were let off with ridiculous, token sentences, no more than a slap on the wrist that allowed you to live. Though it is not in my power to absolve you, I now must lift your sentence of execution, in hopes that the Almighty God will take care of your just punishment. I, The Rat, executioner of the guilty, hereby lift your death sentence in exchange for your cooperation and help, identifying and locating Dr. Horváth Gyula, Colonel Vásárhelyi Ferenc, Lodz Imre, and Lt. Colonel Vida Zoltán. Their death sentences will be carried out, one by one at my convenience and at a place of my choosing.

> *Regretfully,*
> *The Rat.*

"Read it again, Feri," Horváth prompted Vásárhelyi "so our friend can clearly understand why he is about to meet his maker." Vásárhelyi read the note again, getting angrier as he read and spat in Rátz's face when he finished reading. "Thank God," Horváth looked at the others, "The Rat sent me Rátz's note by mistake. He is a traitor to The Ring. What's your verdict, gentlemen?" Just as so many times in the past, the verdict was quick and without hesitation. Vásárhelyi's fist shot out in front of him with his thumb pointing at the floor. The others, holding onto the struggling Rátz nodded their head, and said almost in unison: "Kill the bastard."

"There is no room for traitors amongst us," Horváth said and tightened the rope. Foam bubbled from Rátz's mouth, his swollen tongue sticking out of his face that was twisted by pain and horror into a grotesque mask of death. There was no doubt when his soul left his body to those who held him. His body sank to the floor as Horváth released the garrote, and Lodz and Vida let go of him. He lay in a lifeless heap on the floor. "Good riddance!" Horváth said and savagely kicked the lifeless body. "We'll put him in the rain barrel at daybreak and bury him above the house."

*   *   *

Ben didn't know how Gabi got into his room but woke as he felt her body slide into bed next to him. She hugged and kissed him. He didn't know what to do, how to behave, what to say. He loved the feel of her warm skin, the fantastic sensation of her soft and moist lips against his own, but the gnawing doubts that had been building up for some time, and particularly since they arrived in Pápa, had him tongue tied and wordless. But he made love to her and wondered if she felt his remoteness.

"Do you love me, Hon?" she asked finally and very quietly, her voice betraying her anxiety. Ben lay quietly on his back, watching the first signs of daylight around the edges of the window shades. She lifted her head and repeated a bit louder than before, and with a bit more fear in her voice, "Do you love me, Hon?"

"I love you very much," Ben replied but didn't say anything else.

"I am sorry I had to leave you yesterday." she apologized and tried to explain, "But something came up and I had to go."

"You had to go where?" Ben asked.

"I had no time to explain last night," she was on two elbows now, her face close to Ben's, "but we intercepted a couple of Dr. Horváth's phone conversations, and I had to join the team that came down from Budapest."

"Why?" Ben asked simply, with more than a small amount of resentment.

"Why what?" Gabi's eyes were wide open.

"Why did you have to leave, and why couldn't you let me know, and where does that leave me?"

For a moment Gabi didn't know how to answer but she quickly collected herself. "It's a simple surveillance. Dr. Horváth and the others are holed up in Dr. Horváth's vineyard cottage. We know they are expecting The Rat to come for them, and they hope to kill The Rat."

Ben didn't comment.

"Are you angry with me, Hon?" she asked with genuine concern in her voice.

"You might say that," Ben looked at her, "I came all the way, at your request, from America to help you, and just when a critical situation comes up, you go off without me. Shouldn't I be angry?"

"I am sorry, Love." Her voice was ringing with genuine regret. She kissed him on his lips, chest and stomach, and Ben felt the world, slowly disappear around him.

*   *   *

Inspector Hegedüs, shifted his weight in the small seat of the unmarked police car, and felt the bottom of his pants catch on the rough, plasticized seatcover. His underwear was pinching his privates, as boredom and claustrophobia was setting in. He rubbed his eyes and looked at his watch. Daylight was coming over the mountain and the press house at the bottom of the hill with Dr. Horváth's Mercedes parked alongside it was coming out of the darkness. The cottage above the vines was becoming visible. He thought he saw motion under the stairs going up the side of the house, and reached for his binoculars. As his eyes were getting used to the dim image in the glasses, he thought he saw the figure of a man, looking through binoculars right at him. He felt like waving and smiling at the man, but instead he looked at his watch again and gave out a small curse. His relief should have been here a half hour ago; but the son-of-a bitch, he figured, probably overslept. He knew the local cops couldn't be trusted and hoped that some of their own would be sent to Pápa. Cadet Officer Mohácsi was fast asleep in the passenger seat, but there was no point in waking him. There was nothing happening on the hillside, and even the dogs were quieting down. The dogs drove him crazy throughout the night with their barking, and the night-vision attachment didn't seem to work on his binoculars. There was a bright spot that almost blinded him. In reality it was the window of the upstairs room with the kerosene lantern, but the rest of house was no more than a black blob without detail. Made in the Union of the Soviet Socialist Republics, he thought with a snide expression, as he put the attachment back into its case. But there was no indication that The Rat had come last night, and he was thankful for no murders happening on his watch. He thought this whole stakeout was a circus. His car was covered with tree branches, muddy tufts of grass, anything and everything they could collect at roadside last night to camouflage the car. But there was no doubt that Horváth and the others in the cottage knew that they were there and checked them out through their own binoculars. He got out of the car to relieve himself, and looked down the road hoping to see his relief. But there was no one, no cars, no carts, not even a stray dog on the road and he got back into the car just as Mohácsi was waking up, rubbing the sleep from his eyes. Hegedüs saw Mohácsi lean forward, his eyes now wide open, reaching for the binoculars. "What's up?" he asked Mohácsi.

"I don't know." He handed the binoculars to Hegedüs. "You take a look."

Mohácsi focused the binoculars to his eyes. "I'll be . . ." He said, finding it hard to believe his eyes. In the half light of the dawn he saw four people coming down the steps along the side of the house, carrying what could have been a body in a blanket. They struggled as they, step-by-step, descended the stairs, dragging whatever it was in the blanket. Hegedüs handed the binoculars to Cadet Officer Mohácsi. "What do you make of it?"

"I don't know." Mohácsi kept looking through the glasses. "It sure as shit looks like a body. Hegedüs took the glasses. The four men were dragging the blanket around the uphill corner of the house, and in a couple of minutes came back into view some distance up the hill from the house. Hegedüs saw them drop the blanket, and as it hit the ground, he thought he saw a hand and an arm swing from the blanket. He got really excited and angry. "How could this have happened?" He looked at Cadet Officer Mohácsi who looked back at him with a blank expression. "This is the only way to get up to that house," Mohácsi said. "No one could have gotten past us."

How the hell would you know?" Hegedüs asked with scorn. "You were asleep most of the time."

"I meant while you were on watch," Mohácsi said sheepishly. Hegedüs threw him a dirty look.

Up the hill, the men appeared again from behind the house with shovels and a pick-axe, and started digging. "We better notify Captain Kerek," Hegedüs said, still looking through the glasses.

*　*　*

Ben knew he wasn't quite himself, but overnight, before Gabi showed up, he decided to get on top of things, as he had done in the past when things didn't go his way. He might have completely misjudged the situation; his involvement in The Rat murders, and his relationship with Gabi, but if he did, it wasn't because he wasn't a good cop, or because he might have been mislead by Gabi's youth, personality, energy and beauty. He went by his own feelings and knew that he was in love with her by the dictates of his own heart and mind. Every day, every minute he spent with her drove him deeper and deeper in love with her, and at this point it made no difference any more what she said, did, or didn't do or say, he was in love, and that was that.

Gabi was maneuvering her little car through the mud puddles of the dirt road leading toward the mountain and the vineyards, and up ahead he could see the camouflaged car of the stakeout. Hegedüs was dozing in the front seat when Gabi's car pulled alongside. Mohácsi noticed them first and nudged Hegedüs who collected himself and got out of the camouflaged car and came around to Gabi's side. "Good morning, Captain." He reached into the car as Gabi lowered the window and shook hands with Captain Kerek and Ben.

"We might as well speak English," Gabi suggested, "so Captain Chapman can understand it." Hegedüs nodded. "Anything to report?" Gabi asked.

"Yeah. Plenty!" Hegedüs started. "We didn't see anybody all night, but this morning we saw four of those guys carry a body from the house and bury him up the hill." Ben couldn't believe his ears and thought that Gabi looked puzzled also. "We heard the dogs bark all night long, but as I said we saw no one outside the house. All of them looked up at the house in silence. Gabi spoke finally: "This is amazing. The Rat struck again. Twenty-one down, four to go." She looked at Ben.

"I am not surprised," Ben said finally with an almost sad expression on his face. He no longer was interested in The Rat murders. He heard Hegedüs ask Captain Kerek if they should go up to the house to investigate, and heard Gabi say that at this point it would not be a good idea as it would blow the surveillance, but Hegedüs pointed out that the people in the house knew they were being watched, and that they saw the police car through field glasses. "Yes. I am sure they saw you," Ben heard Gabi tell Hegedüs; "they know they are being watched, but they don't know who is watching them. And as long as they see someone watching the house, it makes little difference if they know that it's the police, or think that it's The Rat." Ben heard Captain Kerek instruct Lieutenant Hegedüs to stay on post, and she would try to arrange for additional people from Budapest. "The body, whoever it is those people buried up the hill this morning, can wait," Ben heard Gabi tell Hegedüs, "the important thing is to stay on post in hopes of catching The Rat."

The whole conversation sounded as if it came to Ben from a distance. He drifted further and further into his own thoughts, and didn't even notice that they had started driving again and were back on a paved road. He came back slowly as Gabi was talking, explaining the details of some of the other cases, pointing out the detail, snickering at the ingenious ways The Rat dispatched his victims, as in the Schiller Árpád case. Ben recalled the name, although when he read about the man in The Book, he didn't quite pronounce the name the same as Gabi just did, but he knew that Schiller Árpád was one of the Hungarian citizens, whose ancestors were brought forcibly from Bavaria in Southern Germany to colonize parts of Hungary under Austro-German rule. He knew that Schiller happily volunteered for the SS, and that he was assigned to Auschwitz, but he didn't know that Schiller was already one of The Rat's victims, or how he died. Now, as they were driving towards Celldömölk on the winding, elderberry tree lined narrow road, he was listening to Gabi, and he had to admit that The Rat, indeed, was ingenious.

According to The Book's author, Ben recalled, SS lackey Schiller was to die in flames, but with ample time to think about the fate of his victims, whom he had fed into the ovens at Auschwitz. He remembered reading those words in The Book, but didn't expect, could not have imagined, how The Rat was to fulfill that prophesy. Gabi was waving her arms, gesticulating, trying to give a three dimensional image to the picture of her words.

*   *   *

"Schiller lived by himself in the woods in the Bakony Mountains, working as a saw operator, cutting railroad ties from huge trees that were cut down by the government operated enterprise to repair the badly mangled railroad system destroyed in the war. He was lucky to get the job. Most of the work was given to people recently released from prison, and in fact, some of the workmen were still prisoners. They were brought to the mill in the morning from a nearby prison, and taken back in the evening. Now, that Schiller was released from prison after serving four years at hard labor, when he was given the opportunity to continue doing the same thing he was doing while serving his prison term, he happily accepted. The work wasn't hard. He walked behind the saw, cutting lumber from the huge tree trunks, moved the fresh lumber into piles, and lined up a new tree trunk on the saw bed when the one he was cutting up was finished. The job didn't pay much, but it didn't matter. It was a job. He knew as an ex-prisoner, he would have had a very difficult time getting work. This job also had lots of advantages. He lived rent free with one other ex-prisoner in a small shack right alongside the mill, and his meals were all provided by the prison kitchen. But as a free man, his food was a little better than what the prisoners ate, and occasionally the foreman left a bottle of wine or home brewed slivovitz that he and his roommate drank as soon as they got it.

Schiller woke up one night," Gabi went on with her narrative, "to the singing of his roommate, who was drunk out of his mind, having finished almost a whole bottle of slivovitz. In the darkness of the shack Schiller could just about make out the silhouette of another figure leading his drunken roommate out of the shack. Schiller was pretty drunk himself, but he sensed danger and tried to get out of his bed. He couldn't. His left arm was tied to the wall of the shack, and both of his legs were roped to the legs of his cot. Only his right arm was free, but he couldn't reach the rope restraints around his ankles, or on his left wrist. The silhouette of the other person came back into the shack and lit a candle. He was dressed all in black; even his face was covered with a black mask, with only his eyes and his lips showing.

"I am The Rat," the silhouette spoke to Schiller, "Have you heard of me?" Schiller shook his head side to side, and said 'no' as his stupor was slowly replaced by intense fear of the stranger. "I have a message for you from your thousands of victims you threw into the ovens, Mr. Schiller, when you were wearing the skull on your cap, as a proud SS man. Do you remember their screams, Mr. Schiller? Don't worry; you will have time to think about it before the flames will consume you."

Gabi looked at Ben, who was looking straight ahead, but Gabi knew that he was listening to every word. She returned her eyes to the road and continued.

"I am giving you an opportunity to think about those innocent victims of yours, or, if you choose, an opportunity to end it quickly, and die right away, as they did. As you can see," The Rat said, "I'm attaching this candle to this tree branch and resting one end of the branch on the windowsill. I will let you hold the other end with your right hand. You can decide how long you want or are able to hold the branch and not let the candle drop into the sawdust and wood chips I spread all over the floor and under your bed. You might want to know that I saturated the sawdust and the chips with your leftover slivovitz, and several liters of kerosene. If you can no longer hold the branch, or decide to let go of it, the candle will drop onto the little heap of sawdust and you will slowly feel the heat as the fire spreads and the rest of the shack catches on fire. Your skin will blister, and you will have the chance to take a deep breath and smell your own burning flesh, just as you smelled the flesh and the skin and the bones of your victims as they burned. The Rat carefully placed one end of the tree branch on the window sill, and placed the other end in Schiller's right hand. Don't worry, Schiller, The Rat turned back from the open door, his outline silhouetted against the feeble light of the clearing, the candle won't go out. It's the best storm candle I could buy. He watched from the doorway for awhile as the muscles tightened on Schiller's arm, and as his arm started to strain and tremble under the weight of the tree branch. His face was distorted by fear, and his screams were swallowed up by the silence of the forest. Schiller's roommate was still sitting on a log some distance from the shack, still trying to get the last drops of slivovitz from the empty bottle, and still singing at the top of his lungs, completely oblivious to the drama taking place inside the shack. The Rat walked rapidly away from the shack and the clearing, as the shack exploded into a ball of flame with a loud whooping sound. "May your soul burn in hell, SS Man Schiller," The Rat said, "turning and walking rapidly into the darkness."

* * *

Gabi threw a sideways glance at Ben, who was looking at her. "Those were The Rat's exact words?" he repeated Gabi, "May your soul burn in hell, SS Man Schiller?"

"They were the exact words on a yellow sheet of paper The Rat left behind, stuffed into Schiller's roommate's pocket."

"And, I suppose," Ben seemed to be in deep thought, "the description of how the shack caught fire, was also described in detail in the note?"

"Our experts put it together," Gabi said quickly, "from what was in the note and what they could get out of Schiller's drunken room mate." But her voice, Ben thought, was not as positive as when she had cleared up other matters previously.

They drove in silence for some time. "Did you ever consider writing books?" Ben asked quietly.

"When I was a kid in school," Gabi smiled at him, "my teacher thought I had a vivid and fertile imagination. Why do you ask?"

"The way you told the story," Ben kept his eyes riveted on the road, "it almost sounded like an eye-witness account," He looked at Gabi, "almost as if you were there."

Gabi looked straight ahead, her face trying to mask her emotions, but she didn't answer. The car pulled up to a broken down wire fence with a gate at the far end of the immense railroad yard at Celldömölk. Near the gate, at the deadhead on the unused siding, the old boxcar Köröndi died in was still sitting in the same place.

*   *   *

It was late afternoon when Gabi's car once again stopped alongside the camouflaged police car. A man Ben had not seen before, in civilian clothes, jumped out of the car and threw a snappy salute at Captain Kerek. Then, as he realized he should not have done that, he gave an embarrassed smile. Gabi must have introduced him, Ben thought, as the man offered to shake his hand. Gabi and he talked for a while in Hungarian and the man offered to shake hands again, and Gabi backed away from the camouflaged car. She turned her car around and headed in the direction of the twin spires of the big church above the skyline of Pápa.

Hegedüs and Mohácsi, "The Bobsy Twins," as Ben now mentally referred to them, were waiting for them in the small lobby of the Golden Griffin Hotel across from the big church. Hegedüs handed a large envelope to Captain Kerek and shook hands with Ben. But the conversation was in Hungarian. That irritated Ben, and after a while he asked to be excused and went upstairs to his room. As soon as he turned on the lights in the entrance hall to his suite, his eyes caught another envelope just like the one Hegedüs had given Gabi, but this one was addressed to Capt. Benjamin Chapman, NYPD. Inside were several smaller envelopes, all from Officer Frank Campanelli. He opened the first one. It contained telephone message slips, some with notes scribbled on by Frank Campanelli, none of which held great interest for Ben. The second envelope was more interesting. An assembled and stapled report, title paged: *Psychological and Physical Profile of the serial killer, k.a. The Rat.*

Ben ignored all items on the cover, the date of the report, prepared by, and so on, and went eagerly to the first page:

> *Based on the data known at the time of the preparation of this report, all of the following must be understood as assumptions based on hard, and soft evidence, and must not be construed as final.*
>
> *At this stage of the investigation, no assumption can be made regarding the subject's gender, but because the many physical difficulties that were encountered, and successfully handled by the subject, it might be safe to assume that the subject is a male of above average physical strength and agility.*

Ben lowered the pages for a moment, and gave out a sigh of relief.

> *It is further assumed that the subject is in an age category of between seventeen and fifty, though it is the assumption of this department that the subject's age is more likely to be just below, or just above forty. Having no hard evidence, such as footprints, to establish or contradict the gender of the subject, the leaning of this department at this time is towards an athletic male of the forty, plus or minus five years, age bracket."*

Ben put the report down. He never liked these kinds of reports. He thought they were high handed, carefully worded crap that went in both directions at once and very seldom offered anything useful to the investigation. But he was happy to read that the perpetrator, The Rat, was thought to be a male. He picked up the report again and made himself read on.

> *Although most of the murders have taken place within the country*

of Hungary, considering the extraordinary planning necessary to carry off several of the murders outside of Hungary, including the most recent Molnár murder in Los Angeles, California, USA, it must be assumed the subject possesses extraordinary knowledge of the grounds of his/her execution in each case, including but not limited to local customs, standards and ways of local practices such as doing business within a certain community, and that the subject has the ability of making decisions on very short notice to accommodate unforeseen situations.

Ben put down the report again, and reached for the bottle of mineral water on a tray on his dresser. He took a swig of the tepid water. The report didn't get him any closer to solving the case than he was when he first heard about The Rat murders. In fact, if he had been given a free hand, he was convinced he would be close to understanding and figuring out The Rat. This report was almost word for word like the German, Hungarian, Polish, and other reports he had already read, all of which were full of 'it's this, or it's that' assumptions. And all of it, he thought bitterly, as wrong as it could be. He didn't want to admit that even though he didn't have hard evidence, his intuition, the deductive powers of his brain, led him to believe he knew who The Rat was. He tried to put the unpleasant thoughts out of his mind, telling himself that assumptions were assumptions, and until the assumptions turned into hard evidence, they were no more than assumptions that could be, as the profile said, right or wrong. He leafed through the report. One of the paragraphs near the end caught his eye.

Based on previous cases similar to The Rat murders, an observation must be made regarding motivation and mindset of the subject. It has been proven in previous cases that most serial killers interviewed subsequently to their arrests, exhibited a strong belief and conviction in the righteousness and justification of their acts, and were pleased at achieving their objective. Not one perpetrator exhibited any sign of repentance and none accepted any responsibility for having committed a criminal act. Some perpetrators evaded capture by committing suicide, some explained in notes left at the scenes of their crimes that their 'mission,' was accomplished. It is therefore advised that investigators consider suicidal tendencies of the subject, and assume the subject might commit suicide right after his/her stated objective.

Ben re-read the paragraph several times and noticed the usual disclaimer on the back page:

The above report is intended to supplement standard practices in the understanding, apprehension and capture of the report's subject, k. a. The Rat. Caution is advised against assuming anything contained within this summary as factual.

"Nothing is to be considered factual," he murmured to himself. "So what the hell good is all this crap?" He reached for the bottle of mineral water but put it back on the dresser. He got up to open his suitcase on the stand and extricated a small bottle of Jack Daniels, unscrewed the cap, and took a large swig straight from the bottle.

The other envelopes had some interoffice garbage he couldn't have been less interested in at this moment. There was a letter from Commissioner Katz, praising him for his exceptional work and progress made in his current assignment. He crumpled the letter and threw it into the waste basket. Just as he expected, the research into Hungarian, Jewish immigrants who ended up in New York after WW II, so far turned up no promising leads. There were several from the city of Pápa, some already deceased, and others that didn't fit into the picture on any level. He never believed The Rat lived in New York, and now, more than before, he was convinced The Rat was a resident of Hungary, more than likely connected in some ways to the author of The Book, and if he was ever going to get on the trail of The Rat, he had to go back to the spot and start his pursuit at the point where The Book was found. He decided to do just that and took another, and another, and another swig from his bottle until the bottle was empty and he fell asleep. Some time later, in a half stupor, he heard knocking on his door, but didn't answer it.

* * *

Dr. Horváth stood on the little balcony of the cottage, looking at the camouflaged police car through his field glasses. "How much longer do you think those halfwits will sit in that stupid little car watching us?" He looked behind him at Lodz Imre, but he just shook his head. "Of course," Horváth commented, "we shouldn't really complain. They're not after us. They hope to catch The Rat," he laughed, "if the dogs, or us, don't get him first." He turned to walk into the cottage and Lodz followed him. "So, you see, Imre, we have double protection. We have the dogs on the hill, and," he laughed heartily, "and we have the dogs at the bottom of the hill." He patted Lodz on the back patronizingly. "I think I'll go into town this morning," Horváth looked at Lodz and the others in the room, "get us some supplies, and perhaps find out what's going on."

"You don't think they," Lodz nodded in the direction of the bottom of the hill, "might stop you?"

"What for?" Horváth asked with righteous indignation. "For being on my own piece of land? For driving my own car? They better not." He looked at the others. "You fellows need anything? Want me to do anything for you?" But they all just shook their head. Finally Vida spoke up: "How much longer do you think we'll have to stay here?" Horváth looked at him. "Now, Zoltán, I hope you're not losing heart. You know as well as I do that The Rat is after us and the only chance for us is to stick together. He would surely get us one by one."

"Yes, but how long?" Vida insisted.

"How the hell should I know?" Horváth was losing patience. "Forever maybe, or until we die or The Rat dies." He forced himself to calm down and show confidence. "We get stronger with every day that goes by if we don't break our unity, but the moment we do, The Rat is ready to pounce. I assure you." He patted Vida's back patronizingly again. "It won't be long." He looked around in the small room. "Maybe you fellows could clean up this place a bit. I won't be long."

* * *

Ben sat on the edge of his bed. His head was still spinning and he held onto the night table, hoping not to fall. Full daylight was pushing through around the edges of his window shades, and the noise of the traffic coming up from the street indicated that he slept way into the day. He thought a cold shower might help, if he could make his way into the bathroom, and stay upright in the slippery little tub while trying to manipulate the hand-shower. But if he didn't want to spend the rest of the day sitting on his bed in his room, it had to be done. He got up slowly and carefully regained some of his balance with every step. He noticed an envelope on the floor at his door. He wasn't sure he should risk bending down and reaching for it, but hoping the note was from Gabi, he overcame his fear and slowly picked up the envelope. It was from Gabi.

"Dearest, I knocked on your door last night, but as you didn't answer, I thought I'd let you sleep. I know you needed the rest, and I hope you're not angry with me. I hope this case will be over soon, and I promise I'll make everything up to you. There are new developments in the case, and I have to go back to Budapest to get the latest, but should be back sometime tonight and fill you in on everything.

Mr. Kovács, my old English teacher, kindly agreed to help if you should need someone to translate for you while I'm not here. You'll find him at the school.

With all my love,
Gabi."

Ben put the note on his dresser, and was pleased to notice how calmly he reacted to Gabi's message. Perhaps the booze quieted him down, or in his stupor he was able to come to terms with his anxieties, but somehow Gabi going away again so suddenly didn't seem to upset him. Perhaps he expected it, and seemed to understand that Gabi would disappear from time to time, before, or just after, there was a new development in The Rat murders.

*   *   *

Professor Kovács, Gabi's English teacher, turned out to be a delightful old fellow. He had a pleasant smile, and his English was faultless, even too perfect. As perfect, Ben thought, as an acquired language could be. He asked no questions about why Ben wanted to go to 36 Bástya Street, and he suggested they walk. It seemed everybody in this town walked everywhere, and Ben thought that may have been the reason why everybody was so trim. They left the old school building and the Professor showed the way. "You are a long way from home." The professor opened up, "Gabriella, my student, told me that you are on a very important case."

"Yes." Ben nodded, but was at a loss to make any other comment.

"And may I ask, how this old house on Bástya Street fits into the case?"

"Actually," Ben was loosening up, "I don't know if it does. But I understand that a certain document, a manuscript, was found there, and if I could find out who wrote that manuscript, or who found it, or some other information surrounding it, Captain Kerek and I would be a lot closer to solving this case."

The professor was listening intently as though searching his mind; "I know about that book. Actually, if my memory serves me right, I think it might have been Gabriella, or another of my students, who found it." Ben stopped in his tracks. This bit of information was out of the blue, totally unexpected, and it hit him with force. If Gabi, or one of her friends found The Book, why did she not tell him so?

Why did she tell him that The Book was sent to the Hungarian Security Agency, and no one knew who sent it. At this point, having this piece of information drop into his lap, he even wondered if it made any sense going back to 36 Bástya Street, or, if he did, what else was he going to look for there. He tried to conceal his emotions, "How do you know that, if you don't mind my asking?"

The professor kept walking, eyes riveted to the ground. "Of course I can't be certain of this, but I seem to recall after the war the city government decided to clean up the portion of the city that just a few years before was part of the Ghetto." He looked at Ben. "Do you know Bástya Street was the main part of the Ghetto, Captain Chapman?" Ben nodded. "Yes, Captain Kerek took me there and introduced me to the people who now live in the house."

"Well then," the Professor went back to his original thought, "housing was badly needed just after the war, and those houses were dormant but in very bad shape. There were not too many young men around. A lot of them died in the war, or were captured," he sad sadly, "and some were taken away." He didn't explain, and Ben didn't ask why. "We put together volunteer teams from the schools, young kids, boys and girls, some no more that ten years old, to help with the clean-up. 36 Bástya Street was in very bad shape. Two of the Landau family came back from the German camps. One was a lawyer, and the other a young fellow who was one of my students just a year and a half before. These two, like everybody who came back from Germany, were in very bad shape. As I hear it, they lived in the house for a while, but when the older of the two, the lawyer died; the young fellow disappeared. I found out later that he went to America. I believe the house lay dormant for a while afterwards. When the clean-up campaign started up again in 1950, my students were the ones who cleaned up this and several other houses."

Why on earth did Gabi introduce him to the professor? Ben's brain was in high gear as he tried to figure out if this was a slip-up, or an oversight on Gabi's part, or if Gabi was trying to send him a message about something. If the professor knew about these things, why did Gabi, who was on the spot, not know who found The Book? Did she want him to find this information from someone else? And if she did, why? With all the other inconsistencies that bothered him, all of which had something to do with Gabi, this was the worse. "Tell me, professor," he turned to Mr. Kovács, "did the young fellow, I mean the one who lived in the house and went to America, could he have written that book?"

"Oh, I don't know that, Captain Chapman. But from what I hear is in that book, I frankly doubt it."

"You know what's in The Book?" Ben was astonished.

"Only what I've heard," the professor answered. "I understand The Book names some of the guilty people who committed crimes in the Ghetto, but that's all I've heard. And I doubt a young fellow would have written that." He thought for a while and added, "Come to think of it, I'm not even sure the young fellow left before his cousin, the lawyer, died, or if it was the other way around. What I seem to recall, this was one of the last houses to be cleaned up and auctioned off. It might even have been as long as four, five years after the war when this house was sold."

They were now standing in front of the two little street front stores, and as they were talking, the young woman Ben met when he and Gabi came to Pápa, came out to them. They chatted for a while. "Did you help with the clean-up?" Ben asked her, but she didn't understand. "Before you bought the house," Ben tried to explain, "when these houses were cleaned up after the war . . ." Professor Kovács translated, and she suddenly understood. "No," she explained, "that was long before we got the house. We are the third people in the house since the war."

"Since this place was a Ghetto?" Ben asked, and she nodded. "What happened to the others?" The Professor translated his question, but he knew what the answer was going to be even before the professor translated it. "She doesn't know," the professor said. "The previous owners sold the house and moved away. She didn't know any of them." He looked at Ben. "Would you like to go in the house?" But Ben had already gotten more information than he had hoped for. "No. I don't think so." He felt he owed the professor an explanation. "I am sorry, Professor Kovács, but I don't think there is any point to put these nice people out." He added with a smile, "Please thank her for her cooperation, and I apologize for bringing you on this wild goose chase." The professor smiled and held up a finger, "Ah, a bit of American slang I suppose."

"Did you tell me, Professor," Ben broke the silence as they walked away from the house, "that the young fellow, who lived in this house and went to America, was one of your students?"

"Yes. He was going to graduate in 1944, but they took him away before he could finish the year."

"And it's interesting," Ben was thinking out loud, "that Captain Kerek was also your student."

"Yes," the professor laughed, "but you know how it is, in a small town like Pápa, everybody knows everybody." They walked in silence for a while. More to break the silence than for any other reason, Ben remarked: "It's quite amazing how well you and your students, like Captain Kerek, speak English."

"Oh yes," the professor nodded, "she was amongst the best. In fact she was so good, we sent her abroad to perfect her English." Ben looked up with a start again. He didn't recall Gabi telling him anything about going abroad to learn English. All he remembered was her saying she learned to speak English in school. But he let it go without comment. "Do you think Captain Kerek might have known the young fellow, I mean the Landau fellow who went to America?"

"It's possible, I suppose." The Professor thought for a bit. "Though I don't think so." He explained, "Gabriella had to be in the lower classes, ten, maybe eleven years old at the time of the clean up. The young Landau boy, the fellow who lived in that house had to be nineteen or twenty when he left here. I doubt it."

They were coming into the center of town, with the huge church dominating the square, and the beautiful seventeenth century castle that at one time before the war belonged to Count Eszterházy, and was now dormant. "Could I ask you to have dinner with me, Professor?" Ben asked as they arrived in front of the Golden Griffin Hotel.

"It's very kind of you," the Professor smiled, "but my wife is waiting for me with dinner. Perhaps another time. Thank you."

Ben offered to shake hands. "Thank you very much, Professor, I appreciate your help and the pleasant conversation." He walked into the hotel and asked for his key. The young woman behind the small counter in the equally small lobby asked if Ben was enjoying his stay, and if he needed anything. "Do I have any messages?" he asked her. She looked in his message box, but there were no messages. "All of you people speak English so well," Ben complimented her. "Where did you learn English?"

"In school," she answered simply, but Ben could tell that she was pleased.

There was no message under his door either, and he went over to Gabi's door and knocked. There was no answer. It was still a bit early for dinner and Ben reached for the crumpled note-covered envelope and pulled out The Book. For the first time the thought hit him that the manuscript, not just the translation, had no cover sheet. Perhaps it never had one, he speculated, but he doubted it. All books, manuscripts, have a cover page with the title of The Book, the name of the author, or just a clean sheet of paper to protect the pages of text. He looked at the copy of the original handwritten Hungarian copy. Why did it not have a cover page? It had a blank end page, obviously there to protect the rest of the pages, but why did it have no cover? "I will never know!" he sighed to himself and started leafing through the Hungarian pages. Even though the photocopies showed some small holes at the left hand margin of the pages, suggesting that the original must have been laced together, he now also noticed for the first time that the pages were numbered, but a few pages were missing and some of the pages were torn. "Why would this book have been so mishandled?" he asked himself "what could have caused pages to be missing or torn, with sections, or just a few words, torn out here and there?"

He missed Gabi. He wondered where she was, why she didn't call, and was very disturbed about Gabi not telling him what he had heard from the Professor this afternoon. Why would Gabi not want him to know about working on the clean-up of the Bástya Street house, and most importantly about The Book being found there? Maybe she didn't know. He had no answers. At least that's what he told himself, while inwardly he was becoming more and more convinced that in fact, he had the answers.

He just didn't know if he didn't want to believe, or accept them.

His stomach was reminding him that the last thing he put in his stomach was a bottle of Jack Daniels yesterday, and he was wondering why it didn't kill him. But his head was totally clear now and he was hungry. He was wondering how he was going to order, or what the different items might be on the menu, so he got out of his room to go downstairs to the restaurant. He knocked on Gabi's door again, but there was still no answer.

A few people were having dinner in the little restaurant, and the aromas that were wafting from the kitchen excited his appetite. He picked up the menu and the waiter came to his table. "Good evening, Sir." He said in acceptable English, "may I help with making a selection?" Ben looked up. "You speak English," he said and immediately realized how ridiculous this might have sounded. But the waiter just said, "Yes, Sir."

"Where did you learn to speak English?" Ben asked, but the answer didn't surprise him. "In school," the waiter said. "I learned to speak English and German and Russian in school, and my mother taught me Slovakian."

"That's five languages," Ben looked at the waiter admiringly. "You speak five languages?"

"Yes, Sir." Came the simple answer again.

Ben shook his head in disbelief. "That's remarkable."

"May I suggest the wild boar? It's delicious. And the asparagus soup would be a great starter."

"Why don't you surprise me?" Ben looked up at the waiter and put down the menu.

Chapter 11

21 down, 4 to go

He could have dialed her room; the phone system was actually pretty state of the art in this little hotel, but instead of calling her, Ben slipped on his pants and shirt, and quietly went to her door and knocked. There was no answer. A few moments later Ben knocked again, a little louder this time, hoping to hear her sleepy voice, but there was no answer. She obviously wasn't in her room, or was deeply asleep; or, Ben hoped this was not the case, for some reason or the other, she didn't want to answer. Whatever the case, there was no point to trying again and Ben went back to his room. He didn't want to think why Gabi was not in her room at four in the morning. He thought he knew the answer, but it was very disturbing, and he wanted desperately to have her explain otherwise. All the barf that was now in his 'barf-box,' everything that caught his attention, pointed in one direction. Of course, he really hadn't even started his investigation, and as he was finding new material, he told himself, his suspicions and assumptions could change easily, but he didn't really believe it. He was hopeful four days ago when Professor Kovács mentioned the young Landau fellow, but that lead turned sour right away when the professor told him the young man had only came back to Pápa once after he left the country in 1946 when one of his best childhood friends died. He could have been a good suspect. The professor told Ben, Lester Landau became a successful cinematographer in Hollywood and traveled the world on various film projects, some of which were seen even in Hungary. This could have given the young man, Ben figured, good opportunities and cover to do The Rat's work, but he dismissed the idea because he knew it was no more than wishful thinking, and because his instinct, and over two decades of experience in police work, told him who the perpetrator really was. He no longer wondered where Gabi might be. When last he heard from her, she said she had to go back to Budapest and she would be back in a day. That was three days ago. She also said there were new developments in The Rat murders, but that was the last he had heard, and he knew there would be no point in going to the stake-out on his own.

He sat on his bed for quiet a while. He knew he had to come to terms with his feelings, emotions, and anxieties, and carry on with the work he agreed to do. Finish it, and go home.

The Book was on his night table and he picked it up. He thought he knew every word on every page, but what suddenly caught his eye were the numerous, bracketed notes within the text, most of which just said [word/s missing] or [text missing.] Why was text and words missing? Why didn't he notice that before? He dug the copy of the original from his suitcase and tried to coordinate and compare the notes in the translation to the original. He figured the cover page—if there ever was one—could have been torn off, gotten lost, but he couldn't understand why a word, or words, or half a page of text should be missing throughout The Book. The pages of the original clearly showed that words were cut out, perhaps with scissors or a razor blade, and here and there carefully torn out by hand. But why? And as circuits were clicking in his brain, the answer slowly came up. He went back to the first deletion, circled it with a red pen and put a number one next to it. He then looked up the first deletion in the original Hungarian copy and numbered it with an identical number. It wasn't difficult to verify the correctness of his numbering. The number of sentences to the next, or previous, paragraph break from the deletion verified that his numbering was correct; and in the English translation, all of these deletions came at a point that could have suggested a name, or some other identification of a person, or a place, or an incident, which might have identified, or gotten him closer to the identity of the author of The Book, or offer a clue, leading to the identity of The Rat. There were several sentences in The Book that didn't quite make sense, but Ben had dismissed them on previous readings, writing them off as something that had gotten lost in translation. Now, as he was leafing through the translation again trying to find them, all he could recall, or thought he could recall, was that whatever it was, it was somewhere near the end of The Book and it had something to do with someone who was murdered by the police Chiefs of Pápa, a Dr. Horváth and a Lodz Imre. Then the name Landau came to him. He bolted straight up, realizing he had heard the name of Landau from Gabi, from the young woman at the house on Bástya Street, from Professor Kovács, and he suddenly realized that the name was in The Book also, but the Landau in The Book could not have written The Book, because he was murdered in the fall of 1944, and The Book was obviously written after the war. He also recalled the first sentence of The Book and leafed back to the opening page, *There were scores of people responsible for our misery and for my family's unbelievably cruel end. It would be impossible to catch up to all . . .*

Of course! It dawned on him that Landau Miklós, whose murder is described in The Book, had to be related to one of the Landaus who came back from the Nazi death camps, one of whom had to be the author of The Book. The Question was which one. Professor Kovács didn't think it was the younger of the two, and Ben had to agree as he recalled another part of The Book's opening statement:

But as time goes by, and as I get older and meeker, I now know this will not be, unless another rat, younger than I, or the offspring of a rat will find this account, and take it upon himself to fulfill my fervent wish to honor the memory of those who perished at the hands of these torturers and murderers, and bring them to their just deserves. The guilty will go on living, unless an Avenging Angel will take up the sword, and deal out the just measure of punishments."

The words, . . . *as I get older and meeker. . .* left no doubt in Ben's mind that the author of The Book was the elder of the two Landaus who survived the Holocaust and came back to Pápa. And it also became obvious to Ben that the author of The Book was related to Landau Miklós. But The Book didn't say that, unless—another circuit tripped in Ben's mind—The Book did say it, but for some reason or the other, the references were removed from the text. The question was why. There could only be one reason. The Rat was somehow tied to, or had a connection with the Landaus, but if this connection was revealed, it would be a clear indication of The Rat's identity. And that's why words, sentences, and pages were missing from The Book.

Ben put The Book down and got up to stretch. The wheels were turning in his mind, claxons were going off, and brilliant flashes of blinkers were telling him that his assumption about the trail leading to The Rat starting in Pápa was right, and if he could find the missing pages, or at least figure out some of the missing words, the next steps would surely lead him to The Rat. His mind was racing. He had to find something to calm himself, but the Jack Daniels was gone, and the only booze in the mini-bar was beer, and some strange little bottles with Hungarian labels. He took a chance on one and unscrewed the cap. A strong, but pleasant scent hit him and he took a little swallow. The stuff tasted good, but it was strong and almost gagged him as it went down the tube. He coughed and cleared his throat, winced a couple of times and took a second swallow. He felt the burning all the way down into his gut but when it settled down he felt a bit calmer and went back to his thoughts.

Who could have censored The Book? He figured he now knew why, but it was the 'who' he had to find an answer for. Then, like a bolt of lightning from a clear blue sky, the answer came to him in a flash. Only the person who found The Book, could have gone over the text and removed part of it. But if The Book was found by one of the youngsters that cleaned up the place, most of whom were ten, eleven, twelve years old according to Professor Kovács, why would they have even read The Book, much less decimate it? The answer was that The Book was not altered by a ten, eleven, or twelve year old. The Book was altered by a person who was in a position to know about, or was old enough to kill Sergeant Köröndi, in a way The Book described Sergeant Köröndi's death sentence. He had to be old enough to assume the identity of The Rat, and send the censured book to the Hungarian Security Agency after Sergeant Köröndi's body was discovered in the old boxcar.

Perhaps, Ben reasoned, he should try to interview some of the people, who as kids, were on that clean-up detail at 36 Bástya Street. Maybe they could shed some light on at least who found The Book, or even more importantly, who held onto it for all the years after it was found, and until after Sergeant Köröndi was murdered. It upset him to have to admit to himself that he already knew who found The Book, who held onto it for all those years, and who might have altered it. He re-read the Landau Miklós case.

[word/s missing] Miklós was a hero of the nation, and was decorated with the highest honor, The Heros' Golden Medallion for bravery and valor as an officer in the Hungarian Army.

Ben took the note pad from his night table and wrote down some guesses that could fit in front of Miklós in the bracketed space where the translation said: 'word/s missing.' The first word he wrote down was Landau. It made sense. It was, he knew, the family name of Miklós, and could have preceded his given name. But why remove it? He went on writing. "My son, Miklós." "My father, Miklós". "My husband, Miklós." "My brother, Miklós." "My friend, Miklós." There was no point to going on. "My friend" didn't make sense right off the bat, if one assumed that The Book was written by the elder Landau who lived in the house for over a year. They had to be related. After all, the author of The Book referred to his family in his first sentence: . . . *for our misery and for my family's unbelievably cruel end.* So it was clear that the two were related. Ben knew from the official files that Miklós was a Landau, and deduced that Miklós could not have been a son, or the father, and certainly was not the husband, but certainly could have been the author's brother. Ben wrote in 'My brother' in the space between brackets [word/s missing]. Then, as a second thought, he added 'dear' between 'my' and 'brother' and went on reading. He stopped now and then to think about and digest what he just read, as if it was for the first time, and now and then leafed back to the early portions of The Book for reference. It was curious that more words and sections were removed from The Book towards the end than at the beginning, and he wondered why. Then, the answer, like all the other sudden revelations that came to him just in the last couple of hours, slowly surfaced. He recalled reading the author's description of some of the thugs of the Nazi regime who still strutted around after the war, brandishing rifles and side-arms, but now wearing the red armbands of the current regime. No wonder, Ben thought, that the author of The Book, whoever he was, was still spooked, scared, and didn't want his identity known. And that's why there were hardly any deletions at the beginning of The Book, particularly where the author identified a guilty German, but there were plenty of deletions wherever the author gave a description of a local event, or a local murderer, who was still free. And, Ben reasoned further, The Rat, whoever he might be, also had all the reasons in the world to protect his identity. But what he found most interesting, a thought that came to him as he was sitting on the edge of his bed leafing through The Book, that at this point the identity of the author, who must have been dead for many years, was no longer really important. The important thing at this point was to find the identity of The Rat, and to find his whereabouts. And the whereabouts, Ben knew, was on Kis Mountain in a small house above the grapes. The cop in him wanted to go to Kis Mountain immediately, but Ben "The Doorknob" Chapman, the man, wanted to pack his suitcase and go home to Forest Hills and retire. His heart was aching, ready to burst in sorrow, but the picture was right before his eyes, and it was clear. He laid back on his bed and closed his eyes.

*   *   *

Things were coming together for Ben. There was a quiet knock on his door. He thought his heart stopped for a second, and that The Rat was at his door. But he told himself he couldn't be sure.

Chapter 12

22 −23

He always knew he was a coward, but this night, as the hours were slowly grinding away, he was more afraid than ever in his entire life. He had his windbreaker on though it wasn't very cold, and turned up the collar as he stood shivering in the dark corner under the steps. He could hear the snoring of the others above him, and it filled him with fear to know that he was alone. He was even afraid to look at his watch to see how much longer he was to stand guard before Colonel Vida was to relieve him, and clutched the large meat cleaver that Dr. Horváth honed to razor sharpness the day they all arrived at the cottage. The dogs were barking in the distance, but otherwise the night was quiet and time seemed to be standing still. His eyes tried to pierce the darkness, but the mountain was shrouded in gloom and he could only make out a few stars as the clouds passed slowly overhead. He thought he heard a small scraping noise, as if something, a small animal perhaps, was scurrying across the flat stones of the back porch, but instead of investigating he pulled deeper into the corner, telling himself that the noise he had just heard was unimportant. Then he heard it again but this time it was louder and a cold shudder ran through his body, telling him that this was going to be the night he was going to die. As scared as he was, he wasn't going to yell, alerting the others of danger because the noise could have been a small animal raiding the garbage, and he didn't want the others to know how scared he was. He recoiled and felt his limbs go weak as he heard the noise again and saw the dark figure emerge from the shadows. His warm urine was running down the inside of his legs as the dark figure waved to follow him. He tried to scream but his throat was dry and no sound came from his mouth. He felt, more than he saw, the lightning fast sweep of the black figure's arm, and felt the searing pain in the side of his face and in his skull. The meat cleaver slipped from his grip as the dark figure grabbed the front of his coat and dragged him away from the building. He had no strength left in any of his limbs. His arms flayed aimlessly at his side, and his legs dutifully followed the dark figure away from the house, deep into the grapes. He desperately wanted to scream but couldn't. The house was slowly swallowed up in the darkness behind them, as they got to the far end of the grapes and the low stone fence that was built from rocks collected from the fields over centuries.

The dark figure spun him around and he felt his hands being tied behind his back with thin wire, just as he ordered his men to tie the wrists of his victims, and hoist them up to beams and tree branches by a rope tied to the thin wire, and leave them hanging for hours. He remembered how much he enjoyed watching the suffering of his victims; hearing them scream in agony as their shoulders were twisted from their sockets, and as his German Shepherd tore chunks of flesh from their bodies. Now he felt his own arms being stretched upwards behind him, and saw the dark figure pulling on the rope, hanging from a thin branch of an old Acacia tree.

"You are very fortunate, Colonel Vásárhelyi." He heard the dark figure speak for the first time. "I am The Rat, your executioner." He felt his bladder and his stomach empty completely and would have sunk to the ground if the rope hadn't supported him. But the pain in his shoulder was excruciating and he tried to get his feet underneath him. "I will hang you, Colonel Vásárhelyi, the way you ordered your henchmen to hang your victims, but your shoulders will not turn out of their sockets, like your victims' did, because, you see," The Rat said almost kindly, "I won't hoist you high. I want you near the ground, where the dogs will be able to get to you. Vásárhelyi's head snapped up at The Rat. A weak, miserable squeak emanated from his mouth as he tried to say: 'No-ooooo.' He heard the barking of the dogs in the distance and he thought that the barking was coming closer. The Rat continued, "You will die slowly, Colonel. The dogs will start ripping your flesh from your miserable bones in a few minutes, but only the bigger ones will reach your innards. You will see your legs disappear slowly and you will see your bones do a death dance as you slowly die. And you will see your friends watching you die. They won't come to your aid, Colonel Vásárhelyi, because by the time they'll hear your cries for help and see you being ripped apart by a pack of wild dogs, it will be too late for them to help you, and because they'll also be paralyzed by fear for their own miserable lives." He stopped talking and looked around. "The dogs are getting closer, Colonel Vásárhelyi. I hear their stomachs growl, their teeth grind, and their tongues salivating for your flesh." He took a yellow sheet of paper from his cape. "Hear now your sentence."

I, The Rat, judge and executioner of the guilty, sentence you to die as you sent your countless victims to their grave. May you suffer the agony of every bite, watching your body disappear into the bottomless stomachs of the hungry dogs. May your soul burn in hell for all eternity. The Rat.

The dark figure folded the paper and tied it neatly to the rope suspending Colonel Vásárhelyi. The Rat stood back as the first of the dogs lunged viciously at the helpless figure dangling from the rope. The dogs ignored The Rat. Their attention was focused on the helpless figure of Vásárhelyi, as he was screaming at the top of his lungs, and as he was slowly chewed up, bite by bite, feeling his life ebbing from his body. He no longer even felt the pain, but saw the dim light of a kerosene lamp being lit way in the distance in the upstairs room of the cottage, and saw the figure of Lodz Imre with the revolver in his hand leaning out the window. But he no longer saw the dark figure and noticed the glowing eyes of more and more dogs emerging from the dark.

*   *   *

Cadet Officer Mohácsi came awake with a start. He was startled by the howling and the loud, excited barking of the wild dogs on the hillside. He reached for the binoculars and tried to attach the night-vision scope, but it was very difficult in the dark interior of the small car. He searched the hillside for the cause of the commotion, but couldn't see anything through the camouflage covering the windshield, and because the Soviet-made scope wasn't working right. Then he spotted a tiny light speck way over to the right and swung the scope in the direction of the cottage. The scope was useless. It showed an immense flare of what probably was a lantern, but other than that, he could just make out some figures coming down the stairs at the cottage, but not much more.

The first sign of daylight appeared over the mountain, but it only flared the scope to the point of rendering it useless. Mohácsi cursed the fucking Ruskies and their god damn garbage and ripped the scope from the binoculars. He sat in quiet, listening to the dogs, thinking that the barking was growing weaker as the sky became brighter. He was startled by a figure knocking on the window of his car, and as he turned he saw Captain Kerek's smiling face. He pulled down the window. "Good morning, Captain." They shook hands. "

"What's going on?" He asked the captain.

"That's what I was going to ask you," Captain Kerek smiled at him.

"I honestly don't know," Mohácsi said. "There was some kind of a commotion going on about an hour," he looked at his scribbled notes, "less then an hour ago. I heard a lot of dogs bark very loud, and I think somebody came down the steps at the cottage with a lantern. But that's about it."

"You didn't see anything, or anyone suspicious?"

"No. Not a soul!"

"And, of course," Captain Kerek added with a smile, "you were awake every second of the time."

"Yes, Captain," he lied, but he didn't think the captain cared one way or the other.

"When is your relief coming?"

Mohácsi looked at his watch. "At eight o'clock. Another 3 hours and some."

"Well then," Captain Kerek said, "report to me immediately if anything should happen."

"Yes, Captain." Mohácsi saluted as Captain Kerek walked away. He was speculating why Captain Kerek didn't park closer to his car as he watched her walk to her car, just a tiny speck in the distance. But he shrugged his shoulder, figuring that the Captain probably didn't want to drive on the dirt road without her headlights, or possibly give away the stake-out if she kept her lights on. It really didn't make any difference to him and he picked up the binoculars to take another look. He thought he saw some figures move through the grapes in the growing daylight, but it still wasn't bright enough to really see who they were, or what was going on. He settled into the seat and closed his eyes.

*   *   *

Lodz thrust the lantern in front of him, but it wasn't much help. A little further ahead, at the end of the rows of grapes, he heard the dogs growl, and fight over something he hoped was a dead animal but inwardly he knew it was probably Feri, or what was left of him. He heard someone scream, but even that was covered by the ferocious barking. When Feri wasn't at his post under the steps as the two of them came to investigate, and when he didn't respond as they called out to him, Lodz Imre was certain that it was Colonel Vásárhelyi who fell victim to the dogs. But if it was him, he was trying to figure out the situation, why did he wander so far from his post? If he needed to relieve himself, he could have done that right next to the cottage. He couldn't understand the situation, unless, he reasoned, Colonel Vásárhelyi did go away from the cottage for whatever reason, and had somehow gotten confused in the dark and gotten lost. Of course, he had to admit, that the only other possible reason behind Vásárhelyi's disappearance was The Rat. That is what he feared, and that is what the situation turned out to be. He stopped in his tracks between the rows of grapes with Colonel Vida behind him, as he saw the dogs and watched in horror. As his eyes adjusted to the darkness, he saw the pack of viscous wild dogs tearing something apart. The something turned out to be a torso with his arms twisted and tied behind his back, hanging from a limb of the Acacia tree, bouncing up and down like a yo-yo when the dogs pulled him down, and the thin tree branch yanked him back up again. Lodz and Vida could see that Vásárhelyi—what still remained of him—was still alive but just barely and that he wasn't going to last much longer. Lodz reached for the revolver in his belt but thought the better of it. Vassarhelyi was beyond help, and if he fired the gun, it could have alerted the look-out at the bottom of the hill that would have brought the police. He didn't want two corpses found, one dangling from the tree branch, and the other buried in a rain barrel up the hill. Instead he released his grip on the pistol butt and watched in horror as the dogs relentlessly gorged themselves on what they could reach. The pack was thinning out as the smaller dogs could no longer reach any part of Colonel Vásárhelyi, and with their bellies full, disappeared into the grapes. But the bigger dogs were still ripping portions of Vásárhelyi's intestines, and Lodz watched helplessly as Vásárhelyi tried to lift his head, and as his face reflected a grotesque plea for help. But there was nothing they could do. Even if they could have chased the dogs away, which of course both of them knew they couldn't, there was nothing they could have done for the half a human being swinging from a rope, whose legs, now reduced to nothing but bones, were doing a macabre jig of death. They couldn't believe that Colonel Vásárhelyi might still be alive. His head moved now and then, as he was swinging back and forth, but as the growing daylight was allowing a better view, his head was slumped onto his chest, and it was obvious that he was dead. A few large dogs were still snapping at and tearing what they could reach, but their hunger was now satisfied and one by one they slinked off and vanished in the grapes.

"We'll cut him down and bury him with Rátz." Lodz Imre crossed himself and fished his knife from his pocket. "Let's get moving," he urged Vida, "before the sun is up and those bastards at the bottom of the hill can see us." He looked down the hill and thought out loud, "I wonder what's keeping Gyula?"

*   *   *

Dr. Horváth sat on the small cot in the tiny cell, and wondered how much longer these bastards were going to keep him there. He didn't understand why they pulled him in, and didn't believe it when he was told that he was in protective custody. He thought bitterly that his office—in the good old days—was directly above him on the top floor of this beautiful building. He knew this cell well. He came down here countless times to taunt some of his victims, and at times extort money, or information about others he hoped to shake down in the future. But now, he was sitting in the same cell, fuming at his own stupidity that landed him there. And, of course he didn't believe these bastards really gave a good crap about protecting him from The Rat, but knew that while he was sitting here in this crummy little cell with his thumbs up his ass, the others were probably going to fall to pieces and give up. In the long run it really didn't matter. Surely it would have been easier to deal with The Rat with all of them together but, if it became necessary, he thought he could handle The Rat by himself. The Ring was falling apart anyhow. Rátz was gone, and at this point he was no longer certain that Rátz really sold them out. Just minutes after he strangled Rátz, the idea occurred to him that perhaps The Rat set them up, intentionally sending him the phony note that was addressed to Rátz, and sending Rátz the note that was addressed to him. No matter, he shrugged his shoulders, Rátz was gone and that was that. No big loss. Rátz was a no account little lowlife that served his purpose in the good old days when Rátz did his bidding and his dirty work. He had no doubt in his mind that, given the opportunity, Rátz would have sold him and the others out without thinking twice about it.

But he wanted to get out of this rotten little cell. He hated the bastards who put him here, and he particularly disliked that little cunt that paraded around as a captain, and insisted on being addressed as "Captain." He yelled at the top of his lung, "Guard!" he repeated louder, "Guard!" And as there was no reply, he kept yelling. He knew that the guard didn't answer, or come to see what he wanted, on purpose. He and his guards let people stew in the cells, ignoring their yelling, and then three or four of them would come down into the cell and beat the shit out of the ones that yelled. He didn't care if he was going to be beaten up. He wanted to get out, and was willing to take his chances. But he didn't expect to see Captain Kerek herself come down the steps with some papers in her hand.

"Good morning, Dr. Horváth," she said pleasantly. "What may I ask is so important that you wake up the entire building with your yelling?"

Horváth didn't quite know how to handle this situation. He sensed that this woman might let him go, and didn't want to risk jeopardizing the situation, but at the same time he didn't want to capitulate too easily. But his better judgment told him to be quiet and find out what this little shit wanted. He toned down his voice: "Why am I being held, and for how long?" he demanded.

"Now, now, Dr. Horváth," she smiled at him, "we are doing you a big favor keeping you here, safe from The Rat."

"I don't need your help," he snarled. "I didn't ask for it, and I can take care of myself."

She didn't answer. Instead, she turned away from him and sat down on the little bench along the wall across from Horváth's cell. Her eyes were fixed on him and Horváth was becoming very uncomfortable under her gaze. "I want to be released immediately." His voice wasn't quite as demanding as before. He knew she had the upper hand, and it made no difference how strongly he protested, or even if he begged, she was going to do exactly as she wanted. He thought all his protests, yelling and screaming wouldn't amount to beans, but the friendly tone of her answer surprised him. "Very well, Dr. Horváth." She got up and came back to the cell. "If that's the way you want it. If you think you can handle The Rat, I'll be happy to accommodate you."

He didn't know if he heard right. She was still looking at him, smiling, and repeated, "Do you think, Dr. Horváth, that you could deal with The Rat if he came for you?"

"None of your fucking business," Horváth felt like saying, but he swallowed his words and just said: "I don't need your, or anyone else's, help."

"In that case," she smiled at him, "I have no legal grounds to keep you."

He couldn't believe his ears, but kept quiet.

"All we have to do," she smiled at him again, "is to have you sign these papers, refusing our help, and you'll be free to go."

Horváth held out his arm for the papers, but she pulled them away. "There is one thing I'd like to ask you, Dr. Horváth, if you wouldn't mind telling me, why is The Rat trying to kill you?"

He knew she was playing with him. He was a past master of these little games, one played with helpless prisoners, and he felt like screaming, his frustration and irritation coming close to the surface again, but he controlled himself, not wanting to give this little bitch the satisfaction. "I don't know why that bastard wants to kill me," he said with venom in his voice, knowing fully well she probably knew more, a lot more, than she let on to. "I thought he sent you a note, telling you why he was going to kill you," she said calmly, still with a condescending smile on her face. But he didn't expect this. How could this slimy little cunt know that The Rat sent him a note? Did she also know what the note said? He decided to play the game. "What note?" he asked feigning innocence.

"Now, Dr. Horváth." She raised her voice, though still being friendly. "I know that The Rat sent you and your friends each a note of your death sentence. You're not going to tell me he didn't?"

"I don't know what you're talking about."

"Oh, I guess I must have made a mistake." She paused, and he knew she was playacting. "I thought that all of you, the five of you in The Ring, all got a note from The Rat with your sentences of death."

This really surprised and puzzled him. The wheels were trying to turn fast in his brain, hoping to figure out where she got this information and how much she knew. There could be no doubt any more, and he felt relieved knowing that Rátz must have sold them out, and that Rátz must have cut a deal with the police also. "What the hell does that have to do with anything?" he blurted out. "So what if I got a note from some deranged killer? It's none of your fucking business. If you know so much, why don't you arrest him, The Rat," he was beginning to stutter, "that miserable bastard that's trying to kill me."

"We are doing our best, Dr. Horváth, to do just that. But I would appreciate your cooperation and help, trying to catch him." She continued calmly, "anything you could tell us would be of help, I am sure."

But Horváth remained silent, and she continued, "You see, we believe The Rat is after you, Dr. Horváth, because you killed a Landau Miklós and his fourteen year old son, János."

"I didn't kill anybody," Horváth said; but it was obvious, judging from the way he said it, that he was lying.

"You didn't kill Landau Miklós and his son?"

"No, I didn't," he said defiantly.

"I thought you were tried and sentenced to four years of hard labor for that murder."

"I was railroaded. But I didn't kill them."

"But, then" she smiled at him, "you obviously know who they were, and that they were murdered?"

"I heard about it."

"What did you hear, Dr. Horváth?"

He didn't want to play this game. It was demeaning to him to be humiliated by this little bitch, but he really had no choice. "I heard that the stupid bastard and his son wandered into an artillery range and were blown up."

"But I thought," she said, "that he couldn't walk because of his injuries from World War I." Horváth remained silent. "And what I would like to know, perhaps you could help me, how did they get to the artillery range from Pápa, thirty miles away in the middle of the night, and why?

Horváth just stared ahead and didn't comment.

"What I had heard," Captain Kerek continued, "was that in spite of their exempt status, you sent them to be deported." Horváth didn't reply. "I read the transcript of your trial, Dr. Horváth, and it said that you robbed them and decided to get rid of them." Horváth didn't comment. "But the transcript also said that the commandant of the internment camp honored the Landaus exempt status and they were sent back to Pápa." Horváth looked at the floor, his lips clamped together. "And that's when you had them shot, and had your henchman, Rátz József take them to the Hajmáskér artillery range, and bury them in a shell crater."

"Even if any of those accusations were true," Horváth hissed at her, "I was tried, sentenced and served my time. You can't hold me here."

"I could hold you, Dr. Horváth," Captain Kerek said kindly, "but I won't, if you don't want me to." She thrust the papers in her hand through the bars of the cell door. "Sign these papers refusing our help of protective custody, and you'll be free to go."

Horváth looked at the papers and took her pen to sign them.

"Thank you, Dr. Horváth. You are free to go as, when, and where you please. I will instruct our look-out at Kis Mountain to let you pass at any time of the day or the night. He will not stop you. We are not after you. He is there to help you. He is there to apprehend The Rat, before The Rat kills you. But if you as much as even look at our people, if you lower your car window, or wave, or try to make conversation, I'll pull you in and put you in this cell and throw away the key. You understand me, Dr. Horváth?" He nodded his head with an annoyed expression. "Do you understand me, Dr. Horváth?" she repeated with a little more force. He was about to nod again, but she stepped closer to him, her face just inches from his, "Do you understand me, Dr. Horváth?" He tried not to buckle under to her, but knew he had no other choice. "I understand," he said quietly.

"You understand what?"

"I understand," he raised his voice.

"You understand, Captain! Yes?"

He knew this was a losing battle. "I understand, Captain." He turned his face away from Captain Kerek.

Two guards appeared with his belt, shoelaces, necktie and some other personal belongings. Captain Kerek stood back and looked after Dr. Horváth, as he walked out of his cell and left the building, accompanied by the guards to the front door.

It was almost daylight and Horváth was wondering how the others were holding up at the vineyard.

*   *   *

Ben thought he was dreaming, but the body pressing him to his bed held him tight. Even before he opened his eyes, he recognized her, more by her scent than by seeing her. Where have you been?" He tried to say, but her lips pressed against his, and her tongue was exploring the inside of his mouth. She said nothing, but her urgency in making love to him told him that she missed him in the last couple of days as much as he missed her. How much longer will this charade go on, he asked himself. He thought that the end of their wonderful times together was rapidly coming closer, but at this point he didn't want to think about how their relationship was going to play out; what was going to happen to her, when and where. He loved her, and wanted to live for the moment only.

"Where have you been?' he said, still a bit out of breath after the intense lovemaking, but she just jumped out of bed and Ben heard her talking from the bathroom: "I'll tell you at breakfast." He got out of bed and went into the bathroom after her. She was already covered with shampoo, her eyes closed, holding the shower nozzle above her head. He got into the tub behind her. "Is that you, Ben?" she asked with shampoo trickling into her mouth. "Who did you expect, The Rat?" She threw her head back and laughed, and playfully felt for his body with her eyes closed. They made love in the tub and soaped each other off and Ben jumped out of the tub to dry himself. "Did you miss me, Hon?" she asked with expectation in her voice. "I did, Love. I missed you very much, and I was worried when I didn't hear from you," he added with concern in his voice. "I thought something bad might have happened to you."

"Like The Rat coming after me?" She was playful, and Ben loved it. He felt young every time they made love, and could never get enough of her youthfulness, and her unabashed, and uninhibited, no-holds-barred way of making love. She was getting out of the tub and Ben turned to dry her back. "There are lots of new developments." She said seriously.

"Well, thanks for telling me," Ben chided, "I thought I was already off the case."

"I am sorry, Hon." She turned and kissed him with both of her arms around his neck. "I'll tell you all about it at breakfast."

"Shouldn't we get dressed first?" Ben tried a funny.

"That might not be a bad idea." She kissed Ben again. "I don't want too many people to recognize me." But her subtlety went over Ben's head. "I'll only be a minute," she said when they were dressed. "I'll have to go into my room and mess up the bed so the maids won't start putting things together." She kissed him again. "I'll meet you downstairs in a minute." She slipped out of the room before Ben could say anything. Ben looked after her, and wondered if all this happiness was going to end in disaster.

*   *   *

The breakfast crowd was gone, and the lunch customers weren't arriving yet. Ben decided to sit outside on the veranda in the small courtyard. The waiter brought him an English language edition of the International Tribune. It was open to one of the back pages and the waiter pointed at a small headline. "The Rat murders continue." There were no secrets in a small town, Ben thought, it made no difference whether it was in Hungary or in the US. He was registered as Mr. Benjamin Chapman, ostensibly an American tourist, but he was sure that everybody in the hotel knew who he really was, an American police officer, and a close personal friend of Captain Kerek. He wondered if they knew how close a friend Captain Kerek really was, but left the thought alone as Gabi came out to the terrace and spotted him. She had to be, Ben thought, the most beautiful creature on earth. She was pretty and her athletic build complimented her stylish clothes. "What's in the paper?" she asked when she spotted the Tribune. "There is something about The Rat murders," Ben said, "but I didn't read it yet." Gabi took the paper and looked at it. "We planted this," she said. "We thought that if we gave The Rat a bit of publicity, she might want more and expose her . . ." she quickly corrected herself, "himself." But Ben didn't miss the slip up, even though he made no comment. "Let's order breakfast before they run out of eggs," he smiled at her and added, "I need a lot of eggs." They both laughed childishly and she blushed as she noticed that the waiter was watching them. "You think he might be The Rat?" she asked in hushed tones with a snide smile on her face. But Ben didn't smile. "I know he is not." He waved to the waiter to order breakfast.

After the waiter took their order he turned to Gabi, "What are the new developments?"

Gabi tried to compose herself. "So many things happened and so quickly, I don't know where to begin," she seemed to be concentrating, organizing her thoughts. "Well," she finally started, "The Rat struck again." Ben looked up and murmured, "As if I didn't know." She looked at him. "Pardon me?" But Ben just shook his head, "Nothing Love. I just thought that might have been what kept you away."

"Yes, it was." She looked at Ben and continued, "The Rat is growing bolder."

She reached down to her shoulder bag next to her chair on the deck. "Two more of his targets are dead and he has sent a full report to us, including copies of the five death sentences, as well as outlining his future plans." She took a Kaiser roll from the basket the waiter brought to the table and buttered a piece. She handed Ben a bunch of papers. "Don't look at them now," she said, "I'll tell you what's in them and you can look at them later." Ben nodded and put the papers down. "Rátz József, you might recall reading about him, one of Dr. Horváth's inner circle, disappeared without a trace, yet the only thing we know, and this is information coming from The Rat, that all five members of Dr. Horváth's inner circle, which incidentally they called The Ring, were sent death notices, and that they are the remaining final five intended target victims. As you know The Rat is fully aware of, and frequently quotes from, The Book. In the past, it was his modus operandi in most cases to fill us in on every aspect of his deeds, but this is the first time that he is tipping us off about who is going to be next, and when."

The eggs arrived. "These eggs," Ben remarked, "are the best I've ever had."

"It's because they are fried in smoked bacon fat," Gabi explained and took a huge bite out of her Kaiser roll with butter and jam spread generously on it. Then, as Ben didn't comment she went back to her narrative, "He," Ben interrupted, "Who? The Rat?"

"Yes," Gabi went on, "The Rat sent us copies of all the death sentences he sent out, and informed us about his time table." Ben looked up. Gabi went on. "We are not certain yet, but we believe that the first two he named have already been executed." Ben set up straight. Gabi went on. "We don't know how this could have been possible, we don't even know if it is true, but according to The Rat's notes, Rátz József was to go first, and this was supposed to have happened two days ago, followed by Colonel Vásárhelyi, supposedly last night."

"Where were you last night?" Ben blurted out, and immediately realized that his question sounded almost accusatory and tried to correct it. "What I mean is," he was looking for words, "did you know that this was happening?"

"Of course," she looked at him with questions in her eyes, "I just told you that The Rat informed us in advance."

"So," Ben seemed to be trying to catch up to all this unexpected information, "if you knew that The Rat was going to strike," he looked at Gabi questioningly, "Couldn't you have prevent it, or even nabbed him?"

"The only thing we could, and did, do is to put an extra lookout at the only road leading to the house all these five people were supposed to be in." She then added, "You know about the stake-out at Kis Mountain."

Ben nodded. "But why was it assumed that The Rat would drive up to the cottage, or use a public road to get to the house?"

"We didn't assume that. We had local constables at every possible place The Rat could have approached the cottage but nobody saw anything."

"Couldn't you have gone in, I mean put an officer in the house with those five?"

"We could only have done that with their permission or direct request. We placed Dr. Horváth under protective custody, but had to let him go when he refused protection."

Ben thought a while. "So then what makes you so sure that The Rat actually struck and killed two people?"

"We are not sure." Gabi continued. "We suspect that The Rat might have carried out his promise. Our stake-out reports seeing only a couple of people around the cottage, one seems to be a guard, standing under the stairs going up to the second floor of the house, and being rotated regularly, but as of this morning we are seeing no guards."

"So, could they have abandoned the place?"

"Some of them might have. As I said we are seeing less then five people, but some might have left, like Dr. Horváth, or have been scratched by The Rat."

"So where is this Dr. Horváth now?"

"We believe he is on his way back to the mountain. We had him for a day and a night, but had to let him go.

"What kind of doctor is he?" Ben asked.

"He was a lawyer." When Ben looked up, she explained. "In Hungary anyone with any kind of doctorate, like a Ph.D., is entitled to be called Doctor."

Ben understood, or didn't care. "So, who are the ones The Rat caught up to?"

"Like I said, we think it's Rátz, and Colonel Vásárhelyi."

"Shouldn't you make sure?"

"We would like to, but how? If we go up to the house and barge in, they'll just tell us that whoever is not there, has left."

"Couldn't you investigate on suspicion? I mean tell those cats that you're investigating two murders and turn the house upside down. Put the fear of God into them?"

"We could Ben. But I don't think it would do any good. All it would do is tip off The Rat, and make him more careful." Ben didn't say anything and she added: "We are after The Rat. Remember?"

"What makes you think you are going to get him? I mean with only three more to go?"

Gabi sighed. "I don't know Ben. Frankly, between you and the fence post; I doubt it."

Ben loved it when Gabi used American slang, and as always, now when she came out with a slang expression so unexpectedly, he wondered where she learned all the slang she used so freely. "We thought of planting someone in the house with them," Gabi backed up a bit, but with only three of them to go we don't want to spook The Rat. We want to catch him." She explained: "When these three are gone, our chances of finding The Rat will be nil. As hard, as I know it is for an American to comprehend, we must at this point consider the remaining three, as bait."

"So, you'll just hang around till The Rat shows, if he does, for as long as it is convenient for him, even if it takes a year or two."

"It won't take a year or two," Gabi said quietly.

"It won't?" Ben looked at Gabi. "How do you know?"

"The Rat set the date," Gabi said quietly, "Dr. Horváth and Lodz Imre are to die on the 24th, exactly five days from today."

Ben was mopping his plate with a bit of his Kaiser roll. "Assuming that two have been dispatched already, that makes four." He looked up at Gabi. "What about the fifth guy?"

"The Rat made no reference to him."

"That means you won't be too busy for the next couple of days," Ben said, and wasn't sure if Gabi considered it a statement or a question. Her answer quieted his anxiety.

"Yes, Hon. Not too busy. We'll have a little time together."

*   *   *

Dr. Horváth was in a rage. His face was red and distorted with anger. "Didn't I tell you fellows to stay away from the wine?"

Lodz tried to protest. "We weren't drinking, Gyula, you must believe me."

"A lot of god damned difference that makes now," Horváth bellowed at them. "You two idiots just watched Feri being torn apart by dogs, and did nothing!?"

"We didn't know, Gyula. He was on guard but he didn't give a warning." He added sadly, "We didn't know what happened. By the time we heard the dogs, he was almost all gone."

"I should close up this place and let you two idiots fend for yourself."

Vida stood up and straightened his stance, adjusted his jacket and came over to Horváth. He clicked his heels, nodded his head in formal military manner and extended his hand towards Dr. Horváth. "I am delighted to meet you Sir. I am Lieutenant Colonel Vida Zoltán, the commanding officer of this Bureau." He swept his hand around the room, as if to indicate his office. He stood in rigid attention in front of Dr. Horváth, who didn't understand what was going on. Lodz broke in, "He's been acting funny since yesterday morning. I think," he made circles next to his temple with his index finger, "he flipped his lid."

Horváth looked at Vida. "We'll have to gag him and tie him up every night from now on.

Chapter 13

The Honeymoon

Lake Balaton glistened in the morning sunshine as Ben and Gabi stood on the mountain top scenic look-out. A gentle breeze ruffled their hair and Ben put his jacket over Gabi's shoulder. If he was ever given an opportunity to write the scenario of a perfect honeymoon, Ben didn't think he could have come up with anything even close to the marvelous time he spent with Gabi the past two days. He felt as though all the problems and cares of his life had disappeared, and that the world had only one purpose; to give him and Gabi the best times of their life. The world and everything in it were there only to make his life pleasant and full of pleasure, without a care. He was in love; more than he ever thought was possible, and knew that Gabi felt the same about him, in fact more so, if that was possible. At every turn of the road as they drove around the lake, new delights waited for them. Little restaurants high on the hillsides looking down on the huge lake with miniature ferry boats, tiny cars and miniscule humanity living out life far below them in the distance. Dinners in beautiful open-air restaurants, sitting in booths surrounded with rosebushes, and the mellow tunes of gypsy music made him feel wonderful and free of care. The two nights they spent in tiny inns, sleeping under goose-down stuffed comforters, and buying knick-knacks from street vendors, old women and young kids, taking in the natural beauty of the surroundings filled Ben with joy, and he was hoping it would never end. The Rat seemed farther and farther away with every passing minute, and as he looked at Gabi enjoying herself, he wanted to discard all the suspicions and terrible thoughts his mind had been filled with for the past days and weeks. He told himself he was wrong, way off in his thinking about The Rat, executions, murderers, all the horrors he came to help solve; a world, he at this point wanted none of. But all good things have to come to an end, he told himself, as Gabi pointed out that in about forty-five minutes they'd be back in Pápa to have dinner with Professor Kovács, her old English teacher.

"Did you like him?" Gabi asked, referring to Professor Kovács.

"Yes I did. He is a nice old fellow. He was very helpful while you were away."

"Did he tell you anything of interest?"

Ben was about to ask Gabi why she asked that question and about working on the clean-up of 36 Bástya Street, and about finding The Book, and the missing pages and cut out words, but thought the better of it. As it was, the honeymoon was almost over, and he didn't want whatever was left of it to be marred with suspicions, and questions he really didn't want answers for. The twin spires of the big church of Pápa were looming in the distance, signaling their return to the real world of crime, passion, human misery, and death.

The single bellhop at the Golden Griffin Hotel spotted Gabi's car and came running with his handcart to get their small suitcases. "We are exactly on time." Gabi looked at her watch and picked up a bunch of messages, official looking envelopes at the front desk. Ben had only one envelope, forwarded to him from New York by the Hungarian Security Agency. He didn't open it. It was too soon and too sudden to go back to the world of reality, and he didn't want to let go of the pleasant memories of the past two days.

"Let's clean up quickly," Gabi told him, "the Professor will be here in half an hour." Ben was surprised as Gabi went straight to her own room and threw him a kiss before she hurriedly slipped through the door. Ben tore the envelope open. It was a standard NYPD inter office memo. Date; Subject; From: To; CC: with a short message:

"To be attached to *Personal and Physical Profile # TR 57194-AA* on page 4, paragraph III. "

Addendum A: Caution is advised re your personal safety. It is the assumption of the profilers of TR 57194-AA that the perpetrator k.a. The Rat might be targeting you as an outsider, who might possibly upset his/her plans, and will make every effort to remove you from the scene. The wearing of bullet-proof undergarment, and heavy caliber personal weaponry is recommended at all times."

Ben threw the memo on his dresser. He did bring his flak jacket and service revolver, but had not unpacked them yet, and he didn't think that old Professor Kovács was much of a threat. He brushed his teeth, put on a necktie, and went downstairs. Gabi was already downstairs with the professor. Ben liked the old man. The professor was unpretentious, had a pleasant way of talking in quiet tones, and most of the time had a smile on his face. They walked through the archway into Kossuth Street and down to Deák Utca to the Staghorn Café. Even before they got there, Ben was beginning to smell the wonderful aroma of food, and was happy to hear Gypsy music he learned to love during their trip around Lake Balaton. The restaurant was already full, but the owner came and solicitously led them to a corner table and snapped his finger high in the air for the headwaiter. As the courses of their food materialized one after the other, Ben thought back to the restaurant where he had breakfast for the past fifteen years on Queens Boulevard, and the Greeks on Ninth Avenue, the Chinese takeout place that consistently lost his address, and the pizza place that was his last resort after a long and tiring day on the job. He loved the food and enjoyed the wine, the Aszu of Tokay, which the professor explained was better than medicine for almost everything that ailed one. They drank the wine from tiny crystal goblets that—as the professor pointed out— were to be sipped but had to be emptied once one picked up the glass. As soon as the goblets were put down, a waiter jumped to refill them. The professor toasted them again and again and put one glass of Aszu after the other away. Ben followed suit. When they got back to the hotel about two hours later, Ben didn't remember any part of the walk from the restaurant, and wasn't quite sure he was going to be able to make the stairs up to the second floor to his room. He almost didn't hear the old prof invite them for a nightcap at the hotel bar, and before he even realized it they were in the bar, the professor handed him a small glass of pinkish liquid. "This is barack pálinka, Mr. Chapman, the nectar of the Universe. It is real Hungarian apricot brandy, and any other apricot brandy is only an imitation." He explained further, "Unlike the Aszu, you must drink this down in one gulp, and must say *Köszönöm, egészségére* immediately. *Köszönöm, egészségére* means 'Thank you, to your health." Ben drank the small shot glass in one swallow and didn't know what hit him. The pink liquid burnt a path all the way to his stomach, his throat was about to explode and as he tried to say '*köszönöm, egészségére*' he gagged on his words. He could hear the professor and Gabi laughing as if from a distance, but his world was slowly disappearing as he fought his eyes that were trying to close. He tried to keep his balance. As hard as it was to have reasonable thoughts, it suddenly occurred to him that the non-stop travel, sightseeing, going from one restaurant to another, having non-stop sex, and the anxieties that crammed his brain, sapped his strength. The huge dinner at the Staghorne Café with endless rounds of Aszu, and now this torpedo-juice called Barack Pálinka, put him completely out of business. He tried to excuse himself to go upstairs, but didn't think he could do it. He sensed that Gabi and the bellhop maneuvered him up the stairs and into his room. He remembered Gabi giving him a glass of Mineral water, and he had the sensation of someone taking his shoes off and arranging his head on the pillow. After that, it was lights out.

* * *

. . . thirty minutes later on Kis Mountain . . .

Dr. Horváth woke with a start. His hand reached for his revolver, as the knocking on his door persisted and became louder than when it woke him. He shook Lodz's shoulder. "Who is it?" He called out, trying to insert some strength into his voice. "Police. Open up!" A commanding voice answered. Horváth and Lodz were getting out of their sleeping bags, Lodz fumbling, trying to find the meat cleaver in the dark. "Open the door, now." The voice demanded. "How do I know you are the police?" Horváth called out meekly. "Don't open the door and you'll find out. You have five seconds."

Horváth removed the heavy wood pole that was braced against the door and reached for the doorknob, but the door exploded into his face as it was kicked in. Horváth raised the revolver, but another ferocious kick sent it flying from his hand. "Put that down, the police woman pointed at the meat cleaver in Lodz's hand, and pushed her way into the room. Horváth stepped back. He didn't expect such ferocity from the dumpy little red faced police woman, in an oversized, ill-fitting long coat, her dirty blond hair sticking out in every direction from under a small hat.

"Put your hands up." She commanded. "One stupid move and I'll blow your brains out." She spun Dr. Horváth and Lodz around to face the wall. The attack was so unexpected, so powerful and swift that the two men, who were scared out of their wits, obeyed, and before they knew it, their hands were cuffed behind their backs. "Which one of you is Dr. Horváth?" The police woman asked. "I am." Horváth answered. "So then, you are Lodz Imre?" She pointed at Lodz. He nodded. "Both of you are under arrest for suspicion of murder."

Horváth became agitated. "For suspicion of what murder?" He didn't expect the incredibly fast and powerful slap across his face that buckled his knees and sent him reeling against the wall. "One more word out of you and I'll blow your head off." She took a piece of paper from her pocket. "You are accused of complicity in the death of Vásárhelyi Ferenc and Rátz József."

"That's preposterous! We didn't kill . . ." But Horváth couldn't finish. Her hand lashed out again and slapped his face with such force that it made Horváth's ear ring in pain. "Let's go." The police woman reached down to pick up Dr. Horváth's gun and indicated for them to get out of the room. "You know the way," she told them, "I am taking you in, in your car. Your car is impounded. Get going." She kicked Horváth in the butt and pushed Lodz forward. The two, with their hands cuffed behind their back, slipped and slid on the steep, muddy path on their way down to the press house where Horváth's Mercedes was parked.

They passed the camouflaged car at the bottom of the hill and Dr. Horváth noticed that Lieutenant Hegedüs was looking at them, but didn't stop them and didn't put his spotlight on. Kis Mountain receded into the darkness behind them, and soon they were on the paved road, going in the opposite direction from Pápa.

Dr. Horváth looked around, "Where are you taking us?" The car came to a screeching halt and the little policewoman jumped out. She almost ripped the rear door off its hinges and dragged Horváth out of the backseat. Horváth felt the blow smash his nose and heard the bone splinter. A kick in his groin doubled him up and a chop to the back of his neck sent him sprawling onto the pavement. He felt the kicks into his ribs and the side of his face, and half consciously felt his body being dragged and stuffed into the back seat. He heard the door slam shut and the front door close also. The car was under way again. Horváth was slumped forward and Lodz was paralyzed with fear. Finally the car slowed and they heard the crunch of gravel under the tires, and the bouncing of the car told them that they were off the main road, somewhere in the country. There were no roadside lights and the car swayed, going with undulating motion and Horváth knew that they were somewhere in a field with hollows, mounds, rocks and potholes. He felt the car stop and heard the front door open. The back door also opened almost immediately and he heard the voice of the policewoman. "Get out. This is the end of the ride." Lodz got out and helped Horváth struggle out of the car. There was enough moonlight for them to make out the outline of a tank, complete with cannon and the open hatch cover at the top of the turret. She produced a short chain with cuffs at each end and slapped them on Lodz's ankles. She unlocked the cuff on Lodz's left wrist and twisted his arms to the front, then re-cuffed them. "Get up there," she commanded Lodz and helped him struggle up on the tank. "Here is what I want you to do. I want you to help me put Dr. Horváth in the tank, but be very careful. I don't want him hurt. I want both of you to enjoy the ride."

In a couple of minutes, both Horváth and Lodz were inside the hollow belly of the tank. Both were seated on the floor and the police woman expertly tied Lodz's hands to a protruding feature with wire. "As you can see," she pointed to the empty interior, "everything has been removed from this deadly machine. Do you know why?" she asked, but didn't wait for an answer. "Everything was removed because this instrument of death is obsolete. It is an old World War II tank of no further military use." She paused, looking down into the cramped cavity in the belly of the tank, with Horváth and Lodz cowering on the bottom. "It can't be deployed in combat; it has no further military use, except one. It is used as a target." The two inside the tank squirmed. She continued, "You see, gentlemen, you are in the target area of the Hajmáskér artillery range, and this old vehicle of past glories is now the main target of the range. At dawn this morning," she looked at the glowing dial of her watch, "about three and a half hours from now, some new army tanks will be concluding their exercise at this range by firing on all the old hardware with live shells." She waited and let her words sink in. "You will hear the tanks and the artillery pieces coming closer from the distance, and you will hear their guns fire. And then, a few seconds later, you will hear the shells hit the targets around you and feel this old tank rock and heave before it too will be hit." She paused for another second. "But to make your experience a bit more interesting and exciting, I have a present for you. These," she dropped some gallon jugs on top of Horváth and Lodz, "are filled with gasoline and old motor oil. They will light up the occasion." She took her bulky long-coat off. "And this will add fuel to the flames. I won't need it any more, and I won't need any of this masquerade." She threw her cap and the blond wig into the tank and unbuckled her belt with the holster on it. "And here is another present, my gun and your gun Doctor Horváth. You might try to shoot yourselves, though I doubt that you could with your hands tied, or that you'd have the courage."

Only her voice gave away her satisfaction in the dark. "I know that by now you know who I really am. I am The Rat, your judge and executioner. I went to all this trouble, bringing you here to these hallowed grounds because, you see, today marks the anniversary of the day when the remains of Landau Miklós and his fourteen years old son were unearthed by an exploding shell, almost at this very spot. You had them killed, amongst so many others, and had them buried here in a shallow grave. Today is your judgment day. But your remains will not be found. A handful or two of ashes maybe, a couple of charred handcuffs, but I will see to it that the world will know why, and how, you died,"

Horváth and Lodz heard the lid of the old tank slam closed above them, and a second later the Mercedes' Diesel engine started to purr.

*   *   *

Ben thought he was paralyzed. His arms and legs felt like lead and it was painful as he tried to open his eyes. He felt Gabi's warm body stir gently against his, and he knew that her leg was wrapped around his stomach but trying to move was painful and he slipped back into a coma-like sleep. It had to be hours later when the aroma of strong Hungarian coffee woke him. The room was bright with sunshine that hurt his eyes, but he could move his legs and arms, and he could sit up in his bed though his head was still pounding. Gabi was pouring coffee, her silk robe was open in front, revealing the most sensuous parts of her heavenly body. "Good morning, Lazy Bones," she smiled and handed him a cup of steaming coffee. "Welcome back from the dead."

Ben rubbed his face. "Holy mackerel." He tried to focus his eyes, "What hit me?"

"I shouldn't have let the old professor put you through 'Drinking Hungarian Booze 101.' She smiled and gently stroked the back of Ben's neck. But Ben didn't think that booze alone could have put him away so thoroughly. He was no teetotaler. He considered himself a graduate of the Jack Daniels School of whiskey sipping, and although he wasn't a drunk, he had demonstrated his capacity for alcohol with some of the best of the NYPD on several occasions. Slowly the images of the night before were floating back into his head. He remembered the old professor holding his glass high, smiling, and urging him on to empty his in one gulp. "What was that poison you guys fed me last night?" He asked Gabi. "It's funny," she kissed him on the forehead, "That stuff has less alcohol than just about any 80 proof whiskey or gin, or vodka. But if you're not used to it," she added, "it has the kick of a mule."

Ben sipped his coffee. It was strong, and it was already helping to clear his head. "I wonder what the Big Cat would think of this." He tried to smile at Gabi. "The big what?" she asked, not understanding Ben. "The Big Cat, Commissioner Katz, my boss."

"Ah, the Commissioner." Gabi let out a small laugh and laughed. "I'll send him a full report."

"Don't you dare."

"But I will." Gabi was mock serious. "I'll tell him all about your heroic and magnificent fight against The Rat. And how hard you are working, helping us catch him."

"Yeah. Right." Ben rubbed his throbbing temples. "And I'll tell him that the only reason you asked for my help is to get at my body."

"Well, . . ." she said coyly, "that is true. But," she added accusingly, "I surely didn't get much of it last night. You were out like a light. El Deado."

Ben couldn't get over her slang. "How did you sleep?" he asked her.

"Very well, no thanks to you."

"I don't remember saying good night to you."

"You didn't. You didn't even move after I put you to bed and I thought I'd stay with you in case you were going to die. I wanted you to go with a smile on your face, but you didn't give me the opportunity."

"You mean I didn't die?!"

"No. I mean give me an opportunity to put a smile on your face."

"You obviously didn't try hard enough."

"You know," she wrinkled her eyebrows in mock puzzlement, "maybe I didn't. Have some more coffee, and I'll try harder."

*   *   *

The road was in pretty good condition, but as soon as they got to the gravel road leading up to Kis Mountain, every rut, pothole, and bump jarred Ben's brain and sent shooting pains through his stomach, spine and neck. He was wondering what he was doing here. Why was he in Hungary? Why was he going to Kis Mountain, trying to corner an elusive killer, The Rat, without having a say in any of what was going on? The whole thing seemed more like a charade than police work. But if he could believe The Rat; if it were true that there were only three more candidates marked for death— After getting away with twenty-two, The Rat was never going to be caught, and as far as he was concerned, that was all right.

"So you think you're gonna get The Rat this time?" He cocked his head towards Gabi, as far as his aching neck permitted him.

"For sure," Gabi used a bit of Americanism, "he has to come to the cottage, and by Saturday morning we'll have him, and the place will be locked up as tight as a drum."

"What makes you so sure he is going to strike Friday night?"

Gabi looked at him. "So far, everything he told us checked out 100 percent. I have no reason not to believe him."

"I agree." Ben said. "In the States, most of these kinds of rub-outs happen in the early morning hours."

Gabi shook her head. "When The Rat says Friday, it doesn't mean Saturday morning." She nodded her head for emphasis. "The Rat will strike before midnight." She pulled up behind the look-out car and turned off the engine. "I am bringing in twelve specialists from BP; Budapest," she explained, "and even my boss is coming down to be part of the take down." Ben listened, quietly rubbing the back of his aching neck. Gabi continued, "My plan is, that exactly at midnight the noose will tighten around the house and, depending on what is going to be observed, or heard, we'll enter the house."

"A big mistake," Ben said quietly.

"Why?" Gabi looked at Ben with a puzzled expression.

"Did it ever occur to you that The Rat might have designated a time just to throw you off?"

"Yes, it did. But our experts don't believe this is the case here. In fact they are convinced The Rat is taunting us. They believe he wants to show us up and do these two in, under our very noses."

"Your experts," Ben almost had a bit of noticeable sarcasm in his voice, "might even expect him to take a bow?"

"As a matter of fact, Ben, some of our experts have expressed a theory that The Rat wants to be captured."

"That's very interesting," Ben replied quietly. "Our experts," he underlined 'experts' with a snide overtone to his voice, "believe that someone like The Rat, might want to kill himself after he does away with his last customers." He looked at Gabi. "I guess I didn't have a chance to show you the Personal Psychological and Physical Profile my experts prepared for me." She didn't answer and Ben figured that if she hadn't, the Hungarian Security Agency had seen the Personal Psychological and Physical Profile, most likely before he had. But her next question surprised him, "What else did your experts have to say, Ben?"

"They said," Ben smiled at her, "this case was in some of its aspects typical and in some of its other aspects atypical. They said The Rat might do this, or might do that, and also that The Rat might not do this or that. They also figured that The Rat might be over six feet tall, unless he is under six feet. But they are pretty sure," Ben smiled, "that The Rat is strong, because of all the evidence that we have about the physical accomplishments of The Rat, and the experts didn't have to guess about that. And I also agree with the experts that The Rat is most probably a man, though could be a woman." He looked at Gabi but there was no visible reaction. Her face remained expressionless.

"Let's go say hello to Inspector Hegedüs," she opened the car door, "see if he has anything of interest to report."

Lieutenant Hegedüs must have seen them get out of the car behind his and he got out to greet them.

"Anything of interest?" Gabi asked as they shook hands.

"Not much," Hegedüs shook his head, and Ben understood and sympathized with the Inspector. There was no job more boring than stake-out duty. He remembered the countless hours of sheer boredom, sitting in a car with nothing happening. It had to be worse here, he looked around and saw the desolate hillside, the little house halfway up the hill, and not a soul in sight. Hegedüs continued, "I saw Dr. Horváth's car leave last night around midnight, and come back this morning. I can't be sure, it was pretty dark and I didn't want to turn the spotlight on, but I think he had some of the others with him."

"When did they come back?" Gabi asked.

"It was just before five," the inspector looked at his notes, "but I almost didn't see them because Horváth had his lights off and I didn't see them until just about the time they passed me."

"You've seen them since?" Gabi asked.

"No." The inspector looked up towards the house, "I think these people sleep during the day."

Ben cut in, "I would, if I were them."

The inspector laughed. "I haven't seen anything this morning."

Gabi looked up the hill at the cottage and scanned the entire hillside. The neat rows of grapes were almost ready to harvest, and their leaves formed solid paths between the rows. "An ideal place for The Rat to attack," Gabi commented. Inspector Hegedüs and Ben followed her look. Hegedüs agreed. "The killer could come from a hundred directions."

Chapter 14

The Night of The Rat

Chief Inspector Albert Szekeres reminded Ben of Commissioner Katz the moment he first laid eyes on him. He seemed to have the same 'I am such a nice guy,' though impatient, overbearing personality, and Ben had no doubt that he was a politician through-and-through. Now that the game was coming to the end, he was going to be in on it, right in the front lines where the cameras were likely to be, and take credit for the whole operation if it was successful, or hand out blame if it was not. At this point he was still handing out praise to those whose work could make him a hero, all of whom knew that they would be sacrificed in a moment if it was in the Chief Inspector's interest. The lavish breakfast upstairs in the private dining hall at the Golden Griffin Hotel was to be followed by a briefing of the staff by the Chief Inspector, which was to be followed by a press conference. Ben was prepared by Gabi that the Chief Inspector expected him to sit next to him at the press briefing, and that Gabi was to act as interpreter.

Ben wasn't looking forward to this event, which he knew was going to be a charade built around an important event without any regard to how that important event was going to play out. The objective was to grab headlines, assert one's importance, and let the world know of the tremendous job one did on behalf of humanity. The fact that 22 people were dead, and that the Hungarian Security Agency, under the leadership of Chief Inspector Albert Szekeres completely bungled the job—Ben thought—didn't seem to be important, nor was the possibility that The Rat might do away with the last three of his victims and get off scott free for all eternity. Frankly, Ben didn't care. He was here, he knew he was part of the charade, and he was going to play it to the end.

He heard the Chief Inspector's fork tapping his water glass, and saw him stand up. The room quieted down.

"Contrary to the expected briefing, I have nothing to add to what information has already been distributed to all of you. The plan, as prepared by Captain Kerek and her staff will commence at eighteen hundred hours this evening and will terminate with the apprehension of the perpetrator known as The Rat. I have been assured that the likelihood of apprehending the perpetrator is high. In the unlikely event that the perpetrator might not be apprehended, the present plan will be considered concluded and we will switch to plan "B" which will be distributed tomorrow, after the standard post mortem. Good luck to all."

Chief Inspector Albert Szekeres motioned to his aide de camp to let the reporters in. The double doors at the far end of the hall burst open and a bunch of reporters and photographers pushed into the room. The Chief Inspector waited till all were situated and the room quieted down. He once again tapped his fork on his glass.

"Good morning Ladies and Gentlemen," the Chief Inspector started. "Now that we are at the eve of a great victory, my gratitude goes out to, and I want to congratulate, all who so willingly and unselfishly denied their personal comforts, and dedicated their life to this very important case. The men and women of the Hungarian Security Agency, and their counterparts world wide, including the efforts of smaller police forces throughout the country, showed exceptional professionalism and dedication, and my gratitude is extended to all. The international importance can not be over-emphasized. Police organizations all over the world lent us their help and expertise. Captain Chapman, the legendary top investigator, the very best of the New York Police Department," he pointed and gave a very broad, theatrical gesture at Ben sitting next to him, "came all the way from America to help us out. We are grateful for his help, and very much appreciate his interest and experience. And I extend my gratitude to Commissioner Arthur Katz of the New York Police Department for his willingness to help us. Captain Chapman will answer your questions now."

Ben wasn't comfortable with this. He didn't like being put on the spot without some kind of notice, and particularly disliked being used, but he remembered Bill Frederick's advice after his meeting with Commissioner Katz. As Bill put it; "The political world of the New York City Police Department spins on bullshit." Not much different from this one, and he figured if these cats wanted to play the game, he would accommodate them.

"Do you think you will catch The Rat?" A young reporter asked. "We'll give it our best shot," Ben answered and Captain Kerek translated and explained the American slang. "Where do you think The Rat is now?" Another reporter pressed him. "We believe The Rat is near by," Ben answered. "How many people did The Rat kill so far?" "Why have you not caught him till now?" "Why did the New York Police get involved?" "Who is The Rat targeting here in Pápa?" "Isn't it embarrassing that the police forces world wide failed in apprehending The Rat?" "Why is The Rat targeting these people?" Ben had enough. "Perhaps Chief Inspector Szekeres could answer that better."

Chief Inspector Szekeres gave a condescending smile. "As in all cases similar to this one, a serial killer is convinced that he is doing a good deed for humanity. In this case, all the subjects The Rat targeted had criminal backgrounds dating back to the days of the persecution of Jews during the Holocaust. All The Rat's victims were involved in those crimes to some extent."

"Is it true that The Rat left notes at every one of his crime scenes?"

The Chief Inspector turned to Captain Kerek. "We'll let Captain Kerek who, incidentally, is the responsible officer heading up this investigation, answer that."

"The Rat did leave notes at every one of his crime scenes."

"Did he name his next victim?" one of the reporters wanted to know.

"That's classified at this point," Gabriella stated flatly.

"Why has it taken this long to inform the World Press?" "Why is it taking all these years to apprehend a killer?" "What if you don't catch him this time either?" The questions went on and on, and Ben thought how all these press conferences were the same here as at home. The Reporters were digging, were never satisfied, and all of them thought they were on a mission of humiliating whomever they were questioning. But the press conference was petering out, and breaking up. One by one the reporters, grabbing a leftover sandwich, or a bottle of soda, were slowly leaving the place. The room was emptying out. One of the reporters, a young man about forty cornered Ben and asked in pretty good English, "Wouldn't you agree, Captain Chapman, that The Rat's victims should have been hanged long ago?" Ben was startled by the question. "What do you mean?" he asked for lack of anything else he could think of. "I mean that they were the worse of the worst. Every one of them should have been quartered years ago!" Ben nodded and the reporter walked away from him. Ben felt badly, but had to agree with the reporter who reinforced his own feelings. At this very moment, catching The Rat was not very high on his priorities. Most of the people, Gabi, Inspector Hegedüs, Cadet Officer Mohácsi and some others he had never seen before were gathered around Chief Inspector Szekeres who seemed to be enjoying the limelight. The local cops, in their dress uniforms were huddling amongst themselves, and Ben decided it was time to leave.

He was glad that nobody noticed him walking out of the hall. He went directly to his room, and as soon as he was inside the room, picked up the translations of the latest communication from The Rat that Gabi had prepared for him. He read, and re-read the death sentences, and was startled to read that Rátz and Colonel Vásárhelyi were indeed, already dead. The note gave a detailed account of Colonel Vásárhelyi's death, but referred to Rátz József's death only as "at the hands of his comrades." The Rat gave no indication where the remains were in either of the cases, other than saying that the remains were handled by the remaining three; Dr. Horváth, Lodz Imre, and Lieutenant Colonel Vida. One sentence jumped out at Ben. He read, and re-read it several times: *It is much to my relief that the Almighty had commuted Lieutenant Colonel Vida's sentence; to be confined to his own world, as it exists only in his mind, for the rest of his natural life.* What did this mean? What was Colonel Vida's own world?" He thought the answer would present itself by midnight, or shortly after.

He was going to be up pretty much the whole night, and he thought he'd grab some "z"s before it was time to go. Ben lay down on his bed and closed his eyes. Suddenly he realized that tonight might be his last night on the case, and more devastatingly, the last night in Pápa, and Hungary, and with Gabi. Panic swept his mind. He didn't think of this before, but now that it was on top of him, the realization was too sudden, too devastating, and he became very upset. He couldn't imagine the world, or his life, without Gabi. He knew he fell asleep, and he thought it was merciful, but his heart was heavy. Thinking about losing Gabi, he felt as if this whole experience was comparable to the condemned man's last meal. His relationship with Gabi, since the first night at the Universal Sheraton Hotel in Hollywood till this very moment, was a meal, the last of a condemned man, but at midnight his life was going to come to its end.

The shrill ringing of the phone jarred him awake. It was Gabi. He figured immediately that with the chief inspector in the same hotel, Gabi—understandably—didn't want to come to his room to fetch him. But as Gabi spoke, he looked at his watch and knew that it was time to go. He hopped off his bed and fished his bulletproof flak-jacket from his suitcase. He strapped on his pistol belt, and knew that both the flak-jacket and the pistol belt would most probably be unnecessary props in the charade.

Gabi was in her car in front of the hotel as he came out to the main square and squeezed into the front seat. The Bobsy Twins, Inspector Hegedüs and Cadet Officer Mohácsi were in the back seat of the little car, and the moment he closed the door, Gabi floored the pedal and the little car screeched away onto Main Street.

The daylight was almost completely gone as they turned off the paved highway and onto the gravel road, which eventually brought them to the dirt road below the vineyards. The camouflaged police car was moved back from where it was before, and Gabi explained that she didn't want to risk The Rat seeing the lookout, and bolting. Ben nodded, but inwardly felt that this, as well as every other aspect of this exercise was a charade, to be played for reasons he thought he understood. But he was with Gabi, and that was all that mattered. He wanted to tell her: "Let's you and I get the hell out of here. The hell with The Rat! Who cares if he kills more of these bastards. It's you and I that matter. Turn the car around, let these clowns out, and let's you and I keep going until we die together. The thought of losing Gabi was exploding in his brain, and he tried to tell himself that his love for her blinded him. He tried to tell himself that his love for her, the thought of possibly losing her, tricked him into believing the worst, and that none of his thoughts were reasonable or right. He had no good, solid reasons to assume that his theories were right, and even the reporter who walked away from him could have been The Rat. A million other people might be The Rat and, it suddenly dawned on him, that if Gabi was The Rat, how could she be sitting in the car with him and the others at the time when The Rat promised to kill two more people. It occurred to him that Gabi would have to kill all of them, before she could kill Dr. Horváth and Lodz Imre. He was confused, but he preferred to be confused with contradictory ideas, than to believe that he knew who The Rat was.

They all got out at the look-out car and stretched their legs. Cadet Officer Mohácsi was to stay behind and Inspector Hegedüs was to drive them to the press house at the bottom of the hill. Captain Kerek turned to Mohácsi, "In the event a motorcycle officer, or any messenger, comes from Chief Inspector Szekeres, direct him immediately to me at the press house. Mohácsi said, "Yes *Kapitan*," and they got back into Gabi's little car. Dr. Horváth's Mercedes was in its regular place alongside the press house, and a uniformed local constable stood by and saluted them at the entrance to the building. Hegedüs took off in Gabi's car with the constable, and Ben followed Gabi into the press house. The smell of mildew hit him and he thought he saw some small animals, possibly rats, scamper under the huge vats and barrels. He could make out a press in the middle of the large place, and followed Gabi to the only window. He barely saw the cottage on the hillside above them, but other than that the hillside seemed desolate and dark.

Moonlight broke through the clouds for a few seconds at a time, only to hide behind another cloud and let the vineyard be buried in darkness again. This whole operation seemed overly dramatic and completely ridiculous to Ben. Nobody would be able to spot The Rat in this darkness, and even if The Rat did show, by the time they realized he was around, and climbed to the cottage on the steep, narrow path in the dark, Horváth and Lodz would be dead, and The Rat would be in the next county before they ever got close to the cottage. All they would find would be two stiffs, possibly buried under a mound of human dung. He suddenly remembered the Köröndi case, and thought about the other victims of The Rat and the circumstances of their deaths. How could she, he looked at Gabi in the darkness of the press house, have dealt with the physical aspects of the Köröndi case? As athletic and energetic as she was, overpowering a man like Köröndi, or SS Hauptsha . . . what's his face, Conrad Hagelhoff in the Venezuelan jungle, or even dealing with the Molnár case, if it was she who killed Mr. Molnár, well, he thought, it just couldn't be. He was so concerned at losing her that these crazy ideas, all based on circumstantial crap, only a stupid flatfoot like himself could've come up with, filled his head with idiotic ideas, and even when some of them made sense, he reassured himself, just plain and simple, it couldn't be. Gabi was two feet from him, even in the dark he could smell the fantastic scents of her body, and he felt better, as he told himself that he was nuts. Gabi was here, and The Rat was supposed to strike in the cottage above them. He felt like reaching out for her, pulling her to him and kissing her. But he didn't. The dark thoughts surfaced in his mind again, and he sadly admitted that there were two people alive who really knew who The Rat was. He was one, and the other had to be Gabi.

He felt Gabi turn to him in the dark. Her silhouette, actually her half silhouette as she was standing to one side of the window was reality; and her voice, almost whispering, came as a reminder that she was there in real life, and couldn't have been The Rat.

"Do you think The Rat will come?" She asked, her voice ringing with anxiety and hope.

"Yes," Ben answered, "The Rat is already here."

"How do you know that?" she asked, and Ben thought he detected a note of fear in her voice.

"You remember our meeting with Hill and his guys in California?" Ben asked.

"Lieutenant Hill?"

"Yes," Ben replied in hushed tones.

"Yes, I do."

"You remember what Lieutenant Hill said about my nose?"

Gabi was puzzled. "What?"

"He said he had me checked out, and heard from the New York guys that my nose could smell a rat from a mile. Remember?"

"I think so," she said hesitantly, not knowing where this was leading. "And can your nose do that?"

Ben nodded. He tapped the side of his nose with his index finger, but realized that she couldn't see him. "This nose can smell a rat from a mile." His hand reached for his revolver under his jacket.

"Can it smell The Rat now?" Gabi tried to force a smile.

Ben nodded affirmatively, but when he realized that Gabi couldn't see it, he whispered, "Yes."

"Is The Rat close?" Gabi sounded anxious.

"Very close." Ben looked at her silhouette and saw that she turned her head away and looked up the hill towards the cottage.

"You think we'll catch him?" she asked tentatively.

"I don't know," Ben replied, "according to the profile my guys sent me from New York, he or she, he emphasized the 'she,' might make a mistake, slip up, and we'll have a chance to get him or her, but according to the profile, he or she," he once again underlined the 'she,' "slipping up is not likely."

"So you don't think we'll get her?" She corrected herself. "Him or her? The Rat, I mean?"

"I think. . ." he emphasized his words, speaking slowly, "I hope, I will get The Rat."

She smiled at Ben. "You, single handedly?"

But Ben was serious. "I'll give it my best shot."

She didn't answer, or comment, and Ben went back to his thoughts. Whatever was going to happen, he told himself, he hoped that Gabi was not going to get hurt. And, if he was right, and he was convinced that he, and only he and she knew who The Rat was, the secret was safe with him, and he was going to take Gabi away from this place, The Rat murders, the Hungarian police, even if he had to hit her over the head. He looked at his watch again. The luminescent dial told him that it was only ten minutes past ten, almost two more hours to go before the midnight deadline. There was nothing to do now but wait. He thought he heard The Rats scamper under the barrels, and noticed that his feet were getting cold. "I hope The Rat is gonna come soon." Ben said. "My feet are getting cold."

"I'll warm them up later," she replied, "but I also hope he is going to come soon. I can think of better ways to spend a Saturday night than standing in the dark in this rat's nest."

"You can?"

"You bet your butt."

"Where did you learn all this slang?" Ben asked.

"In school."

"That reminds me," Ben lightened up a little, "your old professor, Professor Kovács, that drunken bastard, told me that you were the best in his class and that he sent you abroad to learn English. Is that true?"

"Aha. It's true."

"Well, that's something new." Ben tried to see her features in the dark. "You are a real mystery lady. Anything else I ought to know about you?"

"No. That's it."

"No other deep, dark secrets?"'

"No. That's it."

"So how come you don't speak the King's English, like Professor Kovács?"

"I didn't go to England."

"You didn't?"

"Ah, ah."

"Where did you go?"

"I went to the States."

"The United States," Ben was surprised, "like in America?"

"Aha."

"Well. That's a surprise." He paused to think this over a bit. Gabi was a real mystery woman. "Where in America did you go to school?"

"In New Hampshire."

"New Hampshire?" Ben repeated. "How in hell did you wind up in New Hampshire?"

"My school, here in Pápa, had an exchange program with the Phillips Exeter Academy in Exeter, New Hampshire." She added, "I spent two years at the Exeter Academy."

Something was trying to surface in Ben's mind. It felt like 'barf' was trying to come up again, but Ben didn't know what. The strange feelings returned, and Ben was beginning to feel uncomfortable again. "So you really learned English in an American school."

"Yes. At the Phillips Exeter Academy in New Hampshire."

"How did your school, here, pick a school in New Hampshire?"

She laughed. "The Phillips Exeter Academy is probably the best school in America."

"The Phillips Exeter Academy." Ben repeated quietly. "I've never heard of it." Then, the 'barf' came up. Ben suddenly remembered Gabi's laundry bag, the one that had the three, faded large letters, "PEA" on it. He remembered doing Gabi's laundry when she had to go back to Hungary suddenly, and he decided to ask her about the letters on her bag. Now he knew what they meant. PEA, the Phillips Exeter Academy. "No wonder you speak English, I mean American so well." Ben thought for a while. Now I understand. "How old were you when you went to the Phillips Exeter Academy?"

"Fifteen and seventeen." She added, "I lived with one of the teachers and their fac-brats."

"Fac-brats? What's that?" Ben was astonished.

"Their children. Faculty brats. Fac-brats. Their oldest son was a year older than I. I learned a lot from him."

"Well, that's kind of obvious. What else did you learn from him?"

"That's none of your business, Ben Chapman." She laughed and added, "I learned how to say 'Please' and 'thank you' from him . . ."

Ben cut her off. "Did he learn anything from you?"

She laughed. "Plenty. He and I learned everything else from books and magazines like Playboy. He was a nice boy, but kind of simple. He thought that the little thing between his legs was to take a leak only."

"No doubt you straightened him out?!"

"I did. I thought he was going to have a fit when we first made out in the woods behind the football stadium."

Ben looked at his watch again and was surprised how fast the time flew when he didn't pay attention to it. It was twenty minutes to twelve. 'The bewitching hour,' Ben thought and wondered why they were going through with this charade. He knew that The Rat was not going to strike. The Rat was standing next to him, acting out her part, but he hadn't quite figured out what her game was. "In another twenty minutes you can send Chief Inspector Szekeres a message that The Rat failed to show and plan "B" is now in effect."

"He wants me to report to him personally. No matter what time," she said and Ben thought she sighed exaggeratedly, and judging by the tone of her voice, imagined that she was rolling her eyes.

"He probably likes you," Ben said in mock understanding.

"He likes everybody, as long as they have a skirt on. I know he tried to hit on the good looking desk-clerk and, would you know, the simple son of a bitch tried to put the moves on me."

Ben let out a little laugh. "He can't possibly have an idea of what he missed."

"You mean that?" she asked with appreciation in her voice.

"I sure do. I certainly couldn't have."

She quietly moved closer to Ben. He felt her fingers reaching for his belt and his zipper. "Shouldn't you be watching the hillside?" he asked.

"I can do both." She was slipping out of her slacks. "Besides," she said out of breath, "The Rat isn't coming tonight."

"How do you know?" Ben asked, though he didn't really care as he felt himself slipping into her.

"The time is almost up. Even if he showed up now, there is not enough time for him to finish the job before tomorrow." She was breathing heavily. "It's almost tomorrow."

They finished quickly and Ben held on, not wanting to let go of her. The clouds cleared for a second and moonlight shone through the window. Ben looked at his watch. It was four minutes past midnight. He kissed her over and over again. "I guess we are on the job a little longer. It doesn't look like The Rat showed up tonight."

"We'll have to make sure," she said. "I'll give it a few more minutes and we'll go see."

"Then what?"

"Then," Ben could see her turning to him in the moonlight, "When we find Dr. Horváth and his cohort Lodz in a puddle of blood, I'll go report to Chief Inspector Keszeres, and," she leaned over to kiss Ben, "I'll resign."

"Why would you do that?"

"The case is closed, Ben." But Ben could tell that she had more to say. "I am tired of all this killing. I don't want to die an old police pensioner; I want to raise a family . . ." She stopped and Ben did not press her. "But let's finish the job first." She reached for her walkie-talkie. "All units," Ben heard her talk into the microphone. "This is Captain Kerek. On my signal, one red flare, all units converge on the subject building. I repeat, on my signal, one red flare, all units converge on the subject building. Do not fire unless fired upon. Do not fire unless fired upon. Do not enter perimeter "A" until second red flare. Do not enter perimeter "A" until second red flare. Out."

"Are you coming, Ben?"

"Wouldn't miss catching The Rat for the world."

"You might still do that." She smiled at Ben and offered a hand to help him get off the barrel.

The moon played cat and mouse with the clouds as Gabi and Ben were slowly making their way up towards the cottage on the narrow, slippery path. The house was just above and ahead of them, but there was no sign of life inside. Ben could make out the steps going up to the second floor, and reached for his revolver as they got to the stone deck around the base of the house. Gabi already had her pistol and flattened herself against the wall next to the door. Ben tried the doorknob. The door gave and opened easily. Gabi shined her flashlight inside, but aside from a mound of old, rotting potatoes there was nothing in the room. She was about to start up the steps when Ben tapped her on the shoulder. "Me go first," he whispered. She didn't object. The dogs were barking in the distance and Ben looked around, but couldn't see anything other than a few trees and objects around the house. He hunkered down, going under the window to the door, sort of expecting to hear a gunshot and a bullet hitting him in the back. Gabi was right behind him. The door was slightly open. He cautiously pushed it open and Gabi flashed her light in. The room appeared to be empty. They walked in. There were four sleeping bags on the floor, but they were empty. "I guess we got here a little late." Ben bent down to feel the inside of one of the bedrolls "It's cold," he said. "Hasn't been slept in for a while." Her flashlight searched the room and stopped on the garrote hanging from the nail next to the door. The flashlight's beam also picked up some yellow sheets of paper on the table. Ben picked them up. He looked at each of the sheets and showed them to Gabi. "Aren't these the death sentences?" Gabi took the sheets and nodded. "Yes. They are." Ben took them from her and put them in his pocket.

A smaller door was leading into the small kitchen. They entered cautiously. On a long bench, just under the window, Ben spotted what looked like the body of a person. He grabbed Gabi's wrist and aimed her light at the bench. The body seemed to be moving slightly. His eyes were open wide, but his mouth was gagged, and a rope went clear around his body and the bench. "It's Colonel Vida," Gabi said quietly. Ben untied the gag but Colonel Vida couldn't talk. He tried to clear his throat and made hissing sounds, but his tongue was in a knot at the base of his parched mouth. Ben untied the rope and helped him sit up. Colonel Vida slumped back onto the bench. He seemed to be paralyzed. "I wonder how long he's been tied up like this." Ben said. "Looks like too long," Gabi replied. "I guess

---

The Rat missed him," Ben remarked.

"It may be that The Rat didn't need to bother," Gabi nodded her head towards Vida. His lips were moving. Sounds began to come from his lips and he tried to get up but he couldn't. "I am Colonel Vida." He finally managed to say. "How may I be of service to you?" Gabi translated and asked Vida, "Have you seen The Rat?" He smiled, finding his voice returning. "There may be rats in the cells below, Madam, but there are no rats here in my office." He laughed again. "Just one moment." He tried to get up again. "Bring some coffee and brandy for my guests." He called out as if to someone outside the room. Ben and Gabi looked at each other. "The poor slob is nuts," Ben said quietly. Gabi nodded as the Colonel kept talking. "Have you seen Dr. Horváth?" Gabi asked. "Yes," Colonel Vida replied, "I saw him about three weeks ago. He is a good friend of mine. I believe he has decided to join the party."

"How about Mr. Lodz?" Gabi asked.

"Lodz. Lodz. I don't recall knowing a Mister Lodz. Is he from around here?"

Ben whispered something to Gabi. She nodded and turned back to Colonel Vida.

"And what do you do, Sir."

"I am the chief of police of this town." He tried to get up and click his heels, but fell back on the bench. "I live in a beautiful house on Eszterházy street, and I would like you to stop in sometime and pay me a visit."

Gabi translated and stood up. "We better put cuffs on him."

Vida tried to protest but was too weak. "I'll have the hospital pick him up."

She stepped outside onto the little balcony and fired a red flare. Headlights appeared below the hill and a car pulled up behind the press house.

"I guess it's the Chief Inspector coming to check up on you," Ben snickered.

"I doubt it! He wouldn't be up this late unless there were skirts around."

"You are here."

"He can go screw himself," Gabi said.

Ben didn't go on.

They saw a figure making his way into the press house, and a few seconds later coming out, looking up at the cottage.

"It's Hegedüs," Gabi commented, "I recognize the way he walks. As usual, the simple son of a bitch is a day late and a penny short."

Ben smiled at the slang. "I guess that school in New Hampshire is really a good one." He thought for a while. "Where do you think they are? I mean Horváth and Lodz."

"If you ask me, . . ." she looked at Ben, "and you are obviously asking me. Dr. Horváth, Lodz Imre, Colonel Vásárhelyi and Rátz József, might all be fertilizing the grapes around here somewhere."

Hegedüs was coming up the path.

"The vigil is over, I guess," Ben said with an almost imperceptible sarcastic ring in his voice.

"Yes Sir." Hegedüs handed an envelope to Captain Kerek. The envelope was open, but Gabi showed it to Ben and translated the address and the delivery instructions stamped on the envelope:

To: *The Honorable Chief Inspector Albert Szekeres,*
The Golden Griffin Hotel
Pápa, 8500

"Deliver at 24:00 hrs."

She pulled a yellow sheet of paper from the envelope and read it in the light of her flashlight. When she finished, she read it again, this time out loud, translating the Hungarian text:

My sincere apologies to the Men and Women of the Hungarian Security Agency, their colleagues around the world, and to all who devoted countless hours of conscientious, difficult work executing their job beyond the call of duty. I appreciate their effort and am grateful to have been allowed to finish the task that befell me by the grace of God. Twenty four of the worst criminals of the past century were designated by the will and hope of their victims. Their crimes are beyond the scope of anything that is human, and anything that even the most fertile human brain can conjure. I had considered it my sacred duty and privilege to bring justice to these inhuman beasts. I regret that one of the twenty-five, Lieutenant Colonel Vida escaped his just punishment by my hand, but he did not escape the wrath of God, and will be living the rest of his miserable life within the confines of his own, nonexistent little world. As he is, he is no longer one of this world and I need not pursue him.

My job is therefore finished. Although I feel a great relief, and at the same time a great sense of accomplishment, I also know that under the laws of all civilized societies, my actions will be looked upon as crimes without mitigation. It matters not that the courts did not mete out just punishments; that all the ones I was privileged to bring to justice were known killers of scores of innocent victims, for no reason, other than their sick ideologies, material gain, or for sadistic pleasure, or just because they had the power to inflict pain and sorrow, and cause countless deaths. The good Lord put forth His will through my hands, and I willingly and gladly accepted His mission. It was a great privilege to execute the will of God. The countless others, who still walk this earth, having escaped their just punishment like Lieutenant Colonel Vida, will have their reckoning at the hands of the Almighty. My mission is over. My work is finished, and I go to my grave with a clear conscience, my head humbled, and my soul pure.

With the last of the twenty-five gone, I will also cease to be; this is my farewell. I ask that my remains, along with those of Dr. Horváth and Lodz be scattered to the wind over this little country, so that by my death the earth will be purified . . . "

The note went on but for Ben it sounded like it could have been written by one of the NYPD profilers, and he asked himself if he could have been all wrong? The way the last couple of days turned out, most of his theories seemed to go down the drain, none made any sense at this second and he thought that he had to be wrong, very wrong, way off the track. He was sorry, and strangely elated beyond description.

Maybe it was the reporter who accosted him at the press briefing that was The Rat. Maybe he came to the briefing to get a leg up on the latest. Or, maybe it was another reporter or someone who masqueraded as a reporter. Any of them could have been The Rat. Any of a hundred million people could be The Rat. These cops have been investigating The Rat murders for over ten years now and were not even close. And he had to admit, or at least he wished he could admit, he was no further ahead now than he was the day he started listening to Gabi in his office in New York, at Midtown North.

As in the past, the note read on, *it is my privilege to give an account of the judgment God imposed on Dr. Horváth Gyula and Lodz Imre. They died, as they lived, just like the others, suffering an end they imposed on their victims."*

There was another note, a memo from Chief Inspector Szekeres to Captain Kerek. Gabi read excerpts from it to Ben.

You're to investigate why the deception of these murders taking place before the believed date was not suspected and discovered, and why I was made to believe that apprehending the perpetrator on an apparently mythical date was a certainty.

You are ordered to interview Major Hathalomi Sándor at the Hajmáskér artillery range, and investigate the perpetrator's allegations about the murders of Dr. Horváth and Lodz Imre, and killing himself also at the same place. I expect a full report on my desk within five days.

"This is interesting." Gabi paused fort a second. *Unless it can be ascertained that the perpetrator of these murders continues to represent a danger to society, you are hereby ordered to conclude all activity in connection with the so called Rat Murders within thirty days, and report to Central Headquarters for reassignment."*

She read on silently and suddenly laughed out loud. *"P. S. (Off the record.)*

"I want you to know that I very much regret, and I will remember the personal embarrassment I suffered in front of the world press, as a result of the sloppy and amateurish handling of this case, which will probably be very detrimental to my political and professional career."

Two of the local constables approached from between the rows of grapes. More were coming from different directions, and Gabi dispatched one of them to fetch an ambulance for Colonel Vida. She assigned a guard to Colonel Vida and turned to Ben, "I guess it's time to go."

Epilogue

Major Hathalomi Sándor was going to be the concluding step, closing The Book on The Rat murders investigation. He turned out to be a very cooperative, pleasant man. He personally drove Gabi and Ben in a four wheel drive military vehicle to target 35, an obsolete and much shot up World War Two tank, the range still used as a target. The Major explained that this old tank had been stripped of all its interior equipment, and the shell that remained had been on continuous duty as a target since Hungary was allowed to have a self defense force after World War II. He explained that the ammunition used at this range was real, though not full strength. If it were, he pointed out, these targets would have been obliterated a long time ago, but the effect of the ammunition is the same visually as if it were full strength. They explode, he explained, and throw up a lot of dirt when they miss, but produce a high temperature, bright flash when they hit the target. In fact, he pointed out, what directed attention to this particular target during last week's maneuver was the extraordinary large flash and the subsequent burning of the target. It produced a huge fireball, and burned with heavy black smoke. The firing was immediately stopped, and as soon as the flames burnt themselves out, it was discovered that the top hatch of the tank was blown off and was found half a mile from the target. It would not have blown off normally, Major Hathalomi pointed out, as it was supposed to have been in an open position, but the investigation found evidence that it was closed and deliberately wired shut. Several gasoline and oil cans were found inside the tank, along with metal buttons from a police uniform, as well as a standard, police issue revolver and handcuffs, and another revolver, inscribed: 'Dr. Horváth Gyula, from his faithful friends,' and what was ascertained to be burnt human remains." The Major went on: "There was no way for us to determine the identity of the human remains, they were almost totally incinerated, but it is the belief of our forensic experts, and I understand the experts of the Hungarian National Security Bureau, that at least two, possibly three persons were killed and incinerated in the explosion."

"How did they get here?" Gabi translated Ben's question.

"Of course we have no way of knowing exactly," the Major explained, "we found no footprints; the ground around the targets was pretty well plowed up by the explosions, and any footprints or tire tracks, would have been obliterated, but we believe that the victims had to walk to the target from the perimeter. As usual, the range which is several square miles in area, was closed to all civilian and military traffic three days in advance of the exercise, and thoroughly patrolled the day before this part of the range was used. As you can see," he pointed to many green flags all over the range, "at the moment the range is safe, as indicated by the green flags. Three days prior to the exercise these flags were replaced with red ones and many notices were posted at all access points around the area."

"So, where would the people who were burnt to death in the tank, have come from?" Ben asked and Gabi translated the question to the Major.

"We believe that there might be a connection with an old truck that was found abandoned not far from here," he nodded his head to his right, "on a dirt road alongside the range."

We have traced the truck," Captain Kerek cut in, "to one of the owners of a small vineyard on Kis Mountain, who kept the truck at his press house. It was reported stolen the morning of the exercise."

"Was this truck impounded?" Ben asked.

"Unfortunately, the local police in this area returned it to the owner immediately. It was never dusted for prints, or searched for any other possible clues. The owner used it to transport a band of sheep in it the same day, and by the time we got to it, it was full of sheep manure. And," Gabi added, "the cab would have been too small for three people."

"How do you know it was three people?" Ben asked, but Captain Kerek quickly cleared that up. "As the Major here, we also believe it was three people. Besides The Rat's note clearly identified this spot, how it was used, and why it was picked. This is where the remains of Landau Miklós and his son were found. They were murdered by Dr. Horváth and Lodz Imre and, according to The Rat, they were to die at the same place. The Rat also indicated that he was to die with Horváth and Lodz." Ben nodded and Captain Kerek translated her statement to Major Hathalomi.

"I will have to ask for the official report you prepared on this case," Captain Kerek turned to the Major, "and would like to talk briefly to all who were involved in this incident."

The Major nodded and indicated for them to get back to the vehicle. "They are waiting for you," the major told Gabi as they started driving.

*   *   *

His worse fears were surfacing again and Ben felt as though a giant had him in a chokehold, squeezing the air out of his lungs. "Why was he here?" He asked himself again. But the answer was now clear: "He was here, because his being here fitted the The Rat's purpose. The whole New York angle, The Rat possibly living in New York was a ruse to channel attention from where The Rat really was. He knew, and had to admit to himself that the hunches, he didn't want to accept, the hunches he tried to explain away as unsubstantiated assumptions, in fact had to be true. The identity of The Rat was now a confirmed reality. His heart was about to burst, knowing that The Rat was sitting next to him, and was none other than Gabi, Captain Kerek of the Hungarian Security Agency. He also knew that Gabi has been pushing evidence his way for some time now, knowing that he had suspected the identity of The Rat. Gabi wanted him to know. She wanted him to know because she loved him. And he wanted her to know that he knew, but didn't care.

And that was all that mattered, Ben suddenly realized, and felt the heavy pressure lift from his chest, and the gnawing doubts and suspicions suddenly evaporate. He felt relieved and extremely happy.

"This case is closed. It's over!" Ben said with emphasis. "No more victims, no perpetrator; the case is closed!"

Gabi agreed. "Thank God for that."

"There is no doubt," Ben speculated, "that The Rat will go down in the history of criminal cases as a classic, unsolved, perfect chain of crimes."

"Why do you call it unsolved?" Gabi asked. "All the victims were accounted for, and all the clues were reconciled."

Bern cut her off, "All, but two."

Gabi's eyebrows came together; her face turned serious, as she was trying to think of an un-reconciled clue. "What two clues?" she asked.

Ben looked at her. "If there were three people burnt to death in the tank, who was the third person?"

"The Rat. It was The Rat." Gabi looked at Ben. "His note clearly spelled it out that he was committing suicide and even asked to have his ashes spread over the country."

"I have no problem with that," Ben commented quietly. "My question is: if The Rat killed himself in the tank, who wired the hatch shut?"

Gabi's face turned crimson red, but only for one second. "The hatch was wired from inside," she explained and asked, "What's the second clue?"

"Who killed Rátz?" Ben asked.

Gabi's face flushed red again. "Why do you ask?"

"The Rat didn't kill Rátz. His buddies did."

Gabi was quiet. Ben continued, "I asked the young woman, the desk clerk at the hotel to translate this." He handed a yellow sheet of paper to Gabi. "It is not a death sentence." He gave Gabi a couple of seconds to look at the yellow sheet of paper. "This is the sheet we found at the vineyard, but the note, Rátz's death sentence you gave me at the hotel while we were having breakfast, was just like all the other death sentences. I don't know where those came from, but Rátz never received a death sentence like the others. The way I figure it," he looked at Gabi and saw how upset she was, "The Rat set Rátz up by sending a bogus note to his buddies, absolving him of the death sentence, and in return thanking him for his help in getting the others." He looked at Gabi, but she was quiet. "The others figured he sold them out, and killed him." Ben gave her a long, long look. "I guess The Rat slipped up! But now that the case is closed, we'll never know for sure."

The case was closed, and he couldn't care. He was the happiest person on earth.

* * *

The little Lada purred along a narrow, pretty country road. There was no other traffic, except for an occasional local person on a bicycle. Dense woods alternated with picturesque meadows, as the road climbed, or dipped to the bottom of valleys.

"This isn't the way we came to Pápa, is it?" Ben observed.

"No. It isn't." Gabi seemed happy. "I wanted you to see some of this country and the place where I was born."

Ben was interested. "You were born around here?"

"Just around that turn," she pointed forward, "on the top of the hill on the left."

In a few seconds, Ben could see the remnants of what must've been a stately house, partially obscured by large trees on the hilltop above them. Gabi pulled to the side of the road and stopped the car.

They both got out. "That's where I was born." She pointed at the house. "Do you want to see it?" Ben nodded and Gabi led the way up a washed out road leading to the house. Ben looked around as Gabi pointed out the row of crumbling little houses and some other buildings in the distance. The people who worked in the house lived in those little houses, and the stables and the barns were over there."

They rounded the turn on the top of the hill, and Ben could see that the house was a guttted shell, plaster peeling, doors ripped off, and the windows broken, or missing altogether. But the roof was new. "The local government is trying to preserve what's left of the place, hoping to sell it before it all falls down," Gabi explained.

"The government owns it?"

"Yes my grandfather sold it when I was very young and after the war it was looted and abandoned. But it was built in 1778 and it is supposed to be an historical building."

"What's that?" Ben pointed to a small building not far from the main house.

"It's a chapel. All of these types of houses usually had a chapel built next to them for the family and the people who worked on the estate or lived nearby. Come," she turned to Ben, "I'll show it to you."

Like the house, the Chapel was also empty, fallen plaster all over the floor, but above what must have been the altar at one time, were two small windows, one in the shape of a cross, and above it, the Star of David. Ben also noticed a small, red marble plaque near the entrance and stopped in his tracks.

Requiescat in Pace

Kluger Ignác.

Kluger Ignácné - Landau Erzsébet

"They were my grandparents." Gabi said before Ben could ask. "My grandparents on both sides of my family are dead." Gabi smiled sadly. "All of them were killed by the Nazis during the war."

Ben thought that a tear appeared in her eye, and knew that this was not the place, nor the time, to ask any more questions. He hugged her as she sobbed quietly, and he continued to hold her until she stopped crying. He dabbed her eyes with his handkerchief. By the time they got back to her car, she had composed herself and after a while she explained. "My grandmother's family was Jewish, and because of that, both families were taken away."

"What was their name? I mean your grandmother's?"

"Landau," she said quietly, and they both stopped talking.

*   *   *

The road ran along the Danube for some time and in the distance the buildings of Budapest were coming into view.

"Your Boss," Ben broke the silence, "is not going to be happy about you showing up late with the report. . ."

"And I'm afraid the Chief Inspector is not going to give you a letter of commendation either."

"You wanna bet?" Ben asked. "Not that I couldn't do without it, but I think he will give me a letter of commendation. Giving out medals and the like is the very foundation of his existence."

She let out a loud and happy laugh.

"And then what?"

"And then, I'll take two weeks leave of absence and go to Auschwitz to put a small stone on Goldie's parents' grave. Then I'll go back to the states and retire. What about you? What are you going to do?"

"This is the end of my career. I'm washed up. . ." Ben smiled at the slang as she continued, " . . .and even if the Chief Inspector promtes me, I will resign."

"Then what?" Ben taunted her playfully, as they got out of the car in front of the Forum Hotel, as the doorman held the door for them. "What are you going to do?"

She shrugged her shoulders. "Resign, go to the United States and find a good obstetrician."

Ben froze and looked at her for what seemed a very long time. He gently reached for her hand and pulled her away from the immense brass and glass revolving door of the hotel lobby. The majestic Chain Bridge over the Danube, and the Royal Palace across the river seemed to focus on them as they stood quietly, looking into each other's eyes.

"Do you remember what I told you in Los Angeles?" Ben asked.

She looked at Ben, not knowing what he had in mind.

"The night you told me about the two thugs, The Rat wasted in South America?"

She still didn't know where this was leading.

"When I told you that Goldie might have been one of Dr. Hubert's victims?"

But she just shook her head uncertanly.

"I told you then," Ben continued, "that if, and when, I caught up with The Rat, I'd hug The Rat and give The Rat a big kiss."

She looked at Ben puzzled, as Ben pulled her to him, hugged her and kissed her for all eternity.

The end.

Printed in the United States
20287LVS00001B/52-66